ENTICED

Rivenoak pulled the boot from Pandora's foot. His eyes lifted to impale her. ''You are a cursedly beautiful woman.''

Deliberately, he leaned toward her, his hair, straight and black as a raven's wing, falling forward over his shoulders.

Pandora went exceedingly still, her heart seeming to skip a beat. He was going to kiss her, and she, who had never been kissed by a man before, would do nothing to stop him. Then his body, warm and thrillingly hard, pressed against hers, and her hands, as though possessed of a will of their own, were running through the bristling mat of hair on his chest and up over his shoulders to the back of his neck. The ever logical Miss Pandora Featherstone stifled the last, lingering voice of rationale as a probing shock of pleasure shot through her. Good heavens, she had never dreamed the mere touching of lips could have such an intoxicating effect.

Pandora did not know what to expect as she stared, spell-bound, into Rivenoak's eyes. There had, after all, been little reason in the past to speculate what it might be like to find oneself lying on one' ___ ___ a bed of furs. She had the curious premonition ___ ___ ___ ___ out to be changed forever. . . .

Books by Sara Blayne

PASSION'S LADY
DUEL OF THE HEART
A NOBLEMAN'S BRIDE
AN ELUSIVE GUARDIAN
AN EASTER COURTSHIP
A NOBLE DECEPTION
A NOBLE PURSUIT
A NOBLE RESOLVE
THEODORA
ENTICED

Published by Zebra Books

ENTICED

Sara Blayne

Zebra Books
Kensington Publishing Corp.

http://www.zebrabooks.com

ZEBRA BOOKS are published by

Kensington Publishing Corp.
850 Third Avenue
New York, NY 10022

Zebra, the Z logo and Splendor Reg. U.S. Pat. & TM Off.

First Printing: May, 1999
10 9 8 7 6 5 4 3 2 1

Printed in the United States of America

Chapter 1

His grace, Chance True-Son Quincy Ridgeway, the seventeenth Duke of Rivenoak, glided on moccasined feet through the maze of London alleyways, a fleeting, noiseless shadow melting in and out of the deeper rain-driven shadows. At his heels the dog kept pace in the silent, ground-eating trot of the wolf on the trail. And, indeed, the dog was half-wolf, a gift to Rivenoak from his maternal uncle, Laughs-In-The-Rain—a mourning gift to the last of the Three-Rivers People.

It was Laughs-In-The-Rain who had schooled the youthful Chance in the traditional ways of the Clan. From his uncle he had learned how to shape a canoe from birch bark, how to spear fish and stalk game, how to fashion weapons from wood and stone, and how to move through forest and glade with the stealth of the fox—talents that had proven less than useful in his unasked-for role among his father's people. Or at least they had until now, he thought with a mirthless twist of the lips.

The Town House on Portman square stood shoulder to shoulder with the other four-story brick houses of the fashionable

elite. The square itself was held second in prestige only to
Grosvenor Square in which stood Rivenoak's own oversized
mansion that had come to him, along with numerous houses
and estates, a moldering castle, and a title he had neither hoped
for nor desired, from the previous duke, his grandfather.

No doubt the old man would turn over in his grave if he could
see his mixed-blood heir now. Dressed in buckskin breeches and
leather moccasins, his hair the color of ravens' wings allowed
to fall, unfettered, down his back in the manner of his mother's
people, he had the look of his savage forebears, thought Rivenoak with grim humor, remembering that gentle woman, his
mother, who had taught him to read and write, using the King
James Bible as his primer. The irascible old duke would have
disinherited the "Cursed Savage" in an instant in favor of
Chance's Cousin Percival had it not been for the laws of
entailment; and there was a time when Chance True-Son of
the Three-Rivers People had cursed those very laws that bound
him to a life that was utterly foreign to everything he had once
held dear. But no more, he thought, stealing past the uninhabited
carriage house and stables and across the cobblestoned drive
to the back of the great house. The Duke of Rivenoak was a
power to be reckoned with in England. Chance had spent the
past ten years making sure of that.

He was the last of his mother's family, removed from his
mother's people at the age of fifteen and educated at Eton and
Cambridge to take his place as the heir to a venerable dukedom.
At fifteen he had been a man among the Three-Rivers People,
a shaman and a warrior who had tasted danger more than a
few times. In England he had been a boy, a savage to be tamed
and broken, the last vestige of his mother's race eradicated
from him according to the wishes of his English grandfather.
He had learned well. It would be his father's son who sought
redress for the wrongs perpetrated against his mother's clan.
But it would be Chance True-Son, shaman of the Three-Rivers

People, who must first find the sacred things. Mirthlessly, he grinned. There was a certain irony in that, an irony that appealed to his highly developed appreciation of the absurd.

"Stay, Stalker," he said softly to the dog. "Watch."

Reaching with gloved hands for the lead drainpipe, Rivenoak began to climb, hand over hand. He did not have to look to know the dog had sunk instantly to its haunches in the rain. The dog would remain, a silent guard at Rivenoak's back, until his master's return. Prying open the third-story window with his long-bladed knife, Rivenoak slipped inside.

Massingale House, like a large number of those on the square, had been closed for the winter and, save for the staff who kept for the most part to the lower floors, was empty. The furniture, draped in holland covers, wore a frozen, eerie look reminiscent of a graveyard in winter, reflected Rivenoak, his breath forming fleeting, white vaporous clouds in the chill, still air. He could sense nothing in the room in which he found himself. The chamber, containing a bed, a dresser, chairs, a highboy, and a standing wardrobe, had an aura of impersonality about it that marked it as a guest chamber. The things he sought would not be here, he thought, and noiselessly let himself out into the hall.

The next two rooms, a bedroom and an upstairs sitting room, were equally unrevealing. The instant he neared the final door at the far end of the hall, however, he experienced a light tingling at the nape of his neck, a prickle of knowing, like the touch of a warm breath against his skin. He let himself in, closing the door behind him.

Unpretentious and small, this was hardly the room of one who stood high in the household—the governess, he reasoned, or a poor female relative—and yet it exuded a positive energy, a vitality he was quick to sense in the intriguing array of personal articles that it housed. In addition to the few neat, but unprepossessing, dresses hanging on pegs in the wardrobe and a rather hideous bonnet thrust unceremoniously on the single

shelf, objects of an unusual nature littered every flat surface in
the room. On the cherrywood side table was an impressive
brace of matched dueling pistols laid out in a walnut box lined
in blue velvet, while the ottoman hosted a curious array of
albums containing newspaper cuttings detailing every sort of
bizarre occurrence of a criminal nature. The dressing table
boasted a leather-covered case in which resided an intriguing
assortment of powders and liquids in sealed bottles; and on top
of the wardrobe, among various wigs of every sort set on
wooden forms resembling disembodied heads, resided a microscope and a magnifying glass.

Even the recessed windowsill was filled with books of every
description. Clearly the room's inhabitant was eclectic in her
tastes, he observed, noting the titles, ranging from Boswell's
Life of Johnson to Hannah Moore's *Thoughts on the Importance
of the Manners of the Great to General Society,* and from
Charles Burney's *History of Music* to James Hutton's *New
Theory of the Earth.* Music, literature, history, the arts and
sciences—it seemed that nothing was beyond the curiosity of
this singular female.

Who was she? Rivenoak found himself wondering. Obviously not the governess, not with the colonel and his family in
the country. What the devil was she doing here in Massingale's
Town House with the colonel away?

Allowing his fingertips to trail across the strings of a lap
harp, obviously fashioned by an amateur, but with a singular
purity of tone, Rivenoak crossed to a secretary and riffled
through an untidy heap of papers. His fingers paused over a
stack of calling cards, printed in plain block letters and bearing
an inscription:

> Miss Pandora Featherstone
> Confidential Inquiry Agent
> No. 3 South Audley Street

Rivenoak's startled glance swept around the room. A snoop by trade, he thought, smiling faintly. Interesting. And what the devil had Miss Featherstone to do with the Butcher of Bear Flat? he wondered. Could it be that Massingale had employed Miss Featherstone to inquire into the origins of certain artifacts the colonel had acquired during his sojourn in the New World? Or perhaps she was looking into the matter of some anonymous letters the colonel had received of late, letters that must surely have occasioned her employer no little concern. An odd profession for a woman. And a dangerous one if she was poking her nose into the colonel's past.

His eyes fell on a small wooden chest at the foot of the four-poster bed. His heart quickened with startled recognition. Pocketing the calling card, he knelt to trace the letters carved in the lid. "T. F. R. Thomas Fairley Ridgeway," he murmured aloud. Then, aware of a tingling of nerve endings, he tested the lid. Locked. Curious, he thought. Extracting a penknife from a pouch at his belt, he inserted the blade into the keyhole. A grim smile of satisfaction came to his lips at the small click of the lock. He lifted the lid.

Unprepared, Rivenoak felt his throat constrict at sight of the things within. Like a man stricken, he dropped his head to his chest, his eyes clenched shut, as he struggled in the grip of powerful emotions.

The moment of weakness passed as swiftly as it had come, and Rivenoak, lifting his head, stared down into the box at the long familiar objects from a never forgotten past.

The beaded wampum belt fringed with porcupine quills recorded the pact of peace between the whites and the Three-Rivers People. His fingers caressed the beaded work wrought by his mother's own hand, as the memories swept over and through him—Laughs-In-The-Rain singing the story by the campfire of how Ridgeway of the Long Knives had come among the People of the Three Rivers with open palms and words of peace and friendship. They had been true words; and Ridgeway, a man to take into one's lodge. She-Who-Joyfully-Sings *had* taken him into her lodge, even as she had given him the wampum of peace, but not before they had been married by the missionary who had brought the Three-Rivers People into the Christian fold a good three decades earlier.

She had died singing a hymn, Rivenoak reflected, his lips thinning to a bleak, hard line at the thought.

With a hand that trembled ever so slightly, he reached for the King James Bible, the binding cracked with age and stained black with blood—the blood of the innocents, he thought darkly. Turning to the back, he glanced down the handwritten entries, until he came to the fourth from the last. Blurred by time and the elements, it was very nearly rendered illegible. Rivenoak, however, did not have to be able to make out the letters to know what had been recorded there. As a boy, he had read it often enough: "Chance True-Son Quincy Ridgeway, born 27 April in the year of our Lord 1767."

"Chance" because of the wild impulse that had brought Ridgeway, the younger son of a duke, to the New World in search of his fortune, and "True-Son" because the boy was a true son, born in wedlock and, therefore, his father's legitimate heir and, in the way of the Three-Rivers People, his mother's heir as well. "Quincy," ironically, had been chosen in honor of the newborn's paternal grandfather, a distinction that the old duke had notably failed to appreciate.

Setting the Bible aside, Rivenoak reached at last for the bundle wrapped in deerskin. Aware of a heady surge of excitement flowing along his veins, he laid back the soft folds of tanned hide.

He had hoped, even expected, to behold the sacred things. What he discovered were scalps—three of them. Old scalps. Two raven black, the third white. A woman and child of the tribes, and an old man.

Bile, swift and burning, rose in Rivenoak's throat. "The devil," he cursed. That was all there was save for some clothing, a journal kept by his father, and a worn volume of poetry by Herrick of which his father had been fond. Grimly wrapping the scalps back in the deerskin, he replaced them in the trunk along with the other things and refastened the lock. Miss Featherstone, whoever she was, had a deal of explaining to do. But not here and not now.

It would hardly suit Rivenoak's purposes to be discovered in the colonel's house in the process of questioning an apparent guest of Massingale's, especially as he might be called upon to resort to unorthodox methods of extracting the information he required.

Miss Featherstone would be persuaded to talk, he vowed, his hand clenching about the haft of the knife at his belt until his knuckles shone white. Before he was through with her, she would gladly tell him everything she knew about Massingale and the things of power, not to mention the contents of her bloody damned box. In the meantime, he had still to locate and search the colonel's study. The letter had been deliberately vague in all but the certainty that his grace would find what he was looking for in Massingale's Town House.

Rising with swift, agile grace to his feet, Rivenoak stole from the room and along the hall back the way he had come. The sounds of voices issuing from the stairwell brought him to a halt at the top of the stairs.

"You should sit a moment, Lady Pandora, and warm yourself in the kitchen while Jessop lays a fire in your room. You had ought to've let us know when you'd be coming back. We'd have had your room all toasty and warm for you."

"You are very kind Mrs. Caulkins," came in pleasingly low, melodious tones, "and I apologize for the inconvenience of the hour. You and Jessop were ready to sit down at your supper."

"Not at all, miss. Seldom before six. We keep country hours in the winter."

"Yes, well, as it happens, my work here is finished, and I shall be removing to my own house tonight. And about time, too. I daresay Aunt Cora will have had her hands full looking out for the children while I've been away. I only dropped by to pick up a few of my things. I shall send a boy for the rest tomorrow, if it is convenient."

"Anytime, Lady Pandora. You know that. It's been a pleasure having you here. Did you find what you were looking for?"

"Perhaps, Mrs. Caulkins. It is early days yet, but I believe I shall have a full report for Colonel Massingale sooner than expected."

"I daresay the colonel will be pleased. He seemed in a fair taking when he showed up at the Town House. Quite unlike him to come to Town for any reason this time of year."

As the voices grew nearer and more distinct, Rivenoak slipped noiselessly into the guest room from which he had gained access to the house. Leaving the door slightly ajar, he peered through the crack at the two women who appeared at the head of the stairs.

One, a plump, middle-aged female, would be the housekeeper, Mrs. Caulkins. Of the other, he was given only the briefest impression of a slender, straight-backed figure enveloped in a hooded, fur-lined cloak before she stepped briskly out of his line of sight.

Carefully, he closed the door and stood for a moment lost in contemplation. Massingale had come to Town in a hurry. He had engaged Miss Featherstone, a confidential inquiry agent, to look for something. What? And why Miss Featherstone? How the devil had the woman come in possession of his mother's things? And the scalps? What in bloody hell was she doing with them?

Lady Pandora Featherstone and her cursed wooden chest presented a whole new tangle of questions, questions that must be answered before he proceeded any further. Indeed, it would seem that what he needed was the services of a confidential inquiry agent.

Letting himself out the window, he made swift work of sliding down the drainpipe to the waiting dog.

"But you said nothing was taken, Auntie Pandora," insisted twelve-year-old Galatea Featherstone, her freckled face puckered in a frown as she puzzled over the peculiar incident her aunt had just related to those gathered in the parlor that morning before the fire. "Why should anyone sneak into your room and go through your things if they did not mean to take anything?"

"I daresay Auntie had nothing they wanted, stoopid," theorized Galatea's twin brother, Ganymede, who was perched on a tall stool while his Aunt Pandora trimmed his unruly blond curls.

"Or perhaps he heard Auntie and Mrs. Caulkins coming and fled before he could take anything," serenely suggested thirteen-year-old Iphigenia Featherstone, taking neat stitches in a pair of nankeens she was mending for Ganymede, who the previous afternoon had torn out the knee fetching Clytemnestra, the kitchen feline, and her four newborn kittens out from beneath the floor of the garden shed.

"Or maybe there was not a burglar at all," piped up ten-year-old Odysseus, holding up one of the tiny balls of fur in the palm of his hand for inspection, while Clytemnestra looked on from her cozy nest in a basket, her tail twitching in patent motherly disapproval.

"*Someone* was in that room moments before I arrived," declared Pandora Featherstone, tipping Ganymede's head forward in order to get at the hair on the nape of the boy's neck. "And I cannot think it was one of the servants. Whoever it was who stole into my room went through my things. Besides, I detected the faint scent of damp wool on the air mingled with

something else—wet leather, perhaps. And one must not forget
the footprints in the garden bed at the bottom of the drainpipe—
a rather large dog's and a human's.''

She did not add that she had found the footprints in the mud
most peculiar. The intruder, whoever he was, had not been
wearing boots or shoes, but some sort of footwear resembling
soft-soled slippers without heels. Most peculiar, indeed. But
not so peculiar as his apparent interest in the locked box, which
the colonel had placed in her keeping with instructions that it
must on no account be opened. It was, he contended, the box
itself that was to be the object of her research, not its contents.
Blast the box! It had nearly driven her mad with curiosity.

"Furthermore," she continued, "a thorough search of the
room revealed a damp depression in the rug by the box, which
would indicate someone knelt on one knee on the rug for some
little time. I daresay the intruder's unmentionables were wet
from the rain, nor should I be surprised if he managed to pick
the lock in order to search through the things inside. And,
finally, I discovered something caught on a snag in the window
sash in the upstairs guest room.''

Setting the scissors aside, Pandora retrieved a folded scrap
of paper from the placket pocket of her grey serge gown.
Carefully she unfolded it to reveal a single strand of jet black
hair.

"Oh, really, Pandora," declared "Aunt" Cora, a tiny wisp
of a woman whose predilection for order in the midst of chaos
caused her to wear a perpetually frazzled appearance. "How
could you pick up someone's hair and put it in your pocket?
The idea is positively revolting.''

"No it's not," said Odysseus. "It's a clue, is it not, Auntie
Pan?''

"It is indeed, Odysseus," Pandora replied. "A very important clue. Notice its length. If the intruder was indeed a
man—and from the size of the footprints I found in the snow

leading to and from the drainpipe, I sincerely doubt that it was a female—he wears his hair most unfashionably long.''

"I daresay he is a poor fellow who cannot afford to pay a barber," Galatea opined. "Very likely he does not have an aunt like you to cut it for him."

"I should think he is a fortunate chap, then," submitted Ganymede, who, if he were allowed to have done, would have let his hair grow to any unseemly length rather than submit to sitting still for a haircut. "No females to tell him to wash his face or cut his hair or do anything he doesn't wish to do."

"An end, no doubt, to be devoutly desired," Pandora observed without rancor. "I do not think, however, that is the case in this instance." Pandora, carefully folding the clue back in the scrap of paper and replacing it in her pocket, returned to the task of trimming Ganymede's hair. "Upon examining the strand under the microscope, I discovered it came from a head that was well-groomed and kept habitually clean. It was, furthermore, uncommonly healthy, indicating an exceptionally good diet. Whoever scaled that drainpipe and stole into my room at Colonel Massingale's is very probably in possession of a more than moderate income, which tells me that besides being exceptionally fit, not to mention athletically inclined, he is very likely strong-willed, arrogantly independent, and wholly indifferent to what anyone else might think of him. I should not be surprised if he turned out to be among the higher ranks of Society."

"You can tell all that from a single strand of hair?" demanded Galatea in awed fascination. "You must be a magician, Auntie Pan."

"Don't be a gaby, Galatea. What Auntie Pan does has nothing to do with magic. It is science," declared Iphigenia, biting off the end of her sewing thread. "It is all a matter of keen observation, logical deduction, and rational extrapolation, is it not, Auntie Pan."

"It is indeed," Pandora cheerfully agreed. "That and a smidgen of feminine intuition.'' Stepping back to view Ganymede with a critical eye, she gave a short nod of approval. ''There, you will do, Ganymede. I do, in fact, believe I am finally getting the hang of barbering.''

''I liked it better when Sergeant Major Lemkins used to cut it,'' Ganymede submitted grudgingly. ''He was ever so much quicker about it and not nearly so fussy. Do you think he and Papa are ever coming back again, Auntie Pan?''

''But of course I do!'' Pandora, taken off guard by the wistfully uttered question, glanced round her at her nephews and nieces, who, save for Odysseus, demonstrated a marked tendency to avoid her eyes. The poor dears, she thought, her heart twisting beneath her breast. How dreadfully they must miss their papa. ''You mustn't give up on your papa. India, after all, is a great distance from England. Why, it took your papa several months just to make such a voyage. And when once he arrived there, you may be certain he has been kept very busy fighting the Sultan of Mysore. I daresay he is as anxious as you are to get the job done so that he may come home to you.''

''Are you quite sure, Auntie Pan?'' queried Galatea, crinkling her nose at Pandora. ''I have wondered at times if perhaps he had forgotten all about us.''

''He could never forget you, Galatea. Any of you,'' Pandora stated with great firmness. ''Not in a thousand years. Now, why is everyone looking so glum, when it is a perfectly glorious day for a picnic?''

''A picnic?'' exclaimed Iphigenia, her lovely eyes widening in disbelief. ''It has been raining for two days, and everything is a perfect sludge-mire outside. A picnic is clearly out of the question.''

''Not for Auntie Pan,'' declared Odysseus, his face alight with unshakable conviction. ''Auntie Pan can do anything.''

''Indeed, I can, Odysseus,'' said Pandora, laughing. ''One can do anything if one only uses one's imagination. Now, where shall we have our picnic? In the Hanging Gardens of Babylon? Or at the foot of the Great Pyramid at Gizeh perhaps? Or, *I* know. Among the cypress gardens beside the pools of the Taj Mahal! We shall dress in native costumes and dine on native dishes. I'm nearly certain we have most of the ingredients in the house for mulligatawny soup. And certainly we can come up with a reasonable facsimile of Gajar Halva. How difficult can it be, after all, to devise a carrot pudding? Especially as your papa was good enough to send us the recipe in his last letter.''

''May I help make the pudding, Auntie Pan?'' asked Odysseus, returning the kitten to its mama. ''Please? I promise I shall be exceedingly careful not to break anything.''

''But of course you will help,'' Pandora declared. ''We all shall. We shall make a perfectly glorious mess of the kitchens, which we shall have a great deal of fun cleaning up afterwards. Now, everyone off to the attic to rifle through the trunks for costumes. I suggest old table cloths, linen sheets, curtains— anything that can be draped about one in the fashion of a sari for the girls or a dhoti for the boys. While you are doing that, I shall check with Mattie to see what we have on hand in the larder. Dress warmly for your treasure hunt. The attic promises to be positively frosty.''

It came to Pandora as she watched the children rush to the stairs that not in all the time since their papa had brought them home to England in the wake of their mama's passing had they ever once voiced a single doubt that Captain Herodotus Featherstone, their papa and her elder brother, would come back to them. But then, he had been gone an unconscionably long time. Indeed, it was nearly three years since he had deposited his family with the eldest Featherstone, Pandora's brother Castor, the earl, who promptly passed them on to the next in line, the eldest sister, Cleo, who handed them over next to sister Helena, who had been glad to see them go at last to the youngest of the Featherstones—Pandora, who with her Aunt Cora, who was not really her aunt, had been more than happy to take them in, never mind that Pandora's small competence, left to her by her father's spinster sister Philomena Featherstone, had been only just sufficient for Pandora to maintain herself and Cora in something approaching comfort. At least they had had Aunt Philomena's house on South Audley Street, which guaranteed a roof over their heads, and Pandora's determination and ingenuity, which had led her to embark on a career that must be considered as unorthodox for a female as it was singular.

The idea had come to her one evening as she sat going over the weekly expenditures with frequent interruptions from her nephews and nieces, who seemed wholly unable to keep track of the least little thing, such as Odysseus's favorite carved wooden bunny or Galatea's hair ribbon or Ganymede's nightcap, not to mention the mate to Iphigenia's single slipper. It had become a matter of rote, beginning with, "Now, think back. When do you recall having it last? Where were you at the time? What were you doing? Where did you go after that? Did you take it with you or did you set it down?" Leading one of the children through the process of logical deduction for the umpteenth time, she was struck by a most peculiar notion.

It had occurred to her that it was a pity she could not employ her talents for finding things and for solving seemingly insoluable problems for something more gainful than tracking down the children's lost articles. Her papa, a classical scholar, had not only named all his children after famous Greeks (a tradition continued by her brother Herodotus), but, left in his middle age a widower with a daughter fully fifteen years younger than her next oldest sibling, he had not hesitated to give full rein to his love of logic and systematic research in rearing his one remaining chick in the nest. Pandora had been inculcated in the tenets of reason and scientific observation almost from the time she was old enough to talk. Possessed of a keen intellect and a lively sense of curiosity, not to mention an acute appreciation of the absurd, she had taken to classical training like a duck to water. It was, in fact, second nature for her to treat every obstacle in life in the light of her papa's precept that every problem had a solution if only one approached it with keen insight and a calm rationality.

It had come rather on the order of an epiphany that her singular gifts and abilities put her in the way of offering a rather unique service to those in need of help in dealing with conundrums that, to the untrained mind, must seem insoluble. The very next day, she had placed an advertisement in the *Gazette* announcing that P. I. (the ''I'' stood for Ianthe) Featherstone, a noted practitioner of the science of observation and deductive reasoning, was offering her services for hire to discover the seemingly undiscoverable, to determine answers to the apparently unanswerable, and to recover the ostensibly unrecoverable.

In the five months since she had first placed her advertisement in the *Gazette,* she had garnered as many as half a dozen clients and managed to earn all of eighty-five pounds. Not a bad beginning for a female in an unorthodox profession, she had been wont to reflect. Her first assignment, involving the recovery of an abducted pug for a Mrs. Somerset, the wife of a draper, had been easily resolved after interviewing the servants. She had been led immediately to suspect the groom's nephew, who was reported to have suffered numerous painful assaults to the ankle by the ill-tempered little beast. With the assurance his employers would remain in ignorance of the true state of affairs, the culprit had been persuaded to produce the missing pug, which, though considerably chastened, appeared little the worse for wear after its three-day sojourn in an abandoned cellar.

Two missing pets and a misplaced samovar later, she had been summoned into the presence of Lady Stanhope, who had heard from her modiste, Madame Dupres, who had it from Mr.

Somerset, the draper, of Miss Featherstone's uncanny ability
to solve the irresolvable mysteries of life.

Lady Stanhope's irresolvable mystery, involving a ghost in
the attic, had proven rather more stimulating than any of Pandora's previous assignments. Still, it had required little more than
a thorough inspection of the lumber room and an interview of
the household, including Miss Abercrombie, her ladyship's
loquacious companion, (from whom she picked up such interesting tidbits as the fact that the earl and his wife were utterly
devoted to one another, that his lordship had a tendency to the
gout, which had occasioned his physician to prescribe a plain
diet and the curtailment of certain of his lordship's pleasures,
most particularly his fondness for port, and that Lady Stanhope
was possessed of exceedingly delicate sensibilities that made
her prone at the smallest upset to take to her bed with the
spasms) to deduce that the haunting of Lady Stanhope's attic
was attributable not to a phantom, but to a different sort of
spirit altogether. While arriving at a solution to the mystery had
been simple enough, however, Pandora, ever of a sympathetic
nature, had found herself in something of a quandary as to
how, without disturbing her employers' domestic tranquility,
she was to explain the occurrences of footsteps in the attic late
at night, not to mention an occasional eerie glow issuing from
the window beneath the eaves and frequent loud thumps
attended by muffled curses of the sort to bring a blush to the
cheek of any female of refined sensibilities. It came to her that
the most logical approach would be a tête-à-tête with the ghost
itself.

Since she had already reached certain conclusions regarding
the ghost in the attic, Pandora's decision to spend a night in
the haunted lumber room had hardly been the act of heroism
her employer and the servants imagined it. It had, however,
proven of a discomposing nature to the "ghost," who, at Lady
Stanhope's insistence, had not been made privy to Pandora's
investigations into the hauntings. The midnight appearance of

Lord Stanhope, bearing a dark lantern of the sort used by mariners and dressed in a rumpled example of the Deshabille, was only what Pandora had expected. Pandora's sudden materialization from behind the Louis XV standing trunk in which his lordship had been wont to stash his forbidden bottles of port, on the other hand, was almost enough to send Lord Stanhope into a swoon. When some minutes later, Pandora had managed to convince his lordship that she was neither a specter nor a burglar, but a confidential inquiry agent engaged by his lady wife to discover the identity of the ghost in the attic, Lord Stanhope sank with a groan onto a Charles II carved wing chair with a broken arm and, lifting the bottle of port in his hand in a gesture of finality, declared in a voice of gloom, "Alas, I am undone."

"Not necessarily, my lord," replied Pandora, who, while waiting for Lord Stanhope to make his appearance, had come up with a possible solution to both their problems. "If you will only agree to a little playacting, I believe we may satisfactorily explain the mystery of the haunted attic to Lady Stanhope without revealing the true nature of your visits. I'm afraid it will mean, however, giving up your midnight retreats to the lumber room."

"I should agree to anything that would save my dearest Margaret from upset, Miss Featherstone," Lord Stanhope averred with a discernible shudder. "And, besides," he added upon reflection, considerably brightening, "there is always the wine cellar. No doubt it will not be impossible to relieve Steddings of the key long enough to have a duplicate fashioned. I daresay the wine cellar would be a deal more convenient than the attic for my nightly ablutions at any rate."

"No doubt, my lord," agreed Pandora, who privately thought his lordship would do better either to give up his port as the doctor and his wife wished him to do or to manfully insist on indulging in it openly. He was presumably, after all, the lord of the manor. Clearly, Lady Stanhope in a fit of the spasms was something to be avoided at all costs. It was in any case none of her concern, she reminded herself, and proceeded to detail her plan to his lordship.

Lady Stanhope, awakened to the sight of her spouse in the act of prowling the halls, his arms extended straight out before him and his expression most peculiarly blank, was naturally startled to discover that the ghost in the attic was none other than her dearest Wilfred. As disconcerting as it was to suddenly find out the man to whom she had been wed for twenty-three years was given to bouts of somnambulism that had led him to frequent the attic room unbeknownst to himself, she could not but be relieved that the seemingly extraordinary phenomena that had occurred in the house could be attributed to a perfectly rational explanation and not to anything remotely resembling the supernatural. Convinced that Miss Featherstone was blessed with uncommon powers of deduction, not to mention extraordinary courage, she did not hesitate to praise Pandora in glowing terms to her bosom bow, Mrs. Massingale, who promptly relayed the fascinating *on dit* to her husband, the colonel. With the result that, little more than a month after the successful completion of her assignment for Lady Stanhope, Pandora had received a morning call from Colonel Massingale himself.

The colonel, a large man with an overbearing manner, fostered, no doubt, by a lifetime of command and abetted by a sizeable fortune garnered in the New World during the War of Rebellion (by, some were given to speculate, questionable means), had seemed to cause Pandora's cozy parlor to shrink considerably in size. Gruffly, he refused an offer of tea, saying he never touched the stuff, and, eyeing askance her Aunt Philomena's somewhat worn and undeniably dainty appearing dimity-covered settee to which Pandora directed him, declared a preference to remain standing for the interview.

Informing her that she had come highly recommended to him by Lord and Lady Stanhope, he proceeded without further roundaboutation to tell her his purpose in calling. It had come to his attention by means which he preferred not to divulge that he had in his possession certain articles, which, while of little intrinsic value, might very well prove of some historical import. As he, himself, was not of a scholarly bent, he wished to employ Miss Featherstone to ascertain the authenticity of the items and determine, if possible, their history: to wit, when and whence they had originated and an explanation of what, precisely, they were. In order to facilitate her research, he required her to take up temporary residence in his Town House, which was handsomely furnished with a large and comprehensive library, the legacy, along with the articles in question, of the mansion's previous owner, the late Marquis of Selkirk. Massingale had gone on to explain that Selkirk's bereaved father, preferring at the loss of his son never to have to set foot in the cursed mansion again, had sold the entire house—lock, stock, and barrel—to the colonel at a considerably less than exorbitant price.

And little wonder, thought Pandora, feeling a delicious chill explore her spine all over again just thinking about it. The Marquis of Selkirk had been found murdered, nearly twenty years ago, in that very Town House. Newspaper clippings detailing the brutal slaying and the failure to discover any clues to the identity of the killer were carefully preserved in her papa's catalog of interesting and bizarre crimes, along with mention of the sizeable reward offered by the Duke of Rivenoak for information leading to the apprehension of the party or parties unknown who had foully put a period to his eldest son and heir apparent.

From all accounts, Rivenoak had gone nearly mad with grief over his heir's death, coming, as it had, only a few months following the reported demise of his second son in the New World. It was the male offspring of that younger son who had assumed the title upon the event of his grandfather's passing, and it was that scion of the New World who had made the

Duke of Rivenoak one of the most talked about men in England, not to mention reputedly one of the most powerful.

It was common knowledge that he had taken the dwindling fortune left to him by his grandfather and tripled it by investing heavily in the innovative steam-powered mills and factories, an income which he was reported to have doubled yet again in speculations in foreign currency and trade. Having earned the reputation of a modern-day Midas along with a fortune that was the envy of practically everyone who was anyone, Rivenoak promptly turned to philanthropic endeavors, contributing large sums to efforts for the relief of the poor. Not satisfied with employing his considerable material resources for the benefit of those less fortunate, he had not hesitated to wield his not inconsiderable influence in the cause of reform measures, an effort that had earned him the disapprobation of his peers. He was judged a dangerous radical and a law unto himself and would undoubtedly have been given the cut direct had he not been a premier nobleman of the realm, second only to royalty, and had it not, furthermore, been considered exceedingly dangerous to have done.

As it was, he was reputed to have few intimates, demonstrated a disappointing disinclination to lend himself to more than a tepid involvement in the demands of Society, and remained maddeningly elusive to those single females and their matchmaking mamas who would gladly have become more intimately acquainted with him. The truth be told, save for the Prince Regent, who unaccountably had taken a liking to his grace, Rivenoak maintained an impenetrable barrier of aloofness about himself which had caused him at various times to be termed high in the instep, coldly indifferent, and bloody demmed arrogant. But then, he was one of those exalted beings, after all—a duke. No doubt it would have been thought odd had he acted any differently.

It was, consequently, with no little surprise that Pandora, attired in a makeshift sari fashioned from her Aunt Philomena's

tartan decorative shawl, which normally resided on the back
of the sofa, and occupied with balancing a wooden bowl of
mulligatawny soup on one knee as she sat Buddha-fashion on
the floor, looked up to see Aunt Cora ushering a visitor into
the parlor room.

"Pandora, dear," declared Aunt Cora, contriving to appear
a trifle more frazzled even than she normally did, "you will
never guess who has called on us."

Pandora, gazing up into eyes the frosty blue of a mountain
lake on a clear, still day, could not but think that Aunt Cora
had grossly understated the case. Tall and lean, with broad,
powerful shoulders and muscular limbs, all of which showed
to magnificent advantage in a snug-fitting cutaway coat of blue
superfine, skin-tight unmentionables of dove grey, and black
Hessian boots, polished to perfection, her visitor exuded an air
of superiority that placed him far above her touch. Furthermore,
she was reasonably certain that had she ever before had the
occasion to look upon a face, composed like his of a high, wide
forehead beneath raven black hair swept sternly back and done
up in a twisted knot at the nape of the neck, a long, straight
nose, high, prominent cheekbones, and a thin-lipped mouth set
above a strong, stubborn jaw, all of which were finely chiseled
to create an impression of masculine perfection, it was highly
unlikely she would ever have forgotten it. The stranger was,
she did not doubt, the most striking individual upon whom she
had ever laid eyes.

"You are quite right, Aunt Cora," Pandora answered, her
gaze never wavering from the stranger's. "I am certain I cannot
guess the gentleman's identity. Perhaps you would be so kind
as to enlighten me."

She was rewarded with a cold glint of amusement in her
visitor's singularly hard blue eyes, which not only had the
discomfiting effect of infusing a warm rush of blood to her
cheeks, but served to remind her that she was in the act of
receiving a gentleman caller of obvious distinction while

dressed in little more than her Aunt Philomena's tartan decorative shawl.

"Allow me to introduce myself," spoke up the visitor, insufferably bowing. "I am Rivenoak, Miss Featherstone. Charmed to make your acquaintance."

Chapter 2

The Duke of Rivenoak, good God! thought Pandora, who could not but be aware she had in her parlor one of the wealthiest, most powerful men in England. The question of why he should have been there was a conundrum that presented any number of intriguing possibilities, not the least of which revolved around the fact that she was presently involved in an investigation that peripherally, at least, concerned the former Marquis of Selkirk. Obviously, she could not overlook the circumstance that Rivenoak not only just happened to be the former marquis's nephew, but that his grace uncannily fit her deductive description of the burglar who had broken into Colonel Massingale's Town House and searched through her belongings.

But then, Rivenoak *was* the intruder, she was sure of it. She, after all, had never been one to believe in coincidences, and Rivenoak's arrival, unannounced, there in her parlor less than twenty-four hours after the break-in would have been a coincidence of the first water. The question was, why was he here?

From the looks of him, she reflected, taking in his tall, compellingly masculine figure, she would not doubt that he thought to intimidate her by his mere presence. Certainly, he presented a magnificent air of arrogant self-assurance! she mused, acutely aware of the faint curl of the irrefutably handsome lips. But intimidate her into doing—what?

Pandora felt a chill course down her spine, an eventuality that she was sure had more to do with excitement at being presented with a new, stimulating puzzle than with the mere fact that she was staring into the cold, compelling gaze of a man who was reputed to be utterly ruthless with anyone who incurred his enmity—or, for that matter, she mused humorously, with the circumstance that she was rather skimpily attired in her Aunt Philomena's tartan shawl. Unfortunately, in her present state of deshabille, she was at a distinct disadvantage. No doubt his grace must think her extremely unfashionable, not to mention more than a trifle eccentric. Perversely, the realization struck her as enormously funny, so that setting the bowl of soup aside and rising with what grace she could manage in her unwieldy attire, she met the duke's gaze with an unholy gleam of laughter.

"Your grace," she murmured, dipping a curtsey.

The devil, Rivenoak silently cursed, presented, as he was, with a veritable vision of impish beauty. He had hardly known what to expect of a woman who boldly proclaimed herself a confidential inquiry agent capable of solving the irresolvable. An image of a mannish creature with pinched features and calculating eyes had briefly suggested itself, until he had assigned Charles Winthrop, his private secretary, the task of looking into her background. The report, which noted she was the youngest daughter of the previous Earl of Braxton, a recluse who in his lifetime had indulged his passion for classical scholarship to the exclusion of all else, had told him little, save for the fact that Miss Featherstone had long since declared her independence of her eldest brother, the present earl, that she subsisted on a small income left to her by her spinster aunt, and that she had the distinction of being the sister of Captain Herodotus Featherstone, who eighteen years before had been posted in the New World. The report had failed utterly, however, to mention that though clearly out of the ordinary, she was undeniably a beauty of the first water possessed of thick, unruly hair the rich dark brown of the earth of a New World forest and eyes the grey-blue of a sultry summer's day. Nor had it prepared him for a mischievous dimple placed most intriguingly at the corner of bewitching lips. The duke's black eyebrows drew sharply together. The little jade, he thought, to have the temerity to laugh at him! Whatever else she was, Miss Featherstone, he noted, was an impertinent female who demonstrated a total lack of the trepidation, not to mention the proper awe, due to the Duke of Rivenoak, who had gone to a deal of trouble to earn his reputation for being exceedingly dangerous.

In spite of himself and aside from his purpose in seeking her out, he felt his interest irresistibly piqued.

"No doubt I must beg your pardon, Miss Featherstone," he murmured at his coolest, "for arriving unannounced. It would seem I have come at an inopportune time."

"Not at all, your grace," replied the irrepressible Miss Featherstone without hesitation, thinking about another, even more unforgivable breach of conduct. "I daresay one of your exalted station is above the common amenities."

The little devil, thought Rivenoak, his fine eyes flashing at what could only be construed as a masterful set-down. So, the wench was not above crossing swords with him. A pity he was constrained by the presence of numerous children, not to mention the dictates of polite convention, from dealing with her as she had ought to be dealt. Without stopping to consider that he had never before felt a similar urge toward a female of refinement, it came to him that he would not be averse to clasping her to his chest and crushing those beguiling lips beneath his until, breathless and limp, she begged his forgiveness for her impertinence.

"In any case," Pandora blithely continued, apparently oblivious to the ominous glitter of the duke's gaze beneath heavily drooping eyelids, "you are welcome. May I present to you my nephews and nieces—Miss Iphigenia Featherstone, the eldest; Galatea and Ganymede, the twins; and last, but not least, Odysseus, the youngest of my brother Herodotus's hopefuls. Miss Cora Pemberton, my dearest friend and companion, I believe you have already met. As it happens, we were just indulging in a picnic beside the reflecting pool of the Taj Mahal. Perhaps you would care to join us."

A sudden gleam of enlightenment flickered briefly behind the duke's hooded eyes, along with something that might have been surprise.

"Oh, yes, please do, your grace. We have some exceedingly delicious mulligatawny soup," offered Iphigenia in the way of inducement, as she performed a very creditable curtsey in her sari, which had previously served as a white linen and lace tablecloth for the dining room table.

"We made it ourselves," added Odysseus, cutting a dashing figure in a white waistcoat and with a linen towel wrapped about his middle and drawn up between his legs in a manner that, while suspiciously resembling a nappie, managed to give a fair imitation of a dhoti.

Ganymede, similarly attired and balancing on his head Aunt Cora's turban hat replete with a peacock feather fastened to the front by a jade brooch, pressed his hands together before him and executed a solemn bow. "You would bless our humble meal with your presence," he pronounced, clearly immersed in the fantasy Pandora had created for the afternoon's entertainment.

Galatea, not to be outdone by her twin, overcame her instinctive awe of one who not only exuded a commanding air, but gazed down upon them from a commanding height as well. "I should be pleased, your grace,'' she said, swallowing as she looked with determined blue-violet eyes up into the stern countenance, ''if you would sit on the cushion next to mine.''

Pandora, who did not fool herself into thinking the Duke of Rivenoak would be the least enticed by what amounted to a children's party, indeed, who could not at all envision his grace sipping mulligatawny soup while seated, cross-legged, on a cushion on the floor, waited with expectant eyes on her unlooked-for caller.

The baggage, thought Rivenoak, correctly interpreting that coolly appraising glance. She expected him to cry off, probably wished him to do so. Now, what the devil had he done to earn her disapprobation in their exceedingly brief acquaintanceship? he wondered—unless, of course, she guessed his purpose in coming. The scalps and the other things in the locked chest, did she know what she had in her possession? Perhaps she meant to use them to her own advantage. The Duke of Rivenoak, after all, might very well loom to one of her straitened circumstances as a goose ripe for the plucking.

Well, she would soon find that he was neither a goose nor a gull, thought Rivenoak, taking Galatea's small hand in his own strong, shapely member and executing a gallant bow over the child's dimpled knuckles. A man who refused an invitation into an unknown enemy's camp was a fool who forfeited the opportunity to learn that enemy's strengths and weaknesses. ''I should be delighted to sit beside you, Miss Galatea,'' he drawled with admirable solemnity.

It was difficult to say who was more startled—Galatea or Pandora. It was, however, clear who was the more gratified. Galatea flushed with pleasure, while Pandora, overcoming her initial surprise with admirable aplomb, flashed Rivenoak a narrowed glance, which left little doubt she did not trust his motives.

''I say,'' blurted Ganymede, grinning, ''that's simply splendid, your grace. I knew you were a right 'un the moment I laid eyes on you.''

''Ganymede, for heaven's sake,'' blurted Iphigenia, scandalized at such an expression of familiarity to one of obvious distinction. ''What would Papa say if he heard you speak to a duke in such a manner?''

''That I was right about his grace. I know a man when I see one,'' declared her unrepentant younger brother, who saw nothing amiss in having given their caller the highest possible accolade. ''I should wager he doesn't mind.''

''Do you, your grace?'' queried Galatea with an air of childish gravity. ''Mind, that is? I daresay Ganymede did not mean to offend.''

Pandora's lips parted to admonish the children not to pester his grace, when Rivenoak took matters into his own capable hands.

''No, of course he did not, little one. Nor am I offended. How should I be? Among certain of the peoples of the New World, it is quite proper to pay compliments to an honored guest. I daresay had you grown up among the Grandfather Tribe, who, because they are the oldest of all the tribes, are known as 'The People,' Ganymede would have been called 'He-Who-Boldly-Sings-Praises.' And you, *enfant,* would have been 'She-Who-Is-The-Peace-Maker.' ''

''What should I be called?'' demanded Odysseus, who could not wish to be left out of this new game.

''You would undoubtedly be called 'He-Who-Rolls-In-The-Mud,' '' supplied Iphigenia, so far forgetting herself as to screw her face up at the youngest of the Featherstones.

''Can I help it if I like mud?'' demanded Odysseus, who, in spite of the general outburst of mirth, found a certain charm in such a name. ''Mud is all gushy. I like to wriggle my toes in it.''

A lively discussion of ''names'' for the remaining members of the assembled company ensued, as Rivenoak was directed to a seat among the heap of cushions arranged on the floor before the fireplace. It was established amid a deal of merriment that Iphigenia would undoubtedly have been called "She-Who-Mends-Nankeens," while Aunt Cora must surely be "She-Who-Endures-Chaos." It seemed that everyone had a name for Auntie Pan, ranging from "She-Who-Answers-Riddles" to "She-Who-Looks-Behind-The-Ears." Rivenoak, however, stole all the thunder when, gazing thoughtfully at Pandora, he suggested that Miss Featherstone must undoubtedly have been named "She-Who-Shines-With-Laughter."

"Oh," exclaimed Iphigenia, enthralled, "but that is perfect. You do, you know, Auntie Pan—shine when you laugh."

"Do I, dear?" Pandora murmured, her gaze fixed, wonderingly, on Rivenoak. Could it be that she had misjudged the duke? Certainly he would seem to have a winning way with children that she would not have expected of a nobleman with a reputation for ruthlessness. Nor could she believe it was all a sham. She, after all, was an acute judge of character. Furthermore, her brother's four children had been reared among men. They were not likely to be easily taken in by a charming manner. No, there was a deal more to the Duke of Rivenoak than at first met the eye; she was sure of it. She did not doubt, in fact, that he was possibly the most intriguing conundrum that she had ever encountered.

The fantasy afternoon spent beside the reflecting pool of the Taj Mahal proved to be more successful than Pandora could ever have imagined when she first proposed the idea to the children—thanks in large part to her uninvited guest. Rivenoak, who gave every evidence of one perfectly at ease seated cross-legged on a cushion on the floor and sipping mulligatawny soup from a bowl, was not averse to answering any number of questions concerning the native American tribe to whom he was wont to refer as "the People." Obviously, he had spent no little time acquiring a knowledge that was a deal more intimate than could be had from any travel book. Indeed, it came to Pandora, as she listened to his grace's account of a tribal youth's first bear hunt, which was part of the rite of passage into manhood, that Rivenoak was speaking not from hearsay evidence, but from personal experience.

Nor was such a notion in the least farfetched, she immediately reminded herself. Rivenoak's father, after all, had met his demise in the New World. No doubt Rivenoak had become acquainted in his earliest years with the very people that he was describing in such vivid detail. Whatever the case, there was no denying his grace was a gifted storyteller. He wove magic with his words, which flowed with the mystical rhythm of a singer of songs. Indeed, hardly had he begun to speak than they were all transported from the reflecting pool of the Taj Mahal to a wholly enchanting New World forest peopled with animals who spoke in the language of men and possessed personalities as distinctive as those of their human brethren.

"But how *could* Boy-Who-Walks kill Grandfather Bear?" demanded Iphigenia in accents of disbelief, as Rivenoak came to the end of his tale.

"It would be like betraying a friend," Ganymede agreed, clearly disappointed in the youthful hero who had initially captured his boyish imagination, but who would appear in the end to have offended his English notions of honor.

"It was a shabby thing to do," agreed Odysseus, frowning. "Especially after Grandfather Bear saved the boy's life and then showed him the secrets of the forest. If I had been Boy-Who-Walks, I shouldn't have done it. I should have wished to live in the forest with Grandfather Bear forever."

"But that's just it, don't you see?" said Galatea, her sensitive features expressive of rapt understanding. "Boy-Who-Walks *could* not stay with Grandfather Bear. He was to be a man, a shaman of his tribe. His people needed him to protect and care for them; and to be a good shaman, Boy-Who-Walks needed Grandfather Bear's strength and wisdom. Those were Grandfather Bear's final gifts to him. It would have been wrong of Boy-Who-Walks to refuse them.''

"You would have made a good medicine woman yourself, Little-Peace-Maker," said Rivenoak, smiling down at Galatea. "You have an understanding heart. That is precisely why Boy-Who-Walks took Grandfather Bear's life. He was saddened by the necessity, but that is part of becoming a man—or a woman, for that matter. Making choices in life, sometimes no matter what the cost to oneself. It is all part of the great journey. As you grow older, you will discover that it is not always easy to see your path clearly or to follow it, even when you know it is the right path.''

His words had been directed at Galatea and the other children, but at the end his gaze lifted to Pandora, who was watching him with a puzzled frown.

Rivenoak arched an inquisitive eyebrow. "Something troubles you, Miss Featherstone," he said quietly.

Pandora experienced an odd quiver in the pit of her stomach. Faith, she had the strangest sensation that he could see right through to her heart. Could he read her mind as well? "I am not troubled, precisely," she demurred, her gaze searching on his. "I was merely wondering, your grace, what happened in the end to Boy-Who-Walks. Did he become a shaman to his people? The healer and protector for whom they had been waiting?''

It was as if a shadow fell over the chiseled features, or as if the duke were suddenly many thousands of miles away. Inexplicably, Pandora felt a sudden sharp pang in the vicinity of her breastbone.

Then the still, blue eyes, like deep, unfathomable pools, returned to her, and she caught her breath at what she saw in them. "The answer is both yes and no, Miss Featherstone. The boy did indeed become a shaman, but a shaman without a people.''

* * *

An odd sort of pall fell over the party then. Rivenoak, withdrawing into an impenetrable shell of civility, would say no more about the People, and the children, seeming to sense events beyond their meager years, did not object when Pandora shooed them upstairs to change their clothing.

"I shall just go up and see everything is put to rights while you and his grace have your little talk," offered Aunt Cora. "Your grace, such a pleasant afternoon. I do hope you will call again."

"You are very kind, Miss Pemberton," returned his grace, bowing. "Perhaps I shall come again."

"I should go, too, your grace," said Pandora, smiling wryly at her guest. "I confess I am grown weary of this ridiculous costume. Perhaps you would not mind waiting. You may be sure I shan't be long. I daresay you had a reason for coming here today, one that I admit I am exceedingly curious to learn."

"I shall be here when you return, Miss Featherstone," Rivenoak promised, his look sending a small shiver coursing unwittingly through her.

Indeed, Pandora, turning to hasten up the stairs, was acutely aware that Rivenoak would seem to have a most curious effect on her physical functions. The duke was undoubtedly the most fascinating man she had ever before encountered, and she was certain the most dangerous. Still, it was hardly trepidation that quickened her pulse rate or caused her temperature to rise at the merest look from Rivenoak's blue, piercing eyes.

Upon discovering some moments later a hitherto nonexistent compulsion to choose then discard one gown after another in an untidy heap on the floor in what was proving a vain search for something in the least presentable to wear, it came to her that he was having an unsettling effect on her rational thought processes as well.

The devil, thought Pandora, who had never before been

one to pay undue attention to her appearance. Considering the deplorable state of her wardrobe, she was on a fruitless quest, indeed.

No doubt it was due to some perversity in her character that she immediately snatched up the oldest and most unattractive gown in her admittedly uninspiring wardrobe and, telling herself it mattered not a whit what his grace thought of her, flung it on. At last, after a feeble attempt to restore her unruly mass of hair to a semblance of order, she shrugged at the effort and ran quickly down the stairs. It was highly unlikely, after all, that the duke's purpose in calling was due to any attraction he might have felt for one who could only be judged a Nobody.

Whatever *had* brought the Duke of Rivenoak to the house on South Audley Street, however, Pandora reflected humorously, it had been important enough for him to endure a children's party and to keep him waiting while she made herself more presentable. For someone of Rivenoak's stature, that was condescension indeed!

Her curiosity was, consequently, at a fever pitch, as, pausing outside the drawing room door long enough to draw a deep, calming breath, she entered. She was aware of a sharp stab of relief upon sighting the duke's tall figure before the fireplace, his back to the room and his gaze on the fire in the grate. She had not been at all certain that she would find him still there.

"Thank you for waiting, your grace," she said lightly, turning to slide the doors closed behind her. "I beg your pardon for the delay. It was exceedingly kind of you to help me keep the children amused."

"Not at all, Miss Featherstone," replied Rivenoak, with a small shrug of a muscular shoulder. "As it happens, I have seldom been better entertained. They are fine children. Still, I cannot but wonder, Miss Featherstone. Are you not a trifle young to have taken on the burden of rearing your brother's offspring? I should have thought you would be better occupied with establishing a home and family of your own."

Pandora glanced away, aware of a vague feeling of disappointment in the nobleman. Somehow she had not expected him to so easily relegate her to the accepted role of wife and mother, when clearly she was a female of independent thought. "But I have my own home, your grace," Pandora did not hesitate to remind him. "And the children *are* my family for as long as they need me. Furthermore, I now have my career to sustain me. Far from regretting my lot, I consider that I am blessed with the best of both possible worlds." She paused to study him. "In any case, your grace, my domestic well-being can hardly have been what brought you here today."

"As a matter of fact, your marital status does have some little bearing on my purpose in coming," Rivenoak answered, surprisingly. "It seems I require your professional services. I have been informed, Miss Featherstone, that you are a female of rare intelligence and, rarer still, confidentiality. As the matter I am about to relate to you is of a most delicate nature, I must ask your assurance that nothing that passes between us will ever leave this room."

Pandora, startled at the disclosure that far from entertaining an interest in her presence at Colonel Massingale's Town House, the Duke of Rivenoak was apparently proposing to hire her on a matter of his own, was quick to readjust her thinking.

"I should not be a confidential inquiry agent, your grace," she stated firmly, "if I betrayed my clients' trust. You may be sure that whatever you tell me will be treated with the utmost confidence, even should I refuse to take the assignment."

"Refuse, Miss Featherstone?" Rivenoak's lip curled in a manner certain to ruffle Pandora's feathers. "You are a woman, a spinster, moreover, of patently limited means. I am about to offer you a sizeable allowance and the means to enter Society under my aegis and at my expense. I hardly think you will refuse to accept the assignment."

"Do you not, indeed?" lilted Pandora, who, at five and twenty, had long ceased to entertain any notions of moving in polite circles and who, additionally, having not since her one and only disastrous Season at eighteen fostered the least wish to have done, found little inducement in such an offer. Furthermore, while it might be true she had not a feather to fly with, she had determined long ago that she would rather make do with her small competence and what she could earn by her own effort than to sacrifice her independence for any price. She was, consequently, more than a little offended at the assumption that she would find an offer of money and clothes irresistible simply because she was a woman and one of meager resources. Still, she could not deny a strong curiosity to hear the nobleman out. If the duke was willing to go to the not inconsiderable expense to establish her as a lady of fashion, then the matter must be of singular importance.

"I am indeed a woman, sir," Pandora replied with only a hint of irony, "and a spinster of limited means. Nevertheless, I should have to hear what you have to say before I commit myself to anything more than my promise of complete confidentiality. Now, do you intend to tell me what this is all about or not? I should understand if you wished to consult one of your own gender in this matter. You obviously do not entertain a very high opinion of females."

"On the contrary, Miss Featherstone," demurred his grace, smiling faintly. It would seem he had struck a spark from Miss Featherstone. "Even if I did not require the services of a female confidential inquiry agent, I should still have the greatest respect for women and their indisputable strengths. It has been my experience that the gentler sex can make by far the more formidable of foes or allies. They tend by their very nature to be incomprehensible to males, who consequently too often make the error of underestimating them, even going so far as to view them as creatures of lesser intelligence. I should never make that mistake, Miss Featherstone, especially in your case. You are obviously a female of superior reason."

"Am I?" replied Pandora archly, wondering at this new turn

of his grace's. Only a moment ago, he had seemed intent on raising her hackles, and now he was offering her Spanish coin. Obviously, he was intent on testing her mettle. "I should be curious to know on what evidence you have based your conclusions. I am not, I warn you, given to succumbing to empty compliments."

No, she would not be, reflected Rivenoak, having already observed that, though she might be a trifle eccentric and above caring about appearances (he could not but note the grey serge gown in which she had chosen to make her reappearance, while neat and presentable, could hardly have been termed attractive, or that her hair, while glinting glorious gold sparks in the lamplight, failed to conform to even the hint of a fashionable coiffure), the surprising Miss Featherstone was hardly anyone's fool. "I never supposed that you were. I based my conclusions on the manner in which you treat your nephews and nieces. Only a highly rational mind would have devised a picnic in an imaginary setting designed to instruct as well as entertain children on a rainy afternoon."

"No doubt I am gratified that you think so, your grace," Pandora coolly retorted. "On the other hand, I should not be a very good confidential inquiry agent if I were not open to creative ways of thinking. There is a deal more to resolving conundrums than meets the eye. Most people fail utterly to recognize even the most obvious pieces of a puzzle or their true significance, never mind visualizing how each one actually fits into the greater picture. They are too often blinded to the simplest of truths by a deplorable lack of objectivity, not to mention the most basic grasp of deductive reasoning."

"But not you, Miss Featherstone," observed Rivenoak with only a hint of dryness. "I daresay you have already formulated a theory to explain my presence here today."

"As a matter of fact, your grace, I have come to several conclusions concerning you," Pandora did not hesitate to inform him. "Not the least of which is that you are not precisely what you would have people believe you to be."

She was rewarded for that astute observation with the arch of a black, arrogant eyebrow. "Am I not?" murmured Rivenoak in a velvet-edged voice that had quashed the pretensions of far more exalted personages than Lady Pandora Featherstone. "You intrigue me. In what manner am I not what I appear to be?"

If he had thought by that to put her in her place, he was soon to be greatly disappointed. Far from backing down from the challenge, the redoubtable Miss Featherstone proceeded to regard him with frankly probing eyes.

"In many ways, I should think," she answered, a pucker of concentration forming between her eyebrows. "The most obvious, however, is your innate kindness, which you go to great lengths to conceal from the world behind a facade of cynicism. You are, furthermore, despite your reputation for ruthlessness, possessed of a generous disposition and a sensitivity to the feelings of others, both of which you amply demonstrated here today with my nephews and nieces. I daresay people are mistaken in thinking you have taken on the unpopular cause of reform for the benefit of the lower classes out of arrogance and the desire to demonstrate you are above the conventions that govern your contemporaries. I believe you actually care about the plight of the destitute and homeless."

"Do you, Miss Featherstone?" murmured the duke, noting an animated glow tended to light Miss Featherstone's lovely features whenever she was in the process of employing her talent for deductive reasoning.

"Indeed, I do, your grace, and pray do not deny it. I, after all, have seen and heard you here today. You demonstrated a sympathetic affinity for the tale of 'Boy-Who-Walks,' which betrays you. You may not have been born a shaman of your people, but you are a powerful duke. It would be illogical to suppose that a man who would choose to relate such a story for the instruction of children would fail to espouse those noble precepts himself, or to practice them.''

''It was only a story,'' shrugged Rivenoak, marveling at her quick wit and perspicacity. But then, Miss Featherstone was proving to be a most unusual female and a most damned distracting one, he reflected, acutely aware that her plain serge gown failed utterly to camouflage her feminine attributes, even as her absurd tartan sari had had the disturbing effect of all but revealing them. She was a cursedly attractive woman.

Hellsfire, she was far more than that. He had, from the first moment of laying eyes on her, been made keenly cognizant of the fact that she was a creature of rare beauty, not to mention intelligence, and subsequent exposure had served only to reinforce that initial impression. As small and slender as a girl, she was yet amply blessed with well-rounded womanly hips, which served only to accentuate a willowy waist and high, firm breasts that appeared tantalizingly designed to perfectly fit the palms of his hands. In addition, the luxurious abundance of her hair, falling in rebellious disarray from its pins, filled him with an almost overwhelming desire to clasp his fingers in its silken mass. If that were not all or enough, she was possessed of eyes that sparkled with animation, skin that glowed with an ivory perfection, and lips that had a disturbing tendency to pucker when she was contemplating the complexities of a conundrum.

Laughs-In-The-Rain would have said that the powers of the Earth Mother had been generously endowed in Miss Featherstone.

''I believe to say it is merely a story is not strictly the truth, your grace,'' Pandora came back at him. ''There was the ring of sincerity in the telling that would indicate Boy-Who-Walks was someone you actually knew.'' Patently unaware of the disconcerting effect she was having on her guest, she came to stand within a foot of him. ''Furthermore,'' she added gently, ''I believe he was someone who was once very close to you.''

The devil she did, thought Rivenoak, wondering what game

Miss Featherstone was playing. She must know very well what the truth of the matter was. And yet, he could not sense the lie in her. Either she was very deep, indeed, or she was very much in earnest. In either case, she needed, for his own peace of mind, to be put in her place. "You are impertinent, Miss Featherstone," observed Rivenoak, dampeningly.

"Am I, your grace?" replied the singular Miss Featherstone, clearly undaunted by his forbidding aspect. "You did ask, however, and I assumed you wished a straightforward answer."

"You have assumed a great deal in your analysis of my character," drawled Rivenoak, who was quickly revising a host of preestablished assumptions of his own concerning Miss Featherstone. "Most of which, I'm afraid, is far wide of the mark. The truth is you have mistaken kindness for civility. When you come to know me better, you will discover that I am seldom generous and never kind. I am, in fact, precisely as my reputation would have me."

"Naturally you would say so, your grace," returned Pandora, with perfect equanimity. "I daresay you go to great lengths to give that impression." A small furrow creased her brow. "Why, I wonder?"

Rivenoak, who was made keenly aware of her close proximity by the subtle scent of lilacs assailing his nostrils, was hard put not to reach out to satisfy at least one driving curiosity. "Because, Miss Featherstone, it serves my purposes," he answered, drawing forth an exquisite enameled snuff box in order to refrain from crushing one of her rebellious curls in his fist, merely for the pleasure of watching it spring back again. "Upon a proper analysis of the facts, one might just as easily conclude that my purpose in working to improve the lot of the less fortunate is pragmatic, rather than altruistic." Deliberately, he inhaled a pinch of his favorite mixture, then brushing an imaginary speck from his sleeve, returned the box to his pocket.

"Indeed, your grace?" queried Pandora, inexplicably aware of the incipience of an odd sort of flutter in the region of her

stomach. Somewhat belatedly, perhaps, she became acutely
sensitive to the fact that she was alone in the room with a man
who exuded a steely, controlled strength and a curious aura of
power, which had little to do with his exalted station, but with
something that emanated from within himself. Strangely, it was
not fear that attended this awareness, but a quickening of her
own intuitive powers of deductive reasoning.

It came to her that beneath the hard veneer was a man of
sensitivity and compassion who had been deeply wounded at
sometime in his life. Why else should he take such pains to erect
an impregnable wall of cynicism about himself? she reasoned,
overcome by an absurd urge to cradle the side of his face with
her hand. As if that were not bad enough, she discovered her
balance was curiously affected by his mere presence in such a
manner that she felt herself resisting an unwonted tendency to
sway toward his tall frame.

"Indeed, Miss Featherstone," affirmed the duke, seemingly
oblivious to the rosy hue that becomingly tinged her cheeks at
her unwonted thoughts, a circumstance for which she could
only be exceedingly grateful. "It has been amply demonstrated
in the past, after all," he continued conversationally, as though
theirs were a perfectly ordinary meeting, unfraught by undercurrents of wholly irrational emotion, "that the privileged classes
survive according to the light in which the less privileged
perceive their own well-being. As a premier nobleman of the
realm, second only to royalty, I should naturally deplore to see
England follow the example set most recently by France."

It came to Pandora, as she found herself next wondering
what it would be like to be kissed by the stern, handsome lips,
that she had ought to find some excuse to end the interview
before she made a complete fool of herself. Indeed, no doubt
she would have done had it not occurred to her almost immediately upon that thought that Rivenoak was offering her the
elements of a most stimulating conundrum in an area that had

long been a mystery to her—the phenomenon of instantaneous physical magnetism between two complete strangers.

Naturally inquisitive, she had of course wondered, as in the case of Tristram and Isolde, or of Romeo and Juliet, for that matter, what forces might be at work between two people fated to experience an immediate mutual attraction to one another, one, moreover, powerful enough to create a storm of emotion capable of sweeping away all rational thinking. She was, thanks to Rivenoak's riveting presence, beginning to apprehend what could cause otherwise perfectly sane individuals to cast to the wind the most basic instincts for self-preservation.

"And what of the example set by the American colonies, your grace?" Pandora managed, marveling at her power to think and speak at all coherently when she was being overtaken by a wholly disturbing impulse to lift her arms about the nobleman's neck. "You, after all, were born in the New World on the eve of rebellion, were you not?"

Rivenoak smiled sardonically to himself, aware that the redoubtable Miss Featherstone was trying subtly to worm information out of him. No doubt she was perfectly aware that his mother had been a woman of the tribes and that he, himself, as a result was of mixed blood. Miss Featherstone, after all, had his mother's Bible in her possession. If she thought to use it to her advantage, however, she would soon find that she had greatly misjudged the case. The devil knew his grandfather had done all in his power to keep secret that provocative tidbit of information about the heir to the dukedom. The son of She-Who-Joyfully-Sings, on the other hand, was not and never could be ashamed of his blood. On the contrary, he had ever entertained a deep and abiding pride in his heritage, a pride that no one, not even his paternal grandfather, could eradicate, no matter how severe the punishment.

Grimly reminding himself of his purpose in coming, and quelling the almost irresistible impulse to clasp the scheming Miss Featherstone in his arms in order to taste those provocatively pursed lips, he vowed she would get nothing from him, save for a lesson in the folly of aligning herself with his enemies.

Carelessly, he shrugged.

"As the son of an English nobleman," he replied, "I should hardly be expected to feel sympathy for the Americans. You are far wide of the mark, Miss Featherstone, if you think the Duke of Rivenoak could ever be a republican at heart."

"No, not a republican," she agreed, gazing earnestly up at him. "But a nobleman, perhaps, with an enlightened view of human suffering."

Good God, thought Rivenoak, feeling himself drawn into the mesmeric depths of Miss Featherstone's cursedly beautiful orbs. Matters were not progressing at all as he had imagined them. Far from impressing on her a proper understanding of his dangerous nature, he was very close to finding himself seduced by the spinster.

It was time he took hold of the reins.

"I am Rivenoak," growled the duke. "What should *I* possibly know of human suffering, Miss Featherstone? None of which signifies. The point of the exercise in deductive reasoning was not to unravel the complexities of my character, but to delve into the purpose of why I have sought your services."

"But that is hardly a conundrum, your grace," replied Pandora. "It is, in fact, perfectly obvious. You intend to break your usual custom of remaining aloof from the social events of the Season. You are not, however, doing so out of any desire to find yourself a wife. In which case, you would naturally wish to protect yourself from all the match-making mamas and their aspiring single daughters, who would undoubtedly prove a hindrance in whatever your real purpose is. You require my services at the very least as a sort of body guard with the added benefit of a decoy to draw attention away from you. What am I to be, your grace? A newcomer on the scene who has attracted your notice to the exclusion of all the other eligible young ladies, or your betrothed?"

"You are as astute as I was led to believe, Miss Featherstone," murmured Rivenoak, an odd glint in his eye. "As it happens, I had more in mind a promised bride. Such an arrangement would present fewer difficulties. The Season begins in little more than a month," observed his grace. "That should give you time enough to acquire the wardrobe necessary for your introduction into Society."

"That, your grace, might prove something of a stumbling block," confessed Pandora with a wry smile. "I'm afraid I have not the least head for fashion. And, besides, I have not said I should take the assignment. If I were to agree to pose as your betrothed, I believe I should have to have some notion as to your real purpose for this charade. It occurs to me, your grace, that you may be in some sort of difficulty, in which case, to be of any help to you, I should know in what, precisely, I am involving myself."

It was a reasonable request, one that Rivenoak had prepared himself to meet. Unaccountably, he felt a sudden repugnance at giving her the parcel of half-truths he had earlier devised for her benefit. Indeed, he was experiencing the uncanny premonition that he may have done Miss Featherstone a disservice when he assumed she was a scheming female simply because she had had brief residence in Massingale's Town House, not to mention the fact she had the misfortune to be related to Captain Herodotus Featherstone. There was the possibility, no matter how remote, that she was ignorant of the colonel's part in infamy, or her brother's, for that matter.

"I can only tell you, Miss Featherstone, that I would seem to be the object of a plot to discredit me. It is my belief that the malefactor is a member of the *Ton,* which is why I have determined to participate in the Season. You are naturally correct in your assumption that I should require protection from the unmarried females, who have, in the past, demonstrated a singular determination to land me in Parson's Mousetrap. I require freedom of movement while I gather proof against the person or persons behind the plot against me. Equally important, however, I require someone with your particular gift for astute observation to serve as a second pair of eyes and ears at my back.''

Pandora's heart quickened with sudden conviction. ''Then you already suspect someone. Am I to know who that someone is?''

Rivenoak, turning to look at her, shrugged. ''How not? He is a man who has long entertained an enmity toward my house, a man who would stop at nothing to achieve his ends. His name, Miss Featherstone, is Massingale.''

Pandora's heart gave an unwitting leap beneath her breast. ''Colonel Thornton Massingale?'' she said carefully.

Faith, she should have guessed. Why else should Rivenoak have come to her?

''Indeed, ma'am, do you know him?'' Rivenoak queried, his face revealing nothing.

But of course she knew him. The duke knew very well that she did.

''As a matter of fact, I do, your grace,'' she replied, turning away lest he read too much in her eyes. Immediately she came about again to face him. ''Which is why,'' she said, meeting his gaze directly, ''I very much regret that I must refuse your offer.''

She was not sure what reaction she expected from him. Certainly it was not to have the duke loom suddenly over her, so closely, in fact, that she was swept with an overpowering urge to lean her palms against his chest. Worse, it was obvious from the faint gleam of a smile on his lips that he was perfectly aware of the unsettling effect he was having on her.

''Are you sure, Miss Featherstone?'' he asked, noting with interest the flood of color that stained her cheeks. ''I believe we should have made an excellent team.''

Pandora, feeling herself drawn into the blue intensity of his eyes, had to force herself to shake her head. ''I know we should, your grace, but I cannot. It is a matter of ethics. As it happens, I am already engaged on a matter. Clearly, it would be unethical for me to hire my services out to you before I have finished my prior assignment.''

''Ethics. I see.'' Pandora's stomach lurched as Rivenoak lifted a hand to lightly brush a stray curl from her cheek. ''You are a remarkable woman, Miss Featherstone.''

Pandora, struggling against a multitude of bewildering sensations aroused by his nearness, not to mention the compelling urge to fling integrity and Colonel Massingale to the breeze, suffered a sharp stab of disappointment and an equally potent sense of relief when he pulled away. Mutely she watched him cross to the door, then pause, his hand on the door handle. ''Should you change your mind, Miss Featherstone, I trust you will let me know.''

The next moment he was gone, leaving Pandora staring at the door through which he had vanished. Inexplicably, she experienced an unwonted urge to fling something at the oaken barrier.

How very curious, the effect he would seem to have on her, she reflected, willing her heart to cease its ridiculous pounding. She had never before felt a similar urge to forget herself with a gentleman. But then, she doubted not there could ever be another like the Duke of Rivenoak. Obviously he was a man of extreme magnetism, which no female could long resist, and only his innate kindness and highly developed sense of honor had intervened to save her from making an utter fool of herself.

Somehow she was not in the least comforted by the thought.

Chapter 3

"But you could not have turned him down!" exclaimed Aunt Cora, pausing in her never-ending efforts to maintain the house in an impossible state of pristine order. She stared in horrified disbelief at Pandora.

"I did, Aunt Cora. I refused the assignment. I had no choice. There was an unavoidable conflict of interests. I have, after all, accepted a considerable sum from Colonel Massingale. Until I am released from his service, I cannot in all conscience take on a new client, now can I?"

"But he is Rivenoak," Cora pointed out, as if that were the cogent point. "And Colonel Massingale is—is Colonel Massingale. A more disagreeable man I should never hope to meet. He is overbearing and pompous. He tracked mud into the foyer, and then he all but flung his coat and gloves at me as if I were a downstairs maid. Why, he does not like tea! Can you imagine that? Not at all like his grace. So soft-spoken and courteous. You can tell just by looking at him that the Duke of Rivenoak is a gentleman in the finest sense of the word."

"He is, indeed, Aunt Cora," agreed Pandora, smiling at the older woman's assessment of the duke. Obviously, Rivenoak had made a conquest of more than the children that day. But then, he had had a telling effect on her as well, she reflected, recalling her unexpectedly sharp stab of dismay upon hearing him utter Massingale's name.

Indeed, it seemed that her polite words of refusal yet reverberated in the air around her. How empty they seemed in the wake of his departure! And how she wished she might call them back again. Botheration, call *him* back again, she admitted ruefully to herself.

It had nothing to do with the fact that he had the most compelling eyes into which she had ever gazed or that his broad-shouldered, masculine physique was blessed with a sinuous grace that had the curious effect of making her pulse race in a most alarming manner. No, it was only that she had seldom spent a more stimulating afternoon or enjoyed the company of a gentleman more fully, she told herself firmly. Besides, the truth be told she would have liked nothing better than to apply her powers of deductive reasoning on his behalf. His must be a most intriguing conundrum, or he would not have gone to such lengths to make himself acquainted with her. Still, there was nothing for it but to continue as she had begun—in the colonel's service. To do anything else would be to violate every sense of integrity. She had, after all, accepted fifty pounds with a further promise upon completion of the assignment of another fifty from Colonel Massingale. It was to him she now owed her first allegiance, little as she might like it.

And, in truth, she did not like it, had, in fact, come some time past to mistrust the colonel and his motives for enlisting her services. The assignment, after all, gave every evidence of being a drummed-up affair designed to employ her time in a useless exercise.

Pandora had agreed to it in spite of, or perhaps *because* of, the curious nature of the assignment, not to mention the irresistible opportunity to do some investigating of her own into the earlier and far more intriguing conundrum of the marquis's murder. Nevertheless, a hundred pounds to do research in her employer's library could not but seem excessive for the work involved. Furthermore, she had found it not a little strange that she was required to live on the premises during the performance of her duties. Upon having been shown the articles in question, she was made even more suspicious of Colonel Massingale's purpose in employing her to do what might easily have been accomplished, after all, by the colonel's secretary or anyone, for that matter, who could read and write moderately well. While they most certainly presented a conundrum, the articles, of themselves, would have offered little of interest to anyone, save for a confidential inquiry agent trained in the subtleties of observation and deductive reasoning.

The rattle, fashioned from a turtle shell and numerous small pebbles, was easily traced to the native tribes of North America, while the mask of a face rather comically distorted would seem to place the items in the province of several related tribes located along the eastern sea coast, ranging as far north and west as the territory surrounding the five Great Lakes. Neither piece could be considered of a rare or extraordinary nature, as they were quite common among the existing tribes. The beaded leather pouch containing a feather, four smooth pebbles, a few dried kernels of corn, and the small bones of some sort of animal, while interesting, had likewise proven mundane in the context of North American natives. It seemed it was an accepted practice for each adult male of the tribes to keep a pouch on his person in which were contained common objects believed to represent spirits from his personal dream visions.

More intriguing was the long-bladed knife featuring a bone handle, exquisitely carved with representations of a lion and a grizzly bear, the archetype for which could not be traced to any of the tribes. Since lions were not indigenous to either of the Americas, it would have been strange, indeed, if it had. It had been obvious that either it was not of Native American origin, or it owed its existence to an outside influence, the most likely possibility being that Ridgeway, or some other European, had, at the very least, suggested the design to a native artisan. This, and the fact that it was rather unique, might make it an object of interest, but hardly one of historical moment.

Finally, the crude map traced on the back of a tanned hide depicting three rivers was of little help at all, since the reference points appeared not to be recorded on any of the charts available for her inspection. There was nothing, furthermore, to indicate the scale of the territory covered, in which case the rivers depicted might be small streams or rivulets rather than significant waterways. There simply was no way to determine the locality.

She had soon found herself at *point-non-plus*, until she had thought to examine the paint with which the map had been drawn. How very curious that it should have turned out to be a common oil paint used by artists. Even more curious, however, was the certainty that the application was of fairly recent origin, probably dating no farther back in time than a week or two at most. A visit to a local tanner, moreover, had determined that the skin was not deer hide, as Massingale had claimed, but had been derived from the bovine family, most probably a specimen of the West Highland breed of Scotland.

Obviously, the map was a sham, a rather poorly executed one at that, one which had been contrived solely for her benefit with the obvious purpose of insuring her presence in the house on Portman Square. Why? What reason could Massingale have had in luring her to his Town House? And why the elaborate fabrication complete with props to keep her there?

Her first suspicion, that Massingale had engineered the entire scenario in order to make unseemly advances toward a young, unattached female without benefit of a male to protect her, had prompted her to include among the possessions she took with her to Massingale's the brace of pistols Herodotus had left in her keeping. Two days and nights in the Town House undisturbed by anything worse than an odd feeling she was being watched (a sensation she attributed to her own overactive imagination), however, had seemed moot evidence that the colonel had not entertained designs of a lascivious nature toward her and had led her to consider other, less obvious, possibilities.

One which had instantly suggested itself, but which she had no immediate means of ascertaining, was that there was some obscure connection between herself and Massingale of which she was unaware. It was not really so farfetched a notion, she told herself, when one took into account the fact that Massingale and her brother Herodotus had served contemporaneously in the American colonies. There was at least the outside possibility that they had been acquainted. Herodotus, unfortunately, had ever demonstrated a particular reluctance to discuss his experiences as a young leftenant in the New World. Indeed, she had at times suspected that her brother had preferred to put that brief episode in his career out of his mind altogether, but for reasons that she could not begin to determine.

What she *had* determined was that Massingale had wanted her in the house for reasons that were unclear to her and that he had gone to a deal of trouble and not a little expense to contrive that she would be there She was equally certain that whatever Massingale was up to, it had a great deal to do with the Duke of Rivenoak. The duke had confided, after all, that he suspected the colonel of plotting against him. She was convinced, furthermore, that Rivenoak was her Mysterious Intruder. Simple deductive reasoning led her to conclude that Rivenoak's true purpose in seeking her out this morning was to discover her part in Massingale's supposed plot against him.

All of which served only to bring to light a whole new tangle of questions in a conundrum that was growing more complicated by the minute. If, for example, Massingale were involved in a plot against Rivenoak, why should the colonel have brought her, in particular, into it? Surely if he had done it deliberately, it would seem to indicate not only an obscure connection between Massingale and herself (through Herodotus), but one between herself and Rivenoak as well. After all, the contrivance to set her up in the Town House, coupled with the incident of the Mysterious Intruder, would seem a highly unlikely coincidence. No, she very much suspected that Massingale had, at the very least, arranged for her to be a witness to Rivenoak's unlawful entry into the Town House and whatever must have happened had she been where she was meant to be. Only her impromptu visit to the British Museum along with her difficulty in obtaining a hack to bring her home before dark had spoiled everything. She had been away during the crucial break-in.

The break-in, she reflected midway between retrieving a cushion from the floor and plumping it back into shape before returning it to its place at the end of the sofa. How very curious it was, when one stopped to think of it, especially in light of Rivenoak's unexpected call. *Something* had lured him to the house on Portman Square, something important enough for a duke to engage in what on the surface would seem an ill-conceived and most certainly bizarre act of burglary. What he had found was the box, engraved with his father's initials. Was it that for which he had come looking?

What the devil was in the cursed box? she wondered, abandoning all pretence of helping Cora straighten up after their impromptu picnic, as it occurred to her that the box, or its contents, was the key to the conundrum. Indeed, she could only marvel that she had not considered its implications before.

If there was a plot against the Duke of Rivenoak and Massingale had drawn her into it, she had every right to demand to know what was in the box. Indeed, she would be exceedingly foolish if she did not face the colonel as soon as was possible with all that she had discovered. At the very least, she would demand to be released from a contract that gave every appearance of having a nefarious purpose.

It would be not a little inconvenient to travel all the way to Southampton to confront her employer, she reflected, ruefully aware of the expense, not to mention the time, which would be involved in such a journey. Still, she would go even to that extreme, if necessary, to resolve the matter with expediency. First, however, she might as well try the house on Portman Square in the hopes that Mr. Cousins, the colonel's solicitor, had arrived to check on her progress as he was promised to do on occasion. If nothing else, perhaps he could send word to Massingale that Pandora required an immediate interview.

Her mind made up, she turned to inform Aunt Cora that she must go out for a time, when she was interrupted by Mrs. Giddings, her rather sour and less than enthusiastic housekeeper, who announced the arrival of the cart bearing Pandora's belongings from Colonel Massingale's.

"Very good, Mrs. Giddings," Pandora replied. "As I must go out for a while, be so kind as to have everything deposited in my study. I shall see to its proper disposition later."

"As you wish, miss," Mrs. Giddings replied grudgingly. Gazing askance at the clutter before withdrawing, she uttered an audible "harumph" as she pulled the doors closed.

"That woman," Cora muttered, giving the pillow in her hand a vigorous thump.

Pandora, accustomed to the antipathy between the dour-faced housekeeper and the meticulous spinster, smothered a smile. "I know, dear, but she does her work reasonably well, and she *is* all I can afford at present." She gazed about her with a wry grimace. "I do hate to leave you with this shambles. I am afraid, however, it cannot be helped. I really must go out."

"Pray do not give it a thought, my dear." Cora gave a deprecatory gesture of the hand. "Heaven knows, you have enough to occupy you. Philomena was used to leave all the household matters to me. I do wish you will do the same. I daresay it is all I am good for."

"All you are good for!" exclaimed Pandora, her attention

fairly caught by the unwontedly brittle note in the older woman's voice. "What utter nonsense. You know I should not know how to manage without you. I worry as it is that I take too great advantage of your generous nature."

"You could never do that, Pandora," replied Cora with a white-lipped smile. "I know you have had to put up with me because Philomena left instructions in her will to that effect, and heaven knows how I should have gone on without you and the children after she . . ."

To Pandora's consternation, Cora choked, apparently unable to finish, and hastily turned away. What in heaven's name was this? wondered Pandora, her heart going out to her aunt's former friend and dearest companion of thirty years. Cora Pemberton, in spite of her habitually harried air, rather like that of a sparrow who has ever just escaped the clutches of an alley cat, had been a stolid pillar of strength for Pandora.

"Cora, dearest!" Pandora exclaimed. "What is it?"

"For pity's sake," Cora gasped. "Would you look at me? Three years she has been gone, and here I am blubbering like the silly old fool that I am. Pray pay me no mind."

"You are neither a fool nor old. You mustn't think such things. I know you miss Aunt Philomena dreadfully, but you must never for one moment imagine that you are not an integral part of this family. It has nothing to do with any will. It is because we all love and depend on you. You are the mainstay of this unruly mob. Why, we should all be in a perpetual shambles if we did not have you to keep us all in order. Surely you must know that." Drawing a handkerchief from the cuff of her sleeve, Pandora pressed the wisp of linen and lace into the older woman's hand. "Now, pray blow your nose and tell me what has happened to overset you."

"It is nothing, really," said Cora, vigorously applying herself to Pandora's handkerchief. "Only, lately I have begun to feel that I am an unnecessary burden on you, Pandora. Oh, I know you would never say so; but I am, after all, another mouth to

feed, and I am perfectly aware how slender are our resources.
I have wracked my brain trying to think how I should help,
but, short of hiring myself out as a housekeeper, I really have
very little of worth to offer.''

''Now you *are* being absurd,'' declared Pandora, who was
soundly berating herself for not having seen earlier that Cora
was in such a case. ''Indeed, I will not listen to you belittle
yourself, when you are not only indispensable to us, but more
precious than a king's ransom in gold. Now, we will have no
more talk of hiring yourself out as a housekeeper. Your place
is here. We shall all make out just fine, Cora, dear. It is not as
though we were out on the streets, you know.''

''No, but you cannot deny that we are only a step or two
from it.'' Sniffing, Cora Pemberton straightened thin shoulders.
''Pandora, my heart ached to see you in that old gown in the
company of so fine a gentleman as the Duke of Rivenoak, when
by all rights you should have taken your place in Society years
ago. You are a beautiful young woman. If you do not realize
that, you may be sure that his grace was aware of it. Were you
unencumbered, I have no doubt you would have made a splendid match. As it is—''

''As it is, I am perfectly content to be as I am—unwed,
independent, and firmly launched in a new career. I have never
wished to enter Society, and I am certainly not on the look-
out for a husband. Why should I be, when I have you and the
children to look after me. Besides, dare I to point out that
you and Aunt Philomena lived wonderfully fulfilled lives as
spinsters? Why should I be any different?''

''It is not at all the same, Pandora,'' Cora insisted, ''and
you know it. Philomena and I had each other. You were meant
for something quite different.''

''Was I?'' Pandora smiled, an image of still, blue eyes and
a stern countenance springing, unbidden, to her mind. Sternly,
she shook it off, chiding herself for a silly fool. Daydreaming
about a duke, and the Duke of Rivenoak most especially, was

a feckless enterprise for a confidential inquiry agent noted for her objectivity and independent thinking. ''Well, then,'' she said bracingly, the mischievous dimple peeping forth at the corner of her mouth, ''if I was meant for it, then there would seem little point in worrying about it. What will be will be. The future, after all, is one conundrum that only time can resolve.''

Planting a buss on Aunt Cora's cheek, Pandora left the older woman to stare after her with a mist in her eyes.

When she had left the Town House on Portman Square the night before, there had been little to distinguish the mansion from its neighbors, nearly all of which had worn a quiet air of dignified unoccupancy. Pandora was, consequently, not a little startled upon her arrival at ten after three in the afternoon to encounter a scene of utter chaos. Numerous soldiers were tramping about the grounds in a manner that suggested they were searching for something, while a host of bystanders, servants, for the most part, from the neighboring houses, watched and whispered among themselves.

Pandora was stopped at the door by a sergeant of the Guard, who demanded to know her business therein. It was only after Mrs. Caulkins was summoned to confirm that Miss Featherstone was, indeed, in the employ of Colonel Massingale that she was finally allowed to enter.

''Such doings, Lady Pandora,'' exclaimed a wholly distraught Mrs. Caulkins, as soon as they were inside. ''I never expected to see you here today. But then, I never thought to have to live through such a day as this again. If it is about your things, the boy picked them up some little time ago. I do hope you found nothing amiss with them?''

''No, indeed, Mrs. Caulkins. Or, at least I trust everything is quite in order. The truth is I have not taken time to sort through them as yet,'' Pandora confessed, her gaze going beyond the housekeeper to a rotund gentleman attired in a nondescript brown overcoat, yellow waistcoat, and drab short trousers, the plainness of which would seem to place him among the common order. Her first impression, that he was a tradesman, come to demand payment of a bill, she quickly altered upon finding herself under the most penetrating of scrutinies. Certainly, no tradesman would look at a lady in such a manner. A cent-per-cent, then? she speculated, returning her gaze to Mrs. Caulkins. "I came in the hopes I might find Mr. Cousins here today. It is of no little importance that I reach Colonel Massingale as soon as is possible, and I thought perhaps Mr. Cousins—"

"Dear me, but you are too late!" wailed the housekeeper, displaying every manifestation of one on the verge of a fit of the vapors. "The poor gentleman is dead."

"Dead?" Pandora echoed in no little bestartlement. "Mr. Cousins? How-how unfortunate—and how very sudden. He seemed perfectly hale and hearty when I had the privilege of being introduced to him little more than three days ago."

"And so he is yet, I shouldn't wonder," interjected the strange gentleman, stepping forward. "Unless he, likewise, has suffered the curse of this house, Miss—?"

"Featherstone," Pandora obliged him. Upon closer inspection, the pale eyes appeared razor keen, but with a cunning that would seem to have little to do with greed. In addition, she could not but note the heels of his buckle shoes were worn down in such a manner as to suggest a man who spent no little time on his feet. The gentleman, if she were not mistaken, was one of Mr. Fielding's Bow Street Runners. "And you are?"

"Townsend, ma'am. Happy to make your acquaintance, though I must regret the circumstances."

"Must you, Mr. Townsend?" queried Pandora, once again altering her judgment of the man. Not only was Mr. Townsend a Bow Street Runner; he was, in fact, the most famous of that small group of professional constables. It was well-known that he had had the distinction of being on speaking terms with

Mad King George, when the old king had still had his wits about him. "And what circumstances are these?"

She knew before he answered. Indeed, she could only wonder that she had not guessed the truth the instant she laid eyes on the scene outside.

"Unfortunate circumstances, Miss Featherstone. Most unfortunate, indeed. It is not Mr. Cousins, ma'am, who has met an untimely demise, but Colonel Massingale, himself. Foully done in in his very own library, he was. Just like the marquis before him."

"Stabbed in the chest, you mean?" Pandora was quick to respond. "The library door and the windows all locked from the inside?"

She was rewarded for this astute observation with a sharpened glance from Mr. Townsend.

"Precisely, Miss Featherstone. How could you possibly possess such intimate details of a murder that took place nearly twenty years ago? You are far too young to have been aware of them at the time of their occurrence."

"Miss Featherstone is a confidential inquiry agent," supplied Mrs. Caulkins. "I daresay she knows a great deal about such things."

"Perhaps more than she had ought," suggested Mr. Townsend. Hooking his thumbs in the pockets of his waistcoat, he rocked back on his heels, all the while studying Pandora with that keen, speculative gaze.

"I am indeed a confidential inquiry agent and, as such, have made it my practice to study crimes of an interesting or unusual nature," Pandora conceded, not in the least discommoded by Mr. Townsend's obvious efforts to put her on the defensive. "I know little more about the marquis's murder, however, than was printed in the papers upon the event of the crime some eighteen years ago. My father, you see, was used to keep clippings of unsolved crimes. He found them most instructive in my training in logical deduction."

"Highly unusual, wouldn't you say, exposing a female to descriptions of violence for educational purposes?" commented Mr. Townsend, clearly skeptical of what he must have considered a radical concept for the instruction of females.

"As a matter of fact, the Earl of Braxton was noted for his innovative thinking. He was used to pride himself on being a Renaissance man and sought to rear his offspring in those precepts. The fact that I am a female, I believe, he did not consider a relevant detail."

"No, not relevant at all," dryly uttered Townsend, stroking his chin between thumb and forefinger. "Well. Be that as it may, there were dire happenings in this house no later than last night. You were here, I understand, Miss Featherstone. Perhaps you saw something that might give us some insight into what occurred."

"I was only here for a moment or two, long enough to pick up a few of my things. It was all perfectly uneventful, I assure you," glibly lied Pandora, who saw little point in bringing up the subject of her Mysterious Intruder, especially since she had not seen fit to tell Mrs. Caulkins of it the night before, a circumstance for which she could now only be grateful. Pandora did not for a moment believe the Duke of Rivenoak had plunged the knife into Colonel Massingale. The nobleman had, after all, exited before her own arrival at the house at four-thirty. There would, consequently, seem little point in apprising Townsend of the break-in. The least said for the moment, the better. "Perhaps," she suggested, "if you could tell me something of the details . . ."

"It was all perfectly dreadful, Miss Pandora," volunteered Mrs. Caulkins, giving a shudder. "It was Jessop and I who found him, poor man. We had never a notion he was even in the house. It was all by happenstance that I discovered the door was locked, with the key inside. Thinking perhaps the colonel had come during the night and let himself in without bothering to wake anyone, I knocked. When there was no answer, Jessop and I tried the windows on the terrace. They were latched, even as you said. Still, we could see the colonel through a gap in the curtains. Asprawl in his chair at the desk, he was, as if he had merely nodded off. When we could not rouse him by any means, I grew frightened. Jessop broke the door in. It was then we saw the knife in his chest. Oh, the *blood*. May the saints in heaven preserve me, Miss Pandora, from ever witnessing such a sight again.''

"Dear, I *am* sorry, Mrs. Caulkins," murmured Pandora, clasping the housekeeper's hands. "How very distressing for you and Jessop. And have you found nothing, Mr. Townsend, to indicate how the deed was accomplished?"

"Nothing that Mrs. Caulkins has not already related, Miss Featherstone," the Bow Street Runner replied, apparently less than pleased at the revelations that had been made to one whom he must consider at the very most a possible suspect in the crime and at the very least a meddlesome female. "Not that it is any concern of yours, if I may be so bold as to point out."

"Oh, but it is of no little concern to me, sir," objected Pandora, who could not but take exception to the man's patronizing manner. "Colonel Massingale employed me to do some investigating for him. I came today in the hopes of arranging to give him my final report. Naturally, I feel involved, no matter how peripherally, in the fact that he has met a tragic and untimely end."

Townsend, she noted, appeared less than impressed with her reasoning, but then, she supposed she could hardly blame him. The truth was, she was most desirous to see the body and conduct her own search of the premises for any clues that might mean something to her in the context of the little she already knew and suspected about the colonel. Most particularly, she wished to inspect the wooden box, which should most certainly have been returned to the library when she vacated her room upstairs.

She was wracking her brain for a way to broach the subject

of being allowed to examine the scene of the murder, when
Townsend himself opened the way for her.

"You say you were conducting an investigation for the colonel. Perhaps you would not mind telling me the nature of the
work you were doing for him."

"As a rule, I should refuse, Mr. Townsend, out of respect
for the confidentiality of my clients. Now, however, with the
colonel dead, I suppose there can be no harm in telling you.
As it happens, Colonel Massingale employed me to ascertain
the histories of certain tribal artifacts from the New World.
A ceremonial mask, a turtle-shell rattle, a pouch of spiritual
significance, a map, and a long-bladed knife with an anomalous
carving on the handle, whose origins could not be traced."
Pandora, a keen observer, could not fail to note Mr. Townsend's
white, bushy eyebrows twitch ever so slightly at mention of
the final item. "Since none of the articles were of any material
or historical value," she continued in calm tones despite a
sudden leap of her pulse, "I cannot think they are of any
significance to the events of last night. However, I should be
glad to give you what information I can about them."

"What—?" said Townsend, giving every appearance of a
man who had been momentarily lost in reverie. "Oh, yes, yes.
Most cordial of you, Miss Featherstone, I'm sure." The pale
blue eyes narrowed on her face. "There was a knife, you say.
A bone-handled knife. I wonder, could you identify it, if you
saw it."

"I should be an exceedingly poor confidential inquiry agent
if I could not, sir," said Pandora, wondering why the Bow
Street Runner persisted in treating her as if her wits were
wanting. *She,* after all, had not mentioned the knife was bone-
handled. "I have spent the past three days examining it in its
every particular."

"Excellent, Miss Featherstone," Mr. Townsend applauded.
"Then, perhaps you would not mind coming with me to the
library. As a confidential inquiry agent, fully acquainted with

the sordid aspects of crime, I daresay you will not be put off
by the trifling sight of a corpse and a mite of blood.''

''I am not like to swoon, if that is what you mean, sir,''
replied Pandora, who was far too relieved at having so easily
accomplished what she had thought an impossible object to
allow Mr. Townsend's acerbity to touch her. ''I should be most
happy to do what I can to help.''

Pandora was relieved to note upon being admitted to the
library that the scene of the crime, unlike the grounds being
trampled even at that moment by numerous soldiers, had been
left in precisely the condition in which Mrs. Caulkins and
Jessop, the butler, had found it. Colonel Massingale remained
grotesquely asprawl in the leather-upholstered armchair that
had served the great walnut desk, but which somehow had
found itself some three and a half feet from its normal resting
place behind the desk and with the burgundy Oriental rug
intriguingly bunched about its feet. The colonel, it seemed, had
been in the act of enjoying a libation of brandy, as was evidenced by the decanter on the desk in the company of a single,
partly filled glass. A quick, sweeping survey of the bookshelf-
lined room, furnished additionally with two library chairs, an
ottoman, a wine cabinet and grog tray, a cherry-wood occasional
table supporting a globe of the world, and a Queen Anne settee
upon which had been flung a military greatcoat, a tricorn hat,
and a pair of black kid gloves, revealed no sign of the mysterious
wooden box.

''Well, Miss Featherstone,'' said Mr. Townsend, observing
Pandora's examination of the room with a sardonic tolerance,
''I am curious to know what you make of it.''

''No more than you have made of it, I daresay, Mr. Townsend,'' replied Pandora with equanimity. Kneeling down to
touch a damp stain on the rug, she raised the tips of her fingers
experimentally to her nose. ''It is obvious Colonel Massingale

arrived at the Town House between six and six-thirty last night. He let himself in without alerting the household, who were undoubtedly belowstairs partaking, as is their custom at that hour, of their evening meal. The fact that he spent no little time pacing the floor is certain evidence he arrived in an agitated state. Patently he was anticipating the arrival of a second party, someone he perceived as being a dangerous adversary and who would make his entrance without revealing his presence to the rest of the household. The colonel was surprised, however, sometime between seven and a quarter to eight by someone he was not expecting, clearly a gentleman of fashion for whom he did not entertain a similar wariness. Therein lay his fatal error, for it was undoubtedly the Gentleman of Fashion who, in a brief scuffle, put a period to the colonel's existence using the colonel's own knife, which is indeed the very one whose origins I was employed to discover. I should say the colonel met his end at precisely four minutes before the hour of eight, after which the gentleman let himself out the way he came in, with none of the household the wiser.''

This concise explanation of the night's events, far from eliciting an enthusiastic response from Mr. Townsend, was met with a telling silence.

"That *is* the way you see it, is it not, sir?'' inquired Pandora after a moment, lifting an inquisitive gaze from her examination of Colonel Massingale to the Bow Street Runner.

"Ahem," Mr. Townsend replied, his face having assumed a peculiar ruddy tinge of color. "Very astute of you, Miss Featherstone, I do not doubt. Perhaps you would not mind explaining how you arrived at your intriguing conclusions.''

"But it is obvious, is it not?'' returned Pandora, crossing to the bookshelf that lined the inner wall next to the fireplace. "The colonel's greatcoat and hat are perfectly dry, which, since there was no fire in the fireplace to bring them to that condition and since there is no evidence of an umbrella, would indicate he arrived during the brief lull in the storm between six and six-thirty. Mrs. Caulkins, who is a most fastidious housekeeper, sweeps the rugs in the library every Tuesday afternoon, which, as you are well aware, was yesterday. That can only mean the distinct trail in the carpet was made last evening by the colonel's pacing.''

"I see," said Mr. Townsend. "Clever, Miss Featherstone. Very clever, indeed. And the fact that the colonel was expecting a dangerous visitor? How did you come to that determination?''

"Come, Mr. Townsend," smiled Pandora, who, having drawn a magnifying glass from her reticule, was occupied with scrutinizing the leather bindings of a section of books on the shelf. "Surely you did not think I should overlook the granules of gunpowder on the desk. Obviously, the colonel took time to prime and load the pocket pistol in his right-hand coat pocket. As for the time of arrival of the Gentleman of Fashion, that can be assessed from the damp spot on the carpet near the desk. He, unlike the colonel, was caught out in the renewed downpour. His greatcoat shed a considerable pool as he stood talking to his reluctant host. Allowing the colonel time for his extended pacing and the preparation of the pistol for firing would place the gentleman's arrival no sooner than seven.''

"Excellent, Miss Featherstone. But a gentleman of fashion, you said. How could we possibly know that about him?'' demanded Mr. Townsend, who was in the process of shoving himself up after having knelt to feel for himself the damp spot in the carpet.

"The colonel was a man who set great store on appearances. You may be certain he would never have invited anyone less than a gentleman to share a glass of brandy with him.''

"Aha," cried the Bow Street Runner with an air of triumph. "In that deduction at least you are mistaken, surely. There is, after all, only one glass in evidence.''

"Come, now, Mr. Townsend," Pandora said, smiling indulgently over her shoulder at the Bow Street Runner, "you cannot pull the wool over my eyes. I know you are perfectly aware of the shards of glass at the foot of the desk, not to mention the brandy stain in the carpet, both of which would indicate a second glass, broken and spilled in the scuffle, which itself is clearly evidenced by the rug bunched about the legs of the chair. The colonel was thrust backward into the chair in the fight, causing the chair to scoot along with the rug. Upon which the Gentleman of Fashion, wishing to conceal the fact that he had shared a libation with the victim, took time to remove the broken pieces, but in his haste missed those few tiny remnants. He then, ineffectually, tried to blot up the brandy spill. One could hardly expect a gentleman of fashion to be aware of what any good housekeeper knows—that a wine stain must be blotted then rubbed in salt. This, followed by scrubbing with a solution of white vinegar and warm water, is almost the only effective method of removing wine from a carpet.''

Mr. Townsend, who was not himself aware of the only effective method for removing wine stains from a carpet, gave Pandora a look of reluctant admiration. ''Well done, Miss Featherstone,'' he applauded. ''And, now, I suppose you are prepared to explain how you fixed the time at four minutes to eight, not to mention how the murderer was able to escape while leaving the doors and windows locked from the inside. I promise I am eagerly awaiting your explanation.''

''The time of death was easily ascertained from the colonel's desk clock, which, as you have undoubtedly noticed, suffered a broken crystal during the fatal struggle. It is stopped at precisely four minutes to eight. As for the manner of escape, that particular conundrum, I confess, has given me no little pause, for, if you must know, during my stay in the house I spent some considerable time trying to discover the means by which the marquis's murderer was able to enter and exit without being detected. Are you a man who enjoys reading, Mr. Townsend?'' she suddenly asked, with an apparent irrelevancy that was not lost on the gentleman in question. ''Here is an excellent first edition of Milton's *Paradise Lost,* if you would care to examine it.''

Mr. Townsend, who, far from being a slow-top, had come some little time before to the conclusion that Miss Featherstone was no gadabout to jump from one subject to another without purpose, fixed Pandora with an inquisitive look. "As it happens, I am inordinately fond of the Blind Bard, Miss Featherstone." Crossing to her side, he examined the book on the shelf.

"It is a handsome book at that," he observed. "The binding would seem exceedingly well preserved."

"Yes, it is in prime condition, save for one tiny, almost imperceptible flaw. I daresay one would overlook it entirely unless one viewed it through a magnifying glass. Would you care to have a look, Mr. Townsend?"

"Indeed, I should, Miss Featherstone," replied Mr. Townsend, accepting the magnifying glass and raising it to his eye.

"Ah, I do see what you mean. It is very slight, but I should say unmistakable." Lowering the glass, he met Pandora's gaze with a perceptible gleam of interest. "Would you say that is a bloodstain, Miss Featherstone?"

"I should indeed, Mr. Townsend," agreed Pandora, smiling. "A very small, but undeniable smudge of blood, one that I suspect was transferred there from a kid glove, since there is a noticeable lack of a definable fingerprint. Do you think the Gentleman of Fashion was perhaps an admirer of Milton, so much so, in fact, that he stopped after committing murder to examine an indisputably fine first edition?"

"I should say he was a queer cove if he did, Miss Featherstone. I should, in fact, consider the possibility highly unlikely."

"So should I, Mr. Townsend," Pandora stated unequivocally and pulled the book from the shelf.

Instantly, an entire section of the bookcase swung outward, to reveal, concealed behind it, a secret room with an exit. The exit gave access to a private staircase, which led, in turn, to the colonel's boudoir and dressing room.

"By Jove, so this is how the foul deed was accomplished

eighteen years ago," exclaimed Townsend, slamming an open hand against the side of his leg. "And then again last night. I congratulate you, Miss Featherstone, on as fine an example of investigative work as it has been my pleasure to witness."

"Not at all, Mr. Townsend," demurred Pandora, glancing around the colonel's boudoir for some sign of the missing wooden box. "It was a simple matter of observation and deductive reasoning. It still does not identify the person responsible for either of the fatal crimes perpetrated in this house. However, I daresay we may be certain it was someone in each instance who was familiar with the architectural plans of the house. As construction on the square was begun in 1764 and not completed until 1785, it is probable the marquis himself gave orders for the inclusion of the secret room and private stairs to afford him a means of withdrawing from his numerous petitioners. He was, after all, active in the ministry of defence at the time. I daresay he had need of slipping away from time to time."

"Then, whoever killed him was very likely someone who knew his habits. I daresay it is possible the motive might even have had something to do with his position in the ministry of defence."

"Or with something on which his lordship was working at the time. It is at least somewhere to begin, Mr. Townsend. As for the murder of Colonel Massingale, I suggest an investigation into those intimately acquainted with him who additionally would have reason to be aware of the secret room. I, myself, should begin with an interview of the servants. We have a singular advantage in the fact that Mrs. Caulkins as well as Jessop served both men. I daresay they will prove a fountain of information."

"We, Miss Featherstone?" interjected Townsend in ominous tones. "There is no *we*. You will leave the investigation to me. I will not have a lady place herself in jeopardy. These are dangerous men with whom I shall be dealing. I must insist you remain least seen in these affairs."

If the Bow Street Runner had expected to receive an argument from the redoubtable confidential inquiry agent, he was soon to be disappointed.

"You are right, of course, Mr. Townsend," said Pandora, smiling with every evidence of good grace. "I should not dream of interfering with your investigation. Indeed, I wish you every good fortune in what promises to be a most intriguing conundrum. And, now, I shall bid you good day, sir. It is growing late, and I have a great deal to do. It has been a pleasure meeting the famous Mr. Townsend of the Bow Street Runners, I assure you."

A faint flush of pleasure coloring his cheeks, the famous Mr. Townsend bowed gallantly over Pandora's proffered hand. "The pleasure, Miss Featherstone, was all mine."

Ten minutes later, after having taken her leave of a tearful Mrs. Caulkins, who could not but regret the departure of a friend in the most trying of times, Pandora made her way briskly down North Audley Street to South Audley Street and her own residence at number three. Since the distance traversed was a little over half a mile, she was given plenty of time to contemplate the latest ramifications in the deepening conundrum in which she had become embroiled.

Chief among her considerations was the notable absence of the wooden box. The most obvious explanation for its disappearance was, of course, that the murderer had taken the box with him, in which case, it was entirely possible the box itself was the underriding motive for the more heinous crime of murder. If such were the case, then what in heaven's name could have been in the box to incite one to murder? she wondered. And not just a single murder, but very possibly two, she reasoned. After all, Colonel Massingale himself had informed her that the box had previously been in the possession of the Marquis of Selkirk.

She was chiding herself for the umpteenth time for not having peeked into the troublesome box while she had it in her keeping, when she arrived home, and, not wishing to have her train of thought disrupted, proceeded directly to her study.

The one room in the house that was forbidden on extreme peril to all but herself to enter, the study was in the norm a scene of controlled chaos. While Pandora knew perfectly well where everything was, to an outsider, the room must inevitably have presented an aspect of hopeless disorder. The fact that the customary disarray was complicated by numerous wooden crates, a trunk, and a bandbox, all neatly stacked in the small area that was not taken up by bookcases, a paper-littered desk, a worn leather couch, a goldfish bowl, and a long table bearing all the accoutrements of a small, but well-stocked laboratory very likely would not have seemed incongruous to anyone but Pandora, who, flinging into the study and closing the door behind her, was brought suddenly up short at sight of the unexpected addition to her private sanctum.

"Of course," exclaimed Pandora, "how could I have forgotten the arrival of my belongings from the colonel's!"

The apparent eagerness with which she began to unstack the crates would seem to indicate a fondness for her possessions quite out of proportion to any material value that might have been assessed for them. But then, it was not the crates, the trunk, or the bandbox that had drawn her immediate attention or, indeed, caused her to clap a hand to her mouth to quell the cry of discovery that had leaped to her tongue. It was a battered wooden box at the very bottom of the pile and which, she did not have to see to know, bore the initials "T. F. R." carved in the lid.

Chapter 4

"It must have been sent over with my things by mistake," Pandora speculated aloud to Aunt Cora some few minutes later as the two women stood staring down at the wooden chest. "Which is perfectly understandable, considering the state of affairs at the Town House. Can you believe it, Aunt Cora? I never thought I should see the box again, let alone discover it in my very own study."

"Well, now that you have it, what do you intend to do with it?" Cora asked. "If it has something to do with the colonel's untimely demise, you surely cannot intend to keep it. We might all wake up one morning to find ourselves dead in our beds. The sooner it is out of the house, the happier I shall be."

"Then, you needn't worry, dearest Aunt Cora," Pandora laughed. "I intend to take it to the Duke of Rivenoak first thing tomorrow morning. It was his father's, after all. By all rights, it should go to his grace. Unfortunately, Rivenoak was on his way to his hunting lodge in Surrey when he left us and does not plan to return to London until the beginning of the Season.

I'm afraid, Aunt Cora, I shall have to ask you to look after the children for a day or two. Logic, not to mention my women's instinct, tells me it is of the utmost importance to convey the box to him without the smallest delay.''

"But you cannot, Pandora," exclaimed Aunt Cora with every manifestation of alarm. "Not without a female companion. Your reputation would be ruined. At least take me with you.''

"I should like nothing better than to have you accompany me. Unfortunately, it would mean leaving the children to the care of Mrs. Giddings, who very likely would resign without notice at such a prospect, and then what should we have achieved?''

"We should quite happily have rid ourselves of that woman," Cora answered without the smallest signs of remorse.

"Yes, but in the meantime, the children would be without a soul to look after them," Pandora did not hesitate to point out, "and you will admit that is one issue that must leave a great deal to be desired. No, I can see nothing for it but to undertake the journey alone. You may be certain I shall take every precaution. With any luck I shall be able to leave the box with Rivenoak and procure passage on a return coach that very night, in which case, my reputation shall remain as untouched as ever. And, besides,'' she added, an irrepressible gleam of mischief in the gaze she bent upon Aunt Cora, ''even if I am forced to spend the night at an inn, it can hardly matter, now can it? I am unlikely ever to marry and I certainly have no expectations of moving in polite society. My reputation, or the loss of it, would seem a matter of small significance, especially in light of the greater importance of apprising Rivenoak of Colonel Massingale's demise and the circumstances surrounding it, now would it not?''

Cora, who had seen that look in Pandora's eyes before, knew at once that there was little use in pointing out that even a confidential inquiry agent, were she an unmarried female, would have need of a spotless name if she wished to have the patronage of the best clientele. Pandora, once she had set her mind on a thing, was not likely to have it easily changed, especially when it concerned one of her irresistible conundrums. She would go her own way, but at least, Cora consoled herself, this time the child's stubborn propensity for independent action was going to take her once more into the sphere of influence of a man who, if Cora was not mistaken, had seen in Pandora what others had ever failed to see. Slowly, Cora smiled. No doubt Philomena was in the right of it when she was used to insist that matters had a way of working themselves out for the better if one only looked to the bright side of things instead of forever dwelling on the dire possibilities.

It was the dire possibilities, however, of the conundrum surrounding the Duke of Rivenoak that occupied Pandora as she sat in the mail coach facing, on one side, the substantial wife of a miller traveling with her spinster sister-in-law to Horsham and, on the other, the equally imposing bulk of a headmaster on his way to Farley Green to take up his duties at a charitable institution for orphans and destitute children. It had occurred to Pandora that, if the duke had not cut Colonel Massingale's stick for him—and she did not for a moment believe that he had—then it was all too likely that his grace, who was admittedly the object of a malicious plot, might very well be in equally grave peril of his life. Indeed, she could not rid herself of the haunting notion that Rivenoak might even then be lying wounded or dead, the victim of an unsavory villain.

Why she should have been prey to a terrible sinking sensation at such a grave prospect, pertaining as it did to one whom she had had occasion to meet only once and then but for a fleeting ninety minutes, she would have been hard put to explain, especially as she had not experienced anything even approaching of a similar nature upon being given to view the colonel in the reality of what for Rivenoak thus far was only a grim flight of fancy. No doubt it was only that she could not wish to see a man of Rivenoak's generosity, insight and powerful intellect removed from this plane of existence before his time, she firmly told herself, refusing to think for a moment that it might be due to the fact that his compelling masculine presence, not to mention his superb manly physique, wielded a strong influence over her primitive womanly emotions even as an indefinable aura of mystery and the hint of some long past, but deep-seated, hurt appealed to her highly developed sense of compassion.

The truth was she could not have explained in purely rational terms what her feminine intuition had grasped at her first having laid eyes on Rivenoak, that here was a man who must, by his very nature, prove irresistible to her. Feelings, she would have been the first to admit, after all, tend to reside outside the realm of reason.

Had anyone approached her and demanded, on the other hand, to know why she should be convinced beyond a shadow of doubt that Rivenoak could *not* have plunged the knife into the colonel, a sworn enemy, she would not have hesitated to reply that it was all a matter of logic. A man like Rivenoak, after all, was hardly the sort to resort to cold-blooded murder. Had he wished to rid himself of the colonel, he would have chosen a method more suited to his haughty temperament—a meeting at twenty paces at dawn, for example, or a duel with swords, or even the more ruthless means of ruining the man financially or socially, either of the latter of which would have been well within his power.

No, she reasoned, between having to respond in vague mono-syllables to Mrs. Wortham's effusive complaints about her sister-in-law's unnatural ingratitude to one who had ever treated the heartless girl with generosity and to Mr. Thistlewaite's ponderous treatise on the fallibility of the flesh, it was far more likely that Rivenoak was the "dangerous" party whose arrival the colonel had been awaiting with a pistol, primed and loaded.

Indeed, she would even go so far as to speculate that the colonel had lured the duke to the Town House in order to murder him, with herself as an unwitting witness to what was to appear an act of self-defence. Only, the intended victim, as well as the would-be witness, had come and gone before the colonel's own arrival, something he could not have anticipated as he paced in nervous expectation in the library. Certainly, such a theory would seem to explain a great deal of what had hitherto been puzzling about the colonel's motives in employing her in a superfluous exercise made more quixotic, still, by Massingale's insistence that she reside in his Town House during its performance.

As for the wooden box, which had seemed to play a significant role in the deepening plot, it had undoubtedly been the bait to draw the duke to the scene of planned infamy. It and its contents, however, must rightfully belong to Rivenoak. Indeed, his grace must place no little store in them if they had the power to make him so far forget himself as to engage in an illegal entry. That he had not simply removed them was evidence that he had recognized what had all the manifestations of a trap. He was far too intelligent to have fallen for something so obvious.

That final thread of thought brought her once more to a contemplation of what might be contained in the box to cause such a furor. Indeed, she had, perforce, to fight off the renewed temptation to break open the lock and peek inside, an act which her acute sense of integrity simply would not allow. Unfortunately, her equally strong inclination to curiosity, which must be an integral part of any person inclined to be a confidential inquiry agent and was most especially true in Pandora's case, persisted in conjuring up any number of reasons why she should ascertain once and for all the mysterious contents.

Not the least of these was the nagging suspicion that, once Rivenoak had the box in his possession, he would dismiss her from any further involvement in what gave every evidence of becoming a conundrum of truly magnificent proportions, and *that* she could not countenance. She had, after all, already gathered a goodly portion of the pieces of the puzzle. She should, by all rights, be allowed to help put them together. Besides, she knew from experience that there was not the remotest possibility that she would be able to abandon the pursuit simply because the Duke of Rivenoak demanded it of her. In which case, this might be her final opportunity to gain access to the most crucial elements of the conundrum.

Hardly had this exercise in deductive reasoning obtruded into her mind, than, fortunately, perhaps, her reveries were cut short by the coachman's announcement that they were arriving at Shere.

"A pity, Miss Featherstone," remarked Mr. Thistlewaite, who had extended every effort to vie with Mrs. Wortham for Pandora's attention, especially in the matter of his pet project, the establishment of a workhouse for the gainful employment of husbandless mothers and their ill-begotten offspring for the sole purpose of salvaging their souls through virtuous toil, "it seems we have reached a parting of ways."

"We have indeed, sir," agreed Pandora, who could only be relieved at the prospect of disembarking in order to change to a post chaise for the rest of her journey before she had occasion to inform Mr. Thistlewaite that it was not the souls of the single mothers and their unfortunate children that needed saving, but their pitiful lives fraught with poverty and despair. Neither was another workhouse the answer, but decent food and housing, education and training for some trade, along with the creation of meaningful employment for women at a decent wage, none of which could possibly have been within the man's narrow-minded grasp, indeed, seemed beyond the understanding of even the most powerful men in England. As for Mrs. Wortham's sister-in-law, an unemployed governess in her middle to late twenties, Pandora could only feel the greatest sympathy. Miss Laura Wortham could not possibly see anything to recommend in playing auntie to Mr. Wortham's seven hopefuls for the privilege of living in a state of dependence on her brother's questionable largess and in virtual servitude to a woman who must inevitably prove as demanding as she was insensitive.

She, however, would say nothing, Pandora told herself. For once in her life, she would do the sensible thing and mind her own business. The devil, she would, she thought then, as Mrs. Wortham, incensed at her sister-in-law's failure to bring along the bottle of bitters which Mrs. Wortham was in the habit of periodically imbibing, presumably as a tonic for the plethora of complaints that ailed her, launched into a tirade against the unfortunate former governess.

"You thankless baggage!" declared the draper's wife with such vehemence as to set askew her improbable blond wig topped by a tall hat that, aspiring to truly magnificent heights, was adorned with an exotic assortment of fruit, all of which was meant to be a replica of the latest in French fashion. "You forgot to bring my bitters because of the weeping of a scullery maid who had the nerve, mind you, to claim one of my little angels flung a chamber pot at her head? Lud, anyone with a lick of sense would see at once it was all a taradiddle to hide what was obviously the girl's own clumsiness. Anyone, but you, of course. Of all the dim-witted, harebrained—I swear you are not worth your keep, and if it was not that Mr. Wortham insists on doing the charitable thing, I'd see you cast out in the street, I would."

"Then, I suggest, ma'am," Miss Laura Wortham replied in quiet, controlled accents, "you follow your inclinations. No doubt my brother will find some other unfortunate upon whom to vent his charitable impulses, though hardly for a tuppence. Since he has the misfortune to have but one penniless sister, I daresay he will be forced in my absence to put out for a nanny as well as a governess, not to mention a paid companion."

At this composed assessment of the inevitable repercussions to the termination of what could hardly have been described as a mutually beneficial arrangement, Mrs. Wortham manifested every sign of one on the brink of going into an apoplexy. "Ungrateful wretch," she gasped, clasping a hand over what might be presumed to be a palpitating heart. "And after I took you into my home and gave you every consideration, to speak to me in such a manner! Well, I never. Perhaps now you see, Mr. Thistlewaite," she added, turning to her traveling companion for confirmation of the injustice that had been perpetrated against her, "what I have to put up with."

"There is nothing more deplorable than an unrepentant soul," intoned the headmaster with a sympathetic cluck of the tongue, "unless it be a heart hardened against those whose only offence lies in an overabundance of kindness and generosity. You have my sympathies, ma'am."

"I am sure I am much obliged to you, sir," Mrs. Wortham preened before turning a triumphant eye on the unregenerate soul across from her. "Now, what do you have to say to that, Miss High and Mighty?"

"I daresay Miss Wortham is too nice to say anything more in front of strangers," interjected Pandora, quite unable to stop herself. "I do beg your pardon, Miss Wortham," she added kindly to the former governess, who was staring rigidly at a point somewhere beyond her kinswoman's left shoulder, "but I could hardly help drawing certain conclusions concerning you and your probable circumstances. If ever you should find yourself in need of a refuge, I should like you to consider coming to stay with me in London. Here is my card," she added, retrieving one of her calling cards and a five-pound note from her reticule and offering them to Miss Wortham. "As it happens, I am in need of a governess to instruct four children, and, while I cannot offer you what you may have been used in the past to receiving, I am prepared to pay you twenty-five pounds per annum, five of which I shall advance you now if you are inclined to accept."

"You-you are very kind, Miss Featherstone," replied Miss

Wortham, favoring Pandora with a gaze in which the birth of hope vied with helpless disbelief, "but you know nothing about me. Surely you would wish to see references before engaging me in the position of governess."

"I do not see why," Pandora laughed. "You, after all, have not met my nephews and nieces. I am prepared to take you on faith if you are willing to do the same with me and mine."

"She will do no such thing," avowed Mrs. Wortham, who saw the feather in her cap slipping from her grasp. "Mr. Wortham would not hear of it."

"On the contrary, my brother will hear of it," declared Miss Wortham, never taking her eyes off Pandora as she reached out to take the card and the five-pound note. "I shall tell him myself. I haven't many personal possessions, Miss Featherstone," she added to Pandora as the coach came to a halt before the posting inn. "But what I do have I should wish to keep."

"But of course you would." Pandora smiled in complete understanding and, stepping across Mr. Thistlewaite, climbed down from the coach. "I shall see you in London as soon as you have had time to collect them."

"You may be sure of it, Miss Featherstone," Laura Wortham said with a smile that quite transformed her rather pinched features, rendering her more than a little attractive.

"I warn you, if you dare to go through with this piece of nonsense, you will never again be welcome in my home, Laura Wortham," drifted down to Pandora as she instructed the coachman to unload the wooden box from the top of the coach.

She was exceedingly gratified to hear Miss Wortham declare in no uncertain terms that, as she had never been made to feel welcome in her brother's house save as an unpaid servant, that would hardly prove either a deterrent or a disappointment to her. Then a lad with the wooden box in tow conducted Pandora into the inn, and Mrs. Wortham's shrill rejoinder was rendered unintelligible.

* * *

Pandora could not but reflect some thirty minutes later that perhaps she had been somewhat hasty in giving in to charitable impulse. Though she could not bring herself to regret having engaged a much-needed governess for her small brood of nephews and nieces, especially under the singular circumstances that had prompted the act, the five-pound note that had gone to Miss Wortham had, nevertheless, constituted nearly the entire sum she had brought with her to finance the rest of her journey. Indeed, she had quickly deduced that, even foregoing the ha'penny tea at the inn, she could ill afford to hire a post chaise to take her to Farley Green and beyond to the duke's hunting lodge, which was why she now found herself perched on the seat of a farmer's hay wagon.

Still, she was fortunate to have found any sort of conveyance at a sum that did not leave her entirely on the rocks, and she did still have half a dried biscuit and a small wedge of cheese wrapped in a handkerchief in her reticule. Thanks to Aunt Cora's insistence she be prepared for any emergency, at least she was not like to starve. Fortunately, she had just enough of the ready left to stand the nonsense of the coach fare back to London from Shere, and, even if the duke did not offer to drive her to the post inn, she could count herself fortunate that, unencumbered by the wooden box, she was well able to walk the approximately two miles herself. Firmly, she told herself it would not matter a whit that the trek by foot might very well have to be made after nightfall or that very likely she would not find a coach departing before morning for London. Pandora had never been one to be deterred or frightened by a few trifling obstacles.

The view of Surrey from the seat of a hay wagon was one to gladden the heart of any wayfarer. Heathery commons merged on thick beech woods, which would be gay with bluebells by May, but which, even in the middle of March, were already bursting forth with new, green leaves. Hammer Ponds that had once served blacksmiths in the forging of guns for Good Queen Bess's fleet abounded in lush meadows made more picturesque with grazing sheep. All in all, Pandora was not displeased to find herself in the country on what was proving a lovely spring day.

Neither was she to be disappointed at her first sight of the duke's hunting lodge. Nestled at the end of a winding drive in a thick, wild wood and climbing with clematis, the small Georgian manor was hardly the primitive abode one might have expected of a hunting lodge. Still, graced with a small stream over which a delightful wooden bridge arched and boasting half a dozen or so ducks and geese, not to mention a brace of hounds, it exuded a certain rustic charm. There was as well an enticing sense of isolation about the place, due, no doubt, to the encroaching forest of beech wood and fir.

"Be yer certain ye're expected, miss?" queried the grizzled farmer, helping Pandora down from the hay wagon, before setting the wooden box in the drive beside her. "There bain't many visitors come to Briarcroft since the new duke taken over."

"Have there not?" queried Pandora, pretending a confidence she was far from feeling, now that she was actually on the point of coming face-to-face once more with Rivenoak. "But then, I daresay his grace favors the lodge for its seclusion. He probably comes here to escape from people and his many other affairs. You are very kind to be concerned, but I assure you I shall be just fine." Then thanking him for his services, she pressed a coin in the gnarled hand and strode purposefully to the door.

It was soon to prove that the old farmer was not the only one to doubt Pandora's welcome. Indeed, she was informed by the butler, who opened the door to her, that his grace was not at home to callers.

"Then, I shall be pleased to wait in the withdrawing room

until his grace is ready to receive me,'' Pandora declared, dragging the box with her past the astonished superior servant. ''You will inform him that Miss Featherstone begs his indulgence. Indeed, you may be certain he will not be at all pleased if you do not do so with all despatch.''

The butler, apparently recognizing in Miss Featherstone, despite the peculiarity of the circumstances, a member of the quality used to giving orders and having them obeyed, condescended after some hesitation to conduct Pandora into the ''Green Room,'' a ground-story withdrawing room, and even went so far as to instruct a footman to carry the cumbersome wooden box in after her. It soon became readily apparent, however, that he was not prepared to go so far as to summon his master in any great haste. Indeed, it occurred to Pandora somewhat belatedly that she might have done better to send ahead announcing her intent to call on his grace.

Pandora had been left to cool her heels for all of thirty minutes, when the dazzling sunlight of a glorious afternoon drew her out of the French doors onto a small flagstone terrace overlooking the beech wood. What a wonderfully wild and lovely prospect it offered, with the stream gurgling on a winding course through the thick press of trees before her! She was reminded with an unwitting pang of Havenhill, her family home near the Matlocks in Derbyshire. It had been simply ages since she had last strolled through the woods of her childhood or fished the purling stream. But then, her eldest brother Castor and she had never been on anything that approached intimate or even congenial terms. She had rather live the year round in London, even suffering the discomfort of the City heat in the summer, than to endure Castor's platitudinous insistence that she was a foolish, headstrong female on a direct course to ruination.

Still, she reflected, leaving the terrace to wend her way upstream along a path that paralleled the riverbank, she could not deny that she missed Havenhill on occasion or that it was a pity the children, at least, could not enjoy the freedom of the country. Given the chance, they all undoubtedly would have been avid equestrians, not to mention enthusiastic anglers, and the fresh air afforded in the country could not but be more beneficial to growing children than the pall of smoke that hung over the City.

Inevitably, it came to her that perhaps she should swallow her pride and write Castor for permission to come for a visit in July, only to immediately discard the idea as too preposterous by half. Castor would hardly welcome them, and she really could not think the children would greatly profit from being under the stultifying influence of an uncle who had parceled them out almost before they had had time to unpack their few belongings. No, she would not put them through that again, she determined, recalling with a hardening of her lips how, upon their arrival at South Audley Street, Odysseus had been plagued with nightmares and how Galatea had been wont to cling in silent desperation to Iphigenia, who, only a little more than ten at the time, had worn the frozen aspect of one far older than her meager years. Indeed, Pandora could never forget Ganymede's bald assertion that it was only a matter of time before they should find themselves sent off again to some other relative who did not want them any more than any of the others had. There must be another way to remove them all from the City. Somehow she would find more corners to cut, and perhaps with the help of some new clients with conundrums in need of resolving, she would find a way to let a cottage for Aunt Cora and the children at the seaside for a month or two. With Miss Wortham along to keep the children in tow, Pandora would not be given to worry in their absence.

Hardly had Pandora come to what promised a fair solution to the problem of the children than she became aware that, caught up in her reverie, she had walked some little distance from the house, which, hidden in the trees, was quite lost from view. Thinking that she had been gone an unconscionable time, she was on the point of turning to retrace her steps, when she glimpsed through the trees before her what gave every indication of being a crude structure of a sort that was wholly unfamiliar to her.

Her curiosity fully aroused, she strode forward out of the cover of trees into a sylvan glade—and was made immediately to feel that she had stepped outside of time or been transported willy-nilly to some primitive land wholly beyond her ken.

Indeed, she was quite certain that the domelike structure at the center of the glade did not owe its source to anything of an English origin. Constructed of bent poles covered over with what she presumed to be deer hide, the hut lacked anything remotely resembling windows or doors; and yet from the center of the roof rose an unmistakable plume of smoke, and there was, besides, a distinct aroma of burning wood in the air, not to mention a peculiar hissing as of spilled water sizzling on a heated stove top. More deliciously intriguing still, she could not be mistaken in thinking she heard, issuing from the interior of the hut to the beat of a drum, the marvelously deep, vibrant tones of what could only be described as singing.

Pandora halted, listening. Acutely aware of the prickle of gooseflesh, she could not but note that the words were utterly foreign to any of the several languages with which she had even a passing acquaintance. Furthermore, they were couched in a hauntingly captivating rhythm that lacked any resemblance to anything she had ever heard before, but which, like the pulse of her heart in unwitting accompaniment to the beat of the drum, seemed uniquely suited to her natural surrounds.

It was all wondrously primitive and wild and strangely irresistible. She hardly knew when she strode forward, drawn by something that called to her most elemental being.

She was made acutely aware, however, when the singing came abruptly to an end, along with the beat of the drum.

As if suddenly released from a mesmeric spell, she stood blinking in the sunlight, her gaze fixed in rueful amazement on the crude hut set in the glade. Now what the devil? she thought, only to become immediately aware of a flutter of movement in what appeared an unbroken wall of skins.

In the very next instant, a hitherto indiscernible flap was flung outward. Indeed, hardly had she clapped a hand to her breast in surprise than a dark head was thrust through the opening, followed by powerful shoulders and arms, a broad, muscular chest bristling with a raven mat of hair, and a lean, narrow torso—all magnificently wrought and utterly as nature had intended them. Furthermore, below those exquisite examples of masculine perfection, not to mention the insignificant presence of a bone-handled knife at the waist and what amounted to a breechclout, was the added boon of a splendidly firm buttocks as viewed from the side, sinewy thighs, shapely calves, and feet shod in a sort of beaded slipper of soft grey deerskin.

As yet unaware of Pandora's presence, the superb specimen of the masculine gender straightened and stood for a moment, head back, the magnificent chest expanding, as he drew in a deep breath of fir-scented air. Pandora's own breath caught at the sight of the compellingly masculine physique, made more superlative, still, by the shimmer of moisture on the smooth, firm skin. Long raven hair worn unbound and allowed to fall in a natural state down the back and shoulders only added to the splendid image of primitive, untamed manhood.

Primitive? she thought, most singularly struck by the sinuous grace of the man. Faith, if he was a savage, he was certainly a noble representative of his kind. Indeed, she had seen only one other man to match him for pure masculine perfection.

Who was he? she wondered, and what was he doing out in the middle of nowhere clad in little more than a breechclout? She had the uncanniest sensation that she was in the presence of a throwback to the primitive tribes who had once peopled the British Isles before the dawn of civilization or, indeed, to those wild, free peoples of the Americas whom Rivenoak had so vividly described in her parlor only the previous day. But that was absurd, she thought, resisting the urge to pinch herself. This was bonny England in the year 1800. England had long been civilized, and it was highly unlikely that American natives had taken up residence in the woods of Surrey. There was obviously a more logical explanation for the undeniably intriguing anomaly.

She had no sooner reached that conclusion than any further ruminations were cut abruptly short by the incipience of a low, menacing growl, which seemed to emanate at a point immediately to her right. Judging in the circumstances that it was prudent to remain as still as was possible, Pandora peered carefully out of the corners of her eyes to behold, poised in what could only be construed as a menacing stance, its lips pulled back to reveal singularly long, gleaming fangs, what gave every evidence of being an exceedingly large grey wolf.

Good God, she thought, wondering if, indeed, she had been transported to a primeval time. There had not been wolves in England for centuries. It was at that moment, alerted by the snarling of the beast to the presence of an interloper, the "noble" savage reached for his knife and in a swift blur of movement turned.

All in an instant, Pandora found herself impaled by eyes the chill blue of a lake on a clear winter's day.

"Good God," she blurted in startled recognition, "Rivenoak!"

Rivenoak had departed the house on South Audley Street satisfied that, while Miss Featherstone might be a deal too precocious for her own good and more than a little prone to meddle in affairs that should not concern her, any involvement she might have had with Massingale was innocent on her part. It had been his intent to dismiss the confidential inquiry agent from any further consideration, save for the matter of the wooden box in her possession, the responsibility for which he meant to relieve her as soon as possible. It had *not* been a part of his plans to find himself dwelling on the beauty of eyes that had the disquieting predilection for regarding him with a probing intensity one moment, only to be lit the next by laughter that was as disarming as it was captivating.

Miss Featherstone had proven as cursedly alluring as she was innocent. Damn the woman! The last thing he had wanted or expected was to find himself behaving like a moon-stricken cub over a female who was not only meddlesome, but who had the dubious distinction of being related to Herodotus Featherstone. By all rights, he should have found her as false as her brother. That he had not, indeed, had instead been struck to the core by her selfless devotion and generosity toward that brother's brood of young hopefuls, had not been conducive to his peace of mind. Far from it. He had found himself since that fateful encounter plagued with images of Miss Featherstone, ridiculously garbed in a tartan sari that had seemed tantalizingly designed to call attention to her feminine attributes, or Miss Featherstone, clad equally absurdly in a hopelessly unfashionable grey serge gown that, due to its very shapelessness, had had the disturbing effect of stimulating his imagination.

He had come to Briarcroft, as he did every year in the early spring, to escape for a time his existence as the wealthy Duke of Rivenoak. Here, shut away from the world, he could again be Chance True-Son of the Three-Rivers People, a man of the forest. It was a time to remember the old ways, to shed the trappings of the duke for the raiment of a warrior, to feel the sun and wind against his bare skin, to walk in the moccasins of his mother's people. He had ever found it a time of cleansing and renewal. Of all his many holdings, it was only at Briarcroft that he could allow himself to be simply a man.

Little wonder, then, that he should have been more than a little out of temper to discover upon his arrival the previous day that, rather than achieving the serenity his soul craved, he had been utterly distracted by his inability to banish Miss Featherstone from his mind. While taking an afternoon stroll through the woods, with Stalker, a silent shadow at his heels, he had come to his favorite retreat, a small wooded dell over the lip of which the stream tumbled into a sandy pool. Seating himself on the grassy bank, one arm flung carelessly over the wolf-dog's back, he had caught himself picturing Miss Featherstone, wading bare-footed in the pool, her skirts gathered most enchantingly above her knees. Or, again, later that evening, running as he had been used to do as a boy, for the sheer joy of it, he had been visited with an image of Miss Featherstone fleeing in gleeful abandon into the trees, her lovely laughter wafting back to him. He had visualized her, as well, seated across the table from him as he had dined alone, which he too often did, her eyes alight and a small pucker of concentration etched in her brow as it had done when she had engaged him in lively verbal exchange. Then again, when he had availed himself of his nightly ablution of brandy, there she had been, a vision with glorious, dishevelled hair, the roguish dimple in evidence at the corner of her beguiling mouth. In disgust, he had at last flung the glass in the fireplace before stalking off to bed, there to have the enchanting Miss Featherstone invade his dreams.

He had awakened less than refreshed, a circumstance which was remarked by the household in general and most in particular by his Uncle Laughs-In-The-Rain, who did not hesitate to suggest that his nephew had the appearance of a man beset by evil spirits.

"In the old days, we would have known how to chase the bad manitous away. We would have given you a drink of roots and herbs to cleanse the body. You would have fasted for three days before entering the sweat lodge. There we would have sung the songs of healing to appease the manitous and banish them back to where they came from. It would have been a time of visions and power, but those days are gone forever. Now we dwell among the White Eyes. I will tell Stiff-In-The-Neck to send for the white doctor. The doctor will make you bleed, and then you will be too weak to complain, Nephew. It will be well. I am too old to humor the disharmony of a rebellious spirit.''

"You will do no such thing, Uncle," Rivenoak had replied with a sardonic glint in his eye for his companion, who, despite the fact that his hair was turned silver, yet carried himself as erect as a man in the prime of his strength. "I have never been ill a day in my life, and it is not the manitous who have disturbed my rest, but a woman."

"A woman. Ah," nodded Laughs-In-The-Rain, eyeing his nephew sagely. "Then, even the magic of the white doctor cannot help you. I am not too old to remember what it is to walk hand in hand with a woman beneath the moon. The medicine of the Earth Mother is powerful. It can defeat even the strongest of men. Who is this woman who has cast her spell over you?"

"If you saw her, you would call her She-Who-Shines-With-Laughter," Rivenoak said with a faint, reminiscent smile. "Her English name does not signify, since it is unlikely I shall ever see her again. I have no doubt you would like her. She has a quick mind and is both stubborn and headstrong, the sort of woman to drive a man to drink strong spirits. Furthermore, she has the spirit of a mountain lion and the eyes of an eagle: she does not know the meaning of fear, and she misses nothing. Still, she is hardly larger than the English linnet. She walks in beauty and grace, and she is possessed of a generous and discerning heart. She is gentle and yet strong, and her laughter is like the song of a brook."

"She sounds a paragon among women," commented Rivenoak's uncle with a sober mien that did not fool Rivenoak in the least. The old man was deriving great amusement from this new antic of the Trickster's at Rivenoak's expense. "It is well you do not plan to see her again. A woman such as this one would soon invite you into her lodge, and then where would you be?''

"Legshackled, Uncle," Rivenoak declared flatly. "And that is not a part of my plans."

"Be careful, Nephew, when you speak lightly of such things. Only a White Eyes makes plans without taking the Trickster's trouble-making into account. Old Man Hare likes nothing better than to put a snag in the schemes of men."

"And you would like nothing better than to see me squirm in the Trickster's snare. I know you, Uncle," Rivenoak said fondly despite his annoyance. "You would have me married and a parcel of offspring clambering about my knees."

Laughs-In-The-Rain shrugged philosophically. "A man has need of a wife to warm his bed and to provide him with sons to follow in his footsteps and with daughters to care for him in his old age. The Earth Mother gives women magic to bring peace to their menfolk. It is not a gift to be taken lightly, Nephew. I think it has been many seasons since you have known what it is to live in peace."

It had been many seasons, indeed, since he had known any sort of peace of mind, Rivenoak reflected darkly some time later as, slipping into the medicine lodge he and his uncle had erected long ago in the glen, he changed into the raiment of a clansman of the Three-Rivers People. Leaving the hut, he glided on foot through the woods as though pursued by demons. The day he had stood on the docks at Staten Island, waiting with his father beside him to board the ship that would take him forever away from everything he had ever known or loved, had marked the end of his youth along with the joy in his heart. It was as though Chance True-Son had died that day, even as his mother and father and brother and sisters had perished shortly thereafter, the victims of treachery. He had been only just turned fifteen at the time.

What had arisen from the ashes of his youth was a man whose will was tempered by each new, bitter lesson to a steely strength and whose emotions were guarded ever more closely behind a barricade of cold impenetrability—until he was truly Rivenoak, the English duke, a man whom other men feared to cross.

How, then, had this tiny wisp of a woman managed to slip through his guard all in a single moment, rendering him prey to feelings he had thought long since buried and beyond resurrection? he marveled, as, with the wolf-dog ever silent at his heels, he ran to the brink of physical exhaustion.

No doubt it was instinct that had led him at last back to the glen and the medicine lodge. It had come to him upon breaking into the glade that, if he could not banish the woman from his thoughts by will alone, then perhaps he could purge his system of her through the cleansing rites of his mother's people. Whether or not the manitous chose to visit him with a vision, the rite of dream casting would at least take him beyond his present turmoil to a level of consciousness that transcended worldly concerns. In meditation one gained focus and renewed one's inner strength. To the People, it was a sacred practice. To Chance True-Son, it had often in the past preserved his very sanity.

He could not have said how long he sat cross-legged before the fire at the center of the lodge, his body bathed in sweat and the steam rising from the heated stones doused with water. His thoughts gradually stilled, submerged in the rhythmic beat of the drum and the ancient chants of healing. His mind adrift, he entered the waking-dream state in which visions come.

The vision was hardly what he might have expected. A manitou wearing the aspect of a wild boar with a spear thrust through the heart was, after all, enigmatic at best, never mind the addition of a tiny linnet, fluttering in seeming alarm about the head of the boar. But then, one never knew what to expect from the land of the manitous. The boar, obviously on its final journey to the nether regions of the dead, had gazed upon Rivenoak with lingering hatred, and bafflement, too, as if he had yet to grasp he was no longer of the world of men. It was then, as he looked into the eyes of the boar, that Rivenoak recognized his old enemy.

Massingale was dead. Murdered. Rivenoak knew it, even as the vision faded and vanished, leaving the duke's head remarkably clear despite the weakness that always came in the wake of dream casting.

Stiffly, he pushed himself up and stood for a moment, weaving on his feet. Then, eager to escape the stifling confines of the sweat lodge, he reached for the door flap.

The brisk Surrey breeze caressed his skin with cooling fingers. Throwing back his head, he inhaled deeply, savoring the scent of rich, damp earth and the promise of rain on the air.

He felt drained, the demons that drove him momentarily at bay. Massingale was dead by another's hand, but Rivenoak did not fool himself into believing it was over. There had been others—men who would like nothing better than to have Rivenoak silenced, his quest for the truth brought to an end. No doubt one of them had put a period to the colonel's existence. Massingale had been the one weak link, the one man in possession of the proofs that would have brought the others to ruin, and now he was beyond even Rivenoak's reach.

The vision all made perfect sense, if Massingale should indeed prove to be dead, Rivenoak reflected, and he did not doubt for a moment that he would. All made sense, that was, save for the little linnet, fluttering around the boar's head in a seeming dither of excitement. What the devil had *she* to do with Massingale's apparent murder?

As if in answer to that unvoiced question, the wolf-dog's low, menacing growl warned him of another's presence. His hand flashing to the knife at his waist, Rivenoak swiveled on the ball of one foot and crouched, ready to spring to his defence.

It was not, however, a murderous villain who stood at rigid attention a scant dozen feet from him, but the slender form of the very woman whose spell he had sought to purge from his system.

He watched, fascinated, the woman's eyes widen with startled recognition.

"Good God," she exclaimed, seeming to forget the dog, crouched ready to spring at a moment's notice. "Rivenoak!"

Chapter 5

Rivenoak jammed the knife back in its sheath. "Stalker! Come," he commanded. The duke's lips thinned to a grim line at sight of the slender figure, standing rigidly still, her face noticeably pale. The devil, he thought. The vision that had come to him had been astonishingly to the point, it seemed. Indeed, he no longer need wonder whom he had conjured up in the form of an English linnet fluttering about the head of the boar. That part, at least, was made suddenly and abundantly clear.

"Miss Featherstone," he uttered flatly. "I might have known. What the deuce are you doing here?"

"What—?" Pandora stared blankly at Rivenoak as the wolf-dog ceased its growling and glided like a shadow to Rivenoak's side.

"I asked what you were doing here," Rivenoak repeated with a singular lack of amusement. "No one is permitted in this part of the woods. Did Wilkins send you? I shall bloody well have his head for this."

"Oh, no, your grace," Pandora answered, gathering her wits about her. "No one sent me. I was left to wait in the Green Room. When you failed to put in an appearance, I was drawn outside by the sunshine and fell to wandering along the riverbank. I'm afraid I completely lost track of the time. It was purely by accident that I stumbled onto your glen." Then, "Is that a wolf?" she asked, indicating the great creature lying at Rivenoak's feet.

"His father was a wolf," replied Rivenoak, marveling at Miss Featherstone's seeming composure. Any other Englishwoman of his acquaintance would have undoubtedly fallen into a swoon at the mere sight of the wolf-dog, not to mention the Duke of Rivenoak clad in a breechclout. Miss Featherstone, however, seemed perfectly recovered from her initial fright at finding herself menaced by what she must have presumed to be a ferocious wild animal. Furthermore, the troublesome female appeared anything but dismayed at the aspect of a nearly naked man. If anything, she gave every impression of one utterly fascinated.

"He really is quite beautiful," declared Pandora, apparently unaware that she was staring, not at the dog, but at the man. "I believe I have never beheld a more magnificent specimen."

"Have you not?" murmured Rivenoak, who likewise could not but note that Miss Featherstone, wearing a blue pelisse over another of her unfashionable, nondescript gowns and a straw Gypsy hat set precariously askew on top of what had begun as classical coils caught up at the back of the head, but was presently a charming disarray of curls falling down her back, presented an enchanting vision of femininity. She was, he noted wryly, even more lovely than the phantoms that had plagued him.

Mutely, Pandora shook her head in answer. She was quite unprepared for the bewildering array of emotions that threatened to overwhelm her at sight of Rivenoak in the guise of what could only be described as the Essential Male. Even dressed in the garb of a savage, however, he presented the same impression of pride and nobility that he had done when he called on her in South Audley Street. Indeed, the sparsity of apparel seemed somehow as equally well suited to him as had the exquisitely tailored clothing he had affected the previous day in her parlor. No doubt, she told herself, this was due to the fact that Rivenoak's singular aura of controlled strength, not to mention his compelling masculine dignity, was simply an innate part of the man and had little to do with exterior trappings. Inexplicably, the very sight of him caused a most peculiar disturbance in the pit of her stomach, a feeling that was as strangely delectable as it was disconcerting to her rational thought processes.

It came to her that it was little wonder that Rivenoak discouraged visitors to Briarcroft if he was in the habit of practicing a primitive life-style while in the country. No doubt it was a preference he had picked up while living in the wilds of the New World, she reflected, thinking, as she took in the hard ripple of abdominal muscles, not to mention the sinewy definition of his muscular thighs, that there were definite benefits to be derived from living close to nature. Hardly had that thought crossed her mind than, realizing that she had been staring in mute fascination at the duke for quite some five or six seconds, she felt a flush burn her cheeks. Hastily she glanced away.

"I beg your pardon, your grace," she blurted, struck at last by the peculiarity of her position. "I did not mean to intrude on your privacy. It is only that I have never been very good at twiddling my thumbs, and it was such a lovely afternoon. Especially after the confines of the mail coach. Of course, the farmer's hay wagon offered a pleasant means of viewing the countryside and especially the prospect of Briarcroft tucked away in the trees. I quite enjoyed that part of the journey. Still, I really could not resist the allure of an afternoon stroll through the woods, and, besides—"

"It would seem, Miss Featherstone," interrupted Rivenoak,

rescuing her from her hopelessly convoluted explanation, "that it is I who should apologize." Good God, he thought. She had arrived riding on a farmer's hay wagon? It was little wonder that Wilkins had left her to indefinitely cool her heels in the Green Room, knowing, as he did, that he dared not invade his master's solitude on peril of losing his position. Unfamiliar with Miss Featherstone's propensity for independent action, the butler would naturally find such a mode of transportation for a lady questionable at best. The image of Miss Featherstone on the seat of a hay wagon, on the other hand, strangely appealed to Rivenoak. "Had you sent ahead that you were coming, I should have had you met in Shere at the posting inn and thus saved you a deal of discomfort."

"Oh, but it was not in the least uncomfortable," insisted Pandora with a vague wave of the hand. "As a matter of fact, I preferred the hay wagon to the company I was forced to endure in the mail coach, even if the latter did lead to the solution to at least one of my difficulties at home. It is no uncommon achievement to procure the services of a governess, when that is the last thing one is looking to do. Still, I suppose you and I are even now. I really should have let you know I was coming. Unfortunately, I did not know myself until yesterday evening, and by then it was clearly too late to send word ahead. I wonder, would you mind terribly if I sat down for a moment? I feel suddenly a trifle light-headed."

Rivenoak, startled to see the redoubtable Miss Featherstone, in the midst of a discourse that was as incomprehensible as it gave the impression of being disjointed, suddenly sway on her feet, was moved to advance quickly to her aid. "The devil," he said, clasping her by the arms. Gently he eased her down on a hillock of grass. "Why did you not say something? You hardly gave the impression of a female frightened into a swoon."

"Pray do not be absurd, your grace," Pandora retorted, rummaging through her reticule. "I am not such a poor creature,

I assure you. I have never in my life swooned from fright at anything. I am much too logical minded." Drawing forth the small bundle of biscuit and cheese, she unwrapped it. "I have not had a bite since breakfast, and I am prone to dizziness when I miss nuncheon and tea. Would you care for some cheese, your grace?"

Rivenoak's eyes narrowed sharply on Miss Featherstone's pale features. "Do you mean to say you were made to wait in my house without being offered refreshment? I shall indeed have Wilkins's head for this gross dereliction."

"Oh, but it was hardly his fault," Pandora objected. "I should say he is, in fact, an excellent butler. The thing is, he could not be at all sure I was the sort to be made welcome with an offering of tea. I should be the first to admit I must have made a rather odd appearance, especially since I arrived without so much as the benefit of a ladies' companion. And pray do not insist on returning at once to the house to rectify an honest error. I am quite content where I am for the moment." Breaking the wedge of cheese in half, she held out her offering in the palm of her hand. "Are you certain you will not have some, your grace? It may not be mulligatawny soup, but I assure you there is plenty for both of us."

She was rewarded for her insistence with a reluctant gleam of amusement in the chill, blue eyes. "Thank you," replied Rivenoak, accepting with grace. "As it happens, I, too, have missed breakfast and nuncheon. Tell me, Miss Featherstone, is it your customary practice to call on gentlemen unaccompanied by a female companion or have you singled me out for that honor?"

"Dear," exclaimed Pandora, her irrepressible dimple peeping forth, "are you afraid I have come for the sole purpose of compromising you, your grace?"

"The thought, Miss Featherstone, did cross my mind," confessed the duke, who found Miss Featherstone's tantalizing proximity more than a little conducive to unseemly thoughts of temptation.

"Then, you may be easy, your grace. It is not my intention to place you in an untenable position. I shall be on the coach back to London before there is the smallest hint of scandal. As it happens, Aunt Cora wished to come with me. Unfortunately, I dared not leave the children unattended. Besides, I should have been hard pressed to stand the nonsense of two tickets on the mail coach. Due to unforeseen circumstance, I find myself at the present unemployed."

"Then, it is true," Rivenoak stated baldly, his pulse leaping with utter certainty. "Colonel Massingale has met with an untimely end. That is what you have come to tell me, is it not?"

Pandora's eyes flew to Rivenoak's in startled surprise. "You knew," she said. "But how—?"

"Suffice it to say a little bird told me," replied Rivenoak with grim humor. "More pertinent, however, is why you came all this way to make me aware of it."

"But it is obvious, is it not? You did say you were the object of a malicious plot and that, furthermore, Colonel Massingale was a part of it. I thought to warn you, your grace. He was murdered, most curiously, in the same manner as your uncle, the marquis. The weapon employed to put a period to his existence, as a matter of fact, has a marked resemblance to the one at your belt."

"Why, I wonder, am I not surprised?" murmured Rivenoak darkly, his hand instinctively going to the haft of the knife in question.

"Perhaps because you were aware the colonel had such a knife in his possession?" Pandora suggested, calmly munching a piece of cheese.

"No, but I should have done," Rivenoak said darkly. The hard blue eyes deliberately appraised her. "Come now, Miss Featherstone. You are a confidential inquiry agent. You must have wondered at such a coincidence. Did you come thinking to find the colonel's murderer at Briarcroft?''

"Not at all, your grace," Pandora declared with utter conviction. "Pardon me if I point out it is illogical on your part to suppose that I had. I, after all, could not have known you had the knife. And, even if I had known, it would hardly have been convincing evidence that you were involved in the colonel's passing. You are not the sort to resort to stabbing someone in the chest and then to go to a deal of trouble to conceal the fact that you were ever there. It was obviously, however, someone with whom the colonel had more than a passing acquaintance. A gentleman of fashion whom the colonel had an interest in cultivating no doubt for the purpose of elevating his own social status.''

Rivenoak, much struck at Miss Featherstone's unqualified belief in his innocence, paused in the act of availing himself of a bite of cheese. "You amaze me, Miss Featherstone. Did I not know better, I should think you were a witness to the event. How could you possibly know anything about the killer, let alone his supposed social status?''

"I *am* a confidential inquiry agent, your grace," Pandora did not hesitate to remind him. "And I *was* allowed to view the scene of the crime. It was all a matter of observation and simple deduction." Forgetting for a moment in her exuberance for the most intriguing conundrum in her brief career that she was seated on a mound of grass beside the Duke of Rivenoak, who was in what very nearly approached a state of *au naturel,* Pandora proceeded to relate in intricate detail what she had discovered at the scene of the colonel's unfortunate end.

"It is my firm belief that the killer, whoever he was, was familiar with the circumstances of the marquis's equally untimely demise," she concluded, popping the last morsel of her portion of their impromptu repast in her mouth and brushing her hands together with an air of satisfaction. "Why else should he have gone to the effort of duplicating all the singular external trappings of the original crime?''

"Why, indeed, Miss Featherstone?" queried Rivenoak, apparently fascinated by her original thought processes.

"Why, to mislead the investigators into thinking the two murders were executed by the same person or persons, of course," Pandora answered confidently. "Not that they are not related in some manner I have yet to discover, for I cannot but suspect that they are. It is only that I consider it highly unlikely the Gentleman of Fashion had anything to do with the marquis's death, especially as it is my considered opinion that that honor must go to the colonel himself."

"Now you *have* astonished me, Miss Featherstone," declared Rivenoak, who, based on knowledge he alone had in his possession, had long since come to that very same conclusion. "I should be interested to know what led you to suspect Massingale."

"I'm afraid it is more a matter of intuition than hard evidence, your grace," Pandora confessed. It was on her tongue to add that Massingale must certainly have been motivated by events that pertained somehow to the contents of the wooden box in her possession; only at that instant a clap of thunder shattered the tranquillity of the glen, and the very next the heavens opened up with rain.

Uttering a curse, Rivenoak sprang to his feet. "Quick," he exclaimed, reaching down for Pandora's hand, "the medicine lodge."

Pandora, who, even had she not been threatened with a drenching, would have complied with that curtly offered invitation simply for the chance to see inside the curious hut, gathered up her skirts and ran.

As Pandora burst through the opening with Rivenoak close behind her, she was given the immediate impression of a pleasant interior made cozy with furs spread about the floor. At the center, a small fire burned within a circle of rocks, while over the leaping flames was suspended a sizeable shallow iron dish filled with fist-sized stones. A pail of water with a dipper sat next to the fire, and close by was a drum made of a copper kettle with a hide stretched over the top.

"Why, it is a steam-bath!" exclaimed Pandora, gazing up at Rivenoak with wondering eyes. "Now I understand."

"You, Miss Featherstone, are an enormously intelligent woman with a wide grasp of a great many things that should not concern you," replied Rivenoak dampeningly. "You do not, however, 'understand' the first thing about a tribal sweat lodge."

"No, you are quite right, your grace," Pandora conceded without the smallest sign of rancor. "I should, however, like very much to learn about it. I suspect the idea is to cleanse oneself of impurities through induced sweating," she speculated, pulling the wet and considerably bedraggled Gypsy hat from her head, "probably preceded by a period of fasting, and in the process to achieve a sort of meditational trance-state through rhythmic chanting and the beating of the drum." She glanced up from shaking out her damp skirts, a mischievous imp in her eye. "I did not mean to eavesdrop, your grace, but I did hear something of what you were doing. I found it most fascinating, I assure you."

The devil she did, thought Rivenoak, acutely aware of Miss Featherstone's hair falling in glorious, silken disarray about her shoulders. Unlike the other gently born females of his acquaintance, she appeared to care not a whit that she had been caught out in a rainstorm, that her skirts were sodden or that her hat was very likely beyond salvaging. On the contrary, her eyes sparkled with laughter, and her lovely face glowed with exhilaration at their little unlooked-for adventure. Egad, but she was magnificent!

"What I was doing, Miss Featherstone," Rivenoak said repressively, "was attempting to purge you from my system."

"Me?" exclaimed Pandora, the mirth in her eyes giving way to startled uncertainty.

"You look surprised," Rivenoak observed dryly.

"No doubt because I am surprised," Pandora declared roundly. "It is hardly the sort of thing I am used to hearing from gentlemen, especially a gentleman I have met only once and briefly at that. But then, you are not precisely like any other gentleman of my acquaintance. I daresay it must seem perfectly natural to you to be attired in the guise of the Essential Male while conversing in a quite normal manner with a member of the opposite sex."

"Oh, perfectly natural," agreed Rivenoak, who, despite the fact that he had been reared in the customs of the Three-Rivers People, who had not placed a high priority on clothing, hardly made it a practice to appear in tribal costume before English ladies whether they were of his acquaintance or not.

"How I envy you that sort of freedom," Pandora said, with perfect honesty. "I have often thought that, while clothes may offer a means of enhancing one's appearance, they also serve to conceal a great deal of one's essential character. I daresay it would prove most difficult to deceive one another if we were all accustomed to parading around as nature intended."

"You may be certain of it," drawled Rivenoak, apparently much struck at the notion. "We should also be hard put to distinguish kings and dukes from the veriest commoner. Now there would be an interesting conundrum, do you think, Miss Featherstone?"

"I daresay the king would have to wear his crown," laughed Pandora, her eyes lighting up at the absurdity of such an eventuality. "And you, your coronet, your grace. Although I suspect there could never be any doubt as to your superior rank. One has only to look at you to see you are of the nobility."

"And you could never be mistaken for anything other than a lady of quality," countered Rivenoak, who could only be gratified that she had apparently looked. He had not been at all certain from her unruffled composure that she had done more than note he was scantily dressed.

"Now you are roasting me, your grace," Pandora chided. "I may be the daughter of an earl, but I have never been lauded for my aristocratic bearing. My sister Cleo is fond of saying I look like one of the scaff and raff; and I daresay she is in the right of it, for I have never taken the least interest in my appearance and neither, I must say, has anyone else."

"You are mistaken, surely, Miss Featherstone," said Rivenoak, who thus far had not been able to take his eyes off her, who, indeed, was ruefully aware that the disturbing effect of her proximity was soon, in his present raiment, going to be made more than a little evident to her. "You must be perfectly aware that you are not merely a beautiful woman, but an exceedingly desirable one."

He was rewarded for that observation with a widening of disbelieving eyes. "Must I, your grace?" she queried, experiencing a curious fluttering sensation in the pit of her stomach, which she attributed to having missed nuncheon and tea. "Upon what evidence am I to base this highly unlikely assumption? I am five and twenty and have never had a man so much as look at me, unless, of course, you count Squire Thompson, who, in one of his drunken sprees, once cornered me in my father's stables. I was forced to resort to extreme measures to convince him I had not the least wish to frolic with him in the haystack."

She ended that pronouncement with a decided, if unwitting, shudder. Rivenoak frowned.

"It occurs to me that Squire Thompson, though obviously a boor, at least was not a blind fool like the rest of the men of your acquaintanceship," replied Rivenoak, wondering precisely what means she had employed to discourage the drunken squire's advances as he deliberately began to undo the buttons down the front of her pelisse. "You are shivering, Miss Featherstone," he calmly pronounced. "And little wonder. You are wet nearly to the skin."

Pandora, acutely aware of the feather-light touch of Rivenoak's strong fingers moving down her front between her
breasts, was not in the least positive that she owed the quaking
of her knees to the sodden condition of her clothing. On the
other hand, she saw little purpose in arguing with the duke.
Her clothes were indeed wet, and, in spite of the fire, she was
undeniably trembling. Still, as a female trained in the science
of observation and deduction, she could not but find it a most
intriguing paradox that, while she manifested all the outward
signs of one prey to a chill, inside, she felt most peculiarly as
if a slow-mounting fire had been somehow ignited.

It was, she decided, a conundrum worthy of investigation.

"Much better," murmured Rivenoak approvingly, as Pandora, feeling the pelisse slide off her shoulders, obliged him
by pulling her arms free of the sleeves. "You will soon begin
to feel the warmth of the fire now, although I question remaining
in those wet shoes. Pray be seated, Miss Featherstone, and
allow me to remove them. I have no doubt your feet are quite
chilled."

Rivenoak, having been witness to Pandora's calm acceptance
of circumstances that might have caused many another female
to go off in a fit of the spasms, was no doubt understandably
startled to behold the unpredictable Miss Featherstone furiously
blush at the mere suggestion that she bare her feet in his presence.

"You are very kind, your grace, but it really is not necessary
to—"

"But I assure you it is necessary. You will undoubtedly
catch a cold if you stand around in wet shoes, and where would
be the logic in that? Sit, Miss Featherstone. You will do much
better with your feet dry."

"I daresay there is not the least logic in such an eventuality,
your grace," Pandora conceded, sinking down on a soft mound
of furs. Leaning back on her elbows, she resolutely extended
a small foot shod in scuffed velvet half boots to the duke, who

proceeded to untie the laces across the front. "Any more than silly vanity is an excuse for refusing to do the sensible thing. You see," she continued, as Rivenoak, having unloosed the laces, prepared to pull the boot from her foot, "while my papa was perfectly wonderful about giving me the sort of education denied to most women, I'm afraid he neglected those pursuits of a more practical vein."

The boot slid off. Pandora sat perfectly still as she waited for Rivenoak's probable reaction to the undeniable evidence of her father's dereliction in her education.

She was not sure what she had expected, but certainly it was not to behold the hard leap of muscle along the duke's lean jaw at sight of her big toe poking through a hole in her stocking.

"Absurd, is it not," Pandora ventured in an attempt to lighten the moment with humor. "I am conversant in Italian, Russian, Greek, and French, not to mention English. I can discuss Greek philosophy with the best of classical scholars and can read Virgil in its original Latin. I daresay I know as much about classical history as I do about English and have made it practically a vocation to keep abreast of developments in several of the major areas of science, and yet I can do absolutely nothing with a simple needle and thread."

Rivenoak, who was thinking along far different lines, indeed, who had sustained a cold stab of rage at Miss Featherstone's elder brothers for allowing their unmarried kinswoman to live on the edge of what he imagined amounted to penury, was hard put not to give vent to a powerful surge of emotion. Naturally, he was not to know that Pandora had chosen not to reveal her financial circumstances to either of her brothers, who undoubtedly would, if not out of affection, then at least out of a sense of family pride, have taken steps to alleviate her difficulties. The truth was she had rather do without than to accept charity and the inevitable cost to pride and independence that must ever go along with it.

"You are a confidential inquiry agent and a scholar," Rivenoak said, gazing up at her with eyes that seemed meant to make her heart stop. "There is no shame in not knowing how to darn holes in stockings. However, I should be glad to show you the rudiments of mending if ever you should wish to learn the skill." He reached for her other foot. "I was used to watch my grandmother soften hides with her teeth and then sew the hides into clothing with bone needles and leather strips," he said matter-of-factly as he set himself to undoing Pandora's boot laces. "She refused to give up the old ways. My mother adopted the ways of the white men and sewed with cotton thread and steel needles. My father purchased bolts of calico and wool for her on his yearly trips to the coast." His hands went still. "I remember a red dress she wore when—"

Pandora, watching him, had been marveling at the stern features, softened with what could only have been fond memories. Then a swift blur of pain had unexpectedly darkened the marvelous intensity of his eyes. He looked away, and Pandora felt the hard clutch of a hand at her heart.

The moment passed as swiftly as it had come. He looked back at her, his eyes the impenetrable blue of polished steel, and it was as if the moment had never been.

"Your mother was a woman of the tribes," Pandora said quietly, trying to hold on to the memory, trying to make sense of things. "Strange that I did not guess. Yesterday, when you told us the stories. It was you, was it not. You are Boy-Who-Walks."

"Boy-Who-Walks died a long time ago." Rivenoak pulled the boot from her foot. His eyes lifted to impale her. "I am Rivenoak, the English duke. And you are a cursedly beautiful woman."

Deliberately, he leaned toward her, his hair, straight and black as a raven's wing, falling forward over his shoulders.

Pandora went exceedingly still, her heart seeming to skip a beat. He was going to kiss her, and she, who had never been kissed by a man before, would do nothing to stop him. Strange.

It was like feeling oneself caught up in an act of kismet, as if every event in her life, everything she had ever thought or done, had been leading her to this precise moment in time. But that was absurd, she told herself, logic vying against the compelling throb of emotions threatening to run amok in her body. He was Rivenoak, the most sought after man in England and the most feared, and she was a nobody with, of all things, a hole in her stocking. It meant nothing to him to kiss her.

Then his body, warm and thrillingly hard, pressed against hers, and her hands, as though possessed of a will of their own, were running through the bristling mat of hair on his chest and up over his shoulders to the back of his neck. The ever logical Miss Featherstone stifled the last, lingering voice of rationale. Rivenoak was here—now—and for whatever reasons he wanted her, perhaps even needed her. It was one conundrum that could wait to be resolved until some later time.

Intrigued to note not only that Miss Featherstone came to him with a remarkable readiness, but that once clasped in his embrace, she lifted her eyes to meet his with what could only be described as a frank air of expectancy, Rivenoak felt a warning sound somewhere inside his brain.

The Duke of Rivenoak had been hunted by many women intent on marrying him for his title and his fortune. He had preferred to take his pleasures among the barques of frailty who knew better than to try to lay any claims on him. He, after all, had seen what it was for a man and woman to walk hand in hand in love. The memory of his mother and father was still strong in him. The very thought of marriage to a prim and proper lady of noble birth who would have submitted to give him an heir and then frozen him out of her life forever filled him with repugnance. Rather than submit to such a marriage, the cursed title could go to his cousin Percival for all Rivenoak cared. But that was before Miss Pandora Featherstone had obtruded herself into his life.

In all the years since he had been torn from his mother's

people and forced to live in the cold land of the English, he had never known a woman to arouse his primitive male instincts to possess and protect a female of the species the way this one did. But then, she was not like other Englishwomen. She was, indeed, a lady, refined by nature and by her genteel upbringing, but she could hardly have been described either as prim or proper. She was a woman—vital, feminine, blessed with a natural exuberance of spirits, and most damnably alluring.

He did not doubt that she would have been welcomed gladly into the lodges of the Three-Rivers People. Indeed, he suffered an unwonted stab of conscience at the realization that, little as she might deserve it, he would not hesitate to use her to discover everything she knew about Massingale and the wooden box that she had no right to have in her possession. And, afterwards, he would walk away from her. She was, after all, he forcefully reminded himself, a Featherstone and consequently not to be trusted.

Telling himself that the blood quest to which he had dedicated himself for the past ten years was all that mattered, he lowered his head to hers.

Pandora did not know what to expect as she stared, spell-bound, into Rivenoak's eyes. There had, after all, been little reason in the past to speculate what it might be like to find oneself lying on one's back on a bed of furs in a primitive hut with a physically perfect specimen of the Natural Man practically lying on top of one. She had the curious premonition that her life was about to be changed forever. Nervously, she parted her lips to inform Rivenoak that the bone handle of his knife was pressing most disturbingly into her side, and then he covered her mouth with his.

Pandora quivered, shot through with a probing shock of pleasure. Good heavens, she had never dreamed the mere touching of lips could have such an intoxicating effect on one in whom the precepts of objectivism had been inculcated almost from birth and who was noted for what her sister Cleo had been wont to call "an inhuman adherence to rationality." Indeed, in spite of her not insignificant talent for solving the irresolvable, Pandora could find no explanation for why Rivenoak, of all the men she had ever encountered, should have the power to ignite a smoldering heat in her belly or turn her knees into jelly.

Hardly had that delirious thought wafted through her reeling consciousness than Rivenoak thrust his tongue between her conveniently parted teeth. Never had she felt anything to compare to what she experienced then, as Rivenoak probed the previously unexplored sweetness of her mouth. A melting pang seemed to explode somewhere deep inside her belly, sending tiny shock waves radiating outwards to her extremities. Unwittingly she gasped from the pure pleasure of it, a circumstance which seemed only to whet the fires in Rivenoak.

"Witch," he groaned, abandoning her lips to kiss a trail of flames down the side of her neck. "Your medicine is more potent than wine. You should go, Miss Featherstone. Now, before it is too late."

"But I have not the least desire to go, your grace," Pandora did not hesitate to inform him on a long gust of breath. She tilted her head to one side in order to grant him greater freedom for his most intriguing explorations. "Indeed, I am persuaded I should like nothing better than to stay. You see, I have never before been kissed by a man. I must confess I have long entertained a strong curiosity concerning that most elemental of all conundrums—the instantaneous incitement of powerful primal emotions between a male and female in an instance of strong mutual physical magnetism. If you must know, I have never been at all certain I was capable of experiencing, let alone arousing someone else, to a mindless pitch of emotion."

"I believe you need have no doubts on either of those fronts," declared Rivenoak, who was not in the least uncertain as to Miss Featherstone's power to incite a man's primitive passions to a feverish pitch. He was, in fact, painfully aware that he was already in a state of full male arousal. "You are obviously a woman of great passion, and I am testament to the fact that you are fully equipped to inflame a man's primal emotions."

"I-I am?" Pandora quavered, then shivered uncontrollably as Rivenoak's hand, on a titillating journey over her shoulder and down her arm, made a deliberate detour to the fleshy mound of her breast. As if to prove the veracity of his assertion, Rivenoak rubbed the pad of his thumb over her nipple, causing a piercing throb of heat to pervade her nether regions. Mindlessly, she dug her fingers into his shoulders. Then, caught up in the throes of the unexpected and wholly exquisite responses of her body to his manipulations, Pandora writhed sharply beneath his touch and, feeling the knife come up hard against her hip, gasped. "I-I mean, you are?"

"Egad, can you doubt it?" uttered Rivenoak on what sounded very like a low groan of agony.

Pandora's eyelids flew open in quick concern to be met with the sight of Rivenoak, his face set in a rigid mask of control in which his eyes, half-closed, glittered with what gave every evidence of being some terrible torment. More alarming still, the muscles in his arms and shoulders stood out in hard ridges as though his entire body were tensed in fierce concentration.

"Your grace," she exclaimed, "what is it? I felt your knife. Good God, say you are not injured."

"I am—not—injured," Rivenoak obliged her. Dropping his head between his arms braced on either side of her, he gave vent to something between a groan and a laugh. "And that—was not—my knife."

"Not your knife? But I know I felt—!" Pandora, presented with a conundrum, was, in typical fashion, quick to explore the alternative possibilities for the sizeable, exceedingly hard object against which she had come in contact and quicker, still, to arrive at the only logical explanation for it. "Oh, I see," she breathed, her eyes widening with sudden enlightenment.

"Yes, I thought you would," Rivenoak said grimly. "And

now perhaps you realize the wisdom of ending this before you are made to discover precisely how powerful the instantaneous incitement of primal emotions can be between a male and a female of strong mutual physical magnetism.''

"On the contrary, your grace," Pandora did not hesitate to inform him even as she marveled at her own brazenness. But then, she had ever prided herself on being a freethinker and an independent female. And having been given to glimpse what it might mean to have the mysterious power of her own woman's body unleashed, she could hardly wish to curtail the exercise just when it was proving most instructive. "As it happens, I should like nothing more than to continue the investigation to its logical conclusion. If you must know, I have never been one to give up on a conundrum before it is fully resolved."

Fully resolved? Good God, thought Rivenoak, who had no illusions as to the outcome of exploring dangerous grounds with an unmarried female of gentle birth. The last thing he could wish was to find himself legshackled to Herodotus Featherstone's sister, and he was damned if he would wantonly dishonor her. Whatever she was, she hardly deserved that at his hands.

"This time, I fear you have no choice, Miss Featherstone. No doubt you may comfort yourself with the knowledge that I believe I have never known a female more responsive to my lovemaking or one who more thoroughly aroused my primal emotions. And you may be sure if circumstances were different—if this were an earlier time and a different place and if you were not an unmarried female who is a guest in my house— nothing would stop me here today."

"Well, then." With an enthusiasm that must have proven startling to Rivenoak, Pandora clasped her arms about the back of his neck. "I should say there is nothing *to* stop you, your grace. I am indeed an unmarried female, but I am all of five and twenty and quite able to determine my own life. Furthermore, though I may be a guest in your house, let us not forget I am an uninvited one. I daresay that relieves you of all responsibility for me.''

The muscles leaped along Rivenoak's arms. The devil, he thought. Miss Featherstone was obviously a woman of unplumbed passions, a fact that did little to calm the fierceness of his own unexpected attraction to her.

Hell and the devil confound it, he all but groaned, feeling his groin swollen with need. *Attraction* did not begin to describe the power she wielded over him! She was endowed with the Earth Mother's powerful magic, which could drive a man to forget everything in his desire to possess her. Indeed, he had all but forgotten the purpose of his assault on those lovely lips was to breach her defences and force her to reveal all she knew about the cursed wooden box.

''You tax my powers of control, Miss Featherstone,'' he said between clenched teeth, ''not to mention my forbearance. You haven't the least notion of what it would mean to give yourself to me today.''

''I daresay it would mean that we shall have shared a brief moment of exquisite passion,'' opined Pandora, who did not doubt this would be her one and only chance to learn what it was to be a woman in the arms of a man to whom she was overwhelmingly attracted. ''After which, you will undoubtedly go on with your life and I with mine. And that is all there is to it.''

All there was to it! thought Rivenoak, who had little difficulty envisioning any number of complications that must accrue from so foolhardy an act, not the least of which was the most obvious—the unwanted prospect of a nameless bastard. Egad, she had not the smallest sense of what she was proposing.

Still, she was here, and she was willing, it would seem. And he had yet to bring up the subject of the wooden box.

''The logical conclusion to such a conundrum as this, Miss Featherstone,'' he said thickly, his hand beneath the hem of her gown beginning a purposeful quest up the side of her leg, her hip, and over her belly, "is likely to open up an entirely new set of conundrums." His nimble fingers found and quickly undid the string at the waist of her drawers. "None of which may prove remotely solvable." Pandora's eyes widened on his as he delved inside her unmentionables, working his way toward what would seem to be the source of a peculiar moist heat between her thighs of which she had been singularly cognizant for no little time. "Are you quite certain that is what you wish?"

"You forget, your grace, as a confidential inquiry agent, I am dedicated to the proposition of resolving problems," Pandora reminded him on a rising note.

She was about to add that she did not doubt there was any problem that could not be resolved through the process of simple observation and reasonable deduction, but just then Rivenoak apparently found what he had been looking for, a bud of acute sensitivity set in the midst of fleshy, swollen petals between her thighs; and suddenly she was finding it increasingly difficult to bring her faculties to bear on even the most rudimentary steps in deductive reasoning. Indeed, it was most peculiar that, while her powers of observation seemed magnified to include a keen awareness of a bewildering array of sensory input—the spatter of rain against the hut coupled with the spit and crackle of the fire in its circle of stones, the smell of wet earth and smoke mingled with a musky scent from her own body, the glint of blue sparks in Rivenoak's hair along with the smoldering blue of his eyes, and the voluptuous softness of the furs beneath her together with the sensual firmness of Rivenoak's body against hers, not to mention the sensation of a mounting conflagration somewhere in her nether regions that threatened at any moment to engulf her—she was wholly unable to process anything in a rational manner. It was little wonder, she thought feverishly, that Juliet, in the delirious grip of physical sensations, had cast all logic to the wind in favor of her one and only Romeo. Then Rivenoak, pressing the heel of his hand against her swelling bud, inserted a finger between the lips of her body, and it occurred to Pandora, who could not recall having ever performed an illogical act in her life before this, that there was a great deal to be said for the instantaneous incitement of powerful primal emotions between a male and female.

And that was her last coherent thought as a swelling tide swept over and through her and exploded in a final, glorious torrent of release.

Falling back against the cushion of furs, she felt marvelously, gloriously drained. Indeed, she could not recall when she had felt so wonderfully contented, rather like Clytemnestra, the kitchen cat, after a feast of fish heads and cream. No doubt the melting lassitude that filled her could be attributed to weariness after her journey, not to mention the fact that she had arisen that morning before sunrise. She wished nothing more at that moment than to nestle more deeply into the warm nest of furs beneath her and drift off to sleep. Indeed, she was all but oblivious to the fact that Rivenoak, leaning over her, was speaking to her.

"And now that you have reached the logical end to your conundrum, Miss Featherstone," said Rivenoak, who was feeling a deal less sated than his languorous companion, "perhaps you would not mind answering a few questions of my own."

"I shall try, your grace," Pandora responded, smiling beatifically as she stretched luxuriously on the bed of furs. "Feel free to ask me anything. You may rest assured I shall do my best to oblige you."

"You may be sure of it, Miss Featherstone," replied Rivenoak grimly. "I shall, in fact, insist on it. Why do you not begin by telling me everything you know about the wooden box in your possession?"

"Mmm?" murmured Pandora, snuggling her cheek against the cradle of her hand. Helplessly, she yawned. "Box?"

"Yes, the box," Rivenoak persisted. "The one you had with you at Colonel Massingale's Town House."

"Oh, *that* box," Pandora said, curling up on her side and closing her eyes. "Know very little about it, save has caused me no end of speculation. You cannot know how I have had to resist temptation to peek at contents. I have every faith, your grace, you will satisfy my curiosity. Is, after all, one of the reasons I came all this way."

"It is, Miss Featherstone?" prompted Rivenoak, trying to make sense of her ramblings. "Perhaps you could be more specific. Precisely why *did* you come to Briarcroft?"

"Why do you think, your grace?" sighed Pandora, who, experiencing no little difficulty in focusing her thoughts, would have preferred at the moment not to be made the object of a Spanish Inquisition. In resignation, she opened her eyes to gaze up at her interlocutor. "I came to deliver it to its rightful owner of course. It is yours, your grace," she added. Then, her eyelids drifting irresistibly down over her eyes, she sighed, "You will oblige me by showing me what is inside it, will you not? Just as soon as I have indulged in a little nap?"

Rivenoak, ruefully aware that Miss Featherstone had drifted off to sleep, smiled with sardonic appreciation at just how greatly he had misjudged her. She might indeed be the sister of Herodotus Featherstone, but obviously she was cut of a different mold. She had brought him the box, and, more importantly, she had not the first clue as to its contents. Clearly, she could not have been a part of Massingale's sinister plot to destroy him.

Hell and the devil confound it! he cursed silently to himself. It would seem, thanks to her honest endeavor, that she had, nevertheless, placed him in a devil of a coil. At the very least, there was the very real possibility that she would be ruined by this afternoon's events, and, at the most, placed in peril of her life from those who wished to see him dead. It behooved him to find a way to wrap the whole in clean linen and at the same time place her under his protection. Indeed, he saw little other recourse before him save to make the ruse he had constructed to gain an interview with her a reality.

Miss Featherstone would be persuaded to pose as his intended while he took steps to discover the identities of those in the plot against him. He would give her no choice in the matter. And, afterwards, when there was no longer any danger to her, she could go her own way unharmed by the experience.

Rising from the bed of furs, he quickly divested himself of the breechclout and moccasins of his mother's people and reached for the breeches, shirt, and boots of the Duke of Rivenoak.

It was time Miss Featherstone and he returned to London.

Chapter 6

Pandora was teased to wakefulness by a persistent tickling sensation along the side of her cheek, which resisted her every effort to wish it away. She felt deliciously encased in a snug cocoon of warmth out of which she had no wish to be drawn.

Still, she could not but be aware that there was something odd about her surroundings. Instead of linen sheets, she had the distinct impression that she was nestled against a warm, furry animal of some sort, one too large to be Clytemnestra, the kitchen cat, who would not, in any case, have been allowed upstairs in her bedroom. Furthermore, unless Pandora were very much mistaken, she was lying in bed fully dressed, save for the lack of her shoes.

The thought of shoes, rather than the prospect of finding herself abed with a large, hirsute creature of unknown origin, served to jolt her to full wakefulness, her eyes flying open and memory flooding back to her.

"Your grace," she exclaimed at sight of Rivenoak, lying,

fully clothed, beside her. Propped on one elbow, he was occupied with trailing a lock of her hair down the side of her face.

"Miss Featherstone. You are awake."

"I am, indeed, your grace, and mortified that I apparently nodded off in your company. For heaven's sake, how long have I been asleep?"

"Long enough for the rain to stop. Half an hour, I should think. I was reluctant to wake you, you were resting so peacefully."

"Dear, so long?" replied Pandora, smothering the impulse to yawn. "How very rude you must think me."

"Not at all. It was, after all, perhaps to be expected. You are a woman of strong passions." A faint smile touched the corners of his lips as a becoming tinge of color invaded her cheeks.

The remarkable Miss Featherstone, however, was quick to recover.

"Yes, I believe I must be," she agreed with perfect candor. "I never dreamed I should ever experience a moment in which all logic was swept away in a tidal wave of passion, for if you must know, I have been accused of being possessed of an inhuman adherence to rationality. You cannot know what it means to me to be given an understanding of pure physical and emotional transcendence over reason. It was perhaps the most scintillating experience of my life, and I have you to thank for it, your grace."

"Think nothing of it, Miss Featherstone," replied Rivenoak, ironically aware that the experience had possibly been even more eye opening for him. Miss Featherstone had come perilously close to driving him over the edge of his self-control. She had not the least notion how near he had come to casting all caution to the wind in his overpowering need to plunge his shaft into her. Even now, he was ruefully aware of the ache in his loins that his final moment of forbearance had cost him. "No doubt I am gratified that I should have been the one to instruct you. You are not only an apt pupil, but a most inspiring one.''

"It is kind in you to say so, your grace," said Pandora, a frown of concentration etched between her eyebrows. "Even if you do not perfectly mean it. Obviously, I was not quite so inspiring as I should have been. The conundrum, you will agree, was only half-resolved."

Good God, he thought, in sardonic amusement. If she had been any more inspiring, it was doubtful he would be capable at this moment of walking upright. As it was, he could look forward to a wholly uncomfortable hour or two before he was fully recovered from the effects of her power to unleash his primitive inclinations.

"A necessity, Miss Featherstone, that I regret more than you can possibly imagine," he answered with only the barest hint of irony. "I suggest, if my sacrifice is not to be for naught, however, that you set about putting yourself to rights. The servants will undoubtedly have noticed your absence, and there is the unfinished matter of the wooden box. That is why you came to Briarcroft, after all, is it not?"

Pandora, brought sharply back to an awareness of the seriousness of her reason for seeking out the duke, instantly sobered. "I did indeed. That was not, however, my primary concern in coming to you. I am convinced, your grace," she said, her eyes searching on his, "that you are in grave danger. I was in such dread that I should arrive to find you the victim of foul play, and *that* I should not have been able to countenance. I should never have forgiven myself for not having done something to avert it."

"Your concern, Miss Featherstone, no doubt does you credit," observed his grace, struck by the lovely intensity of her gaze. Egad, he thought. She meant it. She had truly been frightened for him. He could not think of another female, other than his Aunt Caroline, Lady Congreve, who would have dared so much for him. Not since the death of his parents. "Had anything so unlikely transpired, I fail, however, to see what you might have done to prevent it.''

"I should have warned you yesterday of my suspicions concerning Colonel Massingale's manipulations. For if you must know, I had already come to the conclusion that the colonel had deliberately established me in his Town House for some nefarious purpose. And after your visit, I was convinced of it. Had I known then of the colonel's unfortunate demise, you may be sure nothing would have kept me silent.''

"You intrigue me, Miss Featherstone,'' murmured Rivenoak, his gaze unreadable beneath drooping eyelids. "What purpose?''

"The most malevolent of purposes, your grace,'' Pandora readily answered. "In light of my employer's peculiar behavior just prior to his demise, I am now of the firm opinion that the colonel intended to cut your stick for you.''

"The plot, it would seem, thickens,'' observed Rivenoak, who could not but wonder how she had come to such a conclusion. "I, however, was not present at the scene of the crime.''

"Oh, but you were, your grace,'' Pandora did not hesitate to inform him. "Or at least you were in my room upstairs sometime earlier that day. Pray do not deny it. There were unmistakable signs of an intruder. I deduced from a strand of hair caught in the frame of an upstairs window, not to mention the footprints at the bottom of the drainpipe, that the burglar was a man of your description. Your unexpected appearance at my house in South Audley Street, I'm afraid, established you as the intruder beyond a doubt.''

"How very clumsy of me,'' remarked Rivenoak in exceedingly dry tones. "And if I were this burglar of yours, what should I have been doing there? I promise I have no need to engage in thievery for a living. As it happens, I am possessed of a not insubstantial fortune.''

"Pray do not be absurd, your grace. You were not there to rob the house. I daresay you were lured there by a message of some sort. Very likely an anonymous letter. What did it promise, your grace? That you might find something of your father's in the colonel's Town House?''

"It was hardly so pointed as that, Miss Featherstone," conceded the duke, resigning himself to the inevitable. Miss Featherstone was far too astute a confidential inquiry agent to be put off by denials. "It promised only that I should discover certain things of interest to me."

"Of great enough interest to entice you to break into the colonel's house," Pandora sapiently observed. "But then, they would have to be, since it was to appear as if the colonel had struck down a burglar in the act of an unlawful entry, with me to serve as an unwitting witness to that effect."

Rivenoak arched an aristocratic eyebrow. "I find this all very extraordinary, Miss Featherstone," he said, marveling that she had penetrated so close to the truth. "The fact remains, however, that it was not I who perished in the colonel's Town House, but the colonel himself."

"Yes, but only because you had the foresight to arrive earlier than expected, and because I, after having been stranded at the British Museum, when by all rights I should have been at work in the colonel's library, determined to move that evening back to my own house. I daresay the colonel was greatly put out with me for my dereliction of duty and with you for failing to put in an appearance for your own murder. We had both come and gone before the colonel arrived."

"How very fortunate for us," said the duke, observing the play of firelight in Miss Featherstone's glorious hair. Of course, he had known from the beginning that the letter was the bait for a trap. The remarkable woman before him, however, had pieced it together from the merest bits of information. And no doubt she would continue piecing things together until she had either figured out the whole of it or she found herself in the sights of a murderer, who would think nothing of cutting her stick for her. Miss Featherstone had not the smallest notion what she was inviting. She was an innocent pitting herself against men who had killed and would kill again, and he was the only one who could insure her safety.

The devil, he thought, foreseeing with sudden clarity that his future relations with Miss Featherstone were likely to be anything but smooth. He did not doubt that her fearless disregard of danger and her stubborn determination to resolve her cursed conundrums would lead them both into any number of perilous situations.

"And now we find ourselves in the midst of a new conundrum," he pointed out, desirous of discovering how much more she had sorted out for herself. "It would seem that, while the colonel has met his just end, we have not the smallest clue why he was killed or who should have done it."

He was rewarded for that observation with an assessing glance from Miss Featherstone. "Are you quite certain you haven't some notion who might have wished him dead, your grace?"

"Other than myself, do you mean, Miss Featherstone?" Rivenoak countered dryly. "I'm afraid not. Not that it need concern you any further. You have delivered the box to me, for which I am grateful, and now it is time you returned to London and put the whole matter out of your mind. You may leave the rest of it to me."

"Pray do not be absurd, your grace," declared Pandora, hardly surprised that the duke wished to deny her any further involvement and yet hurt by it somehow. "There is not the least chance that I shall be able to do that. I am, in case you had forgot, a confidential inquiry agent. It is not in my nature to give up before I have seen a conundrum through—"

"To its logical conclusion," Rivenoak finished for her. "You have already made that much, at least, abundantly clear."

Pandora dimpled irresistibly up at him. "Splendid, your grace. I am so glad you understand. I knew you were a man of powerful intellect the moment I met you. Furthermore, I strongly suspect you have a very good notion why the colonel would seem to have gone to a deal of trouble to try and murder you. Why do you not simply tell me all about it and be done with it?''

''Because, you impossible female,'' growled the duke, shoving himself up to his feet, ''the less you know about these events, the better I shall like it. You have only to see what happened to Massingale to know these are dangerous men with whom we are dealing.''

''Pooh,'' Pandora retorted. ''It is because you cannot bring yourself to trust in a woman. I, however, am not just any woman, your grace. I am thoroughly trained in the science of observation and deduction, which is why I know I can be of invaluable aid to you. That is the real reason why I am here— to offer my services to you. And pray do not try and tell me you have no need of a keen pair of eyes, not to mention ears, at your back. You may be the Duke of Rivenoak and the most dangerous man in England, but I am Pandora Featherstone, a Nobody. People, who would not dream of confiding in you, will think nothing of talking in my hearing. I shall hear and see things you will not, and with no one any the wiser. Surely you must see that I should be an immeasurable asset to you.''

That would undoubtedly be the least of what she would be to him, reflected Rivenoak wryly, as he was treated to the full entreaty of her lovely eyes. It was not enough that she would very likely drive him to an early grave with her propensity for independent action, but she must inevitably be a constant temptation as well.

''Put on your shoes, Miss Featherstone,'' Rivenoak said, resigning himself to the inevitable. ''It is time we were leaving here. If we are to reach London before midnight, we shall have little time to spare.''

'' 'We,' your grace?'' queried Pandora, sitting bolt upright, her eyes questioning on his.

''Yes, Miss Featherstone—we,'' replied Rivenoak, ruefully

aware of the enticing picture she made with her hair dishevelled
from their recent lovemaking and her gown hopelessly rumpled.
It was little wonder he had come to within an inch of dishonoring
her, here, of all places, within the sacred confines of the medicine lodge. Hell and the devil confound it! He was suffering
at that very moment an almost irresistible urge to rectify his
previous omission. "You have a sad notion of my character,"
he said gruffly, "do you think I should allow you to ride on a
hay wagon to the posting inn or, for that matter, the mail coach
to London in your present state—without the benefit of a female
companion. If you are to assume the role of my promised bride,
Miss Featherstone, I'm afraid you must resign yourself in future
to a strict adherence to the proprieties."

"Oh, but I shall, your grace!" Pandora exclaimed, reaching
with alacrity for her worn velvet half boots. "You may be
certain I shall present the very picture of conformability. When
do we begin, your grace? I daresay it would not be amiss to
interview the colonel's servants as soon as is possible. You
may be sure Mrs. Caulkins and Jessop will prove a wellspring
of information. And then there is the ministry of defence. I
daresay the Duke of Rivenoak will have little difficulty gaining
access to the records dating back eighteen years ago. There
might be something in them to tell us if there was any involvement between your uncle and the colonel that might have led
to so disagreeable an end. And then there are always the officers
and men who have served under the colonel. Since my brother
Herodotus is one of them, I daresay they can readily be brought
to confide in me."

"Oh, no doubt," agreed Rivenoak, who had just been given
a glimmering of the sort of difficulties that lay ahead of him.
It would be no simple matter to deter a confidential inquiry
agent of Miss Featherstone's remove from poking her nose into
a hornets' nest if she thought it would reveal some pertinent
piece of a puzzle. Still, that was precisely what he must prevent
her from doing if there was to be any hope of her coming out

of this unharmed. "You, Miss Featherstone, will be far too busy, however, to talk to them. We have less than a month to transform you into a lady of fashion. I'm afraid you will just have to leave any investigating to me for the next several weeks. You, my dear, will be spending all your time with modistes and hairdressers."

"Modistes? Good God," Pandora blurted, only immediately to catch her tongue between her teeth.

The devil, she thought. Rivenoak was hardly the sort to brook an argument. Rather than concede a point to her, he was far more likely to dispense with her services, and that was the very last thing she could wish to have happen, especially while Rivenoak remained in peril of his life. She had every intention of making sure she was in a position to guard his back for him until she had resolved the conundrum of who was plotting against him and why, and to do that, she would clearly have to practice a little more patience and subtlety.

"You are right of course, your grace," she said, awarding the duke a rueful smile. "I was guilty of rushing my fences. Naturally it is imperative that I dress for the part I shall be playing. And that will be no easy matter. It has been no little time since I indulged in anything so costly as a wardrobe. I'm afraid I hardly know where to begin, let alone how I shall bring myself to allow you to stand the nonsense."

"That, Miss Featherstone, is the simplest of our conundrums. My aunt, Lady Congreve, will take you under her wing. You may be certain that she will derive no little enjoyment from seeing you fitted out in the first stare of fashion. And she will not mind in the least sending the accounting to me. She will, in fact, do so with a deal of satisfaction. She is forever fond of saying that I am a deal too wealthy for my own good and that it would benefit me greatly to part with some of my fortune. And now that all that is settled, I suggest we direct our steps to the house." Extending his hand to Pandora, Rivenoak pulled

her to her feet. "You, after all, have still to satisfy your curiosity concerning a certain wooden box."

Pandora had a great deal on her mind on the way back to the hunting lodge, not the least of which was how she should manage to conduct her investigations on the sly without Rivenoak any the wiser. She had not the least intention of allowing the trail to grow cold while she frittered away her time on shopping. With any luck, it should not prove too difficult to slip away from Rivenoak's aunt upon occasion. One could not be expected to be trying on clothes all the time, after all, and besides, she reasoned, elderly ladies were wont to take frequent naps in the afternoons.

The duke, after receiving a string of monosyllabic responses, soon gave up any further attempts to engage her in polite conversation. Consequently, the walk back to the duke's hunting lodge was accomplished, for the most part, in silence.

As they entered the foyer, Rivenoak instructed his housekeeper, Mrs. Reed, to show Miss Featherstone to a room where she might freshen up before an early supper. "Unless," he added to Pandora, "you would prefer a tray sent up."

"Not at all, your grace," Pandora answered, impatient, now that the moment was near at hand, to get on with the business of opening up the wooden chest. "I shall be down in fifteen minutes."

Indeed, as there was little she could do to improve the disreputable appearance of her attire, she took time only to wash her face and hands and to make a valiant attempt to subdue her unruly tresses in a knot at the nape of her neck. Awarding the looking glass a last, comical grimace of disgust, she shrugged fatalistically.

"If Lady Congreve can turn *me* into a lady of fashion, it will be nothing short of a miracle," she declared aloud to the empty room. "Very likely she will only fling up her hands in despair, and who could blame her? I am utterly hopeless."

"I think you do not know Lady-Who-Never-Takes-No-For-An-Answer," came in reply from behind Pandora. "I myself have tried to tell her an old Redskin cannot be made civilized, but she does not listen. She says I am a fine figure of a man, but it is the clothes that make the gentleman. And that is why you see me now in the skins of the White Eyes."

Pandora had come about at the first of this remarkable speech to be met with the sight of a tall, marvelous-looking man with a wonderful, craggy face and long silver hair falling down his back. He was dressed in a claret cutaway coat, a blue waistcoat, and a plain ascot. Cream-colored half-dress pantaloons were decorated with red braid up the sides, and his low patent shoes shone with an uncanny gloss. His dark eyes regarded her with a distinct twinkle in their depths that belied the perfect gravity of his face. She could not but smile in response. "Lady Congreve is right, you know," she said. "You do present a magnificent picture of manhood, Mr.—?"

"I am called Laughs-In-The-Rain, but you may call me 'Uncle.' And you are She-Who-Shines-With-Laughter. I know this because I see it in your face." Eloquently, he shrugged. "And because my nephew has told me about you. I came in here to see for myself the woman who can pierce the steel skin of True-Son-Iron-Heart. Now that I have seen you, I understand why his spirit wars in his breast."

"You are Rivenoak's uncle," surmised Pandora, who could not but be captivated by Laughs-In-The-Rain's peculiar manner of expressing himself, not to mention the engaging twinkle in his eyes. "It is a pleasure to meet you, sir." Then, with a speculative glance, *"Does* his spirit war in his breast?"

"Does the salmon swim upstream to the spawning grounds in the spring and summer?" replied Laughs-In-The-Rain cryptically. "Is the bee drawn to the unfolding petals of the flower? I still do not understand you White Eyes. In the old days,

women did not have to ask about these things. They knew the power of the Earth Mother.''

"Did they?'' queried Pandora, eyeing Rivenoak's uncle doubtfully. "But then, I daresay things were simpler then. There were not the complications imposed by civilization. Indeed, I'm afraid you are mistaken in thinking his grace has a *tendre* for me. I am not even certain he likes me.''

"Come walk with me, Shines-With-Laughter. It is time to eat. I am an old man who does not like to be late for his supper, and you are a young woman with too little meat on her bones.''

"What a whisker!'' Pandora scoffed, as she accepted Laughs-In-The-Rain's arm. "You are not in the least old.''

"I am old enough to know when a man has been stricken by the magic of a woman,'' replied Laughs-In-The-Rain, leading Pandora out of the room and down the hall. "And I know my nephew. Each year he comes here to be Chance True-Son for a while, a man of the Three-Rivers People. Together we remember the old stories around the campfire, the time when our young men hunted in the forest and our women planted beans and corn and squash to feed us through the winter. Laughter filled our lodges in those days.'' Laughs-In-The-Rain sighed and shook his head. "But that is beside the point. This is the time of the White Eyes, and you have asked me a question. True-Son was not himself when he came this time. He was like a man who no longer recognizes his reflection in a pond. He says it is because of a woman. And then you come, and True-Son once more wears the mask of the English Duke. He says he will leave before we have sung the songs of the Three-Rivers People. Now you tell me, Shines-With-Laughter. Why does the bull moose leave the meadow without first easing the hunger in his belly if not because he is filled with a greater hunger that eating will not satisfy?''

Pandora, who had only the vaguest notion what a bull moose might be, and that, thanks to her recent studies of the tribes of North America, was not at all sure why the creature might

leave the meadow before having eaten. Still, as a confidential inquiry agent trained in the process of observation and deduction, she had little difficulty in understanding the overall logic behind Laughs-In-The-Rain's deductive reasoning.

"Dear me," she said contritely. "I am sorry. Your time with Rivenoak has been cut short, has it not. But it is not because of me that the duke is leaving. I came only to warn him. He has enemies, you must know that. I came because I was afraid for his safety."

"And now you will fight for him. I see it in your eyes. True-Son was right about you. You do possess the heart of a lioness and the eyes of an eagle. But you must not forget you are no larger than a small bird. You will be wise to trust in True-Son's strength. He will be the mighty oak upon which you must rely when danger threatens."

Pandora could not but take exception to being thought of in terms of a small bird whose only recourse was to fly before the face of danger, indeed, who must depend on a man to protect her. Having been instructed by her papa in the finer points of marksmanship, she was well able to take care of herself.

She sustained an unexpected thrill of pleasure at the knowledge, however, that Rivenoak had seen fit to ascribe other, more complimentary allusions to her character. Still, while it was true she was possessed of a gift for keen observation and was far too logical-minded ever to be easily frightened, indeed, had never been known to back down from a challenge, it could not but occur to her that saying she had the heart of a lioness and the eyes of an eagle might be coming on a bit strong. Her brother Castor had been used to compare her to an English bulldog, who was too stubborn ever to turn loose of a thing once she had got her blasted teeth in it.

* * *

The wooden box sat on a heavy oak table in the duke's study, when some few moments later Pandora and Laughs-In-The-Rain joined Rivenoak to view its contents. Employing a penknife, Rivenoak soon had the lid open.

"The beaded wampum belt She-Who-Joyfully-Sings fashioned for Ridgeway," exclaimed Laughs-In-The-Rain softly, as Rivenoak lifted the beautifully wrought thing from the box. "I thought I would never see it again."

Reverently, the older man took the belt in his hands. "The pattern of the beads spells out a message of peace between Ridgeway and the Three-Rivers People. Joyfully-Sings will rest easier, knowing it has come at last to True-Son."

"Here, too, is the Bible given to her by the old missionary who converted her and the others," observed Rivenoak. "One can still read the entry of my birth at the back. Then there is my father's journal, ending upon the date of my departure for England. And the volume of Herrick, and that is all, save for these," he added grimly, drawing the deerskin and its grisly contents from the box. "I think I should warn you, Miss Featherstone: These are not the sort of things one would normally show to a lady. You, however, are not in the usual style of gently born females. I do not doubt that, as a confidential inquiry agent of no uncertain talents, you have no need to be told to stand buff."

"Whatever it is, I am not like to succumb to a fainting spell, your grace," Pandora did not hesitate to assure him. "I do thank you, however, for your concern."

In spite of having been forewarned, Pandora could not but pale at sight of the three scalps and the terrible implications of their very existence. "Faith," she breathed, unwittingly clasping a hand to her breast, "pray do not say one of these belonged to your—"

Unable to bring herself to voice the dreadful thought aloud, she caught her bottom lip between her teeth.

"Softly, my dear," said Rivenoak, quick to come to her aid.

"It is true that one of these could have been my mother's, but I do not think that was the case. Somehow, I think I should know it if it was."

"Then who—"

"There were thirty-five men and twenty-seven women at the Old Place when the Redcoats came," said Laughs-In-The-Rain, his eyes distant with remembered pain. "Thirty-four children died with them that day, along with the old missionary. These could have come from any of them."

"Or from none of them," Rivenoak offered, folding the scalps back in the deerskin. "We have no way of telling if these are even from the Three-Rivers People."

With an effort, Pandora put the dreadful sight of them from her until she could think of them without horror. "But then why should they have been in the trunk with the other things?" she queried, taking out a red dress, beautifully adorned with beaded fringe.

"I cannot venture an answer to that until I know how Massingale came into its possession. Perhaps they were meant purely for my benefit, to set me off my balance in the event it came to an even fight. Massingale would have wanted to have an edge in such an eventuality."

"And these other things?" Pandora asked, wanting to turn the subject. Holding the dress up to her breast, she gathered it to her at the waist as she glanced at her reflection in the wall mirror. "Oh, but this is lovely. I have never seen anything like it. Did your mother make it? The workmanship is really quite exquisite."

The muscle leaped along the hard line of Rivenoak's jaw. "Yes, she made it," he answered, staring at Pandora strangely.

Pandora was far too observant not to sense a sudden undercurrent in the room. "What is it?" she asked, glancing from one to the other of the two men. Slowly she lowered the dress.

"Joyfully-Sings wore that dress in honor of True-Son's passage into manhood," Laughs-In-The-Rain said in his deep, peculiarly vibrant tones. "It was at the feast of his leaving, the night before Ridgeway took True-Son to board the English ship. That is why Ridgeway was not with the others."

"The others?" Pandora asked.

"The Three-Rivers People. It was too late to plant in the new place. They returned to the Old Place to harvest the crops they had left behind. I, too, was away. I turned my back on them in anger because they would give up the land of the Three Rivers. They were Christian Indians. They would not fight the English."

Abruptly, Rivenoak crossed to the grog tray and reached for the decanter of port.

Pandora stared with a sense of helplessness at his back, the muscles taut beneath his snug-fitting coat. "Something terrible happened at the Old Place," she said, feeling a nauseous sensation in the pit of her stomach. Her gaze went to Laughs-In-The-Rain. "Please tell me."

"They died." It was Rivenoak. He turned. His eyes, the chill blue of a lake in winter, seemed to freeze her through.

"Your mother? And the children? All of them? How——?"

Laughs-In-The-Rain answered. His weathered face appeared carved from old wood. "The White Eyes came to the land of the Three Rivers as the corn was growing and the squash and the beans were putting out blossoms. They saw that it was a rich land, but they could not see that there was room for all. They wanted it only for themselves. The Three-Rivers People wanted only peace. They agreed to move their lodges away from the land of their fathers. But when the harvest time came, they returned to gather their crops. Without them, many would have died from hunger through the frozen days of winter. Only, the Redcoats came upon them."

"Yes?" Pandora said, when Laughs-In-The-Rain fell suddenly silent. "The Redcoats came, and then what happened?"

Laughs-In-The-Rain shook his head sadly. "The settlers were afraid. They said the Redskin savages would cut their throats while they slept. And so the soldiers took the weapons away from the People. But that was not enough.'' Strong fingers ran gently over the beaded wampum belt. ''I was told the story by the son of the missionary. Joyfully-Sings took the hands of her daughters, Mary Corn-Blossom-Unfolding and Judith Golden-Fawn. She began to sing the hymns of the Christian God. The others sang with her. The singing did not stop until the last of the Three-Rivers People was silenced.''

''Silenced?'' Pandora felt the blood drain from her face. ''But you cannot mean they were—no, it cannot be true. Rivenoak?''

The duke's lean features afforded her little comfort or reassurance. She knew the truth before he answered. ''The Three-Rivers People were shot with their own weapons to save ammunition. Men, women, and children. My mother, my two sisters, and Joshua Little-Wolf, my four-year-old brother—they all died that day, slaughtered by the Butcher of Bear Flat.''

''Good God in heaven.'' Pandora fought down the bile in her throat. ''Massingale?''

''Massingale killed them. Someone else gave the order— the man who brought the settlers into the land of the Three Rivers. He called himself Samuel Butler then. I suspect he, like my father, was the younger son of nobility come to the New World to make his fortune. He is in England now, a man of wealth and influence. Only his name is not Butler, and he has taken great pains to conceal the fact that he was ever in the New World.''

''Then you must know who he is,'' Pandora said, unconsciously gripping the folds of the dress in tight fists.

''I was seventeen when I learned of the death of my parents,'' replied his grace, studying the untouched brandy in his glass. ''Twenty-one at the death of my grandfather. Altogether, it was eight years before I could return to the land of my mother's people. I found Laughs-In-The-Rain, who told me all that had happened that day in the forest. Samuel Butler was long since gone. I traced him as far as Boston, but in eight years the trail had grown cold. Samuel Butler vanished off the face of the earth. Nevertheless, he is alive, here, in England, living under a different identity. Of that much I am certain, and one thing more: I will not rest until I have found him.''

"And your father?" queried Pandora, a chill coursing down her spine at the telling lack of emotion in Rivenoak's voice. "Did he never catch up to the villain?"

"Ridgeway was too late," Laughs-In-The-Rain said, laying the wampum belt carefully in the box. "The Redcoats had finished their killing, and there was no one to honor the dead. They left the bodies where they had fallen, to serve as a warning to others. Ridgeway and one other did what they could for the dead, and then he went after the Butcher. It was in the spring, when the snows had melted, that I returned from the land to the north. Only then did I learn what had happened. The Three-Rivers People were no more, and Ridgeway had been shot down from cover. He lived three days in the care of the missionary's son and the other man who would tell no one his name. They are all dead, and Laughs-In-The-Rain lives in the land of the White Eyes." Somberly he shook his head. "Old Man Hare has played his final trick on me. And now True-Son is the last of the Three-Rivers People. My nephew will find this man Butler and the sacred things of power. And then I can die in peace."

"Pray do not speak of dying, Uncle," said Pandora, going earnestly to the silver-haired tribesman. "You are far from the end of your life, and I promise I am very good at finding lost things. If you tell me what it is that you are looking for, you may be certain that I shall do all in my power to help Rivenoak in his search for it."

"You, Miss Featherstone, will do no such thing. And he is not your uncle," declared Rivenoak, who had not foreseen this new complication, but was telling himself that he should have done. Laughs-In-The-Rain was an irresistible force. The last thing Rivenoak wished was to have his uncle introduce the irrepressible confidential inquiry agent to a new and dangerous conundrum, which she could not possibly abandon until it had been brought to its logical conclusion. "It is a matter that need not concern you."

"Oh, but it does, now that Laughs-In-The-Rain has told me what it means to him," Pandora did not hesitate to inform the duke. "And he told me to call him 'Uncle,' did you not, sir?"

"Oh, I am sure of it," Rivenoak countered, awarding Laughs-In-The-Rain a quelling look. "That does not alter the fact, however, that you are in my employ, and, as such, you will restrict yourself to one assignment at a time. That is the stipulation you yourself laid out to me only yesterday afternoon, was it not?"

"I beg to differ, your grace," Pandora calmly retorted. "I said I could not engage in assignments that offer a conflict of interests. I daresay in this instance that is hardly the case. If I am not mistaken, the one is irrevocably bound up with the other. Uncle, you did say that when we found Butler, we should find the sacred things of power, did you not?"

Meeting the warning light in Rivenoak's eyes, Laughs-In-The-Rain eloquently shrugged. "I cannot speak falsely to Shines-With-Laughter, Nephew. And you should know better than to argue with a woman. They see with the eyes of the Earth Mother, which is to the heart of the matter and not always the way men see. Even if you win, you will lose."

In answer, Rivenoak flung up a hand in resignation. "So be it, Uncle. God knows I have never won an argument with *you.*" Lifting the glass, he drank.

"It is true, Shines-With-Laughter," said Laughs-In-The-Rain. "We believe the man Butler has the medicine pouch and the pipe—both handed down through many generations. They were entrusted to Ridgeway's keeping."

"And you think that whoever killed him must have stolen the sacred things off him. But why? Surely they were of no monetary value," said Pandora, who could not see the logic in such a theft.

"You do not understand," Laughs-In-The-Rain replied, shaking his head in disapproval. He touched his fingertips to his forehead in an eloquent gesture. "You are thinking with the head of a White Eyes. The sacred things are the way to the Sky-People. To steal them is to steal the spirits of the Three-Rivers People."

"Yes, but why should anyone wish to do that?" Pandora persisted. "The People were killed because of their land, not because of anything to do with their spiritual beliefs. I apologize, Uncle, but it just does not seem logical to suppose this Butler would have cared about a pouch and a pipe, even if they were sacred to those he murdered. Are you quite certain they were not buried with Ridgeway?"

"Perfectly certain, Miss Featherstone," answered Rivenoak, who had also questioned the rationale behind such an explanation for the disappearance of the sacred objects. "The missionary's son understood the People. He would not have allowed that to happen."

"Then, I daresay there is a more obvious explanation," Pandora speculated, cradling her chin on the knuckles of one hand. "Ridgeway may have hidden them somewhere for safekeeping. Who was the man who helped him? Perhaps he could tell us something about it."

Rivenoak smiled humorlessly. "Your guess is as good as mine, Miss Featherstone. As it happens, I was able to learn very little about the man, save that he was English. Whoever he was, he apparently went out of his way to help my father. He himself was wounded trying to defend my father when they were fired upon from ambush. He managed to scare the assailants away and then carried my father by travois to the home of the missionary. As mysteriously as he had come, he slipped away in the dark the night my father died and was never heard from or seen again."

"Curious," murmured Pandora, thrilling, in spite of herself, to the tale of the anonymous good Samaritan. "Obviously our man of secrecy had every reason to protect his identity. Perhaps he was an escaped indentured servant or an army deserter or an outlaw of some sort who yet possessed a kind heart. Whatever the case, we may safely assume he risked a great deal in helping Ridgeway. I daresay more than any of us realizes."

Chapter 7

"She is a lovely girl, Rivenoak," said Lady Congreve one morning just past the middle of March. She watched her nephew's profile as he stared out the withdrawing room window at the flow of carriages in the street below. "And she will be a success, never doubt it. However, you really must do something about this propensity of hers to steal out of the house at a moment's notice without so much as a by your leave."

Rivenoak let his hand drop from the lace curtain. "What has she done now, Aunt?" he asked, turning at last to the smartly dressed woman of three and forty who had arrived at his Town House on Grosvenor Square hardly before he had finished his breakfast. "Not another interview with Colonel Massingale's servants, I trust."

"Nothing so tame as that, I'm afraid." Lady Congreve smiled wryly. "This time she contrived to meet in Burlington Gardens with a Sergeant Merriweather of the Guards. We are fortunate that she at least condescended to take Simmons with her, though I fear your Miss Featherstone is in a fair way to corrupting one who has always enjoyed the very highest reputation as a ladies' maid. When I questioned Simmons, she came very near being evasive in her answers. I did manage, however, to pry enough from the woman to understand Miss Featherstone strolled with the sergeant for some twenty minutes. A sergeant, mind you. Really, my dearest Rivenoak, you must see that this will never do.''

''No, Aunt, it will not,'' Rivenoak agreed, though for reasons far different from Lady Congreve's. Miss Featherstone, in spite of all his efforts to curtail her dangerous investigations, was proving as adept at slipping past the guards he had set around her as she was at resisting his every attempt to provide for her greater comfort and that of her small family. She had refused categorically to allow him to move her and her charges into a roomier, more luxuriously furnished house in a more fashionable part of Town, saying it was quite enough that he was paying for the clothes on her back, not to mention a quarterly allowance greater than the yearly competence on which she had been used to provide for herself and the other members of her household. She could not go so far as to accept a house from him as well. It would smack far too much of being a kept woman, and that she would never be, thank you very much.

The infuriatingly stubborn little wretch! he thought, closing his hand into a hard fist at his side.

He could not have explained when it had become a matter of no little importance to him that he make her existence easier. At first he had told himself that it was simply a matter of appearances. It would, after all, be a deal easier to convince the world that Miss Featherstone was his chosen bride if her surroundings presented more the picture of genteel comfort than something that bordered on impoverished gentility. It was not long, however, before he was forced to admit, at least to himself, that he derived no little pleasure from lessening her obvious financial concerns and providing her with a few of the luxuries that she had had to forego since leaving her brother's protection.

Hellsfire, he thought. The truth was he would like nothing better than to provide for Miss Featherstone and her small brood of dependents in such a manner as to relieve her of all material worries. Somehow the irrepressible Miss Featherstone, not to mention the four young hopefuls of a man who was nothing less than a traitor to those who had succored and befriended him, had slipped past his guard and found her way into his heart. But then, the sins of Herodotus Featherstone could hardly be laid at the door of his sister and the children. They, at least, were innocent. And they had accepted Rivenoak into their lives without reservation. To them, he was a friend to be trusted with everything from affixing a square of court plaster to Odysseus's scraped knee to praising Galatea's first uncertain attempts at needlepoint. Even Aunt Cora had overcome her fluster at having the Duke of Rivenoak run tame in her house.

It had been a long time since he had been welcomed into a home in which he was treated with easy acceptance and even regarded as one necessary to the general well-being of all— all, that was, save for Miss Featherstone. Damn the woman! Despite the fact that she had, from the very beginning, professed an unshakable faith in the innate goodness of his character, not to mention an unqualified belief in his inability to commit cold-blooded murder, she yet took issue with everything he tried to do for her. She was stubbornly opposed to anything that might threaten her cursed independence. No doubt she would rather have starved than accept a farthing from him, he thought unreasonably. Pandora, after all, had been managing for no little time to keep food on the table without any help from anyone. That was hardly the cogent point, however, to his grace of Rivenoak, who was ruefully aware that in Miss Featherstone he had at last met a female, who far from coveting either his title or his fortune, would have preferred to have nothing to do with either one of them.

Still, he had managed to see to it that the house on South Audley Street now had a new roof, that the trim was freshly painted, and that, along with the addition of new drapes as well as plush velvet upholstery for the settee and chairs, a new carpet had been laid in the parlor. Furthermore, the dining room now boasted new paper wall hangings and the kitchen a more modern cookstove, while the staff now included a butler, two footmen, two upstairs maids, a new housekeeper (Mrs. Giddings had at last left in a huff, thanks to Aunt Cora's assumption of authority over the household), two scullery maids, and, to go along with the barouche and pair of high-steppers he had provided for Pandora's use, a coachman, groom, and stable lad. All of the latter, of course, had necessitated refurbishing and refitting the carriage house, which had been carried out with the customary despatch commanded by the Duke of Rivenoak.

In spite of these accomplishments, however, Rivenoak was keenly aware that there was yet a great deal more that he would have done had it not been that he could offer no plausible excuse for it. It would have been stretching the bounds of logic, after all, had he included the upstairs bedchambers and sitting rooms in his argument that Miss Featherstone, as his intended, must allow that it was well within his province to render the house more presentable to visitors who, in the very near future, would undoubtedly become numerous. Morning callers, after all, would hardly be expected to venture farther than the parlor or the dining room. Unless, of course, the reluctant Miss Featherstone were to be persuaded that she would be expected to give the occasional dinner party, in which case it was not unusual for the female guests to wish to freshen up after the meal while the gentlemen enjoyed cigars and a spot of brandy, he reasoned. A thin smile curved the handsome lips.

Yes, it would do, he thought. Phillip Westlake, his supremely accomplished private secretary, would be advised to make all the arrangements at once with the stipulation that everything must be finished within two weeks' time. In the meanwhile, it would not hurt to have Miss Featherstone and her brood removed from the premises in order to facilitate matters. It would, in fact, provide a means of killing two birds with one stone.

"It occurs to me, Aunt," he said, turning to Lady Congreve, "that Miss Featherstone would profit from a short stay in the country—merely until Lady Desborough's ball, which will mark the real beginning of the Season. It will remove our irrepressible confidential inquiry agent from any temptation to interview servants or army sergeants until we can introduce her to Society as my future duchess."

"But that is an excellent notion, Rivenoak," Lady Congreve applauded, considerably brightening. "As it happens, we are well along with our shopping, and the modistes have already completed an impressive number of gowns, with more to follow. I daresay it will not be at all disadvantageous to continue our fittings and fabric selections at Hargrove. I feel certain Madamoiselle Veronique would not mind taking up residence with us for a while, along with two or three of her seamstresses, were you to offer her a reasonable incentive; and Edward and the children would be simply delighted to have me home again until we are all ready to remove to the City."

"Excellent. Then, I daresay your esteemed family will not be overly discontent to have some additional company—say, four precocious youngsters, an eccentric aunt, and a governess to swell their ranks. We shall offer Miss Featherstone the excuse that her young charges would profit from a holiday in the country before she herself is caught up in the Season's whirl of social events."

"Yes," agreed Lady Congreve, smiling conspiratorially at the duke, "that should do nicely. If I have learned anything about Miss Featherstone, it is that she is wholly sensible to those things that would benefit her small brood. She really is a remarkable woman, Rivenoak. I find it difficult to believe she did not take on her coming out. I daresay the whole affair was poorly managed. Had she been under my wing, you may be sure she would have made a splendid match.''

"But she has made a splendid match, dearest Aunt,'' murmured Rivenoak with the arch of an arrogantly black eyebrow. "Or had you forgot? Surely, you do not intend to look higher than the Duke of Rivenoak?''

"No, of course I do not. But then, you have said it is all an elaborate charade we are playing. Or am I mistaken, your grace? You did tell me you had employed Miss Featherstone's services as a confidential inquiry agent in order to preserve you from any matchmaking ploys, did you not?''

"Your memory is as keen as ever,'' observed Rivenoak dispassionately. "That is precisely what I told you.''

"Yes, so I believed.'' Lady Congreve gave Rivenoak a long, assessing look. "I wonder, Duke, has it not occurred to you that you are placing yourself and Miss Featherstone in a wholly untenable position? It is not as if she were not well-connected. She is the Earl of Braxton's sister. His lordship is bound to be offended when he hears that Miss Featherstone has apparently consented to become the Duchess of Rivenoak without his ever having been consulted. It is customary, after all, to ask the male head of the family for permission to marry a daughter of an aristocratic house. And what he will think when the whole thing is called off in the end, I simply cannot imagine. It will undoubtedly occur to him that there is something havey-cavey about the entire affair.''

A cold gleam came to Rivenoak's eyes at mention of Miss Featherstone's nominal head of the family, which warned Lady Congreve she had wandered into dangerous waters. "You may be certain I am perfectly acquainted with all the conventions. Miss Featherstone, however, is a female of five and twenty. She is, furthermore, independent of her brother's fortune. You

will agree that in the circumstances, she is free to determine her own life.''

"*I* should never dispute it, your grace," replied Lady Congreve, spreading wide her hands in a gesture of inculpability. "I wonder, however, if Braxton will be so inclined. I have heard he is a veritable stickler for the proprieties.''

"Is he?" murmured Rivenoak, thinking that thus far his lordship had shown a remarkable lack of interest in his youngest sister, not to mention his younger brother's offspring, whom he had to all intents and purposes abandoned to a life of near penury. "Well, then, should he object, he has every right to take recourse to whatever means of redress available to him. You may be certain I shall not hesitate to accommodate him.''

Lady Congreve grew noticeably alarmed at such a suggestion, the possibility for which had already occurred to her no little time earlier. "For heaven's sake, Rivenoak," she exclaimed, her eyes widening in dismay, "you are talking about a duel.''

"I should never be so remiss, Aunt," murmured Rivenoak, clearly unmoved at such an eventuality. "Duels, after all, are hardly suitable topics of conversation for gently bred females.''

"Gammon!" declared Lady Congreve, who, of all her greatly diminished family, had been the only one to take a sympathetic interest in the young American who had arrived in England eighteen years before to take his place as a Ridgeway and, soon after, as the heir apparent to her father, the powerful Duke of Rivenoak. Already married to the Earl of Congreve, she had not hesitated to scout her father's wishes in the matter of the "savage," indeed, had gone out of her way to welcome the youth at Hargrove, the earl's country estate in Buckinghamshire. She had, consequently, come to know him perhaps better than anyone, with the exception of his altogether enchanting Uncle Laughs-In-The-Rain.

When Rivenoak had first come to her with his extraordinary proposal that she sponsor a young woman in Society who had the singular distinction not only of being a confidential inquiry agent, but of posing as Rivenoak's betrothed, she had suspected there was more to the relationship than met the eye. With subsequent exposure to Miss Featherstone and after viewing the two together for little more than a fortnight, she had known positively that the young beauty, at least, was head over ears in love with Rivenoak, whether the child knew it or not. More significantly, however, she was very nearly positive that Miss Featherstone had managed to put more than a small chink in the duke's formidable armor. Certainly, his interest, if not his heart, had been engaged by the remarkable Miss Featherstone. Indeed, Lady Congreve had come to entertain the fond hope that at last Rivenoak had met his match.

That hope, however, had suffered a sudden blight at sight of Rivenoak's steely aspect, not to mention his chilling dispassion at the prospect of finding himself facing the Earl of Braxton at twenty paces. One did not engage in duels with the brothers of a female for whom one entertained any marital ambitions. It was like to put a definite strain on any future relations.

"You cannot hand me such a taradiddle of nonsense, your grace," Lady Congreve declared, awarding her maddeningly aloof nephew a moue of disgust. "You know perfectly well I am no hothouse flower in danger of wilting at the mere mention of a topic judged unfit for my ears. You forget, I was reared with two elder brothers. Dearest Thomas, your father, was fond of saying I was the match of any boy at flinging rocks, climbing trees, and riding to hounds."

She was rewarded with an immediate leavening of Rivenoak's mood, as was evidenced by a distinct gleam of amusement in the look he bent upon her. "Talents which have doubtlessly stood you in good stead, my lady," he observed. "I daresay Congreve goes about in an absolute quake at the prospect of having a missile flung at his head."

"Pooh," Lady Congreve declared, laughing. "He is not in the least afraid of any such thing, and you are trying to change the subject. There is bad blood between you and Braxton, admit it. It is, after all, as plain as the nose on your face. I think you owe me an explanation, Rivenoak. If there is to be any bloodshed, I have the right to know about it.''

"I fear your imagination is running away with you, Lady Congreve," Rivenoak replied, the cold eyes beneath drooping eyelids unreadable. "Far from entertaining any thoughts of enmity toward the earl, I can in all truth say I have never met the man.''

Lady Congreve stared in exasperation at the faint expression of boredom, which had descended like a mask over the duke's handsome features. Really, she had preferred the surly young savage to the impenetrable, world-weary duke. Rivenoak, at his most maddeningly elusive, was enough to try the patience of a saint.

"Oh, very well. Do not confide in me. I am sure I should not expect you to, never mind that I have always held you in the warmest affection." Gathering up her reticule, Lady Congreve stood. "I shall just be on my way now. I have some morning calls to make before I meet Pandora. We shall have to do some last minute shopping if we are to leave for Hargrove day after tomorrow. Shall I tell her you will be joining us sometime during our stay?" she asked, giving Rivenoak a twinkling glance. "Edward complains we do not see enough of you.''

"Then, naturally I should not wish to disappoint Edward," said Rivenoak, accompanying Lady Congreve to the withdrawing room door. "I shall have the travel coach and the landau sent over to facilitate your journey. I myself shall join you later in the week. And, Aunt Caroline—" Taking her hand in his, he looked into her eyes. "I have never, since I have known you, taken your affection for granted. It means a great deal to me to know you and Edward have ever stood my friends.''

Lady Congreve smiled whimsically. Dear Rivenoak. How greatly it must have cost him to admit so much. "I know, my dear," she said fondly. "And I know how difficult it has been for you these many years. Papa was never the same after losing both his sons. I daresay he was consumed with guilt. He never forgave Thomas for giving up his career in the Guards to marry your mother. He never understood how a man could give up everything for love of a woman. And then it was too late. Both Selkirk and Thomas were dead."

"And he was left with an heir of mixed blood. The final bitter disappointment." Rivenoak's eyes chilled to a frosty hardness. "I do understand how it was with him, Caroline."

"Then, do try and forgive him," Lady Congreve pleaded. Impulsively she gave Rivenoak's hand a squeeze. "He was an old, embittered man, who, had he lived long enough, would have realized his mistakes. I know he would have been proud of you."

"Yes, well, we shall never know that now, shall we," Rivenoak said, releasing her fingers. "Nor does it signify. I gave up caring what he thought long before he died."

"Yes, and in believing in anyone, too," Lady Congreve declared, shaking her head at him. "You really must put all that behind you sometime, Rivenoak. You must learn to trust someone again, or one day you will end up just like him—a very hard, lonely old man. What a pity that would be." She drew a deep breath and then let it out again. "Well, now that that has been said, there is no need to see me out, your grace. I do know the way."

Turning, she left him to stare after her with a peculiarly fixed expression.

Trust? he thought with a cynical curl of his lip. He had learned long ago that only a fool allowed anyone to see behind the facade one chose to present to the world. *He* had taught him that—his dear, departed grandfather. Rivenoak doubted he could change that aspect of his character now, even if he wanted to have done.

Hardly had that thought crossed his mind than an image of

grey-blue eyes, which had the disturbing tendency one moment to laugh at him and the next to regard him with an earnest, probing intensity, rose up to haunt him, along with a sudden, overpowering desire to see the female who possessed them.

And why should he not? he asked himself, ironically aware that a tingle of anticipation had supplanted the dark mood that had momentarily threatened. He had promised the children, after all, that he would bring Stalker around to meet them. Still, he did not fool himself into believing that was anything other than an excuse to see Pandora. When he was with her, he was kept far too busy matching wits with the beautiful young confidential inquiry agent to dwell on questions of a troubling philosophical nature.

Strange, but he had the most peculiar feeling that Miss Featherstone had only to look at him to see past the Duke of Rivenoak's mask of proud impenetrability to the man behind it.

The next moment he strode briskly from the withdrawing room and called for his phaeton and groom.

"Pray do not be absurd, Simmons," Pandora admonished her recently acquired abigail, a tall, plainly dressed woman only a year or two older than Pandora. "We are going for a short visit to the British Museum, not the rookeries of Field's Lane. Lady Congreve cannot possibly object."

"Beggin' your pardon, Lady Pandora, but you do not know Lady Congreve," protested Simmons, who was yet smarting from her former patroness's interrogation over the Sergeant Merriweather affair. "She made it quite plain we were to remain at the house until her arrival."

"Never worry, Simmons," Pandora said, giving the abigail a reassuring pat on the arm. "We shall be home in plenty of time. And, besides, I explained all this to you earlier. I really could not ignore the note that arrived at breakfast, now could

I? Especially as it promises pertinent information concerning Colonel Massingale's recent, untimely demise.''

"If you say so, miss," reluctantly conceded the abigail, who, despite the eccentricities of her new mistress, could not resist Miss Featherstone's unaffected manner. Having been in the service of the quality for no little time, she could not but recognize one of those rarities, an unspoiled beauty with a discerning heart and a generosity of spirit, which, coupled with an originality of thought and a vitality for living in sharp contrast to the jaded tastes of the Society into which she would soon be entering, guaranteed Miss Featherstone would become a success practically overnight. Simmons had not needed Lady Congreve's admonitions to guard her new mistress well. Lady Pandora inspired a fierce loyalty in practically everyone who came into her sphere. Still, Simmons could not but wish Miss Featherstone had a little less exuberance for flinging herself into peril and a somewhat greater sense of self-preservation.

"But I do say so, Simmons," Pandora declared. "It is, after all, a significant piece of the conundrum. Who, after all, but the murderer or his accomplice could *have* pertinent information about the crime?"

"Very likely no one," Simmons replied, wondering that she had ever wished for a more adventurous life than serving as a ladies' maid. "Beggin' your pardon, Lady Pandora, that is exactly what has me worried."

"Nonsense. We shall be perfectly safe in the British Museum. No one would dare to try anything there. And just in case something should happen, I have left a note for Rivenoak with the children. It is to be sent to him if we have not returned by eleven."

"How very comforting, I'm sure, miss," commented Simmons with a noticeable lack of enthusiasm.

Pandora, however, was no longer attending. As the barouche, which Rivenoak, against her futile objections, had placed in her use, pulled away from the house on South Audley Street, she had glanced back to admire, as she had often done since she had awakened one morning to discover men at work on the exterior of the house, the new coat of white paint on the trim in sharp contrast to the brown brick. Her attention had been immediately caught by the sight of a curricle and a hackney simultaneously entering the flow of traffic behind her. She could not have explained why the incident should suddenly strike her as particular, save, perhaps, that ever observant, she had not failed to note the two strange vehicles had been situated within hailing distance of the house when she first awakened that morning and looked out upon the new gardener planting roses in her yard. That, and the fact that what she had learned from Sergeant Merriweather coupled with what she had deduced from the information Mrs. Caulkins and Jessop had given her, had served to put her on her guard.

It was no surprise to learn that the only two persons who might have had an intimate knowledge of the colonel's Town House were Lady Congreve, the deceased marquis's sister, and her first cousin, Percival Ridgeway, who, the son of the former duke's younger brother, was presently Rivenoak's heir presumptive. It was patently ridiculous to suppose Lady Congreve, a woman, had struggled with and then brutally killed the colonel and highly unlikely that Percival Ridgeway might have done it. There would, after all, seem little for Ridgeway to gain from such an act. Still, until she knew more, Pandora could not dismiss Rivenoak's kinsman out of hand. There was always the possibility, no matter how remote, that Ridgeway had been involved in the plot against the duke. Perhaps the two archplotters had had a falling out at the crucial moment. Or perhaps Ridgeway had deliberately eliminated Massingale for some reason known only to himself.

Whatever the case, she had not considered her visit with Mrs. Caulkins and Jessop all that productive. What Sergeant Merriweather had had to tell her, on the other hand, had given her a great deal to ponder. An old friend from her childhood, the sergeant had served under Colonel Massingale in the Americas and had little of good to report about his superior. Not only had Massingale used his position to amass a fortune in the fur and rum trade, very often at the expense of the various tribes of Native Americans in the territory under his command, but the sergeant had hinted the colonel was involved in land speculation west of the territories banned from development by the law of 1763, which had restricted colonization beyond the Atlantic seaboard. It seemed certain Massingale had received some sort of remuneration for facilitating the settlement of the fertile lands bordering Lake Erie. He had at the very least been persuaded to rid the area of potential hostiles, not to mention to look the other way when bands of settlers began to arrive. Unfortunately, the sergeant, having suffered a broken leg in an altercation with a tavern keeper, had been reassigned to New York for his recuperation and, consequently, knew nothing of the Three-Rivers Massacre. Indeed, he had nothing further to add, save only that Pandora's brother Herodotus had been posted to the colonel's command shortly before the sergeant's departure.

There it was, thought Pandora, the connection between herself and Colonel Massingale. It had not been by coincidence that the colonel had contrived to have Herodotus Featherstone's sister in the Town House, but what had Herodotus to do with the plot against the duke? Logical deduction had led her to the conclusion that, at the very least, Herodotus knew something about the colonel that was detrimental to his former commanding officer and, at the very worst, implicated Herodotus himself in the events that had gone forth in America. Most dreadful to contemplate was the possibility that Herodotus had had a part in the massacre of men, women, and children. Until she had proof positive, she *would* not contemplate it, she told herself sternly. What she could be certain of was that she now was firmly enmeshed in the dark plot that surrounded Massingale and the Duke of Rivenoak. Indeed, she doubted not the men following her were intent upon instructing her in what her further role was to be. She had been anticipating something of the sort since her meeting with the sergeant.

As the barouche proceeded north along South Audley Street, past Grosvenor Square and on to North Audley Street, Simmons must have been gratified to observe her mistress had apparently taken a new, unwonted interest in her appearance. Indeed, Pandora had such frequent recourse to the small hand mirror she carried in her reticule that Simmons must have begun to worry that Miss Featherstone found something amiss with the way her smart new tulle bonnet with the oval brim sat atop her curls.

As it happened, Pandora, preoccupied with observing by means of the mirror the progress of the hack and the curricle behind her, and Simmons, worrying that perhaps Miss Featherstone was dissatisfied with the abigail's attempts to turn out a fashionably dressed lady, failed to take note of the high perch phaeton, pulled by a magnificent double team of bays and made distinctive by the presence of what gave every appearance of being an exceedingly large wolf crouched on the seat between driver and groom, which met them little more than a block from the house. Nor were they the least aware at the moment they passed, like two ships in the night, that at sight of the passing barouche a thunderous expression descended over the handsome features of the gentleman driving the bays.

Biting off a curse, he swung his team about with consummate skill and fell in a block behind the curricle.

"Do not look now, Simmons, but someone is following us, I am sure of it," declared Pandora no little time later, as having disembarked from the carriage, they made their way up the steps and through the doors of the British Museum. "Indeed, am I not mistaken, there are at least two conveyances that have been with us since we left the house."

"Two? Good heavens, my lady, who? Where—?"

"I said don't look!" Pandora exclaimed under her breath. "They will know we are aware of them. I daresay we shall be safe enough in the museum. Here.'' Drawing the other woman across the foyer, Pandora ducked into the display of natural history. ''We shall wait here to be contacted by the person who sent the note. Pretend to be interested in Sir Hans Sloane's botanical drawings,'' Pandora judiciously advised. ''Actually, that should not be too difficult. They are really quite good.''

''Yes, miss,'' whispered Simmons, who at the moment could not have cared less about the life cycle of a flowering plant and had at no time in her life entertained the smallest interest in the morphology, let alone the taxonomy, of the Plant Kingdom. ''But—?''

''Shh! It would seem I was mistaken in thinking we should not be followed into the museum. There they are, just coming in,'' hissed Pandora, squeezing the abigail's arm. ''Pretend you do not see them.''

''But I don't see them, or at least I don't know which they might be,'' said the abigail, ducking her head in a valiant attempt to assume the posture of one absorbed in the glass case before her, and, indeed, in addition to the two men Pandora had sighted earlier, a trio of gentlemen had just entered, one of whom was apparently delivering the others a lecture on the history of Sir Hans Sloane's contributions both to science and the British Museum.

''The small man dressed in striped trousers, a bottle green cutaway coat, and a perfectly hideous canary yellow waistcoat is one of them,'' Pandora enlightened the abigail. ''The other is taller and hardly bears the aspect of one who would spend his morning browsing in a museum, although it is perhaps wrong of me to judge one of my fellow men by the roughness of his garb let alone the fact that he appears not to have bathed for several days, if not longer. If I am mistaken, I should no doubt apologize. Dear me, he appears to have been joined by two friends. Perhaps they are a fellowship dedicated to the advancement of botanical studies among the unwashed.''

''I don't think so, miss,'' Simmons interjected, her face

blanching at sight of the ruffians, who, giving every indication of having singled out the two women for their dubious attentions, had started to fan out in order to cut off any opportunity for retreat.

"I believe it is time, Simmons," Pandora calmly announced, "that we made a strategic move. I suggest we join the trio of gentlemen on their tour."

"I'm right behind you, Lady Pandora," declared Simmons, who, indeed, had to restrain herself from physically urging her mistress to a faster pace.

Pandora, pretending a lofty indifference to the pack of stalking wolves fanning out to cut off any hope of retreat, strode directly up to the middle-aged gentleman who was in the process of detailing the life and times of Sir Hans Sloane, a former physician who had so generously endowed his collection of fifty thousand volumes and three thousand five hundred sixty manuscripts to the British government for the cost of a mere twenty thousand pounds.

"And that, gentlemen, as you may be aware," the lecturer concluded, "has formed the nucleus of what is presently one of the finest museums in the country."

"But how utterly fascinating," declared Pandora, clapping her hands in appreciation of the gentleman's eloquence. "It would seem we have a great deal for which to thank Sir Hans Sloane. Is it true, for example, that the good doctor promoted the cause of inoculation by performing that office on members of the Royal family?"

"As a matter of fact, madam, it is," responded the gentleman, fairly bridling with pleasure at finding himself in the notice of an exceedingly attractive young woman dressed in the first stare of fashion. "For those very efforts, Sir Hans Sloane was the first physician to be awarded an hereditary title."

"Bravo for Sir Hans Sloane," Pandora applauded, unaware that her sparkling smile had the effect of dazzling the bemused gentleman, not to mention his two elderly companions, who gallantly removed their hats. "I should like to hear more about this remarkable man. Would you object if we joined you on your tour of the museum?"

It was made immediately evident that the gentlemen, all physicians from various towns about England come to the City for the founding ceremonies of the London College of Surgeons, would have been more than pleased to be joined by Miss Featherstone and her ladies' companion. Unfortunately, their tour of the museum had culminated with Sir Hans Sloane's display.

"I regret, Miss Featherstone, indeed, we all do," said Dr. Josiah Grey, "that we were just on the point of departing."

"Dear, that is unfortunate," replied Pandora, glancing past the physician's shoulder to ascertain that, while the little man in the canary yellow waistcoat was still in evidence, the three ruffians had apparently slunk away and were undoubtedly waiting somewhere outside to intercept her. "We were just on our way to the Archives of North American History."

Hooking her arm through the abigail's and turning toward the door, Pandora could only be gratified to have the small conclave of physicians move with her.

She did not have to look to know Canary Waistcoat had followed them. Nor was she in the least relieved to discover the three ruffians lurking about in the foyer. Somehow she did not think Canary Waistcoat or the henchmen would be inclined to simply allow her and Simmons to walk boldly out the door to the barouche. Very likely the unsuspecting physicians, who were hardly in any case to defend themselves, let alone two females, would only be hurt if she were to attempt any such thing.

If only she could contrive a diversion of some sort to draw attention away from herself, she thought, glancing surreptitiously about for a further means of escape. She only needed a moment or two, long enough to slip into the stairwell just a few steps away.

Who the devil were these men and what did they want from her? she wondered, even as it occurred to her that, so long as she was the cynosure of so much unwelcome attention, she could hardly expect the author of the missive that had brought her there to show himself. Unless, of course, one of these four unlikely-looking candidates had sent it, in which case the note had been nothing more than bait to lure her away from the duke's protection. Somehow she did not think the ruffians had authored it. She doubted that any of them could read, let alone write, a note. As for Canary Waistcoat, he offered a far more likely possibility. She had the distinct impression of at least a degree of subtlety in the man that was hardly evidenced by the others.

He was, in fact, making so bold as to approach her!

"I beg your pardon, ma'am, but you are Miss Featherstone, are you not?" he inquired, doffing his small-brimmed hat. "I was hoping I might have a word with you."

"Were you?" replied Pandora, inquisitively arching her eyebrows. "And why should that be, sir?"

At her direct query, not to mention her frankly assessing look, the stranger shifted from one foot to the other, clearly discomfited.

"Well, as to that, ma'am, I confess it is on a private matter." He leaned his head near Pandora with an air of confidentiality. "For your own welfare," he murmured sotto voce and rolled his eyes most peculiarly from side to side in what might have been seen as an attempt to convey some sort of silent message, but which might just as easily have been construed as a threat. Then, for the obvious benefit of the others, "I wonder, Miss Featherstone, if you wouldn't mind stepping outside with me for a moment."

"But I should mind a great deal, until I know what it is you wish from me," answered Pandora, wondering if it were possible he had no real connection to the ruffians at all. Perhaps he was the one who had sent her the note. But, if so, why had he been waiting outside her house? And who had sent the others? Really, it would seem to make little sense. "As it happens," she added judiciously, "I was in conversation with these gentlemen."

"Indeed, sir," spoke up Dr. Grey, observing the intruder with obvious disfavor through the magnifying lens of a quizzing glass, "I fear we must object to your manner."

"Here, here," applauded Dr. Witherspoon, a septuagenarian from Limpley Stoke.

"Why, 'tis obvious the young lady does not even know you," added Dr. Hoskins of Yorkshire, his frail form, hunched over a cane, expressive of outrage.

"Perhaps, my dear," appended Dr. Grey, dropping the quizzing glass and turning to Pandora, "you should permit us to escort you to your carriage."

"But, I say," Canary Waistcoat objected, nearly sputtering at this unexpected turn of events, "you must not interfere. Miss Featherstone has nothing to fear from me. Egad, there is not time to explain," he exclaimed, grabbing her arm. "You must come with me at once."

Pandora, who could not but object to being manhandled, reacted without thinking. Taking hold of his thumb on her arm, she bent it sharply back, with the result that Canary Waistcoat not only let go with a shriek of pain, but dropped, helpless in her grasp, to his knees.

Instantly, she regretted having given in to irresistible impulse. "Dear me, I am sorry," she said, releasing her hold and helping the man up. "It was purely a reflexive reaction. You really should not grab people, you know."

Out of the corner of her eye, she did not fail to note the three henchmen making toward her with obvious intent.

Afraid, in the circumstances, for the safety of her three valiant protectors, Pandora settled on the only avenue open to her.

Reaching into her reticule, she closed her hand around the grip of the small pocket pistol she had had the foresight to bring with her. She could not but be perfectly aware that a single shot hardly afforded ample protection against three men. A single shot in the air, however, might create just the sort of confusion she needed to make a dash for the carriage.

Rivenoak, upon sighting Miss Featherstone and her abigail obviously hot on a trail of inquiry into the conundrum surrounding himself and the late Colonel Massingale, suffered an immediate, dark premonition.

It had not needed his heightened extraordinary powers of perception as a shaman of the Three-Rivers People to apprehend almost at once that she was heading into danger. Trained in his early years in the forest to be ever alert to the presence of enemies, he had not failed to note the hackney coach or, more precisely, its driver and passengers almost directly behind her. The former, besides eschewing the accepted top hat and cutaway coat of a coachman, had had the look of a bruiser who made his living in the art of forceful persuasion; and, as for his two passengers, *they* had hardly borne the appearance of men accustomed to hiring hackneys to carry them about town.

Rivenoak was familiar with men of their ilk. They were a hardened lot, born and bred in the meanest streets of London. He did not doubt they would have killed over a tuppence. That they were clearly following Miss Featherstone boded ill for whatever enterprise the meddlesome confidential inquiry agent had taken upon herself.

Damn all headstrong, meddling females! He could only be grateful that chance had placed him in the way to save her from her own folly, he thought, when, upon arriving at Oxford Street, a dray loaded with crates of live chickens pulled out in front of him and, coming to an abrupt halt, blocked his way. A hard fist closed on Rivenoak's vitals amid the momentary chaos of rearing horses.

Calling to his groom, Fisk, to keep the barouche in sight,

Rivenoak masterfully pulled his team to a halt. Silently, he cursed the clumsy dray and its driver, who, misjudging the turn, had run the rear wheel up against the stone curb. Indeed, it needed only a glance to realize the pair of draft horses, considerably beyond their prime, were unequal to the task of pulling the load over the curb, while the driver, clearly an avid advocate of John Barleycorn, was too bright in the eye to maneuver the dray backwards.

Hell and the devil confound it! thought Rivenoak, grimly aware that Miss Featherstone and the villains trailing her were drawing farther away with each passing minute, soon to be lost in the steady rush of traffic. Damn the chit! He would wring Miss Featherstone's lovely neck for placing him in such a position—if, that was, the rogues who were after her for an undoubtedly felonious purpose did not do it for him, he reflected darkly.

"Fisk, take the reins," he uttered, leaping down from the phaeton. "You," he said to the reeling driver, "come down from there at once. I haven't time for drunken louts."

"Who be yer callin' a drunken lout?" demanded the driver, a hulking brute of a man, whose bearish countenance bore the distinct evidence of a history of pugilism. He bared gaping teeth in a grin of unmitigated delight at sight of the duke's elegantly clad figure. "Right-o, gov. I'll come down. I'll come down and knock yer bloomin' lamps out for yer, I will."

Fisk, observing his employer's loose-jointed stance, his weight slightly forward on the balls of his feet, silently shook his head in pity. The poor drunken bloke was about to discover why Gentleman Jackson himself had once begged off from meeting his grace of Rivenoak in the ring.

It was all over in a matter of seconds.

The brute, all but falling in his clumsy attempt to dismount from the wheel, caught himself and, straightening, let fly a roundhouse swing at the duke. Prepared, Rivenoak ducked

easily beneath the blow, then, in no mood to humor the rogue,
drove an iron-fisted right into the brute's unprotected midriff.

With a sickening gush of air, the fellow doubled over, clutching at his belly.

Rivenoak, ignoring the cheers and catcalls from the growing
number of bystanders, caught the considerably deflated pugilist
by the shoulders. "Easy, old fellow," he said, helping the man
to a seat on the curb. "No doubt I regret having to instruct
you in the finer points of fisticuffs. However, I am in something
of a hurry. A maiden in distress, as it were. You will be so
good as to rest here while I move your wagon from the curb."

Leaving the stunned pugilist to regain his breath, Rivenoak
climbed lightly to the seat of the dray and, taking up the ribbons,
soon had the loaded wagon put to rights.

Still, he was grimly aware that Miss Featherstone, not to
mention her intended destination, was very likely lost to him
as, once more mounted on the seat of the phaeton, he lifted
the bays into motion.

It soon proved, however, that lady luck was riding with him.
Neatly maneuvering his team through the traffic while keeping
an eye out for the barouche and the hackney, he caught sight
of his quarry turning off Oxford Street onto Tottenham Court
Road. He could only be grateful for the bottleneck at St. Giles
Circus, which must inevitably impede the forward progress of
the barouche and the pursuing hackney. Driving at a splitting
pace, Rivenoak wove through the press of vehicles, while Fisk,
clutching to the side rail, clenched his teeth in stoic silence.

"They be turning into Great Russell Street, your grace,"
pronounced the groom some moments later, as Rivenoak,
avoiding a near collision with an oncoming wagon, feather
edged the turn onto Tottenham Court Road. It was only as the
barouche, followed at a discreet distance by the hackney, came
to a halt before the British Museum that Rivenoak realized the
curricle, too, was a part of the small cavalcade.

What the devil, he thought. It did not take four grown men

to subdue two females, even if one of the women was a highly resourceful confidential inquiry agent. Unless, of course, Miss Featherstone was merely the bait to draw a larger, more dangerous quarry into the trap. There was one flaw in such an explanation for the events going forth, however. No one could possibly have known the Duke of Rivenoak would be on hand to witness Miss Featherstone's departure from the house or realized he would follow her.

Too late to stop Pandora from disembarking and entering the museum, Rivenoak passed the ribbons over to Fisk with the curt command to "walk 'em." He was only vaguely aware of the wolf-dog following close on his heels, as he strode purposefully across the street and up the steps to the door. Clearly, the villains were not lacking for boldness to pursue their quarry straight into the public confines of the museum, he reflected, coldly assessing the danger to Miss Featherstone. Their intent could not have been to cut her stick for her. It was far more likely they meant to abduct her. The question was why?

Obviously, someone had paid them to carry her off—perhaps because she had uncovered something in her investigation of Colonel Massingale's death that posed a threat to the killer, Rivenoak reasoned. Or perhaps it was because someone knew of her association with the man who had sworn a blood oath against those responsible for the massacre of his mother and the Three-Rivers People, not to mention the murders of his father and uncle.

It was all too possible that the Duke of Rivenoak was the reason Miss Featherstone was now in danger, and so long as she was allowed her damned independence, she would continue in peril of her life.

The devil, he thought, reaching for the door to the museum. It was time he took matters in hand.

* * *

"Now see what you have done," gasped Canary Waistcoat accusingly, holding his greatly mistreated thumb in his other hand. "I'm afraid, Miss Featherstone, you will be made to pay for this."

Miss Featherstone, however, was not attending. She was far too busy calculating the best place to send a bullet into the ceiling. The last thing she could wish, after all, was to injure some unsuspecting inhabitant of the floor above. No doubt the corner would do nicely, she reflected, preparing to draw the pistol from her reticule.

Hardly had that thought crossed her mind than it seemed that utter chaos broke loose in the form of a large, grey shape that glided past the physicians and fairly launched itself at two of the startled ruffians. The third, making a lunge for Pandora, was caught in a hard grip on the shoulder and spun around to receive a bone-cracking fist to the jaw.

"Simmons," commanded a masculine voice, "to the carriage."

A strong hand closed about Pandora's wrist.

With screams of terror, the ruffians broke and ran.

Simmons bolted through the museum door, and Canary Waistcoat ducked judiciously behind a great potted palm.

"Stalker, come." The hand about Pandora's wrist pulled her without ceremony into the stairwell and up the stairs. The grey shape glided after her to leave the physicians in sole possession of the foyer.

"Good Lord," uttered Dr. Grey on an explosive breath. Slowly lowering the walking stick, which he had been brandishing in the defensive posture of a fencing master, he glanced around at the bewildered faces of his fellow physicians. "Did my eyes deceive me, old chaps, or did we just narrowly escape being attacked by a wolf?"

Chapter 8

"Rivenoak," gasped Pandora, some few moments later, as they reached the head of the stairs, "what are you *doing* here?"

"More pertinently, Miss Featherstone," Rivenoak replied with scant humor as he pulled her into an unoccupied reading room filled with shelves lined with ancient books and manuscripts, "what the devil are *you* doing here? It was my understanding you were to be at home for Lady Congreve to call on you this morning."

Pandora, taking in the grim line of the duke's profile, felt her heart sink. He must know perfectly well what her purpose had been. His grace was obviously in a rare taking. "Not until later. I should have been back home in plenty of time. Unfortunately, I seem to have run into a little unexpected trouble." Sinking down on her heels, she fondly pulled the grinning dog to her. "Stalker, you big, beautiful wolf, you. I was never so pleased to see anyone in my life. You frightened them off, did you not—those dreadful bad men—an act for which I am ever so grateful."

"No doubt he was glad to oblige you," observed Rivenoak in tones heavily laced with irony. "You have not, however, answered my question."

"But I should have thought it was obvious, your grace," Pandora replied. Giving Stalker a final pat, she rose to her feet. "I came in search of answers to a conundrum."

"Naturally, why did I not think of that?" Rivenoak mused sardonically, drawing Pandora farther back in the stacks of books. "What conundrum, Miss Featherstone?"

"Why, your grace, there should be strange men watching my house, for one. And for another, why I should have received this as I sat down this morning to breakfast." Pulling a twist note from her reticule, she handed it to the duke.

" 'British Museum,' " read the duke aloud. " 'Nine o'clock, the Sir Hans Sloane display, if you wish to learn pertinent facts about the colonel.' Obviously a trap, Miss Featherstone," Rivenoak pronounced, crumpling the bit of paper in his fist. "I should not have expected *you* to fall for something so patent."

"On the contrary, your grace," Pandora did not hesitate to inform him, "it was not intended as a trap. If it were, you may be certain the perpetrator of the plot would hardly have chosen the British Museum for such a dangerous scenario. He would have picked an isolated place in which there would not have been witnesses about. No, whoever sent the note had some other purpose in mind. Unfortunately, I daresay all the commotion has most certainly frightened my would-be informant away."

Silently Rivenoak cursed. Damn the woman and her bloody passion for conundrums that must inevitably lead her into danger! The pressure in his chest, which had been occasioned by the grim realization of how near she had come to falling a victim to unscrupulous villains, was only gradually subsiding, leaving behind a hard knot in the pit of his belly.

"If there was an informant, you may be certain he will contact you again," Rivenoak said with bitter certainty. "In which case, you will inform me of it immediately. Is that understood, Miss Featherstone?''

Pandora, meeting the hard glitter of his eyes, could not but note his grace was in anything but a conciliatory frame of mind. Really, he was making a great deal out of something that in the end had proven a trifling affair. She had not the smallest doubt that her own solution to her earlier difficulties would have worked perfectly well had he not interfered. Obviously the villains who had tried to abduct her were neither particularly bright nor of an overly courageous disposition. But then, Rivenoak, she reminded herself, was a man of noble intentions. He must inevitably feel concern for the safety of a woman in his protection, even one who was perfectly capable of taking care of herself. ''But I did inform you, your grace,'' she replied in calm, rational tones. ''I left a message with the children to that effect, with the instructions it was to be given to you in the event you asked about me.''

''How very far-sighted of you,'' commented Rivenoak, who found little that was comforting in the thought that, had he not given into impulse to call on her that morning, he should have been left to learn of Miss Featherstone's abduction by dangerous villains when it was too late to have done anything to prevent it. ''No doubt I should have enjoyed a pleasant time contemplating your probable fate long after the fact.''

With ominous deliberation, he took a step toward her.

Pandora, who was perhaps belatedly gaining an appreciation of his particular point of view, backed before him. ''I wish you will not be absurd, your grace. I was perfectly prepared to deal with any unforeseen eventualities. Had Stalker not intervened, I should simply have frightened the ruffians off with my pocket pistol. I assure you I am a crack shot.''

''An excellent solution, no doubt. One, which would have had the added benefit of making you instantly famous throughout England. I can see it now: 'The Earl of Braxton's Sister Engages in Shoot-out in British Museum.' Such a charming *on dit* must undoubtedly make the rounds of every fashionable salon in London, not to mention the front page of every newspaper." With a single stride, he closed the intervening distance between them. "Naturally, you did not stop to consider the possibility that the villains might likewise be armed or that you had only a single shot against three, possibly four, assailants."

Pandora, coming up hard against a bookshelf at her back, decided, in the circumstances, to stand her ground. "I was not so remiss as that, your grace. You may be sure I had taken all the possibilities into consideration, which was why I had decided to fire in the air. The pocket pistol was clearly a last resort to create enough confusion for Simmons and me to escape."

"And trusting me was not even on your list of options," observed the duke with an odd sort of bitterness, even as he took rueful note that Miss Featherstone had never looked more beautiful than she did at that moment with her cheeks flushed from the lingering excitement of her recent adventure and her eyes great pools of uncertainty, which nevertheless seemed able to see right through him. Damn the woman and her uncanny power to make him forget who he was and the dangerous game he was playing! Propping a lean, strong hand on the shelf next to her head, he closed his other hand around the front of her lovely neck. "Did it never once occur to you, Miss Featherstone," he demanded, savoring the tremor that shot through her small frame at the caress of his thumb along the line of her jaw and over her lips, "that we have a vested interest in working together?"

Pandora, who was wholly unprepared for this unexpected turn of events, who, indeed, could not but think his grace had determined upon an exceedingly unfair method of weighting the argument to his advantage, failed utterly to stifle a gasp. "If you recall, your grace," she breathed, irresistibly closing her eyes against the instantaneous awakening of those unruly passions inevitably aroused between two persons possessed of a strong mutual instantaneous physical magnetism, "I did suggest that two heads are better than one in resolving a conundrum. As a confidential inquiry agent, however, I should have been exceedingly remiss not to pursue every avenue open to me.''

A faint, bemused smile played about Rivenoak's lips at sight of Miss Featherstone's instantaneous melting to his practiced manipulations. Egad! He had never met a female who responded so readily to his touch—or one, for that matter, with the power to so utterly inflame his own passionate nature, kept rigidly under control in the normal course of events. ''Which you have done with a single-minded determination behind my back,'' the duke said thickly, undoing the top button of her bodice, which, styled in the ''waistcoat bosom,'' conveniently fastened down the front. ''I said nothing when I learned you had returned to the colonel's Town House to interview the servants.''

Pandora's eyes flew open in instant, startled awareness. ''I should think not, your grace. Mrs. Caulkins asked me to come. She was very upset and wished some reassurance she and the others did not risk being slain in their beds. Besides, I told you,'' Pandora reminded him a trifle breathlessly, as he lowered his head to press his lips to the excruciatingly tender flesh below her earlobe, ''they knew of no one out of the ordinary who was familiar with the secret room.''

''You did,'' agreed his grace, his nimble fingers finding and undoing the second and third buttons of her bodice with a cool deliberation that both fascinated and robbed her of volition. He reached for the next. ''And though I had specifically asked you not to return to the Town House, I decided to dismiss the matter from any further consideration. I was even prepared to overlook the fact that only yesterday you flouted the proprieties to meet with a Sergeant Merriweather of the Guards.''

''The proprieties, your grace?'' echoed Pandora, who, though she might be inexperienced in the art of lovemaking, yet could not think it was quite the accepted thing for a gentleman to disrobe a lady in the British Museum. Strangely, the realization served only to intensify her physical reactions to Rivenoak's steady progress down the front of her bodice. She was, in fact, finding it increasingly difficult to keep her mind on the duke's thread of conversation. "Sergeant Merriweather," she said on a gasp as Rivenoak, having successfully bared her to the waist, cupped a hand beneath her breast, "is an old friend of the family's. His father has been the groom at Havenhurst since before I was born. I—"

"Heard he was returned from India and naturally wished to inquire about your brother Herodotus," Rivenoak finished for her. "You do not have to explain." Pandora groaned and arched her back as he caressed the hardening bud of her nipple with the pad of his thumb. Rivenoak grimaced, feeling his groin painfully taut against the confines of his breeches. Miss Featherstone had not the smallest notion of her power to incite him to madness. But then, she was generously endowed with the Earth Mother's magic. She had cast her spell over him the first time he made the error of gazing into her bewitching eyes, and now he saw but one course before him. "I could not care less at the moment about your Sergeant Merriweather," he uttered with a velvet-edged softness. "I do care, however, that you placed yourself in danger today. That, I fear, I cannot tolerate. Before we are through here, I shall have made certain, my impossibly headstrong confidential inquiry agent, that it will never happen again."

Pandora's eyes flew open in bestartlement as Rivenoak, clasping his hands beneath her posterior, without warning lifted her to him. Feeling her feet precipitously leave the floor, she instinctively flung her arms about his neck. "Your grace?" she gasped. "What is the meaning of this?"

The duke, carrying her to a table, presumably reserved for those interested in doing research, arched black, arrogant eyebrows. "You are the confidential inquiry agent trained in the science of logical deduction. I suggest it is not beyond your capabilities to resolve that particular conundrum yourself."

As he had set her on the edge of the table and was in the process of working the hem of her dress up over her legs, Pandora could hardly deny the truth of that statement. "Here, your grace?" she demanded, experiencing a wholly unladylike thrill at such a prospect. "Now? But what if someone were to come in? They would find us in a wholly compromising situation."

Briefly, Rivenoak lifted his head. "Stalker—guard," he commanded. Then, as the dog instantly sprang to its feet and padded away, to sink down on its haunches before the door, he returned to the far more important business of lightly planting a trail of kisses from Pandora's navel up to the delectable valley between her breasts. "No one will come in," Rivenoak assured her. "Not that it signifies one way or the other. It is my intention to compromise you beyond question."

Pandora, who was experiencing a resurgence of those primitive passions to which Rivenoak had briefly introduced her before, in the medicine lodge, failed to grasp fully the significance of his last remarks. Indeed, between the sublime distraction of his lips caressing the swelling bud of her nipple and his hand stealing its way up along the tender flesh of her inner thigh, she was having a deal of trouble thinking about anything at all—save for a sense that Rivenoak was a man moved by a strong purpose, and her overpowering desire to run her hands over his chest without the impediment posed by the fabrics of his coat, waistcoat, and shirt.

"Your grace, I cannot think . . . this is at all . . . fair," she protested on a sharp breath, as she became acutely aware that he was in the process of divesting her of her drawers.

"No, I daresay it is not," agreed Rivenoak, demonstrating no discernible inclination to leave off what he was doing. Egad, but she was beautiful, he thought, his groin leaping at sight of her breasts, perfectly rounded to fit the palms of his hands. She was all small and slender and yet womanly, and she responded so sweetly to him. She inflamed his senses like no other woman before her. More importantly, however, she had breached the walls he had built around him and awakened a part of him he had thought forever frozen. She was indeed a true descendant of the Earth Mother, a woman who wielded a powerful medicine. He wanted her as he had never wanted any other woman before her. Lowering his head, he ran his tongue over the peaking nub of her nipple beneath her thin, lacy chemise.

Pandora's breath whistled in her throat, even as her fingernails dug mindlessly into Rivenoak's shoulders. A faint, wondering smile touched Rivenoak's lips.

"On the other hand," he said huskily, mercilessly turning his attention to her other breast, the nipple already taut with arousal, "you have only to tell me to stop. I shall naturally heed your wishes."

Pandora, prey to a slow, swelling heat in her nether regions, which had the curious effect of filling her with a seemingly insatiable need to wrap her legs around the duke and pull him to her, could not but think that his was a deliberately obtuse observation. "But I have not the least desire for you to cease what you are doing," she breathlessly assured him, and even went so far as to lift herself in order to facilitate the removal of her underthings. "It merely occurs to me that thus far I have been the only one to benefit from our investigation into the conundrum of instantaneous magnetic impulse. Your grace," she uttered on a keening note, as she felt his fingers parting the fleshy petals between her thighs, "if we are to be granted a true understanding of the pure physical and emotional transcendence over reason, I should wish at least to *see* your crowning glory!"

Rivenoak, who had been marveling at the discovery that Miss Featherstone, already flowing with the sweet nectar of arousal, was fully prepared to receive him, was startled from his single-minded purpose by that unabashed avowal from her innocent lips.

"Naturally, I should never wish to deny the request of a

lady,'' he said, experiencing an unwonted pang of conscience at the further realization that she was as generous as she was passionate. Hell and the devil confound it! He had not the smallest doubt that she would give herself to him freely and fully; and then, when it was all over and there was no turning back again, she would refuse categorically to place any claim on him other than her determination to risk her life to resolve the conundrum that threatened him. She deserved better than what he had cold-bloodedly planned for her, and yet he was grimly aware that there was no turning back now. He would have her, and she would be made to suffer the consequences. He would make sure of it. ''I believe it is only fair to warn you, Miss Featherstone, that, should I go so far, I shall very likely be unable to contain the instantaneous incitement of my primal emotions.''

Had he thought to impress her with the dangers inherent in deliberately unleashing the powerful forces inherent between two people of strong mutual physical magnetism, it was soon made clear that he had failed abominably.

''But that is the point, is it not, your grace?'' queried Pandora with perfect equanimity. ''To experience the sublime transcendence of pure emotion over rational thought processes.'' Giving in to the purely instinctual impulse to return in some small measure, at least, the pleasurable sensations that he was so generously arousing in her, she reached to undo the buttons of his waistcoat. ''A conundrum that is only half-resolved is no answer at all, but only an enigma, which cries out for enlightenment.'' Having successfully loosened the confining fabric of his waistcoat, Pandora did not stop until she had tugged the shirt out of his waistband. Marveling at her own brazenness, she slipped her hands beneath the fabric. ''I wish to be enlightened, your grace,'' she said, gazing up into the rigid contours of his face as she explored the marvelous lean hardness of his torso and chest. ''More than anything, I should like you to be the one to instruct me.''

Rivenoak groaned, a shudder shaking his strong frame. Instruct her? Egad, she was a seductress who cast her spell without even knowing it! Clearly, a future with Miss Featherstone would be anything but the frozen detachment he had been led to expect from a female of refinement, he reflected ironically, and hastened to oblige her by reaching to undo the fastenings at the front of his breeches.

Pandora, whose sole instruction in the masculine physique was derived from statues and paintings, had yet considered herself reasonably well informed on the subject of anatomical correctness. She was wholly unprepared, however, for the sight of the Essential Male in full masculine arousal. Rivenoak's male member, released, was hardly the sort of thing one encountered in classical renditions—examples of Etruscan phallic symbols magnificently cast in bronze came to mind perhaps, she reflected, stunned by the stark beauty of the idealized male member rendered in flesh and blood.

"How magnificent you are," she breathed, and reached out to touch him with a wholly innocent lack of self-consciousness. "I never dreamed I should produce such a-a dramatic effect in a male of the species."

Rivenoak, who was keenly aware of it, indeed, who was very near to a dramatic climax as a result of it, clenched his teeth against the exquisite anguish of her caresses. The devil, he thought, wondering if indeed he had taken leave of his senses. Not only was he about to wantonly despoil an innocent, but he was going to do it on a tabletop in the British Museum! It was a conundrum he doubted he would ever fully resolve if he lived to be a hundred.

"How not?" he uttered thickly. Laying her down on the table, he lifted himself on top of her. "You are a woman to inflame a man's passions." Spreading wide her thighs, he inserted himself between them. "More than that, you are an innocent who is about to discover what it means to delve into the conundrum of primal emotions between a male and a female of powerful magnetic attraction.'' Deliberately, he inserted the tip of his swollen manhood into the lips of her body. ''This is going to hurt, Pandora. Trust me to carry us both through.''

''But I do trust you, Rivenoak,'' Pandora smiled to give him encouragement. She was about to add that she had every confidence in his ability to see them safely through anything, when, covering her mouth with his, he drove himself inexorably into her.

His mouth over hers stifled her cry of pain and surprise. Going perfectly still, he held her. How small she was, and tight, his marvelously sweet Pandora. He cursed himself for a merciless brute to have used her so, even as he gloried in the feel of her, snug about his shaft.

Feeling the sweat standing out on his forehead from his effort to control the overpowering need to finish what he had started, he lifted himself on his elbows to look down into her face. ''Pandora,'' he murmured huskily. ''My sweet, the worst is over. I promise enlightenment lies before us.''

Pandora, already considerably enlightened by the mere fact that she held him inside her, indeed, seemed somehow a perfect fit for his manly proportions, slowly unclenched her eyes, first one and then the other. ''There is more, your grace?'' she queried. ''What we have already accomplished looms to me as nothing short of a miracle—or a conundrum, at the very least. I confess, when I saw your crowning glory, I did not think I should be able to accommodate you.''

Rivenoak dropped his head in a laugh that threatened to break his tenuous control. Her spirit intact, she was unharmed in all but the loss of her maidenhead, and that she had given him freely. He would give her in return the resolution to at least one of her precious conundrums.

''You need not have worried.'' Carefully, he began to move inside her. ''You might have been designed especially to accommodate me. Together, little earth mother, we are a perfect fit.''

Pandora, who could not deny the truth of his assertion, who,

indeed, was experiencing a distinct resurgence of primal passion
at each slow, probing stroke of his shaft, was moved instead
to lift herself to him. "Oh, your *grace!*" she breathed, clasping
her arms around him.

"Yes . . . you do . . . begin . . . to see it," uttered Rivenoak
between panted breaths. He groaned, feeling her start to reach
for the thing that loomed just beyond her grasp. "How beautiful
. . . you are. So small. So generous. Tell me you want it, Pandora."

Pandora clung to him, her fingertips digging into his shoulders, as she felt herself carried on a magnificent, rising swell
of rapture. Want it? she thought feverishly. Good God, she was
like to die from it! "I want it," she hastened to assure him.
With her legs clamped about his back, she raised herself to
meet him. "Please, Rivenoak. I feel enlightenment is upon us."

"Egad," groaned Rivenoak for whom the moment of truth
loomed a far more urgent reality. Driven beyond mortal endur-
ance, he drew up and back.

Pandora, in the grip of impending enlightenment, cried out
in protest. Just when she knew the resolution to a conundrum
of truly magnificent proportions was within her reach, Rivenoak
had abandoned her. It really was too much.

Then, without warning, Rivenoak drove himself into her in
a single, savage thrust.

It was as if he had burst the floodgates of her resistance.
Even as she felt him spill his seed inside her, Pandora exploded
in a glorious blaze of magnificent revelation.

At last, trembling and weak, they collapsed together in a
tangled heap of arms and legs.

Pandora had never in her wildest fancies dreamed what it
would be like to lie gloriously sated in the arms of a man. How
strange, she thought languorously, that the unleashing of her
primal passions should have had the effect of magnifying her

every physical sensation while at the same time rendering her acutely sensitive to the undercurrents of emotion behind Rivenoak's practiced lovemaking. At their very first meeting she had perceived at once he was a man who held himself aloof from others—a lonely man, she had thought, who had been deeply hurt at sometime in his life. Then, she had suffered an almost irresistible impulse to breach the walls he had built around himself, perhaps to chase the chill from his marvelous eyes with the warmth of her laughter—only she had not known how. How different it had been in the throes of their magnificent, unbridled passion! She had felt his need, couched in some driving purpose that had made him ruthless and yet tender somehow in his manipulations. It had come to her then that Rivenoak, whether he knew it or not, had been a man at last reaching out to someone. That she was the one he had chosen filled her with a fierce tenderness. It would be enough, she told herself. Indeed, she would never ask anything else.

She felt him stir against her then. Hugging her newfound knowledge to her, she steeled herself to meet his gaze.

Rivenoak lifted himself on one elbow. He studied Pandora's face for a moment before dropping a kiss on her forehead. "You look beautiful, Miss Featherstone," he said. "How are you feeling?"

Pandora smiled languidly. "Considerably enlightened, your grace. And you?"

Rivenoak, no less enlightened than she, could not but be keenly aware that she had surrendered herself to him with a sweet abandon that was as selfless as it was boundless. He had thought never to meet such a woman as the remarkable Miss Featherstone, and now, because of him, she was in peril of her life. It was time she learned that he was prepared to do everything in his power to keep her from harm.

"Regretfully aware that it is time we were going." Easing

himself off her, he stood and helped her down from the table. Quickly he went about putting himself to rights again. ''We have a long journey before us.''

Pandora, who, somewhat reluctantly, had followed his suit, paused in tying the drawstring about her drawers to look at him. ''I beg your pardon, your grace? I was not aware that we were going anywhere. Indeed, I'm afraid any sort of trip is out of the question. The children—''

''Will be joining us at Hargrove, along with their governess and Miss Pemberton. Naturally, you will wish them in attendance at your wedding.''

Pandora stared aghast at the stern, handsome face. ''Pray do not be absurd, your grace,'' she declared. ''There is not going to be any wedding. You do not have to marry me because of-of—some silly convention. There is no need for it.''

''I'm afraid, Miss Featherstone, there is every need. I did warn you. I have compromised you, and now you must pay the consequences. You will marry me. You have no choice in the matter.''

Pandora blanched, recalling with sudden clarity his avowal that he meant to compromise her without question. Faith, he had done precisely that, and with a single-most purpose that posed a conundrum more baffling than any that she had ever encountered before. Certainly, he had not done it out of love for her. She was hardly the sort to engage his affections. Indeed, she would seem to have a singular gift for arousing his temper. Still, she could not discount what she had felt as he had carried her to the heights of passion. She could not be mistaken in thinking for that glorious span of time in which they had been melded as one he had allowed her past the barriers to his innermost self. On the other hand, she did not believe for a moment it was because he desired her as his wife. Then, why had he done it?

The most logical answer would seem to be that he had been motivated by his highly developed sense of honor. She had, after all, practically begged him to help her in resolving the conundrum of the instantaneous incitement of primal emotions between two persons of strong mutual magnetic attraction, and he had said he could never wish to deny the request of a lady. Faith, he had warned her of the consequences, and she, in her blind determination to resolve the irresolvable, had discounted them.

Clearly, it was all her fault that he now found himself in the position of having to offer for a female he could not want for his wife! But it was all a tempest in a teacup. She was dashed if she would docilely permit him to sacrifice himself out of some silly notion of honor. Indeed, it was not to be thought of.

Deliberately, she straightened to her full five feet, two inches in height.

"You mean you are offering me no choice in the matter," she said, a dangerous glitter in her eyes. "Well, I will not have it, your grace. We are long past the age of forced marriages. I thank you for the honor you would do me, but I regret I must refuse."

"Yes, of course you do," replied Rivenoak, hardly surprised. He had, after all, been watching the play of emotion across her face as she went through the steps of logical deduction. "You are, after all, an infuriatingly stubborn female who would rather accept ruination than give up what you conceive to be your independence. You are also a highly intelligent woman, however, who prides herself on her grasp of logic. I suggest, before you discount becoming my duchess, you consider the advantages."

"Very well," Pandora returned in reasonable tones. "The advantages are obvious, are they not. I should have position and a title, I should never have to worry about money, and, most importantly, I should be married to a man who is as kind as he is honorable. That does not change the fact that I cannot marry you. I should not wish a marriage of convenience on either one of us, your grace. And certainly not because of this. I asked you to help me in resolving a conundrum. You owe me nothing because you were kind enough to oblige me. Certainly, it would be illogical to expect you to marry me for it."

Oblige her! thought Rivenoak, who was only beginning to glimpse the difficulties before him. One must suppose from Miss Featherstone's train of logic that *she* had seduced *him!* "Very generous of you, to be sure, Miss Featherstone," he observed acerbically. "You may be certain, however, that I do not contemplate a marriage of convenience. You will be my wife in the full meaning of the word. I daresay between two people of strong mutual magnetic attraction, anything else would be to ask the impossible."

Had he expected to win her over with that cogent argument, he was soon to be proven far short of the mark.

Pandora, swept with a wave of tenderness at this further evidence of his generosity, gazed up at him in such a manner as to rob him of his breath. "Then, take me to be your mistress, your grace," she said, touching her palm to the side of his face. "It would be a far more logical arrangement for two people of rational thinking. You could continue to come to me in my house, just as you have the past few weeks, and still keep your freedom. We should have the best of both possible worlds."

Good God! thought Rivenoak, contemplating the prospect of openly undertaking a liaison with the Earl of Braxton's unwed sister in the presence of Herodotus Featherstone's four young hopefuls, not to mention Aunt Cora. Naturally, it must be supposed that he would relish such a proposition.

"An intriguing suggestion, Miss Featherstone," he said with only the barest hint of irony. "I wonder, however, if you have considered the complexities involved in such an affair, especially where there are children in the household. I cannot think either of your brothers would look favorably in such a circumstance upon allowing you to continue as guardian to the children.''

It was true. She had not considered that particular aspect of the problem, which was decidedly unlike her. Clearly, having indulged her primal emotions had affected her rational thought processes to the extent that she was not thinking at all coherently. ''Then, we shall just have to be exceedingly circumspect. I daresay if we are careful, Braxton and Herodotus need never find out.''

She knew, even as she said the words aloud, just how vain was such a hope. No matter how discreet they were, there was bound to be speculation. Sooner or later, the truth would come out, and, while she did not mind for herself, she could not wish the children to be made to suffer for her indiscretions.

''Very well, you are right,'' she declared before Rivenoak could point out the obvious flaw in her argument. ''A liaison is out of the question as long as the children need me. In which case, I'm afraid, your grace, that we cannot see one another again.''

That announcement from Pandora was met with a heavy sigh from Rivenoak.

''That, Pandora, is the one resolution I am not prepared to accept for this particular conundrum,'' he said, deliberately reaching out to finish buttoning her bodice for her, as if she were a child in need of adult supervision, she thought half-resentfully. ''Or had you forgot? I have engaged your services as a confidential inquiry agent.''

It was the trump card he had been saving for the coup de grace. Furthermore, it was obvious she *had* forgotten that pertinent fact, momentarily at least. Rivenoak smiled mirthlessly, wondering when it would have come to her that she was a confidential inquiry agent who prided herself on her integrity. Obviously, her stringent code of ethics would bind her to their earlier agreement.

''Well, Miss Featherstone?'' murmured Rivenoak, taking

little pride in having sprung the trap. No doubt he could salve his conscience with the knowledge that he had chosen the sole means at hand of preserving her from her own propensity to dash headlong into danger. As the Duchess of Rivenoak, she would be under his constant, personal protection.

No doubt Rivenoak would have been surprised had he been able to read Pandora's mind and, consequently, discovered she had been following a similar train of thought. Indeed, no sooner had she been recalled to a sense of what she, as a confidential inquiry agent, owed to Rivenoak, than she had immediately seen how impossible was her situation. Certainly, she would have been less than useless to Rivenoak in the role of his mistress. Forced to remain inconspicuous in order not to attract undue notice to herself, she could hardly have moved freely among the *Ton*. As his duchess, however, every door would be opened to her. Furthermore, he must be perfectly aware that she had not the wherewithal to reimburse the not inconsiderable sum of money he had already invested in her, even had she wished to be released from their earlier agreement, which she most decidedly did not, not so long as Rivenoak was in danger and not while she had yet to discover why she herself had been made a part of the strange chain of events that would seem to owe its origin to the massacre of the Three-Rivers People.

Marriages, she reflected philosophically, had been founded on worse premises than a mutual magnetic attraction between two people, coupled with an abiding interest in resolving a conundrum of murderous intrigue, not to mention the fact that she, at least, loved Rivenoak, as she had never thought to love anyone.

It was a truth that she had discovered in answer to the conundrum of why, following the events in the medicine lodge, she should have become prey to periods of extreme irrationality, exemplified by sudden fits of temper over inconsequential things, the frequent awakening to the circumstance that she had been sitting for heaven knew how long woolgathering about

eyes the chill blue of a mountain lake on a crisp day in January,
and a previously unheard-of loss of appetite, coupled with a
sudden compulsion to gorge herself on sweetmeats and marzi-
pan while indulging in spates of melancholia—*she,* who had
ever been known as a wholly sensible female without the least
inclination to delicate sensibilities, let alone a sweet tooth!

The explanation for these anomalies in her behavior came
to her in something of the nature of a sublime revelation occasioned by the arrival of the duke one afternoon when she was
least expecting it. She had spent the entire morning standing
on a stool while Madamoiselle Veronique and Lady Congreve
(who had turned out to be anything but the elderly aunt in need
of frequent naps that Pandora had expected) planned their battle
strategy. Faced with the prospect of an afternoon of shopping,
when she was chafing to be about the far more intriguing matter
of the colonel's untimely demise, she had not been prepared
for the sudden swift stab of unmitigated joy that had shot
through her at the appearance of the duke in the doorway to
the upstairs sitting room.

All her feelings of long-suffering, irritability, and barely
suppressed impatience were instantly banished as if they had
never been, and she was left with a glowing warmth that came
perilously close to rendering her giddy.

It had been a sobering realization, upon retrospection, that
she could undoubtedly attribute both her earlier malaise and
the instantaneous blaze of joy she had experienced to his grace's
influence over her. She had come, through logical deduction,
to the inescapable fact that either she had totally taken leave
of her senses or she had irrevocably lost her heart to the Duke
of Rivenoak. She had leaned immediately to the latter, since
she seemed perfectly able, in all other aspects of her life, to
comport herself in a rational manner.

The dramatic events in the British Museum, however, had
served, if nothing else, to clarify her feelings, leaving not the
smallest doubt that she loved Rivenoak wholly, so much so,

in fact, that she was seriously contemplating abandoning her scruples and marrying him.

"It would seem, your grace," said Pandora, lifting her eyes at last to Rivenoak, "that I am in a toil of my own making. I deeply regret that, by the very nature of my dilemma, you are embroiled in it, too. Indeed, I can only speculate that my normally unerring adherence to logic was affected by our powerful mutual magnetic attraction, not to mention my strong primal passions. I failed utterly to see this particular outcome to something that should have been above mundane convention."

Rivenoak, who had seen it, indeed, had deliberately manipulated it to his own ends, felt little of triumph at her show of capitulation. He should have known she would blame herself for what she supposed to be his sacrifice in marrying her. Undoubtedly she would feel obligated to him for it, and that was the last thing he had ever wanted from his beautiful, headstrong Pandora. Still, it could not be helped. She would marry him; he had seen to that. Once she was his duchess, there would be plenty of time in future to correct any misconceptions she might entertain concerning what had happened this afternoon in the British Museum.

"The world, I'm afraid, is not so enlightened as you or I," he answered, attempting to put her bonnet straight. "Nor am I as reluctant for this marriage as you would seem to believe. Given the chance, I daresay we shall rub along well enough."

"But I have not said I would marry you, your grace," Pandora instantly objected. "Only that I regretted having placed you in the position of feeling you must offer for me. The truth is, I cannot feel it is in the least necessary. Since there is no one to know what has happened, then I can hardly be considered truly compromised. Consequently, I see no reason why we cannot continue as we originally agreed: I shall be your pretend promised bride for the Season, and that is all there need be to it."

Rivenoak, apparently much struck at this new solution of

hers to a conundrum he had thought satisfactorily brought to a close, stared at her with a peculiarly fixed expression on his handsome countenance. Good God! he thought. He could not but wonder to what extremes he would have to go before Miss Featherstone could be brought to consider herself "truly compromised."

"You are mistaken, surely," he said, having summarily dismissed a fanciful image of making love to Pandora on a bench in Hyde Park at the fashionable hour of five. "Are you not discounting the irresistible impulses occasioned by the close proximity of two persons who entertain an overwhelming mutual magnetic attraction for one another? I'm afraid I could not promise to contain my primal emotions where you are concerned, Miss Featherstone, any more, I daresay, than can you. We shall undoubtedly find ourselves tempted to indulge our passionate natures on more than one occasion in the near future. Come, Pandora, admit it. We should do much better married."

Pandora, who was not prepared to admit any such thing, especially under the circumstances of a forced marriage, and in spite of her personal belief that he was perfectly in the right of it when he pointed out they should be hard put to resist temptation, parted her lips to observe that they would just have to agree that henceforth they would keep their relationship on a purely professional footing, when Stalker came suddenly to attention, his bushy tail waving gently and a low whine announcing the presence of a newcomer on the other side of the door.

Rivenoak closed strong fingers about Pandora's wrist. "Softly," he murmured, the side of an index finger to his lips in warning. Then, quietly, "Stalker. Come."

The wolf-dog padded to Rivenoak's side. Pandora went suddenly still as the door handle turned. Rivenoak stepped deliberately in front of her, and the door opened.

"Oh, I say," announced a pleasant, drawling masculine

voice, which seemed peculiarly suited to the well-knit, distinctly rakish gentleman in his middle to late forties who poked his head in. "Rivenoak, old chap, you *are* here. Fisk said you were. Said you might be in need of some assistance. Didn't believe it m'self, but what would you. Had to see for m'self." Keen hazel eyes strayed speculatively to Pandora, peeking around Rivenoak's shoulder. "Beg your pardon, old man. Didn't realize you weren't alone. Hope you'll pardon the intrusion."

"Not at all, Percy." Smiling faintly, Rivenoak turned to draw Pandora forward. "Miss Featherstone, allow me to introduce to you Percival Ridgeway, my cousin. As it happens, we were just finalizing our wedding arrangements. Lady Pandora has just agreed, you see, to become my wife."

Chapter 9

Ridgeway's handsome features registered surprise and something else—an exceedingly brief, but unmistakable, sharpening of his glance. The next moment he was smiling, something, Pandora judged, that he did rather easily.

"I say, old man," he declared, shooting his hand out to Rivenoak with alacrity. "My congratulations and all that sort of thing. Indeed, couldn't be happier for you both. When, may I ask, is the ceremony to take place?"

"I am in no mood to put the happy event off longer than it takes to obtain a special license," Rivenoak unhesitatingly professed, despite the sharp jab of a feminine elbow to his ribs. He released his cousin's hand. "I find that I am inordinately impatient to embrace marital bliss."

"Then, naturally you will require someone to stand up with you. Only name the time and the place, and I shall be there."

"I'm afraid, Mr. Ridgeway," interjected the intended bride, a glint of warning in her eye for her would-be bridegroom, "his grace is rushing his fences. A special license is out of the question." She bit her tongue to keep from blurting that, indeed, any sort of wedding was clearly impossible. Obviously Rivenoak's intent had been to enlist a witness to his cause. She, however, had no intention of allowing him to force her into a marriage for all the wrong reasons, especially since she was very much afraid her brother Herodotus may have played some part in the massacre of Bear Flat! Which was all the more reason she must not fling away her one chance to remain in Rivenoak's service, she told herself. If Herodotus was involved in the conundrum that surrounded Rivenoak, she must be allowed to find the truth out for herself, if only to make it up to the duke in some small way by helping him to find whatever it was he was looking for. Reminded that Ridgeway was a possible suspect in the colonel's untimely demise and recalling the fleeting look in his eyes at Rivenoak's announcement, she turned her full attention on the duke's cousin. "What woman, after all," she added, assaying a sweet (and hopelessly inane smile, she did not doubt), "does not wish a little time to show off the fact that she is betrothed before she becomes a bride?"

"Miss Featherstone has a point, Rivenoak," observed Ridgeway, seeming to tear his eyes off the young beauty, who had affixed him with an unnervingly direct gaze. Indeed, he had the deucedly odd suspicion that he had never undergone a more thorough scrutiny than the one he received at that moment from Miss Featherstone. "Never known a female who did not set great store by all the folderol surrounding betrothals and weddings and all that sort of thing. Featherstone, did you say? Not related to Braxton are you, Miss Featherstone?"

"The earl is my brother," replied Pandora. "Are you acquainted with him, Mr. Ridgeway?"

Egad, thought Percival, who could scarcely imagine a familial relationship between this vibrant young beauty and the overly starched Earl of Braxton. "Knew him at school. Eton, you know. Were in the same form together. The demmedest thing. Absolutely no sense of humor. Regular nose to the grind-

stone sort of chap. But what would you? Took honors. M'self,
I was sent down. As it happens, couldn't have been happier
about it. Deucedly unpleasant place, boarding school, what?
How is the old chap?''

"Precisely as you have described him," Pandora laughed,
finding that she could not but like Percival Ridgeway in spite
of the fact that he was obviously little better than a charming
ne'er-do-well and a rake. But was he a cold-blooded killer?
she wondered, sensing that there was a deal more to the duke's
cousin beneath the frivolous surface than met the eye. "Do
you come often to the British Museum, Mr. Ridgeway?" she
queried, hooking her arm in his as they departed the reading
room.

"Never set foot in the place before today," confessed that
worthy with the slightest of shudders. "Deucedly dreary, don't
you think?"

"Not at all," Pandora replied. "I find it a stimulating envi-
ronment abounding in information. One can discover the
answers to any number of intriguing questions here. If you feel
that way about museums, Mr. Ridgeway, why did you drop
in?"

"I believe it may be safe to assume, Miss Featherstone,"
offered Rivenoak in exceedingly dry tones, "that my cousin's
original intentions were financial in nature."

"Could not have hit closer to the truth, dearest cousin,"
agreed Ridgeway with charming affability. "Only stopped
because I recognized your bays out in front. Thought maybe
you'd see fit to advance me a pony. Naturally, when Fisk
mentioned there might be some trouble inside, I did not hesitate
to come to your assistance."

"For which I am no doubt grateful," drawled Rivenoak with
commendable sangfroid, and reached for his purse. Extracting
a handful of notes, he pressed them into his cousin's hand. "Is
there anything else I can do for you, Percy?"

"Nothing to signify." Ridgeway smoothly transferred the

sum to his inner coat pocket. "But since you mention it, there
is the trifling matter of my tailor. Seems he is hot under the
collar. Has taken to bivouacking on my doorstep these past
several days."

"No, has he?" queried Pandora with a wry gleam of amusement. Considering the exquisite cut of the ne'er-do-well's
morning coat of blue superfine, not to mention his flowing
neckcloth tied in the Mathematical, his immaculate waistcoat
of striped toilenette edged with pearl binding, and his tights
tucked into Hussar buskins, she did not doubt the "trifling"
matter concerned not an insignificant sum. Clearly, Ridgeway
was accustomed to living beyond his means. "How very odd
of him."

Ridgeway awarded her an approving look. "Precisely what
I thought. Wouldn't even have bothered to bring it up, save he
has become bloody demmed inconvenient. Blasted tradesman
is forever underfoot. Ain't as if he don't know I'm good for
it."

"Naturally we cannot have your peace cut up over trifles,"
observed Rivenoak without the smallest hint of irony. "Feel
free to send the accounting to my secretary."

"Ever so good of you, Duke," Ridgeway said, clapping a
hand to Rivenoak's shoulder. "Knew I could depend on you."

"Quite so," observed Rivenoak, who had more pressing
concerns on his mind than his cousin's habitual failure to remain
beforehand with the world. He, himself, after all, had deliberately compromised Miss Featherstone with the intention of
placing her permanently in his protection, and now that she
had, out of some stubborn twist in logic, maneuvered herself
out of his net, he was faced with the untenable prospect of
having to live with his error in judgment or discover a means
of overcoming her unreasonable aversion to becoming his duchess. The former was not to be thought of, and the latter promised
to be a deal more difficult than he had previously imagined. The
devil take all confidential inquiry agents, he thought, especially

those with the power to cut up his existence. "I am no doubt happy to oblige you, Percy," he said, suddenly impatient to be rid of his kinsman. "But, now, Cousin, I'm afraid I must ask you to excuse us. Miss Featherstone is expected at home."

"Certainly. A pleasure, ma'am," said Ridgeway, doffing his hat to Pandora. "I daresay we shall see a deal more of one another. You are, of course, planning to take in the Season's social events."

"As a matter of fact, Aunt Caroline will be taking Miss Featherstone about Town," replied Rivenoak, noting, as they left the museum, that there was no sign of the four men who had earlier accosted Pandora. Neither was the barouche in sight.

"Splendid." Taking her hand in his, Ridgeway gallantly saluted her knuckles. "I shall be sure to be the first in line to claim a place in your entourage of admirers."

"I shall look forward to it," smiled Pandora, and was hardly surprised that she meant it. Ridgeway, she doubted not, would prove a welcome presence amid the host of unfamiliar faces.

Some moments later, having relegated Fisk to the perch at the back of the phaeton, Rivenoak set the team in motion. In spite of the necessity of paying close attention to the press of traffic, he could not but be acutely aware of Pandora, sitting in contemplative silence, one hand affectionately patting Stalker stretched out between them, his head and forepaws across Pandora's lap. The duke was struck with an unwonted feeling of uncertainty, not to mention a distinct uneasiness of conscience at the possibility she was experiencing pangs of remorse for what had occurred that morning between them. Indeed, it was all too likely that she would eventually come to despise him once she had time for lengthy retrospection.

He found such a prospect left him with a peculiarly hollow sensation, which was as disquieting as it was unfamiliar. Indeed, it came to him that, far from wishing a return to the even tenor of his existence before he had had the mischance to discover and open the cursed wooden box among Miss Featherstone's possessions only to find himself embroiled in a conundrum far more disquieting than the one on which he had originally embarked, he could not envision a life without the meddlesome confidential inquiry agent. Clearly, it behooved him to discover why she held the notion of marriage to him in adversion if he were to have any hope of overcoming it.

Rivenoak glanced speculatively at Pandora's lovely profile. The small pucker of concentration between her delicately wrought eyebrows was an ominous sign that she was engaged in the process of logical deduction. Hell and the devil confound it! He would have given a deal more than a penny for her thoughts at that moment.

Doubtless he would have been gratified to learn that, far from holding him to blame for what had transpired in the museum reading room that morning, Pandora had arrived, through the application of reason, at the conclusion that she owed Rivenoak far more than she could ever repay for the experience of gaining enlightenment in that most splendid of all conundrums—the power of a man and a woman to raze the barriers imposed by logic and rationale in order to achieve a sublime communication of kindred spirits. Were it not for her dread that Herodotus might have been a part of the dark secret that cloaked Rivenoak's past, she would have been sorely tempted to grasp at the happiness she had momentarily glimpsed in the duke's arms. With him, she had felt what it was to be a woman, and that was something rare and priceless, especially for a female who had thought never to know what it was to love a man for whom she had felt an instantaneous magnetic attraction.

He was everything she had ever dreamed of in a man and much, much more; and, had things been different, had she not to worry that Rivenoak's wrath of vengeance would fall on her brother Herodotus and his four young offspring, she would

have embraced his offer with all the boundless love she held
in her heart for him.

That, however, was not to be, she sternly told herself. The
most for which she could hope was to stand between the man
to whom she had irrevocably given her heart and the brother
and children who were an inextricable part of her.

It was hardly a felicitous prospect Pandora envisioned before
her. Indeed, she did not doubt that she would be sorely tried
to keep her true feelings hidden from Rivenoak. Furthermore,
she had not the smallest hope she would be equal to the task
of preventing her unruly primitive passions from overriding
her better judgment. And why should she? she thought rebel-
liously. As a female of independent thinking, she saw not
the slightest reason why she should not be allowed that one
concession to her happiness. After all, what was the worst that
could happen? There might be a child come from their joining,
and that could hardly be a bad thing. Indeed, how could it? A
child would be a living extension of herself and Rivenoak.

Having come to that wholly logical conclusion, she nearly
jumped as she became aware that Rivenoak was addressing
her.

"I-I beg your pardon," she stammered, a blush staining her
cheeks at her lapse of attention, not to mention the nature of
her ruminations. "I'm afraid I was not attending."

"That much was obvious," observed Rivenoak, neatly
feather edging the turn off Oxford into North Audley Street.
"You have not spoken since we left the museum. Would I be
presuming too much to ask if, in your preoccupation, you were
led to reconsider my offer?"

"I'm afraid the answer is no, your grace, I have not. Nor
am I likely to do," Pandora answered, forcing herself to meet
his gaze. "It would hardly be fair of me to give you any false
hopes. I shall not be brought to change my mind, Rivenoak.
There are—reasons why I cannot marry you."

"You are a confidential inquiry agent dedicated to the scientific application of logic," Rivenoak observed matter-of-factly. "I naturally assumed you had *reasons,* Miss Featherstone. I do not suppose, however, that you intend to share them with me."

"No, your grace, I do not, save only for what I have already stated—that I cannot marry anyone simply to satisfy a point of honor. I cannot believe that would be a solid foundation for a lifetime commitment. Besides, it is my firm conviction that two people who share the sort of feelings we have shared should be above mere convention."

"Sublime enlightenment transcends the purely mundane, is that it, Miss Featherstone?" queried Rivenoak, who was more inclined to the tenet that enlightenment resided in accepting the reality of a conventional world, at least in England, which prided itself on being a civilized nation.

"That is it precisely, your grace," applauded Pandora, who could not but be relieved he had so easily grasped the obvious.

"You relieve my mind, Miss Featherstone," Rivenoak said, shooting her a penetrating glance. "I had thought perhaps you were coming to regret our investigations into the conundrum of instantaneous physical magnetism."

"Now you are being absurd, your grace. How could I regret our attempts to resolve a conundrum of such magnificent proportions? On the contrary, it was everything I should have hoped for, and more. If anything, I am exceedingly grateful to you for your guidance in an area of investigation that should otherwise have remained a mystery to me."

Rivenoak, treated to the full intensity of her gaze, not to mention the becoming tinge of color to her cheeks, could only be heartened to extrapolate from that effusive admission that she had taken as much pleasure from their lovemaking as had he. "It would seem, at least," he ventured carefully, "it is not the physical and emotional aspects of our shared passion that have determined you against marrying me. In which case, may I assume you do not find me personally objectionable?"

Pandora's head came up, her eyes earnestly seeking his. "Oh, no, your grace," she blurted, then, seeing him accept that pronouncement in startled silence, "I mean, yes, your grace. You may make such an assumption. I could never find you personally objectionable. How could I, when I consider you to be the kindest, most generous man I have ever met, not to mention the most devastatingly attractive? Indeed, I should vastly prefer it if you did not wield so powerful an influence over my mental and physical states."

"No doubt I should be happy to oblige you," offered Rivenoak with an air of humility, "were I not myself in a similar circumstance where you are concerned, Miss Featherstone. Still, I cannot but be gratified to learn of your dilemma," he added, glad to have cleared what he had privately believed to be his greatest hurdle. "Especially, as I had hoped you would wish me to continue as your mentor."

"But of course I wish it, your grace," declared Pandora, wondering that he could ever have entertained any doubts in the matter. "I should be pleased to pursue with you the conundrum of instantaneous mutual magnetic attraction for as long as you are of a similar inclination."

"You may be assured I am of just such an inclination," Rivenoak assured her. He was, in fact, ruefully aware that he would have liked nothing better than to repeat the rudimentary steps of their investigations no later than three days hence in the more congenial surrounds of the master suite of bedrooms in his house on Grosvenor Square. Unfortunately, Miss Featherstone had proven unreasonably obdurate in her refusal to make that a practical consideration. "Indeed, I cannot recall having felt a stronger inclination for anything of recent date. A circumstance which can no doubt be attributed to my naturally inquisitive nature."

"I have sensed that in you. It is a facet of character that we share," Pandora returned, wishing she might divulge her latest findings to him. He was possessed, after all, of a powerful

intellect coupled with what she had felt from the very beginning
to be an instinctive understanding of things beyond the awareness of most men, a peculiarity that might have developed due
to his early training as a shaman. Indeed, she did not doubt
that, together, they might have made short work of the conundrum before them.

As it was, however, she dared not, for the sake of Herodotus
and the children, reveal all that Sergeant Merriweather had
confided. His belief, for example, that Herodotus had incurred
the enmity of an exceedingly powerful man, a man who had
not hesitated to wield his considerable influence to the detriment
of her brother's career in the army.

As much as she would like to have done, Pandora could not
dismiss the facts before her. Her brother Herodotus had served
under Colonel Massingale in the Americas. Massingale had
been instrumental in the murder of Rivenoak's mother and her
people, and Rivenoak was one of the most powerful men in
England. Clearly the most obvious conclusion to be deduced
from those three facts was that Rivenoak not only was aware
that Herodotus had played a part in the massacre at Bear Flat,
but that the duke was the powerful enemy whom Herodotus
had to fear. In which case, Rivenoak's initial purpose in seeking
her out could only have been to further his pursuit of vengeance
against those whom he held responsible for the deaths of the
Three-Rivers People.

Anyone else would have logically deduced that Rivenoak's
insistence on marriage was a part of that ulterior purpose—to
place his enemy's sister under his sole power in order to use
her against that enemy.

Pandora, however, had never been one to accept the obvious
without first eliminating all the other possibilities. Indeed, she
could not dismiss out of hand her powerful woman's instinct,
which vehemently denied the apparent facts. Herodotus simply
could not have sunk so low as to murder innocent men, women,
and children. It was not in his nature. Nor could she accept

that Rivenoak, whatever his original motives, would marry her
solely to use her to his own ends. It would have been contrary
to his character, which was as noble as it was generous, and
counter to his intellectual grasp of the obvious, which must
have made clear to him that marriage to a woman he detested
would have been far more punitive to him than to Herodotus.
And then there were the children to consider. She did not
believe for a moment Rivenoak could have so completely won
their affections if he were not the man he gave every evidence
of being.

No, the facts simply did not add up, she reflected, as the
phaeton drew up before her house on South Audley Street.
Rivenoak must surely be unaware of Herodotus's possible
involvement, which would mean someone else with considerable influence was responsible for her brother's failure to
receive the recognition he had earned. Furthermore, she did
not doubt that the Man of Influence was the one who was
behind the pall of mystery surrounding Rivenoak. When she
found *him,* she would discover Colonel Massingale's murderer.

"Of course it is in the *Gazette,*" Pandora declared two weeks
later above the confusion generated by Odysseus and Ganymede, who, its being Laura Wortham's afternoon off, were
involved in a rough and tumble on the floor of the parlor, and
by the influx of painters and wallpaper hangers, who were
presently occupied with renovating the entire second and third
stories. "That does not mean I have changed my mind about
marrying him. I did agree to pose as Rivenoak's future bride.
It was all a part of the original plan."

"Yes, but to announce it in the *Gazette,* Pandora," replied
Aunt Cora, for once oblivious to the chaos going on around
her. "Surely that is carrying things a trifle too far. Braxton is
sure to read it. If you had no intention of going through with

an actual wedding, might it not have been wiser to be more circumspect?"

"I feel sure his grace knows what he is doing," Pandora glibly lied and reached down to disengage one of Clytemnestra's kittens from its determined ascent of her skirts. "Odysseus," she said, perhaps rather more sharply than she had intended, "the kittens have escaped the kitchens again. Please gather them up and return them to Clytemnestra at once."

"But we were playing with them, Auntie Pan," objected Odysseus, glancing up from the headlock in which he triumphantly held his older brother powerless.

All in an instant the tables turned. Ganymede, sensing the younger boy's attention was momentarily distracted, broke loose and flipped Odysseus to the floor, one arm pinned behind his back.

"Gotcha, little dandyprat," he chortled in triumph. "I shall teach you to sneak up on me from behind."

"The devil, Auntie Pan," wailed Odysseus. "Now see what you have done. And just when I had him."

"Odysseus, I shall thank you not to use such language," Pandora declared, reaching in pursuit of a second feline, who darted under the cherry-wood sofa table. "Ganymede, be so kind as to release your brother at once and help him catch the kittens. You may take them up to the schoolroom to play if you promise to return them to the kitchens when you are through."

"I shall as soon as the gnome cries uncle," asserted Ganymede, demonstrating no discernible inclination to release his brother. "Odysseus stole my sack of marbles, and I shall have them back before I am through with him."

Red-faced, Odysseus broke into a furious struggle, nearly unseating Ganymede in his effort to dislodge the older boy. "Never did . . . any such thing. My bloody marbles. Won 'em fair and square."

"Boys!" exclaimed Aunt Cora as the escalating scuffle

threatened to set the gimcracks to rattling. "Here, here, now. You will turn the place into a shambles!"

The youngest Featherstone, noted for having the agility of an eel and the ferocity, when his temper was aroused, of a cornered badger, twisted out of Ganymede's grasp and was poised, ready to spring at his brother, when a powerful hand descended seemingly out of nowhere and, catching Odysseus by the waistband of his trousers, lifted him, kicking and blustering, off his feet.

"Now, what have we here?" drawled a thrillingly familiar voice, one which had the peculiar effect of making Odysseus go instantly rigid in his precarious position, dangling, facedown, a good two feet off the ground, of freezing Ganymede where he lay, asprawl on the floor, and of causing Pandora, caught ignominiously on all fours, her posterior up and her head and shoulders down as she peered after the delinquent kitten, to bring the back of her skull up with a solid thump against the underside of the table.

"The devil!" burst unbidden from her lips.

"Quite so, my dear," came in immediate reply, couched in tones of sardonic masculine sympathy. "How fortunate that I have arrived in time to witness you in the midst of domestic bliss. No doubt I now understand why I could not persuade you to go away with Lady Caroline to Hargrove. I see you are being vastly entertained by these two young thatchgallows, not to mention Clytemnestra's unruly progeny, so much so that I doubt you will be the least tempted to join me for a drive."

"In the circumstances, your grace," said Pandora, who, still clutching a kitten by the scruff of its neck, had managed not only to extricate herself from her wholly unfeminine position on all fours, but had risen with admirable aplomb to her feet to meet Rivenoak's gaze full on, "I should like nothing better than to go for a drive. But then, you knew that the instant you walked into this room. Unfortunately, it is Miss Wortham's afternoon off, and, the way the boys are behaving, I should not dream of leaving them alone with Aunt Cora.''

"You could always take us with you," suggested Odysseus, seemingly perfectly content to be dangling from the duke's powerful grip.

Pandora favored the young rapscallion with a grimace at such a prospect. ''I should rather ask his grace to invite Clytemnestra's litter of kittens along for the ride. Besides, you hardly deserve a reward for your deplorable language.''

"Then take *me*," spoke up Ganymede, having climbed to his feet. "I at least cannot be faulted for using speech of which no gentleman could approve."

"Toad eater," declared Odysseus, lifting his head to eye his brother in no little disgust. ''You're as much at fault as I am. Ain't he, your grace?''

"Isn't he, Odysseus,'' Pandora corrected.

"Of course he is, Auntie Pan. I just said so, didn't I?''

"I give up.'' Pandora flung up her hands. ''You are obviously fated for a career as a barrister.''

"Am not. I'm going to be a soldier, like Papa.''

"If you continue on your present course, you are far more likely to end up a candidate for the penal colonies,'' Rivenoak observed dryly. All in a single, swift motion he swung Odysseus high into the air and, flipping him in a half-hitch around, caught him between his hands beneath the boy's arms. ''You, my lad,'' he said, holding Odysseus on a level, eye-to-eye, with himself, ''are about to be put in the care of a man who knows all there is to know about the instruction of unruly boys. Before he is through with you, you will have learned the wisdom of doing your best to live in harmony with others, and most especially with your Auntie Pan.'' Setting Odysseus on his feet, Rivenoak dropped a firm hand on the boy's shoulder. ''Make your bow to my Uncle Laughs-In-The-Rain. He is going to be in charge of your lessons this afternoon.''

"Lessons!" groaned both boys in unison, even as they eyed

with interest the tall, silver-haired warrior, who, attired in a bottle green cutaway coat trimmed with braid, leather breeches, and knee-high boots of soft doeskin, stood a pace or two behind Aunt Cora.

"Is not every day a lesson in the journey of life?" queried Laughs-In-The-Rain with an eloquent shrug. "A man who does not learn the teachings that this world has to offer is a man who goes blind into the next world."

There were light footsteps in the foyer, followed by the entrance of Iphigenia and Galatea, who had been outside helping the new gardener tend the roses.

"Look," exclaimed Iphigenia, "it is his grace, and he has brought someone with him."

"You are Laughs-In-The-Rain," Galatea pronounced without preamble as she strode directly to the newcomer. "His grace has told us all about you. I am Galatea, and I am pleased to meet you, sir." Smiling shyly, she dipped a curtsey.

"Chance True-Son has told me about you, also," said Laughs-In-The-Rain with a dignified gravity to match the child's. "You are She-Who-Is-The-Peacemaker, and this must be She-Who-Mends-Nankeens."

"I am He-Who-Rolls-In-The-Mud," declared Odysseus with an air of importance, as he marched up to the duke's uncle. "How do you do, sir?"

"I am He-Who-Boldly-Sings-Praises." Having made this announcement, Ganymede bent in a bow. "Do you know any stories to tell us?"

"Please, sir, will you not come in and have a seat," said Iphigenia, awarding Ganymede a frown of disapproval. "Perhaps you would care for tea and biscuits."

"I am an old man who has known what it is to have an empty belly," replied Laughs-In-The-Rain, allowing Galatea to take his hand trustingly in her own. "Such a man learns never to turn away the offering of a meal. In the old days if there was food to be had, all had a share in it. It was the way of the People that, if one cooking pot was empty, then so, too, were all empty."

"Our cooking pot has cabbage in it today," Odysseus declared, wrinkling his nose in disgust. "You may have all of my share that you want. I should rather have licorice and sweetmeats."

"Yes, and a bellyache, too," Pandora pointed out with a comical grimace. "Before you have anything, however, you will return the kittens to their mama. At once, if you please," she added for good measure, as she extended a wriggly bundle of fur to the boy. Then, turning her attention to Laughs-In-The-Rain, she smiled and held out her hand. "Uncle, how good it is to see you again. I believe you have yet to meet Miss Pemberton. Aunt Cora, this is Mr. Laughs-In-The-Rain."

"A lodge which has a capable woman to tend it is a lodge blessed by the Earth Mother," solemnly pronounced Laughs-In-The-Rain.

"Yes, well," uttered Aunt Cora, seemingly a trifle uncertain at the picture the warrior presented of masculine dignity. "A pleasure, I am sure. And, now, if you will excuse me, I shall just ring for the tea tray."

"And I shall just go and fetch my bonnet and pelisse," Pandora added, eager, now that the children appeared to be in capable hands, to have Rivenoak to herself in order to read him a curtain lecture on the subject of sending in wedding announcements to the *Gazette,* when she really preferred he had not. "I shall be back in a moment. Children, I depend on all of you to make sure our guest is made to feel welcome."

"Can the otter be made to feel unwelcome in friendly waters?" queried the warrior, taking a seat on the sofa next to Galatea.

"What is an otter?" demanded Odysseus, sitting cross-legged on the floor at the feet of their guest.

"An otter, stoopid," replied Ganymede, following Odysseus's suit, "is a furry creature who lives in a hole along the bank of a stream and eats fish. He is generally thought to be a rollicking good fellow, though Papa said they can be the very devil when cornered.''

"Like trolls, who live in caves under bridges?'' asked Odysseus, his eyes alight with the spirit of adventure. "If one came after me, I should wrestle it to the ground and make it tell me where its treasure was hidden.''

"Silly, otters haven't any hidden treasures,'' Iphigenia scoffed. "They are only animals.''

"Then, you do not know Grandfather Otter,'' observed Laughs-In-The-Rain with a sober mien belied by the twinkle in his wonderful eyes. "Grandfather Otter, because he could swim as fast and dive as deep as the fish in the water, was given a great treasure to keep by Nanabozo, the protector of the People. All the manitous, the spirits that inhabit living things, tried to make Grandfather Otter tell them the secret of the treasure. Grandfather Otter would only laugh at them and tell them not to waste their time worrying about things that did not concern them. Then he would bound away and slide, laughing, down the riverbank on his back into the river. When all the other animals saw how Grandfather Otter played all day, even through the winter, romping and sliding over the snow, they were filled with envy. 'Why should Otter have all the fun?' they asked themselves. 'It is because of the treasure,' said Fox, who had let Old Man Hare slip through his paws and thus had not eaten all day long. 'If we had the treasure, we would feel like laughing, too.' But no one, not even Badger, who was chosen to search Grandfather Otter's hole in the side of the riverbank, or Beaver, who was sent to look up and down the river, or Raven, who searched to the top of the tallest mountain, could find where Grandfather Otter had hidden the treasure. The more discontented the animals became, the more Grandfather Otter laughed at them and played. It is the same even to this day.''

"But what happened?" demanded Ganymede, who, like the others, had been hanging on every word.

"Yes, pray do tell us. Did the animals discover the secret of the treasure?" asked Iphigenia.

"I think Grandfather Otter *was* the treasure," spoke up Odysseus, frowning. "He would be to me if I were sad or unhappy. I should only have to see him having such a splendid time to feel better myself. I daresay I should jump right in and play with him."

"You are wise for your age, Boy-With-The-Heart-Of-The-Otter," rumbled Laughs-In-The-Rain, smiling. "A man who knows the secret of a joyful heart is a man who is blessed with the greatest of all treasures. It is the same for a woman," he added for the benefit of the female contingent. "You have only to look to Shines-With-Laughter to know this is true."

His gaze lifted to Pandora, who, caught up in the spell of the story, had yet to leave to fetch her pelisse and bonnet. Inexplicably, she felt the blood stain her cheeks as her eyes met those of the silver-haired warrior.

"I am afraid the children would not agree with you today, Uncle," she said, her lips twisting in a rueful smile. "I seem to be all on pins and needles lately."

"Your heart is troubled, Shines-With-Laughter," replied the warrior. "I see this in your eyes. And my nephew goes about wearing the face of a man who has eaten unwisely of the root of the raccoon berry."

"The raccoon berry?" Pandora queried with an uncertain lift of her eyebrows.

"An herb that causes nausea," Rivenoak explained, giving his uncle a censorious look. "The Three-Rivers people used it for medicinal purposes, varying from a purgative to a wart remover."

"Oh, I see," said Pandora, her sober mien belied by the shimmer of mirth in her eyes.

"Quite so," Rivenoak drawled in sardonic appreciation.

"Yes, that is better," commented Laughs-In-The-Rain, nodding his head. "You both have the gift of laughter. You would be wise not to forget, in your preoccupation with worldly matters, the story of Grandfather Otter."

"I shall not forget, Uncle," Pandora murmured, smiling fondly at the warrior. "Not so long as I have you to remind me."

Pandora was still smiling to herself when, some moments later, she allowed Rivenoak to help her to the seat of his curricle. Perhaps the warrior was right, she reflected, glancing surreptitiously up at the duke's stern profile as the curricle was set into motion. Perhaps one should not allow one's worldly concerns to deter one from the joy to be had in living. Certainly, Laughs-In-The-Rain had cause enough to feel acrimonious, and yet he had managed somehow not to allow what must surely have been a terrible grief and rage, as well as a loathing of the Redcoats who had murdered his people, to turn him bitter. He, of all people, showed what it was to view life through the philosophical eyes of the otter.

Would that Rivenoak could do the same, she thought wistfully, recalling to mind the impossibility of her own situation. How could she embrace the joy that might be hers as Rivenoak's wife if she were unable to find proof of Herodotus's innocence of any wrongdoing at Bear Flat? What Laughs-In-The-Rain's tale of Grandfather Otter did not take into account was the practical outlook of the wise old English owl, who, when approached by anyone, no matter how seemingly fair or familiar, always demanded to know "Who-o?" Clearly, she could not give in to the temptation to grasp at a happiness that might in the end prove to be only a chimera.

Reminded all at once why she had wished to have Rivenoak to herself, she steeled herself to broach the subject of the wedding announcement, when Rivenoak himself opened the door to her.

"You are angry with me, Miss Featherstone," he said baldly, glancing down at her. "It is because of the announcement in the *Gazette,* one must presume. Pray do not be afraid to open the budget."

"You may be sure that I have every intention of doing just that, your grace," Pandora declared, glad to have the matter out in the open. "I do hope you realize what you have done. It is the shabbiest thing. It is not enough that you will be forced in future to publish the fact that your intended bride has changed her mind, but we may undoubtedly expect Braxton to bear down on us at any moment."

"A hideous prospect," ventured the duke, apparently unmoved at such an eventuality. "Am I to take it that the earl will object to such a match?"

"How detestable you are," observed Pandora, giving a helpless choke of laughter at such an absurdity. "You know very well he would not object in the least at seeing his sister a duchess."

Rivenoak eloquently shrugged. "Then, I fail to see the difficulty," he replied, "or the necessity for a retraction."

"Fiddle!" Pandora retorted, in no mood to make light of the matter. "I have made my position perfectly clear, your grace. I cannot marry you."

"On the contrary, Miss Featherstone," objected Rivenoak, maddeningly cool, "you have not made yourself clear at all. As I recall, you have categorically refused to tell me what impediment, precisely, you see to such a union. Until you do, I shall not accept no as your definitive answer."

"Then, you are uncommonly stubborn, your grace."

"Rather say I am utterly determined, Miss Featherstone, to have you as my wife, even so far as to venture to discuss the matter with the head of your family."

"I am the head of my family," Pandora asserted, as close

to being angry with the duke as she had ever been. "You may be perfectly sanguine at the prospect of having my brother descend upon us. I, however, am not. I have been content to have my elder brother play least seen in my affairs, and I have no wish to alter our arrangement at this or any other date."

"Then, you may rest easy, Miss Featherstone," Rivenoak answered, turning the bays into the entrance to Hyde Park. "I am reasonably certain the earl has no such intention. I should, in fact, be greatly surprised if he exerted himself to come to London at all in the very near future."

Pandora eyed the duke askance at that unexpected assurance. "I fail to see how you could possibly know that, your grace," she said, wondering if he had been spending time in the sweat lodge again.

"Suffice it to say that I have a certain gift of Sight, which tells me your brother is content to remain at home. I daresay he could not be dragged from his morphological studies of the songs of the various English members of the thrush family, *Turdidae,* with a special emphasis on the mavis as compared to the nightingale."

Pandora stared at Rivenoak in undisguised amazement. "How could you possibly know of Braxton's obsession with those particular members of the thrush family—unless?" She stopped, her eyes widening with sudden comprehension. "Rivenoak, you have been to see him."

"It did seem the logical thing to do, Miss Featherstone," observed his grace with a humble air that did not fool Pandora in the least. "Lady Congreve assures me his lordship is a stickler for the conventions. I felt, in the circumstances, you would appreciate my efforts to avert any unpleasantness. You will admit a meeting at dawn would hardly have served our purposes."

"No, I daresay it would not," agreed Pandora, struck with an image of the bull-headed, slightly short-sighted Castor, flinging the gauntlet down before the powerful Duke of Rivenoak. Really, it was too absurd. And yet she could not dismiss the possibility out of hand. It was, in fact, just the sort of nonsensical thing one might expect from Braxton if he imagined his honor had been impugned. Castor had always been a stickler for what was due the family name. But then, save for Herodotus and the children, she had long since distanced herself from the rest of her family. It should not have been any of his concern what she did.

Unfortunately, since that was *not* the reality, Pandora could only view the duke's actions in averting such a disaster with a mingling of relief and the sense that she was caught in a slowly closing snare from which there would be no escaping.

If she did not solve the conundrum of the colonel's death very soon, she would be left little choice but to tell Rivenoak the truth, and that she could not countenance—not before she had had the chance to prove Herodotus's innocence!

"Am I forgiven, then?" queried Rivenoak, when he judged he had allowed Pandora sufficient time to arrive at the only logical conclusion possible regarding the announcement in the *Gazette*.

"I suppose there is little point in crying over spilt milk, your grace," Pandora said, wryly noting the considerable attention they were attracting from the passersby. "On the other hand, I am not so green that I do not know the real reason you did what you did was out of the mistaken notion that you would make it impossible for me to refuse your generous offer." Suddenly, Rivenoak found himself impaled by grave, blue-grey eyes that had the power to render him peculiarly susceptible to distinct pangs of conscience. "My dearest lord duke, I am deeply touched by your persistence in trying to make an honest woman of me, but I do wish you would stop. It really is not necessary. Perhaps you would be relieved to learn that I am far from being in a delicate condition. In which case your notions of honor are entirely misplaced. There is no reason for anyone ever to know I am a ruined woman."

It was true: a wave of relief did wash over the duke at the news that Miss Featherstone was not increasing, but not for the reasons she must have supposed. If she were ever to bear him a child, he meant to make most damned certain it was in the wedded state. At least, with the news, he was granted more time in which to persuade her to his frame of mind. "You are mistaken, surely, Miss Featherstone," Rivenoak said with cool deliberation.

Pandora's eyebrows arched. "I beg your pardon, your grace?"

Rivenoak smiled grimly. "*I* know, and that is sufficient to warrant my continued assault on your unreasonable objections to our joining in wedlock. I will have you as my wife, Pandora, or I shall know the reason why. And now that that is settled, I suggest you turn your not inconsiderable powers of observation to the more pressing matter of the colonel's murder. Approaching us in the carriage drawn by the showy pair of matched greys is the Countess of Inglethorpe. As it happens, her husband, the earl, was killed in a duel little more than three months ago."

"Dear me. How perfectly dreadful," declared Pandora, looking to the carriage in question. "And you think the countess might have some connection with the colonel's murder?"

"I think the lady will not have been overgrieved at the colonel's death," replied Rivenoak, pulling the team to a halt as the two carriages came together. "It was the colonel who shot Inglethorpe. The lady has the further distinction of having once entertained aspirations of becoming my duchess."

Chapter 10

Pandora was aware of a sudden twisting sensation in the region of her stomach. And little wonder, she thought upon gaining her first close-up view of the countess. She had hardly expected that particular revelation from the duke.

Lady Inglethorpe, a red-haired beauty who looked twenty-five, but was in reality closer to thirty-one, exuded that certain air of self-assurance that marked her as an acknowledged diamond of the first water. Obviously, she was accustomed to being paid the homage due to one blessed with china blue eyes, a flawless, creamy complexion, and regal, classical features. Dressed to the height of fashion in a Madras muslin gown beneath a very smart half-Curricle cloak trimmed in lace and topped by a beehive bonnet of fine moss, she might just have stepped from the pages of *La Belle Assemblee*.

It was not her attire, however, that caught Pandora's immediate attention, or even the countess's beauty, breathtaking though it might be. It was an instantaneous impression of ice beneath the glittering facade that caused Pandora's glance to narrow sharply on the lovely countenance, even as the countess called out a greeting from the rose velvet depths of her carriage.

"Your grace," she exclaimed with an elegant wave of a daintily gloved hand. "What a marvelous surprise. I had not thought to see the Duke of Rivenoak in Hyde Park at the fashionable hour of five." Her cool gaze swept over Pandora's trim figure becomingly attired in a pale blue pelisse over a rose sarcenet gown. "Well, and little wonder. I daresay we have your companion to thank for this unexpected honor."

Pandora's smile felt stiff on her lips. Indeed, she could not but marvel to discover her hands had clenched into fists in her lap. It was not in the least logical.

"As it happens, I have a great deal for which to thank my companion," replied Rivenoak smoothly. "Not the least of which is she has agreed to become my wife. Lady Inglethorpe, allow me to present Lady Pandora Featherstone, my intended."

"Miss Featherstone," Lady Inglethorpe said, condescending to incline her head a bare fraction of an inch in Pandora's direction. "My congratulations. I had not thought there was a woman alive who could lure Rivenoak into Parson's Mousetrap. Naturally, I wish you happy. However did you manage it? Sometime you must tell me your secret."

"Secret, Lady Inglethorpe?" Rivenoak interjected before Pandora could summon a reply. Lifting Pandora's hand to his lips, he kissed the palm. "There is no secret. There is only Lady Pandora in whom I have discovered an instantaneous mutual magnetic attraction."

Pandora, treated to the gleam of humor in the duke's marvelous eyes as they met hers, could not but respond in kind. "Indeed, my lady," she said, dimpling irrepressibly at Rivenoak, "we were instantly drawn to one another. But then, you must realize as well as I that Rivenoak is possessed of a compelling presence. It will always be a conundrum to me why he should have felt the same about me."

"But you are too modest, Miss Featherstone," Lady Inglethorpe returned with a faint hardening of her eyes. "I myself can only marvel that we have never met before. I have always prided myself on knowing everyone who was anyone. This cannot be your first Season in London?"

"The first in many years, my lady," admitted Pandora, not in the least disconcerted at being placed in the category of a Nobody. "My come out, I'm afraid, could only be accounted a dismal failure."

"Indeed?" Lady Inglethorpe lilted with uplifted eyebrows. "How very fortunate that your second Season promises to be altogether different."

"Oh, quite different," Pandora blithely concurred. "Until now, after all, I had considered myself quite firmly on the shelf, a circumstance with which I was more than content, never having entertained any real aspirations to marry. His grace, however, has proven most uncommonly persuasive."

"No, has he?" murmured Lady Inglethorpe, a distinct edge to her voice. "But then, Rivenoak has always enjoyed a reputation for ruthlessness. I daresay, Miss Featherstone, you must have something that has attracted his interest."

"Do you think so?" Pandora glanced archly at the nobleman. "What, I wonder, could it be?"

"You know very well what it is, my dear," drawled Rivenoak, an answering gleam in the look he bent upon her. "Obviously, I covet your fortune."

"Dear me, a fortune hunter," Pandora dramatically sighed. "I should have known. What a pity I haven't a feather to fly with. I am afraid I am going to prove a great disappointment to you, my dearest Rivenoak."

"On the contrary, Miss Featherstone," said Rivenoak with a singular lack of his earlier playfulness, "you are proving a never-ending delight and will no doubt continue to do so."

Pandora furiously blushed. Good God, if she did not know better, she would have thought he was perfectly earnest in his declaration. But that was absurd, she told herself firmly. It was all a part of the charade they were playing.

Neither noticed Lady Inglethorpe's startled reaction.

At the lively exchange between the powerful duke and the Nobody, the beauty's eyebrows fairly snapped together. No matter how rumor might have it, theirs was to all appearances a love match. The duke had made it a point to demonstrate his approval of Miss Featherstone.

In the days that followed, it was to become increasingly evident to everyone that Rivenoak was pursuing his chosen bride with a single-most determination—everyone, that was, save for Pandora herself.

It was remarked early on that whatever social function Miss Featherstone attended, the duke was certain to make an appearance, even going so far as to dance two waltzes with the young beauty at Almack's Assembly Rooms, a wholly unprecedented occurrence that quickly made the rounds of every fashionable salon in London. If that were not enough to fuel the fires of speculation, it was to be noted that on almost any given evening at the fashionable hour of five, the duke could be seen tooling his matched bays through Hyde Park with Miss Featherstone at his side, that he had been spotted more than once strolling along Bond Street in the company of the lady, various parcels clasped about his august person, and that he had taken to attending musicales, soirees, and dinner parties with a shocking regularity that put at grave peril his previous reputation as the "Inaccessible Duke."

It was variously theorized that Rivenoak, having succumbed to Love's potent influence, had discovered a previously hitherto unsuspected flair for Society, that Miss Featherstone's vital presence had had a leavening effect on the nobleman, or that, his impenetrable defences breached at last, he was simply moon-struck. Others, less given to romantic inclinations, were prone

to the more cynical view that Rivenoak was simply playing a
deep game with an as yet to be discovered ulterior purpose.

As for Pandora, had she stopped to think about it, no doubt
she would have thought it peculiar that Rivenoak, openly inviting
speculation, seemed overly intent on living in her pocket or that
he had developed a penchant for intimidating her numerous admirers by sweeping her away onto the dance floor without a moment's
notice. As it was, however, she was far too occupied with the
more important matter of resolving the conundrum of the colonel's
demise to consider that the duke might be acting out of character.

Naturally, Rivenoak was often with her. They, two, had joined
forces to expose the real identity of Samuel Butler, who must
figure significantly in the dark plot encompassing recent, as well
as past, events. Indeed, Pandora had come to wonder if it was
the mysterious Butler who had sent the anonymous letter summoning the duke to Massingale's Town House. Had the colonel
been the recipient of a similar missive? she wondered as she
allowed Rivenoak to lead her from the ballroom out onto Lady
Desborough's terrace.

Rivenoak believed it was entirely possible. The duke had confided as much to Pandora only moments before, as an enticement,
had she but known it, to lure her away from her promised dance
with Viscount Estridge, the most importunate of her admirers.

It was, Pandora noted, a spectacularly lovely evening with
a crescent moon clean-cut in a sky brilliant with stars more
dazzling than the ballroom's crystal chandeliers or the beautiful
people dancing the quadrille in their fine silks and glittering
jewels. Pandora, herself a vision in cream-colored satin, her
unruly tresses subdued in a Roman coiffure of tight curls gathered high atop her head and ringlets framing the oval of her
face, could hardly believe she was now accepted as one of
those "Beautiful People"—she, whose only adornment was
her mama's single strand of pearls clasped about her neck!

Thank heavens Simmons was a master artist when it came
to turning a sow's ear into a silk purse. Pandora smiled to

herself. Unbelievably, she actually looked the part of Rivenoak's intended bride. But then, the crowning touch, of course, had been Rivenoak himself.

Her glance strayed to the tall figure of the duke at her side. Pandora was quite sure she had never seen a more elegantly turned out gentleman or one more certain to cause a flutter among the female contingent. Faith, but he was handsome dressed all in black, save for the immaculate white of his marcella waistcoat, his neckcloth, and his silk shirt devoid of ruffles or frills. His magnificent raven hair drawn back in a knot at the nape of his neck accentuated the strong masculine profile, chiseled to perfection, even as his French suit called attention to his broad-shouldered, slim-hipped build.

He was a man who must inevitably stand out in a crowd by the sheer force of his masculinity, and yet for all intents and purposes he was conservatively appareled. Indeed, save for the solitaire diamond in the folds of his neckcloth, there was nothing in his raiment to draw undue attention to himself.

Still, it was little wonder they had been the cynosure of all eyes upon making their appearance at the top of the stairway that curved gracefully down into the ballroom, Pandora wryly reflected. Could it truly have been only a bare two hours ago? Pandora, even knowing she walked at his side solely in the capacity of a confidential inquiry agent engaged in an elaborate charade, had yet experienced a swell of pride at his show of attentiveness. And, in truth, he had been most damnably convincing. She doubted there was a soul present who did not believe the Duke of Rivenoak was well pleased with his chosen bride.

She, however, knew the real truth of the matter. She was there to fulfill an obligation, she reminded herself, and, more importantly, to discover the identity of the villain who was plotting against the man she loved.

Pandora never paused to consider that she was a Nobody, who had failed miserably in her one and only attempt to join the ranks of the Society into which she had been born. She was a confidential inquiry agent on a mission. It mattered not a whit what anyone thought of her so long as she was allowed to move freely among the members of the *Ton* in pursuit of the elusive Samuel Butler. As a result, she conversed easily with all who came into her sphere, displayed a natural warmth of manner that was immediately judged both charming and unexceptional, and dazzled not a few of the gentlemen who swarmed about her in the hopes of earning her regard.

In the process, she had overheard a great many things to which she would not otherwise have been privy were she not under the aegis of the Duke of Rivenoak. Miss Elsbeth Effington, for example, had, while in Pandora's hearing, confided to her bosom bow Lady Jane Garth that Lady Inglethorpe had reportedly gone into a distempered freak over the news of Rivenoak's betrothal to an Unknown. Furthermore, it would seem that everyone who was anyone was perfectly aware that Lady Inglethorpe, before she had become Lady Inglethorpe, had openly pursued the heir to the former Duke of Rivenoak during not only her first Season in London, but, foolishly, her second and third Seasons as well. No doubt it was equally common knowledge that the old duke had been violently opposed to the match. After all, the daughter of a less than affluent baron would clearly have been beneath the touch of a future duke. In the end she had been left little choice but to accept Inglethorpe rather than to be left penniless and on the shelf. It had been the crowning jest of the Season that hardly had the imperious young beauty found herself properly wed to the earl than the old duke had been struck down by an apoplexy brought on, it was rumored, by his own vitriolic temper. From all accounts, the new countess, spurned by the new duke and relegated to the wilds of Northamptonshire by a jealous husband, had sworn a terrible vengeance on the duke and his entire line for perpetuity.

It was little wonder, thought Pandora, allowing her escort of the moment to leave her seated next to a potted fern while he went to fetch her a dish of punch, that she had detected a

certain frostiness beneath the beauty's veneer of graciousness
in the park. No doubt Lady Inglethorpe, treated to what gave
every appearance of the cooing of lovebirds, had been wishing
the devil would fly away with them both!

She was just in the process of digesting that intriguing thought
while wondering if it could have any bearing on the death of
the colonel and the plot against the duke, when she was treated
to a snatch of conversation between Lord Fontesquieu and Sir
Robert Winslow, who had taken up station on the other side
of the fern. It was made immediately apparent from Lord Fontesquieu's aside to Sir Robert Winslow that Viscount Estridge
had only the previous night lost a small fortune at the Faro
table. The viscount, however, was good for it, indeed, was
hardly likely to notice his purse was the lighter because of it.
"Ain't at all like it was when the old viscount sent the family
fortune down the River Tick at the single draw of a card,"
observed Sir Robert. "Who would have thought when the son
went into exile, he would return rich as a nabob?"

Lord Fontesquieu's reply that some men had all the luck left
Pandora pondering what he had meant by that. After all,
Estridge, it would seem, had not been in the least lucky at the
tables the night before. Obviously, the two noblemen must
have been referring to the greater fortune that had come to the
viscount while he was away from England. It came to her to
wonder just how he had amassed that fortune. She had, in fact,
been on the point of discreetly wooing the information from
the viscount himself, when Rivenoak had loomed out of the
crowd to claim Estridge's promised dance for himself.

"I fear, my lord," murmured Rivenoak, regarding the viscount from beneath heavily drooping eyelids, "you must excuse
Miss Featherstone. I believe," he added, holding his hand out
to Pandora, "that this dance is ours."

Pandora had required only a single look into the stern, hard
countenance to realize the duke did not intend to take no for
an answer. Viscount Estridge, a slender man in his early fifties

who exuded the smooth, silky confidence of a cruising shark, was less easily persuaded.

A pale gleam flickered in the viscount's colorless eyes.

"But I must protest, your grace," he said, affecting a smile that was as passionless as it was meant to be ingratiating. "I have waited the entire evening for a dance with the lovely Miss Featherstone."

"No, have you?" drawled the duke, apparently unmoved at the other man's plight. "Then, you will understand my own impatience to claim what is mine. My dear?" he said at his most maddeningly cool.

Pandora, noting the faint tinge of color touch the viscount's pale cheeks, laid her hand in Rivenoak's palm. "I do beg your pardon, Viscount Estridge," she said, smiling sympathetically. "Another time perhaps."

Estridge graciously bowed. "You may be sure of it, Miss Featherstone. I shall be looking forward to it."

"I suppose it would be pointless to suggest you have nothing further to do with the viscount," murmured Rivenoak moments later, as he led Pandora out onto the dance floor.

"Pointless in the extreme, your grace," Pandora, still nettled at the duke's untimely interference, did not hesitate to confirm. "Why?"

"Because he is a dangerous man utterly without scruples."

"Yes, I sensed that in him, but he is also possessed of an intriguing past. Did you know his father lost everything on a single turn of a card? Or that Estridge, faced with certain ruin, fled England to return an enormously wealthy man?"

"I should hardly be unaware of it," replied the duke, continuing on past the country square, just then forming, and proceeding to the French doors leading out onto the terrace. "It was my grandfather who won the Estridge family fortune." Glancing down at her, he arched an inquisitive eyebrow. "You did not really care to dance, did you, my dear?"

Pandora stared in perplexity at the duke's impassive features.

"You knew it?" she exclaimed, wondering what else he had
omitted to inform her. "And you did not think it was pertinent
to tell me about it?"

"Viscount Estridge has, from all accounts, garnered his fortune from diamond mines in India. It hardly seemed significant
to the case in point. It did occur to me, however, that you might
be interested to learn I have discovered Colonel Massingale
had, for the past several weeks, been selling out of the Funds.
I suggest, Miss Featherstone, that someone extorted a considerable sum from the colonel before he died and that he mistakenly
believed it was I. I should even go so far as to speculate that
he had been the recipient of numerous anonymous letters and
that, further, it is quite possible he was summoned to the Town
House that night by the same means as was I. Now, would you
care to join me in a stroll on the terrace or would you prefer
to take up where you left off with Viscount Estridge?"

Biting her tongue to keep from flinging back a withering
retort, Pandora stepped wordlessly onto the terrace.

"But if Colonel Massingale was receiving anonymous letters
threatening to expose his part in the massacre at Bear Flat,"
she said as Rivenoak, apparently not satisfied that the terrace
afforded the privacy he desired, led her down the steps into
the topiary garden, made to resemble a bizarre assortment of
animals, ranging from an African lion to an Egyptian crocodile,
"why should he believe you had written them? Surely, he must
have realized how very illogical such a conclusion would be.
You are hardly the sort of man who would resort to extortion.
You already have all the flimsy you will ever need. It would
be more true to your character to simply face him with what
you knew and demand satisfaction."

"How very well you would seem to know me, Miss Featherstone," observed Rivenoak in sardonic amusement. Indeed,
he could not but find it singularly ironic that, while his elusive
Pandora could apparently so easily gauge his character, she
could not perceive the one significant truth—that he was in

earnest pursuit of her. "As it happens, I did not hide the fact
that I was looking into the colonel's part in the massacre. I
informed him of it and of what I intended to do when I had
the proof I needed to publicly condemn him."

"Just as I expected," said Pandora, not in the least surprised
at that revelation. "And what was the colonel's response?"

"He replied rather peculiarly that it was about time I ceased
to hide behind a veil of threats," Rivenoak answered, wondering how long it would take her to deduce what he himself had
surmised almost from the moment he had learned of Massingale's death, that which had only been made more apparent by
the attempted abduction at the museum. "From which I surmised that he was the victim of an extortion plot. He might
naturally draw the conclusion that I had determined on such
a course with the intention of ruining him financially. Here,
however, the course grows muddy. No more than a fortnight
after our confrontation, I received the anonymous message
informing me the proofs for which I was searching resided in
the colonel's Town House."

"It was a trap, of course," Pandora pointed out. They had
already agreed on that.

"Obviously, and yet I could not ignore the possibility, no
matter how remote, that there was something in the colonel's
study to condemn him."

"And so, contrary to the usual rule of burglars, you chose
to carry out your search in daylight," deduced Pandora. "Excel-
lently done, your grace."

"No doubt I am gratified that you approve, Miss Featherstone," murmured Rivenoak, who would rather have been
discussing the intriguing tendency of her eyes to appear deep
pools in the moonlight. Deliberately, he pulled her into the
leafy arch formed by the trunk of an elephant beneath which
was a cunningly placed marble bench. "In light of the events
of that evening, I consider it highly probable Massingale had
been goaded into the belief he had no choice but to eliminate

me.'' Seating himself, he pulled Pandora down beside him.
"Unfortunately, it is also probable someone had determined
the colonel was become a liability he could no longer afford.
In which case, we were both being manipulated toward that
evening at the colonel's Town House.''

"Yes, he might very well have been set up either to cut your
stick for you or to have it appear you had done the same for
him,'' speculated Pandora, struck by an even more startling
possibility, one that she dared not share with Rivenoak. It had,
in fact, occurred to her that *she* might very well have been the
intended victim!

It would seem to make a deal more sense, she mused, only
vaguely aware that Rivenoak had taken the opportunity to wrap
his arm about her waist in order to draw her near enough for him
to inhale the sweet fragrance of her hair. What if Massingale,
learning from his wife of Pandora's existence, not to mention
her singular vocation, had immediately connected her with
another figure from his past—Herodotus Featherstone, who
might very well know a deal more than anyone about the events
in America? As a confidential inquiry agent *and* the sister of
his former subordinate, she would naturally fall immediately
suspect in the colonel's mind. Indeed, he might very well suppose that she was the one sending the letters of extortion, if
indeed the letters had ever existed. Shortly after that possibility
reared its head, he had been confronted by Rivenoak, who had
not hesitated to inform the colonel of his own suspicions.

It must have come to him that he might very well dispose
of two birds with one stone. Hence, the elaborate plot to bring
Rivenoak and Herodotus Featherstone's sister together in the
colonel's Town House. Only Pandora had been the intended
victim with Rivenoak posed to take the blame for her heinous
demise. No doubt the colonel would have been forgiven for
disposing of the murderer of a defenseless woman under his
protection. To add sauce to the gander, the contents of the
wooden box, once revealed, would have been sufficient not

only to discredit the duke in the eyes of the *Ton,* the scandal of his birth, which his grandfather had taken such pains to keep secret, enough to make him the object of vilification, but it would have provided a convincing motive for the killing as well. No doubt the colonel would have been sure to claim the box belonged to the deceased and to further suggest the possibility Miss Featherstone was extorting money from the duke to keep its contents a secret.

Faith, it would all seem to make perfect sense! No doubt the colonel had stolen into the house night after night to hide and wait in the secret room for the moment Rivenoak would appear in response to the anonymous summons. She recalled with a slight shudder the feeling she had had at the time that she was being watched. How very put out he must have been on that final night not only that his intended victim had failed to put in her customary appearance in the library, but, finally, to surmise she had flown the coop altogether! Still, he had waited for Rivenoak. After all, if he could not frame the duke for the murder of Miss Featherstone, he might yet at least shoot the nobleman and claim afterwards he had mistaken Rivenoak for a burglar.

It was all so tidy, except for the fact that nothing had transpired as the colonel had so carefully planned it. Ironically, he himself had become the victim of his own infamous plans. Why? she wondered, not for the first time. Who had intervened to put an end to the colonel? And who had been extorting money from him?

"Why did you wait until now to tell me about your confrontation with Massingale?" she said suddenly, turning to face the duke with searching eyes. "And your theory concerning the letters. Surely you could not have considered them an insignificant piece of the puzzle."

Rivenoak, who had been watching the play of emotions across her face as she went through the steps of logical deduction, smiled ruefully with the knowledge that for quite some four or five minutes, she had completely forgotten his existence. The realization was hardly the sort to add to his self-esteem, especially as he had maneuvered her into the garden with some vague notion of truly compromising her beyond any thought of redemption. He stifled a sigh. "Because, my impossible confidential inquiry agent," he said, cradling the side of her face with the palm of his hand, "I still had hopes of keeping you out of this."

Pandora's pulse inexplicably quickened. "And now you no longer feel that you can. Why?" she persisted.

Rivenoak's lips twisted in a mirthless smile. "I believe you know why, Pandora. And if you do not, I daresay your infallible sense of logic will soon lead you to the answer."

"The devil, Rivenoak," Pandora blurted. "You do not intend to tell me."

"Correct as always, Miss Featherstone. I prefer to hear it from you, when you are ready to trust me."

"Trust you?" exclaimed Pandora, as close as she had ever come to exasperation with Rivenoak's propensity for the enigmatic. "I believe, your grace, the shoe is on the other foot. Indeed, I cannot but wonder what else you are keeping from me."

"Nothing, I assure you, that you do not already know for yourself." Rivenoak, his face a stony mask in the uncertain light, heaved a sigh. He let his hand drop to his side and stood. "Pray do not let it concern you. Come, it is time we went back inside."

Pandora stopped him as he made as if to turn away. "Your grace."

"Miss Featherstone?"

Pandora's heart gave an uncertain twist at the distance in his voice.

"I do trust you." She rose from the bench to gaze earnestly up at him. "I always have, Rivenoak. It is only that there are some things I—"

She was not allowed to finish. Uttering a low hiss, Rivenoak clamped a hand over her mouth and pulled her into the shadows.

"Softly," he murmured close to her ear. "We are not alone." Carefully he uncovered Pandora's mouth. "There, lurking near the giraffe."

"Yes, I see him. And there." She pointed to the fanciful rendition of a zebra. "What in heaven's name is Canary Waistcoat doing here?"

"Canary Waistcoat?" queried the duke with an inquisitively arched eyebrow. "Someone of your admirers, my dear?"

Pandora choked on a helpless burble of laughter. "I do wish you would be serious. Canary Waistcoat was the man who accosted me at the museum just before you turned Stalker loose on the three ruffians."

"Ah, yes. I do seem to remember an odd sort huddling behind a potted palm. He would appear to have a happy knack for following you."

"He would, indeed, your grace. Only, this time I believe it is the other fellow who has his attention."

Rivenoak, observing the little man work his way from hedge to hedge, could only agree with her. Curious, he thought. There was something about that other fellow. . . .

"You will remain here, Pandora," Rivenoak uttered shortly and, without warning, glided forward, to disappear into the shadows.

"Rivenoak!" Pandora called in a whisper. "Wait!" The devil, she thought, and started after him, only to be stopped by a distinct rustle of movement behind her. Heedless of her gown, she stepped hastily into the cover of the foliage.

Her immediate reaction to hearing the approach of a light step, followed by a low gurgle of feminine laughter, was to expel a silent breath of relief. Obviously she was not about to be set upon by villains intent on some nefarious deed. Undoubtedly, it was a pair of lovers, stealing a few moments alone in the starlight.

Still, it would hardly do to be discovered, apparently unaccompanied, in the garden. The last thing she could wish was to become the object of speculation and rumor of the sort that would breed. Ignoring the needling prick of branches, she set herself to wait until the couple passed.

That they did *not* pass, indeed, seemed intent upon a tête-à-tête on the marble bench Pandora and the duke had only recently vacated, soon became all too readily apparent. In spite of the fact that her view of the couple was obstructed by the facsimile of an elephant's leg done in artfully pruned yew branches, she could hear all too distinctly the muffled sounds of the sort to bring a blush to her cheek.

Good God, Pandora groaned, silently to herself. It was bad enough she was forced into the role of unwitting eavesdropper on a scene of intimacy, but she must do so in the discomfort of prickly evergreen needles. Really it was too much. A curse on Rivenoak. It was all his fault for leaving her to cool her heels while he dashed off presumably in the pursuit of danger. One day he would discover she was not the sort of female who needed his protection, or any other man's, for that matter. She was a confidential inquiry agent, fully prepared to meet the dangers of her profession.

She was on the point of mentally reviling Rivenoak's character, his past, and his family connections, when her attention was diverted by the unknown woman's throaty laugh.

"Really, my lord. You grow too bold. Need I remind you I am not one of your Paphians?"

"You need remind me of nothing, my lady," responded the gentleman, his voice harsh with lingering passion. "I have a keen memory, and it tells me that you lured me into the garden with the promise that I should not be disappointed."

"And I daresay you have not been—disappointed, my lord," countered the lady in tones highly suggestive of the sort of activities in which the two had earlier been engaged.

Apparently the nobleman was put in mind of them. Uttering an oath, he exclaimed, "No, by the devil, I have not."

There ensued more muffled sounds of the sort to evoke images of behavior on the most primal level, when once again the lady, whose voice, though hauntingly familiar to Pandora, eluded her immediate identification, called a gasping halt.

"Enough, my lord, I beg you. Remember where we are and that soon we shall have to return to the ballroom. You cannot wish me to appear as if I have been mauled by a wild beast. Faith, but your own appearance is most deceptive. How very powerful you are!"

"Unlike your Town Beau, Ridgeway, is that what you mean?" returned his lordship in accents of loathing. "I may have been born a gentleman, Countess, but I have not always lived the life of one."

"No, I believe you have amply demonstrated that, my lord," provocatively laughed the lady, even as Pandora vibrated to the familiar name of Ridgeway. Surely she could not mean who the name would seem to imply, thought Pandora with a sickening sensation in the pit of her stomach, as the lady continued, "It is what I find so devilishly attractive in you."

"You surprise me, my lady. I had thought it was my fortune you found particularly attractive."

"Now, you are perilously close to being a bore, Estridge. You must know very well Inglethorpe left me more than well provided for even after the entailment to his younger brother. I have no need of your fortune in diamonds, or was it furs from the New World? My husband's former business associate was never able to get anything straight."

Pandora, made instantly aware of the lady's identity, not to mention that of the gentleman, only just managed to stifle a gasp.

Still, she must have made some noise, or an involuntary movement, perhaps. Lady Inglethorpe gave a short hiss.

"Faith, my lord, did you hear something?"

"No, nothing, save for the breeze in the shrubbery," Estridge's voice came back, hard with impatience and something else beneath the surface—menace, thought Pandora, wondering that Lady Inglethorpe would seem curiously oblivious to it. "Tell me about this business associate of the late earl's. I was not aware Inglethorpe dabbled in trade."

"Oh, not in trade, my lord." Lady Inglethorpe gave vent to a scornful laugh. "Inglethorpe would never have dirtied his hands in something that so much as smelled of trade. It was more in the nature of a 'Gentlemen's' enterprise."

"You mean he was a smuggler," surmised Viscount Estridge.

"If you must speak plainly, yes," replied Lady Inglethorpe with the barest touch of pique. "It was, in any event, a lucrative enterprise, until the colonel got wind of it and decided to make himself a part of it. Such an arrangement was doomed from the very beginning. Not only was the colonel a boor, but he was greedy. He wanted everything for himself, including me. Fortunately, he was also easily manipulated. I could almost be sorry he is gone, if I had not formed such an aversion for him and had he not become something of a problem. He did do me a favor, after all. He made me a wealthy widow."

"And now you want a favor from me, is that it? I warn you, Lady Inglethorpe, you will find I am not so easily manipulated."

"No, I daresay you are not. On the other hand, I believe it is I who may be able to do a favor for you. And I shall ask nothing in return, save only that you do not fail me. We, after all, have at least one common interest."

"You are, if nothing, sure of yourself," observed the viscount, his ardor no longer in evidence. Pandora, sensing the shark uppermost in him, felt a sudden chill for the lady. "I am all eagerness to hear what you have to say."

"Not now, my lord. And certainly not here. Come to my house." The soft rustle of skirts signaled Lady Inglethorpe had risen from the bench. "Shall we say tomorrow night? Eight, I should think. We shall dine together."

"You will do more than feed my appetites, Lady Inglethorpe," Estridge promised darkly. "You will satisfy my every curiosity."

"Shall I, my lord? No doubt I shall be looking forward to it. Certainly, you will gain a deal more in the way of enlightenment from me than you would from the duke's promised bride. Oh, yes, I saw the way you looked at her. I daresay everyone did, especially his grace of Rivenoak. Pray don't worry." Lady Inglethorpe laughed, as the pair moved out from beneath the sculpted hedge and started back the way they had come. "Personally, I should be greatly pleased if she were made to satisfy your darkest desires, my lord."

Pandora clenched her hands into fists at her sides. The devil, she would, Pandora thought, her earlier feeling of concern for Lady Inglethorpe's safety at the hands of a man who gave every evidence of being utterly ruthless suddenly and instantly dispelled. Lady Inglethorpe, not to mention Viscount Estridge, had a great deal to learn about confidential inquiry agents trained in the scientific application of deductive reasoning.

The countess had as good as murdered her own husband. She had all but admitted it. Colonel Massingale may have pulled the trigger, but he had been little more than the instrument of Lady Inglethorpe's cold-blooded manipulations. Had she, then, arranged for his sudden demise, even as she was obviously hatching some new evil? What could it be? Pandora wondered. And against whom was it to be directed? But, perhaps more significantly, what had it to do with Viscount Estridge?

All of Pandora's considerable powers of woman's intuition warned her that it was somehow imperative that she discover the answers to these conundrums. Indeed, it was time she learned a deal more about the viscount, and what better way than to pretend an infatuation with him? she thought, listening to the sounds of the couple's retreat down the flagstone walk.

Obviously, she would have little difficulty initiating a light
flirtation with the nobleman. She did not doubt she could learn
a great deal from Estridge without his ever being aware that
he had been subjected to the keen investigative probing of a
trained confidential inquiry agent. Of course, Rivenoak promised to be something of a stumbling block. On the other hand,
if she proceeded with every care, the duke need never know
about it.

Hardly had she formulated that thought and, judging the way
was clear, had proceeded to extricate herself from the yew's
prickly branches, than she turned—and came instantly up
against a hard, immovable object.

A low gasp burst from her lips, even as strong hands clamped
implacably about her arms.

"The answer, Pandora, to this newfound conundrum of
yours," pronounced a stern masculine voice, "is no. Whatever
harebrained scheme you have concocted to discover the object
of Lady Inglethorpe's machinations is unequivocally out of the
question."

"Good God, Rivenoak!" Pandora breathed, sagging in sudden relief. Then, "The devil, your grace," she gasped. "You
nearly frightened me out of half a year's growth."

"I shall gladly do much more than that if I do not have your
immediate promise that you will not strike up a flirtation with
Viscount Estridge."

"A flirtation, your grace?" lilted Pandora, more than a little
startled at Rivenoak's apparent gift for reading her thoughts.
"With Viscount Estridge. Whatever gave you that idea?"

"What, indeed," replied the duke in tones of sardonic
appreciation. "I daresay between two people of strong mutual
magnetic attraction there must inevitably be a certain melding
of minds."

"Fiddle!" declared Pandora, her lovely eyes lit with rueful
amusement. "You overheard everything, did you not? And,
being of a highly rational mind, you followed the same line of

reasoning as did I. Naturally, we arrived at the same conclusion.''

''A sobering thought,'' commented Rivenoak, apparently much struck at the notion. ''As it happens, however, you are in the right of it. I did hear most of it. And, while it was clear to me you, as a confidential inquiry agent, would choose the direct approach to gain your objectives, I determined on a more subtle method of achieving the same ends.''

''Stealing into Lady Inglethorpe's house in order to spy on them is hardly subtle, Rivenoak,'' Pandora observed dryly. ''It is a blatant breach of the law. Or had you intended to bribe one of the servants to do it for you?''

''What an odd notion you must have of my character, Miss Featherstone,'' drawled his grace, taking her arm and leading her back toward the ballroom. ''As it happens, I have no intention of breaking into Lady Inglethorpe's house or bribing her servants. Apparently, I have come up with an option, which you, despite your many investigative talents, have overlooked.''

At this bald-faced assertion from his grace, Pandora came to an abrupt and determined halt. ''Devil!'' she asserted, her gaze accusing on the duke's handsome face. ''How dare you tease me, when, obviously, you know something I do not. You will tell me everything, this very instant, or you will leave me no choice but to pursue my own course in this matter. You may begin by revealing where you went when you so precipitously abandoned me in that cursed shrubbery and you will include what it was you discovered.''

''Not 'what,' my dear,'' replied the duke without the smallest hesitation. ''But 'who.' ''

''Or 'whom,' as the case may be, but what is the point in quibbling? Tell me, whom, other than canary Waistcoat, did you discover?''

''As it happens, Canary Waistcoat managed to elude me in the dark. Whom I did discover was my Cousin Percy, who, as it happens, was intent on following Lady Inglethorpe and her companion without being detected. Having been on exceedingly intimate terms with Lady Inglethorpe for the past several years, he has a vested interest in the lady.''

''No, has he?'' exclaimed Pandora, suddenly and greatly enlightened. So, it was *that* Ridgeway who was dangling after the countess, she thought with a sigh of relief. ''How very curious. I should not have thought Percival Ridgeway the sort to suffer pangs of jealousy over a woman. What, I wonder, would have happened had you not intercepted him before he could witness his inamorata in the arms of Another?''

Rivenoak shrugged a single broad shoulder. ''Nothing,'' he said, ''you may be sure of it, unless Estridge had so far forgotten himself as to do some injury to the lady. It was not jealousy that led him to follow Lady Inglethorpe, but something altogether different.''

''What, then? Pray do not tease me, Rivenoak. Tell me.''

''I suppose one might say he has been something of a guardian angel to her. Percy has helped the lady out of countless coils of her own making. I daresay he has loved her since she was little more than a green girl straight from the schoolroom.''

''Only, she does not return his love,'' breathed Pandora, who, after having witnessed the object of Ridgeway's affection in what could only have been termed ''compromising circumstances,'' doubted not Lady Inglethorpe was wholly incapable of anything approaching that finer sensibility. ''How very sad for him! I daresay he is not plump enough in the pocket for her. Still, if he does have a *tendre* for her, can you really think he will spy on her for you?''

''I think, Miss Featherstone,'' replied Rivenoak in tones of finality, as he led her once more toward the house and the waiting ballroom, ''only Percival can ever say what Percival will do.''

Chapter 11

Rivenoak was displeased with himself. More than that, he was displeased with his world in general. It was a novel experience for one who had ever followed the precept that a man, if he was a man, ruled his own existence. The inescapable fact remained, however, that the fate of one of the most powerful men in England rested in the hands of a woman who had become as necessary to his happiness as she was determined to fling it all away.

No doubt Rivenoak's Uncle Laughs-In-The-Rain would have found his nephew's dilemma more than a little amusing. The silver-haired tribesman had warned him often enough to beware of the Trickster—Old Man Hare—who delighted in wrecking the plans of men. The Trickster had outdone himself this time, the duke was wont to reflect cynically of late. In spite of Rivenoak's determined campaign to demonstrate to the world that he was earnestly on the hunt, Miss Featherstone continued to elude him at every turn.

Had he not incontrovertible evidence that the lady was not

so indifferent to him as she was determined to make him believe, he would have come long ago to the conclusion that he was embarked on a feckless course. As it was, however, he could not dismiss the events of the fateful morning spent in the British Museum.

The duke was far too experienced in the art of love not to know his impossibly headstrong, wholly desirable confidential inquiry agent had not only given herself to him with a sweet, wild abandon that had been as generous as it was selfless, but that she could only have done so if she entertained a more than moderate affection for him. Certainly, no other woman in his rather extensive experience had ever had the power to so far make him forget himself as to seduce an Innocent on a research table in a public reading room of the British Museum!

He had told himself often enough since that day that he must clearly have been mad. However, while it might be true that he had momentarily taken leave of his senses, he knew beyond a doubt that he had not been nor was he now insane. The simple truth was Lady Pandora Featherstone was the woman he had thought never to find, and now that he had found her, he would be demmed if he would let her slip through his fingers.

If he had to carry her forcibly off to Gretna Green to convince her he was in earnest, he bloody well would, he grimly told himself the morning following Lady Desborough's ball. It was not a course that he would wish to pursue. He would far rather his sweet Pandora arrive on her own at the realization that she could trust him with the truth. And, therein, lay the crowning achievement of the bloody Trickster.

The truth was, Pandora would never give in to her heart's desire so long as she believed her duty resided in protecting her brother Herodotus from the vengeance of the man she loved.

Damn Herodotus Featherstone and his traitorous heart! The man had for too long been a thorn in his side.

Rivenoak found it singularly ironic that a man he had never met before should have the power to rob him of everything he had ever loved. And now that same man was to be the instrument of denying him even the woman he would have as his wife! Rivenoak, after all, did not fool himself into believing that the gloriously stubborn, infuriatingly independent Miss Featherstone would ever forgive him, let alone learn to give him her trust, if he forced her into marriage. He, better than anyone, knew she must come to him of her own free will, and *that* she would never do, so long as she feared Rivenoak's wrath against her brother.

"Hell and the devil confound it!" Rivenoak cursed, slamming the side of his fist against the fireplace mantelpiece in his private study. It was a conundrum to baffle the most persistent of confidential inquiry agents.

Instantly, he berated himself for a bloody fool. He, after all, was the Duke of Rivenoak, he reminded himself, a man of far-reaching power and influence. He had not made himself what he was without learning a deal of patience. Indeed, he would not have survived, his pride intact, his dear departed grandfather's every attempt to break him had he not the stoic strength of his mother's people.

The memories of that seemingly endless battle of wills reverberated through this study, which had been the old duke's fortress of impregnability. It was here, and the similar study at Rivenoaks, the duke's principal estate, that the young savage was used to be summoned to demonstrate his progress in being transformed into an English gentleman. It had not mattered that Ridgeway had made sure his son had a proper understanding of his English heritage, that he could both read and write and do numbers, or that he had, thanks to the old missionary, an excellent grasp of history, not to mention a fair proficiency at Latin and French.

It was not the boy's mind or his intellect that the old duke had been determined to break and re-create in his own narrow image. It was his spirit.

Rivenoak's eyes glittered, cold with a never-forgotten rage, as the memories crowded around him.

"Who are you, boy? Tell me who you are!"

He was Chance True-Son-Iron-Heart, a man of the Three-Rivers People, who had endured at fourteen the rite of death and rebirth in the spirit of the Grandfather Bear. The old duke had never understood that, any more than he had understood that his heir was also Chance Quincy Ridgeway, the true son of Ridgeway, who was a man of truth and honor, a man who had loved the gentle Joyfully-Sings, a Christian woman of the tribes, who had taught her firstborn to read from the King James Bible.

It had taken three able-bodied men to hold the savage down while his hair, the pride of his manhood, was cropped close to his head and then shaved to accommodate a horse-hair wig. That had been his grandfather's answer to the boy's silence, born of bewildered hurt and instinctive defiance. It had been a shameful thing, one never to be forgiven or forgotten, only added to the legacy of hurts and insults, the canings, the tongue-lashings, the scathing scorn of an embittered old man who could not see the gift that his younger son had bequeathed him from the New World for what it truly was.

Only Aunt Caroline had seen and understood. The young savage from America had come prepared to honor and revere the old man who was the father of his father. He had come with a naive heart, which he would gladly have surrendered to the stern old man who was his paternal grandfather. He had never offered so much again. His grandfather had made sure of that.

Until now, Rivenoak thought wryly, when a hopelessly obstinate female with a warm, loving, generous nature had breathed new life into that frozen core of emotion. Bitterly and in cynical wonder at himself, he faced the truth.

He loved Lady Pandora Featherstone, as his father before

him had loved Joyfully-Sings, with the boundless passion of a man who could not face the thought of a life without her.

The realization brought him no comfort, not now, when he was so close to finding and bringing to justice the man behind the massacre at Bear Flat. He needed all his faculties on the task at hand. Instead, he found his powers of concentration impaired by emotions over which he seemed to have lost all control. As if that were not all or the worst of his problems, he was faced with the nearly impossible charge of keeping Miss Featherstone from harm.

Grimly, he recalled his failure to illicit a promise from the headstrong confidential inquiry agent that she would not engage Viscount Estridge in a dangerous flirtation. Miss Featherstone had not the smallest notion what she would be inviting were she to do anything so patently foolhardy. Rivenoak did, however. The duke was all too aware of what the viscount was capable.

Estridge was ruled by an overweening hatred of the house of Ridgeway, and he was not hampered by principles. The previous Duke of Rivenoak had ruined the viscount's father. He would stop at nothing to do harm to the heirs of the man who had robbed him of his birthright and sent him into exile. It was cold comfort to Rivenoak to discover Estridge was on the point of joining forces with Diana, Lady Inglethorpe, whose loathing of the dukes of Rivenoak was surpassed only by that of the man she had recruited for her unsavory purposes, but he was hardly surprised. It had, perhaps, been inevitable the moment Rivenoak presented Miss Featherstone as his intended bride.

The duke did not have to look far to determine the object of Lady Inglethorpe's malevolence. It would be Pandora, and through her, himself. Equally and chillingly apparent was how she intended to use Estridge to achieve her ends. Lady Inglethorpe herself had all but revealed it the previous night in Lady Desborough's garden.

Their object, at the very least, would be Miss Featherstone's ruination and, at the very worst, her abduction and rape. Hell and the devil confound it! Pandora, in her stubborn determination to pursue her cursed conundrums, would be playing into their hands—unless, of course, he could find a way to direct her interests elsewhere.

A faint smile flickered across Rivenoak's stern lips. Yes, he thought, the germ of an idea having taken root in his fertile imagination. It was perhaps time he took his troublesome confidential inquiry agent further into his confidence. No doubt a red herring would do nicely to distract her.

The duke was not alone in his dissatisfaction with the manner in which things were progressing. Pandora, too, had spent a sleepless night pondering the evening's events, not the least of which was the fact that she had come within a hairsbreadth of confessing everything to Rivenoak, indeed, would have done had it not been for Lady Inglethorpe and the viscount's timely interruption, with the result that she had arisen that morning in something less than her usual good spirits.

The ensuing events of that ill-starred morning were hardly conducive to an improvement either of her temper or her frame of mind. She had, in fact, found herself snapping the nose off Aunt Cora and all because the poor dear, just when Pandora, free of any appointments, had been particularly looking forward to a quiet morning undisturbed by anything more unnerving than an hour or two spent in quiet cogitation, had set the entire household into a flurry of dusting, sweeping, and mopping. It had required a good twenty minutes of earnest entreaty to soothe a tearful Aunt Cora's wounded sensibilities not to mention convince the distraught woman Pandora had no wish to see her dearest friend and companion remove herself permanently from the premises.

Nor had that been all or the worst of it. Hardly had Pandora

seen Aunt Cora once more happily occupied with ridding the
entire house of the smallest speck of dust, than she was met
with the daunting aspect of the normally unrufflable Miss Wortham in what could only have been described as a stew of
anxiety. A few words from the governess had served immediately to initiate a frantic search for a missing Odysseus, who
had been found at last in the tool shed trussed up in imitation
of a French captive of the American Indian Wars as had been
described to the boys by Laughs-In-The-Rain. Pandora would
gladly have wrung Ganymede's neck, not because he was the
gleeful perpetrator of this exceedingly unfortunate incident, but
because, feigning an innocence she should in the norm have
found exceedingly suspect, he had allowed her to imagine for
an unconscionable thirty-five minutes that Odysseus had fallen
the victim of any number of possible dire fates, running the
entire gamut from accidental death by drowning in the neighbor's fountain and goldfish pond to being abducted by the same
villains who had tried unsuccessfully to kidnap her.

A succeeding series of lesser crises on the order of minor
household disasters, ranging from the new cook's insistence
that she must resign at once if she could not be assured she
would no longer have to tolerate the necessity of forever shooing
inquisitive kittens out of the cupboards, off the worktable, and
away from the cooking pots, to Galatea's horrified discovery
that Cassandra, her favorite doll, had apparently been sealed
up in the nursery wall by the paper hangers who had covered
over the child's secret place for hiding her treasures, behind a
loose wallboard.

At last, at her wit's end, not to mention her tolerance, Pandora
had fled to the peaceful confines of her private study, where
no one dared to trespass, there to pace and ponder what she
must do concerning the new conundrum of Lady Inglethorpe
and Viscount Estridge.

It was not long, however, before she found herself preoccupied, not with brilliant thoughts of strategy, but with the conun-

drum of how a single glance from eyes the chill blue of winter
could ignite a warm glow inside her, or how she could know
instantly when a certain tall nobleman had entered a crowded
room simply by the sudden acceleration of her heartbeat or a
tingling along the length of her spine. It was not in the least
fair that the mere scents of shaving soap, clean linen, and
tobacco at close range were enough to scatter her thoughts or
that the fleeting touch of a strong, masculine hand had the
power to render her knees weak.

Obviously, those physical manifestations of the phenomenon
of the instantaneous incitement of powerful primal emotions
between a male and female in an instance of strong natural
physical magnetism were beyond the realm of understanding
of the purely rational mind. Pandora, who had always prided
herself on her ability to resolve any conundrum, had long since
given up trying to explain the effect Rivenoak had on her. It
was enough to know that she loved him, indeed would always
love him, with her whole heart and mind, for as long as she
lived.

The devil of it was she *could* not have him, even if he could
have been brought to return her love, which was ridiculous in
the extreme even to contemplate. Rivenoak might marry her,
indeed, had made every effort to persuade her that such an
eventuality was not so distasteful to him as she would seem to
imagine, but he would do so only out of a misguided sense of
honor and because he was not accustomed to being denied
having his own way. Certainly it was not because he entertained
any sort of affection for her beyond what one must naturally
feel for a confederate in arms, for that was what they must
consider themselves, she thought, two fellows who had joined
forces in the face of a deadly peril. Her brother Herodotus had
told her it was not unusual for soldiers to develop a certain
bond for one another when in circumstances of extreme danger.
And when the danger had passed, no doubt they went their

separate ways, each carrying with him naught but the memory
of that shared moment in time.

All of which was just as it should be, Pandora told herself,
snatching at a potted plant she had nearly upset on its stand in
her furious pacing. The devil, she thought, setting it right again.
If this was what love did to one, she was like to end up like
Miss Peevey, her one and only governess whose sole duties
had been to instruct Pandora in the social niceties in preparation
for Pandora's come out and who, due to having walked in on
Pandora and her papa in the act of dramatizing the bloody
scene of a most bizarre murder involving an axe and a killer
who seemingly had vanished without leaving a single clue
behind, had developed the nervous habit of stumbling into
things, simply because she was forever looking over her
shoulder.

Really, it was too much, Pandora reflected, settling with a
heavy sigh on the edge of the writing table. If she had learned
nothing else from her near confession to Rivenoak, she had
learned that she could not carry on the pretense much longer.
It really was imperative that she find Samuel Butler posthaste
before she made a complete and utter fool of herself.

The realization that that would mean the end of her brief
dream of happiness with the man she loved filled her with a
terrible hollow sensation.

The devil, she thought, out of all patience with herself. The
real conundrum was that, while she did not know how she
could go on seeing Rivenoak without revealing the true nature
of her feelings for him, she could no more wish to have the
charade come to an end than she could wish to stop breathing.

Hardly had that thought crossed her mind than her ruminations were interrupted by a firm rap on the door, which had
the peculiar effect of making her leap to her feet. Furthermore,
she was swept, as she wheeled around, by a sudden giddy
sensation sufficient to cause her to knock over the ceramic
inkwell on her desk.

"Hell and the devil confound it, come *in!*" she blurted, and, snatching up the closest thing at hand, which just happened to be a hand-stitched white linen and lace table scarf that bore the embroidered inscription, "Labor of Love," blotted ineffectually at the spreading puddle of ink over the paper-littered tabletop.

She did not have to look to know, when the door opened, who had entered. She had known it was Rivenoak the moment he announced his presence on the other side of her door.

"Now look what you have made me do," she gasped, feeling herself unaccountably on the verge of tears as she held up the ruined linen scarf. "My Great Aunt Agatha made this on the event of her first affair of the heart. She was thirteen at the time, and the object of her misplaced affections was twelve. I believe her infatuation was brought to a sudden end when she discovered the boy she had sworn to love for all eternity had exposed her to the chicken pox."

"Indeed, and who could blame her," observed his grace with perfect gravity, as he took in the image of Miss Featherstone, less than immaculately attired in a somewhat rumpled morning gown of sprigged muslin, her hair threatening to fall from its pins, and a small smudge of ink marring the purity of her brow where she had impatiently brushed at a wayward curl. She had never looked more adorable—or more desirable, he realized, experiencing a distinct stirring in his loins. "Allow me," he added, drawing forth his linen handkerchief.

"Dear," said Pandora, still staring from the ruined scarf to the inky mess of papers on the desk top, "what the devil shall I do next? It seems I am doomed to make a mull of everything."

Rivenoak, stepping near, gently tilted her head back with a hand beneath her chin and wiped the smudge from her forehead. "My poor Pandora, what has happened to overset you? You have done nothing worse than spill some ink. It is nothing which cannot be put right again, I assure you."

Pandora, suffering a sudden urge to burst into tears, vehemently shook her head. "No, it is a great deal more than that. You know very well it is. And it can never be put right again."

Pulling away from Rivenoak, Pandora began to pace in a fit of distraction.

"The ink, if you must know, is only the tip of the iceberg. I have been plagued with any number of similar mishaps. And it is all your fault, Rivenoak. Indeed, I shall not soon forgive you. If it were not that I am a confidential inquiry agent who prides herself on her integrity, I should tell you that I cannot continue with this ridiculous charade. It is simply too much to ask of a woman with strong primal emotions. If you must know, Rivenoak, I was used to be considered a female of uncommon sense, and now look at me. I am become a stumblebum and-and a watering pot, and I doubt not I shall soon be the sort to take to my bed with the spasms. And all because I was foolish enough to let myself fall in love with you! But then, I really cannot see what choice I had. Logically speaking, I had no control over it, anymore than do the salmon or the poor bull moose who must go without his dinner. It really is the shabbiest thing!" At last, feeling tears of utter frustration well up in her eyes and spill over her cheeks, she realized what a fool she must appear. "The devil!" she gasped, abruptly turning her back on the duke in mortification. "What a ninnyhammer you must think me. I pray you will pay me no mind."

Rivenoak, who had suffered an unexpectedly fierce stab of elation at Pandora's unwitting declaration, had to restrain himself from clasping her roughly in his arms. *Pandora had said she loved him!* Good God, he had almost despaired of ever hearing those words from her lips. Still, he did not fool himself into thinking it had changed anything. There was yet the barrier of her brother Herodotus between them. Furthermore, she was obviously overset and quite possibly had not the slightest notion what she had just said. In a more rational moment, she quite possibly might take it all back again. Rivenoak was all too aware that to rush his fences now might very well serve only to drive her farther from him.

"My dear Pandora," he said and, deliberately, turned her to face him. "You are stubborn and headstrong, and far too prone to independent action for my own peace of mind, but you are hardly a ninnyhammer. I daresay I have never met a woman less prone to behave in a manner that might be construed as other than exceedingly rational. Save, perhaps, in this determination of yours to set up a flirtation with Viscount Estridge."

"I-I beg your pardon?" Pandora convulsively sniffed, wondering if the duke had failed to hear her correctly. Certainly, it would seem to have made little impression on him that she had just declared that she loved him, she thought, hardly knowing whether to be hurt or relieved at his apparent intention to completely overlook it.

"Viscount Estridge, my dear," Rivenoak prodded, handing her his handkerchief and instructing her to blow her nose. "I cannot think your plan to engage his interests one of your finer endeavors in logic."

"But of course it is not," Pandora retorted, blowing into the piece of fine linen with an exuberance that brought a wry hint of a smile to Rivenoak's lips. "It was hardly a well-thought-out idea. I have, since last night, had a great deal of time to reflect on its fallacies." She had, in fact, spent the greater part of the night debating them while fighting a losing battle with her pillows. "Not the least of these would be how it would reflect on you. The last thing I should wish would be to damage your reputation, Rivenoak."

"Perish the thought," agreed Rivenoak with every appearance of gravity. *His* reputation, good God! he thought. He could not recall the last time anyone had given his already dubious reputation the least consideration. His name had long been equated with ruthlessness and an utter indifference to what anyone might think. Rivenoak, it was universally agreed, was an unprincipled rogue, a heartless rakeshame, and a dangerous radical. He was, in short, a law unto himself.

"Exactly so," continued Pandora, dabbing at the end of her nose with the duke's handkerchief. "Besides, I have the children to take into consideration. I cannot think how I should have explained to them why their Auntie Pan was comporting herself in a manner to invite speculation, when in only five short years Iphigenia will be making her come out. She might very well take it in her head to follow in her aunt's footsteps, and who would I be to tell her differently? It is hardly logical to expect children to do as one says and not as one does."

"Oh, entirely illogical," Rivenoak nodded as he gingerly accepted the return of his soiled handkerchief. "I should say with children, it is always better to teach by example."

"I could not agree with you more," Pandora returned, glad that the duke was proving so amenable to her way of thinking. "Which is why I have decided the better course would be to conduct the investigation under the benefit of cover."

Rivenoak, who had been congratulating himself on so easily having achieved the goal of dissuading Pandora from a flirtation with the viscount, was instantly aware that he had just suffered a sudden setback. "I beg your pardon. I fear I am not conversant with all the terminology of a confidential inquiry agent. What, precisely, do you mean by 'under the benefit of cover'?"

"But of course you would not know!" exclaimed Pandora, with an apologetic flutter of the hand. "How thoughtless of me to expect that you would. I sometimes forget that not everyone is trained in the art of criminal investigation. In this case I am talking about a covert undertaking in which one employs the use of a disguise," she patiently explained.

"I see," murmured Rivenoak, who, though he did not perfectly comprehend how Pandora intended to employ a disguise to her benefit, could not but suffer alarm at the dire possibilities. "And what particular disguise did you have in mind?"

"But that is easy, your grace," Pandora did not hesitate to

reply. "I have it from Simmons, my abigail, that Lady Inglethorpe has a deal of difficulty keeping a ladies' maid, no doubt because of her less than felicitous temperament. She is, in fact, interviewing candidates for that recently vacated position this afternoon at three."

"And you, I must suppose, intend to present yourself as one of them," offered the duke with a noticeable lack of enthusiasm. Egad, he thought, recalling with a sense of enlightenment the exceedingly odd assortment of less than attractive hats and wigs that had resided in Pandora's room at Massingale's Town House. Pandora meant to spy on Lady Inglethorpe in the guise of a servant! It did not bear thinking on, and yet he doubted not that, short of tying her hand and foot and confining her to a cellar, that was precisely what she would attempt to do.

"How quickly you catch on, Rivenoak," Pandora applauded, pleased at this new evidence of his ready grasp of things. "But then, I have always known you are a man of powerful intellect."

"I do try my humble best," confessed the duke, contemplating the feasibility of flinging a sack over her head and transporting her immediately to Gretna Green. At least if she were his wife, he would be well within his rights to keep her safely locked up in his dungeon. "I wonder, however, if you have fully considered every aspect of this new plan of yours. I daresay you will be missed if you fail to make an appearance tonight at your various scheduled social engagements."

"Not at all, your grace," said Pandora, surprised that Rivenoak, of all people, could think she had not approached the matter in a wholly logical manner. "I have taken care of everything."

"Of course you have. Anything else, naturally, would be too much to hope for."

"I beg your pardon?" queried Pandora, who had not quite caught the gist of the latter part of his comment.

Rivenoak gave a vague wave of the hand. "Nothing, my dear. Pray continue. You were saying?"

"Yes, well," Pandora answered, wondering if the duke were feeling quite the thing. "I have already sent to Lady Congreve to inform her I am indisposed with a headache and intend to remain at home to rest. I daresay she will not be displeased to have an evening alone with Congreve and the twins, who, if you must know, have been pleading with their mama to take them to Vauxhall Gardens in spite of the fact that they are only seventeen and will not have their come out until next Season."

"How fortunate that Aunt Caroline can never deny the girls anything," observed Rivenoak dryly.

"Yes, but they are nevertheless well-brought-up young ladies. I think I have seldom met two girls with more agreeable manners, and, for all that they are doted upon by their mama and papa, they are not in the least spoiled or high in the instep. No doubt they take after their mama."

"I should not be at all surprised," conceded Rivenoak, who, despite his own affection for the twins and their parents, could not at the moment care less that Pandora approved of their genteel manners. "And what of the matter of references? You did not, I suppose, overlook the fact that Lady Inglethorpe will require a recommendation from your supposed previous employer?"

"I have, as a matter of fact, just left the employ of Lady Fitzsimmons of Killarney, who was inordinately pleased with my services. Unfortunately, I have a terror of sea travel and could not bring myself to accompany her ladyship to Lisbon where she is to join her husband, a foreign diplomat there on a mission for the Crown."

"How unfortunate, indeed," murmured Rivenoak, less than gratified to be presented with a copy of a letter supposedly written by the conveniently inaccessible Lady Fitzsimmons. Pandora, it seemed, had indeed thought of everything, everything save what would happen if Lady Inglethorpe saw through the confidential inquiry agent's disguise to Miss Featherstone, the Duke of Rivenoak's intended bride. "You would seem to be inordinately sure of yourself. Still, I cannot but wonder what makes you think Lady Inglethorpe will hire you over the other candidates.''

"Well, naturally, I cannot be sure, Rivenoak," Pandora replied with a suspicious gleam in her eyes. "Except, perhaps, that I have every reason to believe, due to a notice I have caused to be sent around to the employment agency used by Lady Inglethorpe to the effect that the interviews have been postponed until tomorrow, I shall very likely be the only candidate.''

"Very clever, Miss Featherstone," Rivenoak congratulated her in tones heavily laced with irony. The devil, he thought. Next she would be assuring him there was not a chance her disguise would fail because she had learned Lady Inglethorpe was inordinately short-sighted and out of vanity refused categorically to be fitted with eyeglasses! "Naturally, I must wish you every success in your endeavor. I have only one other question. What, precisely, do you hope to gain from this elaborate scheme? Unless I have overlooked something, I fail to see what Lady Inglethorpe could possibly have to do with the job at hand, which, if my recollection does not fail me, was to discover the identity of the illusive Samuel Butler, not to mention that of the Gentleman of Fashion who cut Massingale's stick for him. I should not like to think you have allowed yourself to become distracted by a conundrum that, while undeniably intriguing, yet cannot but be considered unrelated to our other, more immediate, endeavors.''

Pandora, who did indeed find herself suddenly and greatly distracted, not by an unrelated conundrum, but by the duke's unexpectedly determined advance toward her, backed a step and then another. "But I believe the two are related, Rivenoak," she hastened to reply. "Indeed, I should be greatly surprised if they were not. After all, Lady Inglethorpe was obviously instrumental in engineering her husband's death. And she all but admitted Massingale had become something of a problem to her. I daresay it is not beyond the bounds of reason to suppose she might have been involved in the colonel's murder as well. At the very least, I daresay she might know a great deal about Massingale and his acquaintances, especially if, as she would seem to imply, he was at one time her lover.''

Rivenoak, who had not overlooked those possibilities, who, indeed, had ceased sometime before the cock crowed that morning to hope against hope that they had not occurred to the irrepressible confidential inquiry agent, unerringly maneuvered Pandora so that she came up with her back against the closed door. It was, in fact, something in the order of the red herring he had meant to offer her in the way of a distraction.

"Very astute of you, my dear," he said, reaching down to turn the key in the lock. "I daresay you will be trying next to convince me that it was my Cousin Percival who shot Massingale. And why not? After all, he knew about the secret room, and he would hardly be squeamish about putting a period to one who could only have been considered a dangerous rival for Lady Inglethorpe's affections. Perhaps he was even a party to the plot to lure me to the Town House. If I had fallen a victim to murder, he would now be the Duke of Rivenoak with all that that implies. A compelling motive, would you not agree?''

"*Compelling* is hardly the word for it," Pandora answered, apparently so struck by the possibilities that she failed to note Rivenoak had removed his coat and was presently in the process of undoing the buttons down the front of his waistcoat. "It is not inconceivable to suppose he would have all the pertinent information from Lady Inglethorpe herself," postulated Pandora, her fertile thought processes clicking into motion, "if, indeed, she was the one who planned it all.''

"And how not?" Rivenoak interjected in the way of encouragement as he turned to the task of ridding himself of the constraints of his neckcloth. "She might very well have learned all about my past from the colonel, who possibly was not averse to talking a great deal in bed.''

"And one must not overlook the peculiar circumstances of the three ruffians at the museum," Pandora did not hesitate to bring up, failing, in her preoccupation with the unfolding plot surrounding recent events, to register the plot in steady progress under her very own nose. "I noticed at the time that they bore distinct evidence of being seafaring men—tar-blackened hands, brown, weathered faces. Strange that I did not make the connection sooner. One might even go so far as to speculate that they could be members of that secret society of free traders who abound along our coasts and that Lady Inglethorpe, through her late husband's unsavory connections, might very well have recourse to engage their services. I daresay either Lady Inglethorpe or Percival could have sent the note summoning me to the museum for the purpose of discovering how much I knew about the colonel and his demise. I have always thought it was a trifle too coincidental that Percy just happened along when he did. No doubt he planned to save me himself from the ruffians in order to engage my complete confidence.''

"Only I came along and ruined his grand gesture. Brava, Miss Featherstone," applauded the duke, who, having occupied himself with ridding the wing chair, arranged with a long stool *a la Duchesse,* of a stack of dusty tomes on various subjects ranging from *The Symbolic Significance of Mutilation in Ritualistic Assassination* to *The Phrenological Study of the Skulls of the Criminally Insane,* a well-preserved feather duster, and an untidy heap of graphic illustrations of particularly heinous crimes, among various and sundry other oddities concerned with conundrums of a singularly violent nature, straightened from his labors, a particularly fine example of a steel and beech-wood meat cleaver held gingerly between the thumb and forefinger of one hand. "I believe you may just have put a significant number of the pieces of the puzzle together. Speaking of which," he added, "I cannot but wonder—?"

"Oh, *that!*" exclaimed Pandora, making haste to relieve him of the undeniably intriguing object, which, she could not but realize, he had been scrutinizing with the air of one caught up in profound contemplation. "As it happens, this is the meat cleaver that figured prominently in the significant depletion in the year 1734 of the LaRouche family, who had the misfortune to include among its members a victim of maniacal excitement. My father was exceedingly fortunate to gain its possession at an auction of bizarre and unusual historical artifacts some few years ago."

"Fortunate, indeed," agreed his grace, wondering what other bizarre and unusual historical artifacts Miss Featherstone might have waiting for him to stumble upon stashed about the house. "As to the case in point, however," he added, returning to the more pressing matter upon which he had been occupied some moments earlier, "I should advise you to employ your unique investigative abilities on Cousin Percy without delay. I daresay he would be more inclined to confide in a beautiful young confidential inquiry agent than would Lady Inglethorpe in a newly employed abigail."

"Yes, well, I suppose the idea has merit," doubtfully concurred Pandora, who, perhaps understandably, was more than a little reluctant to give up her elaborately laid plans, not to mention the rare opportunity they afforded to put her not inconsiderable talent for disguise to the touch.

Rivenoak, recognizing the voice of dissension when he heard it, moved quickly to nip rebellion in the bud. "You may be sure of it," he stated firmly, reaching to ease from Pandora's hand the meat cleaver, the flat side of which she had been absently tapping against her chin as she contemplated the pros and cons of his advice. Carefully, he laid the instrument of historical mayhem aside. "Trust me, Pandora," he said, as, slipping an arm about her waist, he drew her to him. "You must know I should never deliberately mislead you."

Pandora, quivering to the touch of his lips against the sensitive flesh below her earlobe, was moved at last to give him her full and undivided attention. Indeed, though she was perfectly aware that this was precisely what she should not be doing, a long, shuddering sigh burst from her lips, seemingly summoned from her very depths, and her head lolled as if of its own accord to one side, allowing the duke greater freedom for his explorations.

"Liar," she breathed, wondering distractedly how her arms had come to be clasped about the back of Rivenoak's neck. "You are guilty of misleading me at this very moment." A small groan sounded deep in her throat as the duke's hand, trailing down her arm to her unprotected side, unerringly paused to cradle her breast in his palm. "And you are doing it deliberately, when, really, Rivenoak," she gasped, "you know that we shouldn't."

Rivenoak, having successfully distracted his sweet Pandora from any thoughts of a dangerous undertaking, covert or otherwise, could only thrill to her instantaneous response to his lovemaking. She was all fire and innocence, his magnificent Pandora, and she had said that she loved him! It came to him suddenly that he had never wanted anything more than he wanted Pandora at that moment.

"You are mistaken, surely," he uttered thickly, bending down to sweep her up in his arms. "We did agree, did we not, that there was yet a great deal left to be discovered concerning the phenomenon of instantaneous arousal between two persons of mutual magnetic attraction. It occurs to me that I have been grossly neglecting my duties as your guide in those particular endeavors."

"What, precisely, did you have in mind, your grace?" queried Pandora, smiling whimsically in spite of herself. "We have, after all, already explored the possibilities of seduction in a public museum, not to mention the sacred environs of a medicine lodge. I daresay, in contrast, the couch in my study must seem rather conventional."

" 'Conventional'?'' Egad, thought Rivenoak, who, recalling the collection of oddities it had been his privilege to remove from the couch alone, could hardly imagine an adjective less suited to describe their present location. "No, how can you say so? This is hardly any study. It is the private domain of a confidential inquiry agent, who has surrounded herself with all the trappings of a life dedicated to the resolution of conundrums." Laying her deliberately on the couch, he leaned purposefully over her, a hand propped on the cushion on either side of her shoulders. "What better place than this to explore the range of possibilities?"

Pandora, who had never had occasion before to view her private sanctum in that particular light and who, furthermore, was become suddenly and acutely aware of the sensual manner in which the strong, masculine column of Rivenoak's neck minus the usual neckcloth emerged from the open V of his shirt, gazed up at the duke with rueful eyes. "You are determined to make me forget my resolution not to allow myself to delve into the conundrum of the unruly nature of my primal emotions, are you not. Really, Rivenoak, it is too bad of you."

"Perhaps now, my little English linnet," Rivenoak smiled in what could only be described as a diabolical manner and lowered his head to sample with his lips the delectable swell of her bosom above the square neck of her bodice, "you will believe me when I tell you I am not the paragon of virtue you would have me."

Pandora quivered in a helpless thrill of unruly primitive passion. "Now you are being absurd, your grace," she protested, mindlessly arching her back as he worked his way down the valley between her breasts, down over her torso and the firm mound of her belly. "I never said you were a paragon of virtue. Only that you are generous and kind and noble and honorable and—! You *devil!*" she gasped as Rivenoak, having pulled the hem of her dress up to her waist, arrived at the nub of her primal sensitivities.

"Softly, my beautiful Pandora," Rivenoak uttered huskily, lifting his head. "There is nothing to fear in what I am doing." Leaving off what he had been doing, he hastily proceeded to divest her of her unmentionables. Equally swiftly, he undid the fastenings at the front of his breeches, releasing his swollen manhood. "We are on the threshold of a whole new plane of investigation into the conundrum of the instantaneous incitement of primal emotions."

Pandora, who did not doubt it, indeed, who had already been given startling evidence of it, yet was troubled by a lingering voice of reason that reminded her how precarious were her already battered defences. Every tenet of logic cried out to her to call a halt to any further investigations into that most dangerous of all conundrums before it was too late, her resolve to remain nothing more than Rivenoak's comrade at arms utterly and irrevocably forgotten.

Faith, it was not in the least fair, she told herself, for the first time truly angry at Herodotus for having left her to be beleaguered with doubts and uncertainties concerning his mysterious stint in the New World. Still, it could not be helped. She simply could not allow matters to progress any farther and hope to maintain her professional objectivity. Indeed, it was quite impossible.

"Rivenoak," she said, steeling herself to be firm, but gentle, in her refusal, "I really cannot help but think we should be making a grave error to-to . . ."

At that moment Rivenoak turned to her, and suddenly even that last, persistent voice of rationale was silenced by the fierce look of tenderness in his eyes.

". . . to overlook Estridge as a possible suspect," she ended feebly and just a trifle breathlessly. "After all, Lady Inglethorpe did let it slip that his fortune may have come not from diamonds, but from furs. And a fortune made from furs, you will agree, would hardly have come from the Orient, but from the New World."

Rivenoak, who at the moment could not have cared less if the viscount's bloody fortune had come from a string of bordellos in Asia Minor, sat on the edge of the couch and leaned over Pandora. "I should never dream . . . of disputing your logic," he said, between planting a string of kisses along the side of her neck, over her cheek, to her eyes, first one and then the other, and down again to the corner of her mouth. "Only your timing. I am afraid I am in no case . . . to engage in a rational discussion . . . of the conundrum of . . . Viscount Estridge's . . . years of exile."

Pandora gave vent to an audible gasp as Rivenoak's nimble fingers, having found and unfastened the small buttons at the back of her dress, proceeded to explore the exquisitely sensitive region of her back clear down to the firm mound of her buttocks. "You may be sure I understand your reluctance, Rivenoak," she uttered in tremulous accents. "Still, I cannot but think it is of some little importance to-to . . ."

Whatever had seemed important was suddenly and quite thoroughly relegated to obscurity as Rivenoak, covering her mouth with his, kissed her with a savage, tender passion that was quite unlike anything she had ever experienced from him before.

Rivenoak needed her, was reaching out to her with the hard, driving passion of a man who had known too much of bitterness and far too much of loneliness. It came to her that nothing, not the most scintillating of conundrums or the most brilliant of resolutions, could compare with the wonder of that simple revelation. With a low groan, Pandora surrendered to the instantaneous arousal of her purely feminine instincts to succor and to heal. To Rivenoak, she would give unreservedly of herself in answer to his overwhelming need. And if it came to her to wish that Rivenoak might in some small measure return her love, she did not hold it against him.

He was Rivenoak, she told herself, and she loved him. It was all that truly mattered.

Rivenoak, sensing her capitulation, marveled at the sweet generosity of his Pandora. He had never known a woman to give so freely of herself, or one who so utterly breached his defences. She had burst into his life like a sudden shaft of sunlight into the frozen heart of darkness, and she had stayed to burn away the chill of memories he could wish forgotten. To be with her was to know what it was to be whole again, his spirit at one with the two disparate worlds that had fostered him and made him what he was. For her, he would have laid down the blood oath against the man who had misled and betrayed the Three-Rivers People to their death. For her, he would have allowed Herodotus Featherstone to live in peace.

All this, he would have done, if only Pandora would ask.

Still, for this moment she was his, he told himself with a fierce joy that was as new to him as was his need to possess and protect her. With Pandora, he need never be alone again. With Pandora, he could know what it was to be once more in harmony with the world.

Spreading wide her thighs, he inserted himself between them. He needed to drive himself into her, if only to banish for a time the phantoms of the past that drove him, and Pandora, his sweet generous Pandora, was already flowing with the nectar of arousal. She was ready for him. Bracing himself on his elbow, he pressed the tip of his shaft against the swollen lips of her body.

Pandora gazed up at him, her eyes grey-blue gems, unshadowed by doubt. With a sense of wonder, he felt her open to him.

"Pandora," he whispered. "Little earth mother." Then, with a groan, he plunged deep into her.

It was to come to Pandora no little time later that making love in her private study was not in the least mundane or conventional. Indeed, not even the mystical heights of that fateful morning spent in the reading room of the British Museum could match the glorious ecstasy that it was given to her to experience that afternoon on her own wing chair with the long stool arranged *a la Duchesse.*

Carried on a delirious wave of rapture, she had seemed to shatter into a thousand quivering pieces at the very moment that Rivenoak, covering her mouth with his, had, with a low cry of triumph, spilled his seed into her.

She had felt wonderful, glorious, as collapsing together on the couch, their energies spent, they had lain side by side, one of Rivenoak's arms flung carelessly across her chest. Even as she had listened to the soft sound of his breathing in sleep, she had been torn by the knowledge that she could not bear a life without him.

It had come to her then that she must find a solution to the seemingly irresolvable conundrum, and the only way she could hope to do that was to discover what Lady Inglethorpe knew about the colonel's past.

Carefully, she slipped out from under Rivenoak's arm and rose from the couch to quietly put herself back to rights again. At last, reluctant to leave, she stood for a long moment gazing down at Rivenoak's dear beloved face.

How young he looked, the hard lines about his eyes and mouth banished in sleep! Would that she could erase them forever from his face, she thought. Bending over him, she placed a feather-light kiss to the corner of his mouth; then, straightening, she let herself silently out of the room.

Consequently, she did not see Rivenoak's eyes instantly open or his stern lips thin to a grim line at the faint sound of the door closing behind her.

Chapter 12

It was doubtful that anyone observing the plainly dressed female leave the house at Number 3 South Audley Street by means of the service entrance would have paid any undue attention to her. She appeared to be of no more than an average height, her figure rather unremarkable beneath a nondescript grey serge gown. Her hair, mousy brown beneath a plain bonnet, was severely drawn back into a knot at the nape of her neck, and a pair of rimless spectacles sat squarely on the bridge of her nose, which gave the distinct impression of pinched nostrils. Her features, while not precisely homely, could hardly have been described as comely either, due principally to the peculiarity of her mouth to pucker in a most distracting manner over rather large, protruding front teeth. Still, she was neat, even prim, in her personal appearance as befitted an obvious woman of the serving class.

Climbing into the hackney coach, which had apparently been summoned for her use, she settled back against the plain squabs and stared straight ahead as the hired conveyance pulled away from the curb. At last satisfied that no one, not even Miss Wortham and the children who were just returning from an outing to the neighborhood park, had recognized beneath the guise of a servant Miss Featherstone, the children's aunt and the Duke of Rivenoak's promised bride, Pandora relaxed ever so slightly.

Pandora could only hope that, if Lady Inglethorpe did see fit to take her on, the countess would not require her new abigail to do anything too elaborate. Pandora doubted not that she was well able to prepare a bath, lay out her ladyship's clothes, even dress her. She might even manage to do a creditable job of combing out the lady's tresses, which, cut in the newest fashion of short curls clustering about the head, should not offer too great a challenge to Pandora's limited talents for hairdressing. Were she to order her new abigail to employ a curling iron, mend a rip, or press a gown, however, the results were likely to be rather less than satisfactory, Pandora reflected with a wry smile. Fortunately, it would be only for one night; and, after all, it was a deal safer than her original plan involving Viscount Estridge.

Pandora could not but feel a measure of relief at her decision not to engage the interests of the viscount. She had never fooled herself into believing he was anything but an exceedingly dangerous man. Which was why she was determined to learn a deal more about him. If it was true Rivenoak's grandfather had ruined Estridge's father, then there was every reason to suppose the viscount entertained anything but charitable feelings toward his grace. Indeed, it was not inconceivable that Estridge would do anything in his power to harm the duke. One of the most obvious avenues for him to achieve such an end was to make it appear, at least, that he had turned the duke's intended bride against her betrothed, and Pandora was hardly so naive as to suppose, to do just that, he would scruple to resort to forceful means of persuasion with a female.

At least as Lady Inglethorpe's exceedingly temporary abigail, she would be in a position to do some nosing about for anything that might link the countess to the colonel's death, or to any of the other pieces of the puzzle. And then, of course, there was the possibility, no matter how remote, that she might be able to eavesdrop on Lady Inglethorpe and Viscount Estridge at their tête-á-tête that evening. Pandora would have given a great deal to be a fly on the wall during that no doubt informative discourse. Failing that, however, there was still the chance she might learn something from the other members of the household staff. There was always a deal of gossip belowstairs concerning those who inhabited the upper floors.

Inexplicably, that thought led her to wonder what her own household staff must make of the duke's rather lengthy stay in their mistress's private study. Poor, dear Rivenoak. He would be terribly angry with her when he awakened to discover she had slipped out of the house while he slept. She doubted not he would deliver her an exceedingly stern curtain lecture when he saw her next.

The arrival of the hackney at Number 15 Portman Square interrupted any further ruminations on that particular subject. Pandora, steeling herself for the coming interview with her prospective new employer, stepped down from the carriage and, handing the driver a coin, walked primly to the front door.

Never having had recourse to interview for a position, Pandora was not precisely sure what she expected upon being admitted by the butler. Certainly, it was not to have Lady Inglethorpe, attired in a flowing negligee of lemon-colored silk, descend on her in a flurry of impatience.

"You are late," announced her ladyship without preamble. "I distinctly remember stipulating to the agency that I should have a replacement for ladies' maid here no later than half past two. But at least you are here. I suppose I must be grateful that you showed up at all. Bolton," she added, for the benefit of the butler who was standing at starched attention, "I am indisposed to callers for the rest of the afternoon. There will be no exceptions, is that understood?''

"No exceptions," repeated Bolton, bending stiffly at the waist. "As you wish, m'lady."

Lady Inglethorpe, who had already turned to ascend the staircase, paused suddenly to look impatiently over her shoulder at Pandora. "Well?" she queried imperatively. "What are you waiting for? I haven't all day. I am plagued by a splitting headache, and I have a guest coming for dinner. I cannot be expected to entertain if I haven't all my wits about me. You do know how to minister to a headache, one must hope."

"Indeed, m'lady," Pandora replied, moving at once to follow in Lady Inglethorpe's wake. "Lady Fitzsimmons, my previous mistress, was wont to say I had a fair gift for it. No doubt you'll be wantin' to see the letter she wrote in the way of a reference."

"No, no. I cannot be bothered now. I'm sure you come with the highest recommendations. Your kind always do. A pity none of you ever live up to your reputations."

Having made that pronouncement on the reliability of abigails in general, Lady Inglethorpe swept through a doorway into what proved to be a luxurious suite of rooms done frivolously in chantilly laces of blond silk and Genoa velvet of rose against an ivory background.

"Pray remove your hat and gloves, Miss—Miss—? What the devil is your name? You do have one, one must presume."

"'Tis Potts, m'lady," supplied Pandora, dipping a curtsey. "Miss Prunella Potts."

"Good heavens, is it indeed?" declared Lady Inglethorpe, raising gold-handled scissors eyeglasses to better scrutinize the unfortunate bearer of the name of Potts and, most particularly, in conjunction with Prunella. The hint of a frown etched itself in the purity of the countess's brow. "Strange," she murmured, "there is something—"

"I beg your pardon, m'lady?" queried Pandora, tinglingly

aware she was at the moment of truth, that, indeed, the countess
had recognized something familiar in her new abigail that she
could not quite place. Having laid aside her hat and gloves,
Pandora returned to respectful attention. "Is there something
amiss?"

Frowning, Lady Inglethorpe shook her head. "No, no, it is
nothing. Just for a moment you seemed to remind me of . . .
But that is ridiculous. Why are you just standing there?" Dropping the scissors eyeglasses on the dressing table, the countess
flounced to a roll arm couch in the Egyptian style, with crocodile feet, and flung herself facedown on it. "I am in the most
dreadful torment, and you do nothing but bother me with
silly . . ."

Whatever she had been about to say was lost in the shuddering
release of a long sigh, as Pandora, leaning over the countess,
began to rub the tips of her fingers with telling effect over her
ladyship's temples.

"That's the thing, m'lady," Pandora crooned, applying the
pads of her thumbs in a circular motion to the back of the
countess's neck below the skull. "Just you lie still and relax.
Prunella Potts will have you feeling right as a trivet in no
time."

"If you do, you will have done what no one else has ever
been able to accomplish," murmured the countess in thickening
accents. Then, "Mmm, you do seem to have a way with your
hands."

"You're all tied up in knots, m'lady," replied Pandora,
kneading the taut muscles down the countess's back with such
effect as to produce a low moan from the object of her manipulations. " 'Tis easy to see you've a great deal that's troublin' on
your mind. In my experience, when a beautiful lady like yourself
is all twisty inside, 'tis usually because of a gentleman."

"You have no idea," groaned the countess, sinking deeper
into the couch. "Only the gentleman is no gentleman. He's a
snake."

"What man isn't," said Pandora sagely, pressing one thumb at a point to one side of the countess's vertebra below the base of her skull and the other at a second point in the soft flesh of one buttock. "Breathe slow, m'lady. Let everything go lax."

The countess, who could hardly have gone any limper than she already was, exhaled a low moaning breath.

A satisfied grin played about Pandora's lips as, some few minutes later, she was rewarded with the distinct susurrus of a feminine snore issuing from the prone Lady Inglethorpe. It was the Oriental pressure points. Her papa had taught her all about them. They offered a nearly infallible relief for pains brought on by tension and, in this case, Pandora did not doubt, a guilty conscience.

"That's it, m'lady," Pandora whispered, carefully withdrawing from the sleeping countess. "You rest for a while now, while I have a little look around."

A hurried search through the dressing table, two bureaus, and three clothespresses revealed nothing of interest beyond a small, deadly looking pistol with pearl handles, a wardrobe that must have put a dent in even the countess's sizeable purse, and an apparent fetish for shoes, of which she must have possessed upwards of fifty or sixty pairs of every possible style and color. Still, Pandora told herself, standing back to carefully assess her next move, there should have been some sort of a safe for the lady's much vaunted jewels.

A search of the wall paintings and a thorough exploration of the floor coverings proved disappointingly unrevealing. Indeed, Pandora, despite her considerable talent for resolving the irresolvable, was on the point of acknowledging failure, when her eyes came to rest on what presumably was a bust of the late Earl of Inglethorpe set on a marble dais.

Curious, mused Pandora, who could not be mistaken in thinking the countess could hardly have entertained an overly great affection for the man she had very probably caused to be cut down in a duel. It was, in fact, highly illogical to suppose Lady

Inglethorpe would choose to honor her dead husband in her bedroom with a bust that hardly suited the otherwise feminine decor.

A closer inspection of the unlikely *objet d'art* revealed an almost imperceptible anomaly in the texture of the marble at the top of the dais. As if compelled, Pandora leaned her palm against what could only be described as a faint depression in the molding.

Coincidentally with the anomaly giving way a fraction of an inch beneath her hand, the earl's head gave a fair imitation of an instantaneous decapitation. Swinging backward on cleverly wrought springs, it revealed beneath its former resting place a compartment in which resided a jewelry box and a slender leather-bound volume, which had the distinction of bearing the initials "T. W. M." imprinted on the cover.

"Thornton William Massingale," breathed Pandora, her heart leaping beneath her breast. "It must be." Eagerly, she reached for the book, only to freeze at the sudden stir of movement behind her, followed almost immediately by what sounded ominously like the interruption of peaceful snoring by an audible snort.

All in an instant, Pandora settled the earl's dissevered head back in place and, whirling about, made her way back to the countess.

"Mmm," murmured Lady Inglethorpe, coming awake to soothing fingers kneading the back of her neck. Licking dry lips, she swallowed. "Faith, have I actually slept? Pray, what time is it?"

"Nearly four o'clock, m'lady," Pandora replied, consulting the clock on the mantel. "I hope you're feelin' some better. Lady Fitzsimmons was used to say Prunella Potts worked miracles when m'lady suffered a spell of the megrims."

"I could not care less what Lady Fitzsimmons was used to say," the countess said, waving Pandora away. "Enough, girl.

I shall only just have time to prepare myself for the viscount's arrival.''

"But your headache, m'lady?''

"Is gone, if that is of any satisfaction to you. Now, pray stop gawking and ring for my bath to be sent up.''

The ensuing four hours were to prove an education to Pandora in the feminine art of toiletry on a grand scale. While m'lady soaked in her cucumber bath, Pandora was kept busy filing the countess's fingernails and plucking her eyebrows to a delicate arch, tasks which she managed to carry out without giving herself away. The business of mixing a mask for m'lady's face, on the other hand, called on all her considerable ingenuity. Fortunately, she was not entirely unfamiliar with almond paste, which the countess already had in goodly supply. Adding a dash of lemon verbena and crushed violets for a pleasing scent was a masterstroke of genius, she decided as she spread the mask on Lady Inglethorpe's face.

No doubt Pandora would have taken the opportunity to retrieve the colonel's book while the countess was rendered oblivious with a cucumber slice over each eye had she not to contend with a constant stream of maids fetching cans of hot water from the kitchens in order to maintain m'lady's bath at a constant, steaming temperature.

Indeed, between laying out the countess's evening dress, a violet sarcenet robe over a shimmering petticoat of dark purple shot through with silver, locating the matching French heels with the diamond buckles, hurrying to wash the countess's hair and remove the facial mask, then helping her ladyship from her bath, wrapping her in towels warmed before the fire, and seating her before the dressing table to make a clumsy attempt at rolling the red tresses in curling papers, Pandora was kept far too busy to allow for so much as a surreptitious look at what she greatly suspected was Colonel Massingale's private journal.

Nor was that all to test Pandora's patience. Lady Inglethorpe, besides being a spoiled beauty with never a thought for anyone but herself, was fond of talking about her past lovers in the context of what fools they had made of themselves over her, from which Pandora was able to deduce that a Mr. Whitfell, of the Sussex Whitfells, had once sent a fortune down the River Tick purchasing jewels and other folderols for the imperious beauty, not the least of which were a matched set of greys and a phaeton to go with them, before she had grown bored with being constantly compared to a "goddess of Immortal Love and Beauty" and severed the relationship. And then there was poor Lord Sommersby, who had gone into a sharp decline upon having "his hopes blighted." Lady Inglethorpe, it seemed, had been pleased to lead the poor youth on so long as he was heir to his grandmother's fortune. Naturally, however, she had had to put an end to the infatuation when she learned the elderly lady had disinherited her grandson for dallying after a Woman of Questionable Virtue. But that, Lady Inglethorpe could not resist prattling on, was nothing compared to the greatest fool of them all—the Duke of Rivenoak, who, before he had ascended to his lofty title and position, had been the callowest of youths. He had, in fact, been utterly deficient of Town Bronze and demonstrated a deplorable lack of backbone. The old duke, she did not doubt, had told his grandson when to piss in the pot.

At that pronouncement, Pandora, in the act of combing out the lady's tresses, gave a sudden jerk on the comb sufficient to bring a yelp of pain from the countess.

"I beg your pardon, m'lady," Pandora hastened to apologize in apparent heartfelt contrition. "'Twas a snarl I wasn't expectin'."

"You fool. See that it does not happen again."

"You may be sure of it, m'lady. I was just that caught up

in listenin' to you. The old duke was a hard man, was he. But the grandson lost his heart to you. Belike there was trouble betwixt the two of 'em over it.''

"Hard," Lady Inglethorpe had gone on to say, led by her vituperative loathing of anything Rivenoak back into her previous train of thought, had not begun to describe the former duke. He was a wicked, mean-spirited, ill-tempered old goat, who, she knew for a fact, had once caused his grandson to be starved and beaten to within an inch of his life and all because the heir to the dukedom had refused to eat with a fork. But at least the old duke had been a man in his day, indeed had been reputed to service a number of mistresses, with the rumor of numerous by-blows. It was unfortunate the heir, while obviously enamored of m'lady's attributes, had proven something less than an ideal lover. He had, in fact, been a very great disappointment. Since Lady Inglethorpe had never encountered that difficulty before or since, she could, indeed, only speculate that perhaps his grace was of the sort to prefer men or even young boys.

The devil he did, thought Pandora, applying the comb with greater and greater vigor. She doubted Diana, Lady Inglethorpe, far from luring his grace to her bed, had ever been so fortunate as to have Rivenoak favor her with more than a glance in passing. As for her assessment of Rivenoak's sexual preferences, it was obviously the venom of a woman scorned. A man like Rivenoak would hardly be attracted to a female who was as crass in her thinking as she was vulgar in her pursuits. Pandora, hard put not to voice her thoughts aloud, fairly ripped the comb through the countess's tresses.

"*Oh!* You bungling idiot!" shrieked Lady Inglethorpe, clasping a hand to her smarting scalp. "What in the deuce do you think you are doing? Grooming a horse? Give me that comb before you do any more damage. It is little wonder that your precious Lady Fitzsimmons let you go. I daresay the unfortunate woman must resemble a plucked chicken.''

"I beg your pardon, m'lady," Pandora replied, only too glad

to relinquish the comb to Lady Inglethorpe. "I don't know what's wrong with me this evening. I fear 'tis my rheumatism actin' up again. I bain't used to the damp chill of London."

"Yes, well, we shall discuss your rheumatism in the morning. You may be sure of it. In the meantime you may set about tidying up this mess. The viscount will be here any minute. We shall be dining in my sitting room, and I expect you to be finished and gone from here before I go below to greet him."

"As you wish, m'lady," said Pandora, her heart sinking at this new complication. She did not see how she was to retrieve the colonel's book, not to mention escape the premises undetected, if the countess meant to entertain the viscount in the adjoining room. Really, it was too bad of her.

Unless, of course, Pandora could contrive to leave the bedroom window unlatched. If she recalled her initial impression of the house correctly, there was a ledge running just beneath the windows along the entire front of the house. How difficult could it be to slip into the room next to this one and make her way over the ledge to the bedroom and then back again? No doubt it would be a deal simpler than contriving a facial mask or pretending a knowledge of the application of Spanish papers to the cheeks in such a manner as to leave the impression the lady's complexion was naturally rosy, Pandora reflected, recalling this night's efforts, her first ever, with makeup.

In the midst of busying herself with gathering up and putting away her ladyship's dressing gown, slippers, and discarded negligee, mopping up the floor with the countess's used towels in the wake of the maids' efforts to empty the tub, and putting the dressing table back into order, Pandora took occasion to approach the window.

"What are you doing there, Potts?" demanded the countess, pausing in the act of examining her elegantly clad figure in the oval looking glass. "You haven't time for woolgathering."

"No, m'lady." Coughing to cover the small click of the latch, Pandora made a show of straightening the drapes. " 'Tis a lovely evening, though," she said, turning back to the countess. "Will there be anything else, m'lady?" she queried.

"You may fetch me my folding fan."

"Yes, m'lady."

Pandora, slipping the loop of the folding fan over Lady Inglethorpe's slender wrist, stood back to view the countess admiringly. "You look a vision of loveliness, m'lady. I expect the viscount will be fair taken with you."

"Pray do not be absurd, Potts," declared Lady Inglethorpe, giving her hair a final pat. "Of course he will. I hardly need you to tell me the obvious. You may go now. Have Mrs. Walters show you to your quarters. I shall not be needing your services again tonight."

"Very good, m'lady," said Pandora, dipping a curtsey. "And may your evenin' be everything you so richly deserve it to be," she added, a comment that caused her ladyship's gaze to narrow sharply with suspicion and Pandora to make a hasty departure.

Once in the hall, Pandora stood aside in order to allow three footmen bearing trays laden with victuals to enter the countess's suite. As soon as she was alone, she made directly for the next room in line.

Hardly had she reached for the door handle than the knocker sounded below, announcing the arrival of the countess's anticipated guest. Her heart accelerating, Pandora turned the handle.

Locked! The devil, she thought, and turned her back to the door. Desperately, she sought another avenue of escape.

Too late, she realized, at the audible click of a door latch. The countess was coming!

Without warning, the door gave way behind her. A strong hand clamped over her mouth and dragged her backwards into the previously locked room. Swiftly, but silently, the door was pushed to before her startled eyes, and the next instant the hand over her mouth was withdrawn to be replaced by ruthless lips, which would have served utterly to silence her screams, had she been tempted to give vent to any, which she most decidedly was not.

"Rivenoak!" she gasped when no little time later her assailant finally saw fit to release her. "Devil! I might have known you were in here."

"And how not?" grinned the duke, his teeth flashing in the light of a single flickering candle. "You did not really think I should allow you to conduct your investigations without me? By the way, I must congratulate you on your disguise. For the barest instant, as I kissed you, I was overcome with the unnerving suspicion I had got the wrong female."

"The teeth!" exclaimed Pandora in instant comprehension and reached up to extract the theatrical set of dentures that had been the key element of her transformation. "I had quite forgot them in all the excitement. It's a wonder you did not dislodge them in your ardor, your grace. I should hate to think of the shock that might have caused you."

"No more than the shock of coming awake in your study to discover you had gone on your cursed undercover mission without me," affirmed the duke with a noticeable lack of humor. "The devil, Pandora, did you not once stop to consider what would have happened to you if the countess had seen through your disguise?"

"I was fully prepared to deal with just such a circumstance had it arrived," Pandora was quick to assure him. "I am far too logical minded ever to undertake a plan of action without having prepared for every possible contingency; surely you must know that by now, Rivenoak."

"I know you did not bring your pocket pistol with you," countered the duke, wondering what his impossible confidential inquiry agent had planned to use in its stead. "I found it on your desk where you left it."

"But of course you did," Pandora agreed with perfect equanimity. "Why else should I have put it there? I hardly needed a weapon, your grace, when I knew you would be near to protect me.''

''The devil you did,'' growled his grace, snatching Pandora close with every apparent intention of crushing the breath from her small frame.

''But I assure you I did,'' Pandora asserted, not in the least daunted at such a dire prospect. ''It would have been illogical to suppose that, having been made privy to my plan, you would not have come after me.''

Rivenoak, who could dispute neither her flawless exercise in logic nor the conclusion to which it had led her, was hard put not to throttle her for the agonizing five hours he had been made to suffer waiting with his ear to the door for the first sign her disguise had been penetrated. And that did not even take into account the trouble to which he had been put to gain entry to the house by means of scaling the neighbor's trellis to the roof and undertaking to make the perilous leap of no less than four feet across to that of Lady Inglethorpe's, which had given him access through the dormer window to the attic. It was mere chance that, having stolen, undetected, down to the third story, he was in time to overhear Lady Inglethorpe extolling the dubious virtues of abigails in general and, in need of a hiding place, had slipped into the first empty room, which had proven to be no less than the master bedroom, conveniently adjoining that of the countess. But then, he reasoned philosophically, the pure exercise of logical deduction was a science in abstracts and, as such, was clearly above such mundane concerns as the specifics of achieving the already determined logical conclusion. That he was here was all that really mattered.

''And now that I have satisfied the dictates of logic,'' he said, ''I trust you intend to tell me what you have managed to discover. I believe I have earned at least that much, my dearest Pandora.''

''But of course you have, Rivenoak. How could you doubt it. As it happens, I have discovered a book with the initials 'T.

W. M.' inscribed on the cover. I haven't the least doubt that it belonged to Massingale and that it contains information of no little value, at least to Lady Inglethorpe, who keeps it in a secret compartment in a bust of her dear departed husband. Unfortunately, I was unable to get a look inside it before Lady Inglethorpe was so disobliging as to wake up from her nap. Nor was I given the opportunity later to retrieve it. I am afraid, Rivenoak, that the secrets it contains are still safely tucked away in Inglethorpe's bust.''

"How very disobliging of the earl," observed Rivenoak, who, having come to a fair understanding of the conundrum presented by Pandora, could not but visualize any number of harrowing resolutions to which she might already have committed herself.

"Yes, is it not," agreed Pandora, pressing her ear to the door in anticipation of the countess's return in the company of the viscount. "Although one can hardly blame poor Inglethorpe. I daresay he would not care in the least for the idea of being made the repository for the secrets of his widow's former lover." Pandora crossed to the window and, releasing the latch, pushed it open. "The footmen have exited the countess's suite. I might have just enough time to retrieve the book, if I hurry."

Rivenoak stopped her with a hand on her wrist. "Not that way, however," he said in grim appreciation of the extremes to which a confidential inquiry agent was willing to go to achieve her ends. "I suggest the door connecting the master suite with her ladyship's. This way."

It was little wonder that Pandora had failed to detect the door between the adjoining suites. Cleverly camouflaged as part of the oak wainscoting, it was almost invisible to the naked eye. The hinges, it seemed, were from lack of use also in need of an oiling.

A loud creak accompanying the opening of the door caused her hair to stand up on the nape of her neck.

"The devil," muttered Rivenoak, admitting Pandora into the

countess's bedroom and then stepping in after her. "I suggest you make haste, my girl. I have little liking for the thought of a tête-á-tête with our unwitting hosts."

Pandora, who could not have agreed more with the duke, went directly to the earl's bust and released the lock. Snatching the book from the secret compartment, she shoved the earl's head back in place and turned, preparatory to making her escape.

The duke's low hiss, followed almost immediately by the distinctive trill of Lady Inglethorpe's laughter, lent wings to her feet. Still, she had hardly slipped into the late earl's bed chamber, the duke hard on her heels, than the countess and her gentleman guest entered the sitting room—and were greeted by the telltale creak of the closing door.

"What was that!" shrilled the countess, then, with utter conviction, "The master suite door! Good heavens, my jewels! Summon the servants. Someone is in the house!"

Instantly aware that to try to escape into the hall would only mean certain discovery, Pandora and Rivenoak froze for the barest instant in the middle of the floor. It took even less time to realize it would be utterly fruitless to attempt to conceal themselves in the clothespress or under the bed, where someone was sure to look for them.

Pandora and Rivenoak exchanged a pointed glance, then, as if of a single accord, sprang for the window.

"There was someone here, I tell you," declared Lady Inglethorpe to Viscount Estridge as they reentered the sitting room at half past eight. Little caring that she was observed, the countess crossed directly to the bust of her late husband and sprang the lock.

"A clever device," commented the viscount, plopping into his mouth a plump grape from a tray filled with fruit presumably intended as refreshment to accompany the evening's entertainment. "It would appear that the burglar, whoever he was, was unsuccessful. Your jewels would seem to be intact."

"Don't be a fool. The burglar was not a 'he,' and she was not after my jewels. The sly little mouse got what she came after." Slamming the head of her late husband down over the secret compartment, the countess uttered a blistering oath. "I thought there was something queer about her. Whoever heard of anyone with a name like Prunella Potts."

" 'Prunella Potts,' egad," said the viscount, elevating an incredulous eyebrow. "And who, my dear countess, is Prunella Potts?"

"My new abigail, or so she pretended to be, though I should have known instantly she was an impostor. She was inordinately inept at her duties. Faith, she came near to plucking me bald. I should give a great deal to know who the devil she was."

"Yes, I daresay you would, if she had the temerity to yank the hair from your head. Odd behavior for a ladies' maid."

"You may be certain she was never a ladies' maid. Indeed, I should doubt she was ever employed as a servant. There was something about the wretch that put me in mind of someone, though I cannot think it could be anyone of any importance. She was most distractingly unattractive. I daresay I should have remembered her if I had ever seen her before."

"Perhaps her identity may be determined by the object of her thievery," speculated the viscount, helping himself to a glass of champagne, which his hostess had been thoughtful enough to have set out along with a cold collation of potted lobster, soused oysters, French barley cream, cucumber slices, buttered oranges, and saffron bread, not to mention various tangy cheeses. "What, precisely, did she take?"

"What did she take?" echoed the countess, who had been preoccupied with following a similar line of reasoning. "Nothing, actually, that really matters. A journal, as it happens, which has already served its purpose."

"Well, then," shrugged the viscount, pouring a second glass

of champagne and carrying it to his distraught hostess, ''I fail
to see why the incident should be allowed to interfere with our
evening, do you? No doubt the culprit is long gone. In which
case, there would seem to be little you can do about her at the
moment—unless, of course, you intend to call in the Bow Street
Runners?''

''The Bow Street Runners?'' exclaimed Lady Inglethorpe in
tones of what might have been construed as alarm. ''No, of
course not. I see no reason to involve them in what, after all,
is a purely domestic matter. I daresay tomorrow is soon enough
to decide what to do about this unfortunate incident. Come,
my lord, let us dine. As you said, the girl is undoubtedly far
away from here by now.''

The ''girl,'' who was at the moment a deal closer than either
the viscount or the countess could ever have imagined, could
only be grateful for Rivenoak's reassuring presence as, grimly
quelling the almost irresistible urge to sneeze, she fervently
wished Lady Inglethorpe and her companion to the devil. Even
clasped breathlessly in Rivenoak's arms, her lips only a tantalizing two or three inches from his, she was not in the least
enamored with the thought of having to remain in her present
position for any great length of time, especially should the
evening's entertainment turn to activities of a more intimate
nature. Being forced to lie silent and listening while Estridge
and Lady Inglethorpe sported in the bed underneath which she
and Rivenoak had sought refuge would hardly be conducive
to comfort. But then, neither was the memory of inching over
the narrow third-story ledge from the former earl's master suite
to the countess's window. It was, in fact, an adventure that
promised to occasion her second thoughts if she ever again
entertained the notion of engaging in burglary.

Still, she consoled herself, painfully aware of the slender
volume digging into her breast beneath her bodice where she

had lodged it for safekeeping, it would have been worth all the trouble if she and Rivenoak managed to escape their present predicament with whole skins and if the book did indeed prove to contain pertinent information concerning the conundrum of Samuel Butler's true identity. In spite of Lady Inglethorpe's claim that the book had already served its purpose, Pandora's every feminine instinct told her its loss had been no little unsettling to the countess.

Rivenoak, faced with the conundrum of how to extract Pandora and himself from their present predicament without an exceedingly unpleasant confrontation with the two people who would derive the greatest enjoyment from such a scandal as that must be, was far less convinced that the colonel's alleged volume was worth the difficulties he envisioned before him. He was damned if he would endure another such moment as he had lived with Pandora beside him on that cursed ledge. Never had he known such fear as he had felt then for his dauntless Pandora. Thinking at each perilous step to see her plunge to her death had been torment enough to last him a bloody lifetime.

He would take her over the viscount's dead body and straight down the stairs and out of the house if he had to, but he preferred something rather less dramatic. Something in the way of a diversion perhaps, he thought, keenly aware, even in the absurdity of their present circumstances, of Pandora's body pressed to his, indeed of the fresh scent of her hair, tickling his chin.

The devil, he thought, a slow anger igniting somewhere in the pit of his stomach. The bloody charade had gone on long enough. It was time Pandora was brought to realize that he would have her as his wife and, furthermore, that he would no longer tolerate her stubborn insistence on flinging herself into danger. Certainly, he did not intend to spend another minute cringing ignominiously beneath Lady Inglethorpe's bed.

It was then, as the indistinct sound of voices issuing from the adjoining room impinged on his consciousness, that an idea took root in his mind. If he could make his way back along the ledge to the master suite and through there into the hall, he doubted not he would have little difficulty finding his way outside. Then he would make so bold as to call on Lady Inglethorpe. He would in fact demand to see her on the pretext that he had irrefutable evidence of her culpability in Pandora's attempted abduction. That should draw the couple in the other room downstairs long enough for Pandora to make good her own escape.

No doubt he owed it to Pandora's influence that he found himself even considering something that could only be described as impudent at best and brash at its worst. But then, if anyone had told him only a few hours earlier that he would be hiding under the bed of a woman who had vowed to destroy him, he would have thought that person clearly mad. It was, indisputably, a long shot, but, short of remaining the night in the company of Lady Inglethorpe and her newest conquest, he could see no other viable option before him.

"I believe, Pandora, love," he whispered, pressing a kiss to her forehead, "it is time we were bidding our hosts *adieu*. I am grown damnably weary of their hospitality. If I am to lie with you in my arms, I should vastly prefer it to be *in* the bed rather than under it."

"I could not agree with you more, your grace," Pandora whispered back with a rueful grin. "How do you propose to effect our departure?"

"Through the door, my sweet," replied his grace with a glint in his eye. "Like the civilized people we are."

Pandora, listening to Rivenoak detail his plan, did not think it at all impudent or brash, but brilliantly daring, rather. Indeed, her only objection was to the method of its implementation. While it was all very well for Rivenoak to insist on being the one to brave the ledge for a second time, she could not but think it was unfair that he should take the risk. After all, she was the one who had got them into the fix they were in. Rivenoak, however, proved uncommonly obdurate in his refusal to countenance the mere thought of Pandora on the ledge, even going so far as to vow he would openly confront the countess and the viscount if Pandora did not swear to follow his instructions to the letter.

Obviously, Pandora reflected some few moments later as she slid out from under the bed and, stealing across the room, slipped behind the door to the sitting room, it had been of little use to propose that they both escape to the adjoining room by means of the ledge, which, logically speaking, would have been the simplest means of achieving their end. She did not doubt Rivenoak would have done precisely as he had threatened, and that she could not allow. Apart from the scandal, it would have meant exile or death for the duke.

Still, she thought, as she peered through the crack between the door and the jamb at Lady Inglethorpe seated on the viscount's lap, there were certain compensations for being left to wait for Rivenoak's signal.

"But I told you I want nothing in return," drifted distinctly to Pandora's ears. "You cannot know how long I have waited for the opportunity to see his grace pay for his arrogance. And you, I daresay, have more reason than I to wish to see him humiliated and ruined. He holds Claverly, and what is Viscount Estridge without his hereditary estate?"

"A man who has already taken steps to have it back again." Pandora, watching, felt her blood go chill as the viscount's hand pointedly slid around the lady's throat. The countess paled, her sudden fear an almost tangible thing in the room. "I suggest you do not take too much for granted, Countess. I take little pleasure in being reminded of my father's humiliation. He was a man of honor who took his own life to atone for his loss of Claverly. I, on the other hand," he murmured, allowing his hand to slip down over the countess's bared shoulder and along her arm in a manner that was intimately suggestive, "am not burdened with any archaic sense of a gentleman's code. I shall have Claverly back, along with the satisfaction of seeing the cursed line of the man who usurped it brought to ruin. The fact that a Ridgeway will be the unwitting instrument of that destruction will only make it all the sweeter."

"A Ridgeway, good God," breathed the countess, a false ring to her trill of laughter. "You cannot mean Percival. You are mad."

"Am I? But then, you naturally are unaware that your dear Percival has hit a losing streak. He has, in fact, incurred a considerable gambling debt. As it happens, his promissory notes have only just recently fallen into my possession."

"And, naturally, you intend to collect," said Lady Inglethorpe, with an effort recovering her poise. "One can only wonder what you intend to exact in the way of payment. It could not be that you have Claverly in mind, now could it?"

"You are quick, Lady Inglethorpe," the viscount applauded. "Cleverly is, in fact, the only payment that I shall find acceptable. And only the Duke of Rivenoak can deed it over to me. It is, you will admit, a finely spun web. Your friend Percival must make remuneration, or his reputation as a gambler and a gentleman is finished. I shall see to that, and then what would he do with himself? Poor Percival. Somehow I cannot see him retiring to the country."

"Even so, you cannot think Percival would kill his cousin to pay off a gambling debt? No, it is impossible. Percival may be a fribble and a ne'er-do-well, but you are mistaken if you think he would ever turn his hand against Rivenoak. He hasn't the stomach for it."

"With the title of duke at stake, and the considerable fortune that goes with it? You surprise me, Countess. It would seem you grossly underestimate your cicisbeo. In fact, I believe you do not know him half so well as you think you do. Percival Ridgeway will do what is necessary. I shall lay you odds on it. His cousin, the duke, would not be the first man he has killed in this tangled web, you will admit.''

Lady Inglethorpe appeared to involuntarily wince.

''It would seem you have things well in hand, my lord,'' she said, slipping off the viscount's lap with the apparent intention of refilling the champagne glasses. Pandora, however, could not be mistaken in thinking the lady's hand shook more than a trifle. ''And Miss Featherstone? What of her? You do understand that she has become something of a nuisance, poking her nose about where she has no business to do. Had the colonel not been a bumbling fool, the girl would no longer be a consideration, and Rivenoak would be on trial for murder. Now there is no telling what she might uncover. She might even stumble on to that business of yours with . . .''

Pandora, who was holding her breath in a heightened sense of expectancy, nearly jumped at the hollow clang of the front door knocker. Rivenoak! Good heavens, she had nearly forgotten.

''The devil,'' exclaimed Lady Inglethorpe. ''Who could that be at this hour?''

''I daresay we are about to find out,'' observed the viscount, calmly sipping his champagne. ''Could it be you were expecting someone?''

''No, how should I, when I already had made plans to have you here tonight.''

The muffled sound of voices lifted in argument penetrated to the upper stories, then abruptly fell silent. Pandora, wholeheartedly wishing the approaching moment of her salvation had waited a mere ten seconds longer to arrive, drew deeper into the shadows in anticipation of whatever brilliant ploy Rivenoak had come up with to serve as a diversion.

She had not long to wait before Bolton, the butler, arrived to announce the presence of callers.

''*Who* did you say was here?'' demanded Lady Inglethorpe in accents of incredulous disbelief.

"Bow Street Runners, m'lady," Bolton patiently repeated. "They claim they have been alerted to the presence of a burglar in the neighborhood. I beg your pardon, m'lady, but they insist on speaking to you in person to ascertain nothing ill has befallen you."

"The devil they do," exclaimed the countess, wearing a forbidding aspect. "Well, we shall just see about this. I beg you will excuse me, Viscount. It seems I must leave you for a moment or two."

"On the contrary," came the oily reply, "I shall go with you. I have a curiosity to meet these Bow Street Runners."

Pandora, some five minutes later, having stolen down the servants' stairs and let herself out the back entrance, inhaled a deep breath of fresh air. Never had the stars looked so magnificent, even veiled in a thickening mist. It could not but occur to her, recalling to mind the first birth of fear in Lady Inglethorpe for a man who was clearly more dangerous than the countess had ever imagined, that she, Pandora, was not in the least cut out for a life of crime, no matter how fraught with adventure. Very likely she would not care in the least to be caught in the act by someone like Viscount Estridge, let alone face the possibility of being shut up in a prison or transported to the penal colonies. At this very moment she wanted nothing more than to be at home with her four boisterous young wards and Aunt Cora, not to mention a tall nobleman who had a way of letting her draw on his strength when she seemed most in need.

Hardly had that thought crossed her mind than she experienced a sudden tingling sensation at the nape of her neck. Inexplicably, her heart quickened, and she was assailed with a feeling of weakness in her knees.

"Rivenoak," she breathed, turning to meet the tall shadow that loomed out of the night. Instinctively she stepped into his waiting arms. "Thank heavens."

Chapter 13

Grim-faced, Rivenoak pulled Pandora close. "Softly, my girl," he murmured. "It is over now. You are safe."

"But of course I am safe," said Pandora, glad, nevertheless, to lean against his powerful frame, if only for the few moments it would take to truly realize he was there and unharmed. "I never doubted you would succeed in effecting our escape. Still," she added with an involuntary shudder, "if ever I have to go out on a ledge again, I daresay I should prefer it to be a figurative one."

"The devil," Rivenoak cursed softly to himself. "You are trembling." Hastily he removed his coat and draped it around her shoulders. "And who can blame you," he said with only the hint of irony. "I daresay you missed nuncheon and tea."

"Not to mention dinner," Pandora smiled ruefully. "It would seem Lady Inglethorpe does not believe in feeding her abigails. It is little wonder she is forever losing them." She lifted her head to favor Rivenoak with a wry smile. "Would it be too much to ask if we departed from here directly? I suddenly find

I actually am devilishly sharp set. And for once, I believe I have had enough of resolving conundrums for a while.''

"I could not agree with you more." Rivenoak smiled, relieved to see that Pandora's spirit, not to mention her keen appreciation of the absurd, was fully intact. He felt the pressure in his chest subside ever so slightly. "Come," he said, leading her along the alleyway away from Lady Inglethorpe's Town House, which was presumably being thoroughly searched for the presence of a burglar. "My lady's carriage is waiting.''

"Summoning the Bow Street Runners was a brilliant diversion," Pandora declared some few minutes later as she sank gratefully back against the squabs of the duke's closed carriage. "Much better than your original plan, which I cannot but think might have miscarried.''

"I am glad you approve, Miss Featherstone," said Rivenoak, drawing her irresistibly into the circle of his arm.

"Oh, but I do," Pandora insisted. "Very likely Lady Inglethorpe would have found your sudden appearance at her door exceedingly curious in light of the evening's earlier events. She might even have gone so far as to connect Miss Prunella Potts with Pandora Featherstone." She glanced up at Rivenoak's stern profile limned against the passing street lamps. "But how in heaven's name did you manage to find two Runners so quickly? Surely you did not have time to send to Bow Street.''

"Hardly," replied Rivenoak, who was remembering the feel of Pandora earlier as she had stepped so readily into his arms in Lady Inglethorpe's kitchen garden. She had felt then, just as she did now, cradled against his shoulder, as if she belonged there. "Strangely enough, I happened to run into them as they were leaving the house next to Lady Inglethorpe's. It seems a burglar was spotted scaling the trellis next door. Apparently, it was the neighbors who sent for the Runners.''

"Indeed?" queried Pandora, who could not but think that an exceedingly fortunate coincidence. "How very odd. And did they catch the intruder?"

"Fortunately, they did not," Rivenoak said philosophically, "or we should not be here now. As it happens, I was the burglar they were after."

"You?" Pandora pulled away, the better to see Rivenoak's countenance. "Good heavens. What the devil were you doing on the neighbor's trellis?"

"You may well ask," replied the duke, wondering when it would have occurred to her to ponder how he had managed to gain entrance to Lady Inglethorpe's Town House. "As it happens, I was in pursuit of my future wife."

Pandora, feeling the blood rush to her face at all that was implied in that bald-faced assertion, could only be glad for the concealing shadows of the carriage. Faith, why had it not occurred to her to realize how much he had braved for her? She had never asked herself *how* he would come. She had known, logically, he would find a way, and that had been enough. Or had she known it in her heart? she wondered suddenly. Laughs-In-The-Rain had said women were used to know these things without having to ask. Could it be that her woman's instinct was telling her something her trained intellect could not accept, that Rivenoak did truly care for her, indeed, might even love her, if only a little?

But, no, it was absurd, she told herself, settling once more against his shoulder that he might not see her face. Indeed, she must not be so foolish as to give into pure fancy. The duke could have anyone. And thus far, she ruefully reminded herself, she had proven nothing but a deal of trouble for him. Besides, even if by some wild chance he did imagine that he loved her now, he would soon change his mind were he to learn of her brother's possible involvement in the massacre at Bear Flat. It would be too much to hope, after all, that that would not prove an insurmountable obstacle.

"I suppose it is pointless to say that you should not have taken such a risk," she said at last. "Not for me, Rivenoak, and certainly not for the sake of a charade. I should have found my way out somehow without your intervention. I am well able to take care of myself."

"So you have assured me on more than one occasion," replied Rivenoak, hardly surprised that she had decided to misconstrue his meaning. The muscle leaped along the hard line of his jaw as he visualized her stealing alone along the cursed third-story ledge, or perhaps she would have chosen to slide down the drainpipe. Hell and the devil confound the girl's obstinate disregard for her own safety. "You will pardon me if I fail to see any evidence of it. You, my dear Miss Featherstone, seem remarkably prone to mishaps of a cataclysmic nature. And, just for the record, I assure you I should never have gone to so much trouble for a charade. I am not in the habit of risking my neck for a mere whimsy. You *will* be my wife, Pandora. Between two people of strong mutual magnetic attraction, to suppose anything else would be wholly illogical."

Hastily Pandora averted her face. If only he knew the truth of it, she thought, dismally aware that in different circumstances she could not but have agreed with him. "In our case, I am afraid there may be other variables that point to a different conclusion," she said, feeling the colonel's book, hard against her midriff. "I have told you, Rivenoak, that I cannot marry you. Why will you not simply accept it?"

Rivenoak, vibrating to the note of distress in her voice, was hard put not to give in to the impulse to end what was rapidly assuming all the manifestations of a stalemate. Only the wish that she might bring herself to trust him with the truth about her brother kept him silent. "But it is obvious, is it not? I have every intention of changing your mind, and the sooner we discover the answers to the conundrum of Colonel Massingale's murder, the sooner we can turn our efforts to the more important matter of why you will not marry me. I will know, Pandora,

one way or the other. I should prefer, however, that it came
from you. In the meantime, we have gone to a deal of trouble
to obtain Colonel Massingale's bloody journal. I suggest we
have a look in it. Indeed, I find I am all eagerness.''

Pandora, who was a deal less eager in spite of all that she
had gone through to obtain the volume, who, indeed, would
have much preferred to glance through it by herself in case
there was anything concerning Herodotus in it, reluctantly
extracted the book from her bodice. She could only hope Rivenoak did not feel her heart ridiculously start to pound as she
opened the leather binding.

''But this is very curious,'' Pandora murmured a few seconds
later as she held the scrawled writing up to the uncertain light
shed by the street lamps. ''It would appear to be not so much
a journal as a narrative of some sort. Yes, here it says these
are the recorded memoirs of Colonel Thornton William Massingale, lately of His Majesty's Army, concerning his sojourn in
the American colonies and encompassing certain events, which,
if they should ever be brought to light, he wishes it to be
understood that he was acting in conjunction with Another. It
would seem the narrative begins with the colonel's assignment
to what he clearly considered an insignificant outpost in the
territory south of Lake Erie.''

''In the land of the Gnanaenhutten Valley, where the three
rivers flow,'' supplied the duke. ''There was a small British
outpost. In the year before the British ceded the Northwest
Territory to the United States, one of the officers under Massingale advised the native inhabitants of the Three-Rivers to abandon their lands to the white colonists rather than engage in a
war that would mean many would die on both sides, a war the
Red Man could not possibly win. The native tribesmen, seeing
the wisdom of the officer's words, did as he suggested. They
abandoned their village and the rich lands that had been theirs,
but they could not abandon their crops. They returned for the
fall harvest. The rest you know.''

"Yes, but that is not all," Pandora said, her hand going out to Rivenoak. "It is written here that your father, Lord Thomas Fairley Ridgeway, petitioned his brother, the Marquis of Selkirk, for an intercession on the part of the native people. He asked that the People be allowed to remain in peace in the land of their fathers. That intercession was granted by the king himself. It says so right here in Massingale's own words."

Pandora, handing the volume to Rivenoak, felt a hard lump rise to her throat. "I daresay your grandfather had a hand in it. The Duke of Rivenoak, after all, was a formidable influence at court. Oh, do you not see, Rivenoak? He did it for your father."

"I see only that it came too late to save the Three-Rivers People," replied the duke coldly. "Whatever my grandfather did or did not do, it proved of little consequence. The Three-Rivers People had been sent to their graves before the word ever reached my father. It is clear from this that Massingale and Butler made certain of that. But even had they not, the following year saw the end of the King's influence over the land of the Gnanaenhutten Valley. The entire Northwest Territory was lost to the Crown."

"Still, they did try," Pandora insisted, wondering at the steely hardness in Rivenoak's voice. One would almost suppose he blamed his grandfather for the events at Bear Flat. "They could hardly have known their efforts would come too late. Or that greedy men would take advantage of the distances separating the two continents to make a profit. I daresay that, had your uncle lived, Massingale would have been hanged for the murder of Lord Thomas Ridgeway, for it is clear that he could not leave your father alive to testify against him. Your father was far too well connected for that."

"Nor could he leave Selkirk alive," observed the duke, relinquishing the volume once more to Pandora, "which is why the marquis was killed little more than three days following Massingale's return to England. How the colonel was able to learn of the marquis's secret room is open to speculation, but you may be certain he did learn of it and that, furthermore, he used it to silence the only man who could have brought him to justice.''

Pandora, who had continued to read from the colonel's confession even as she listened to Rivenoak, could not but be relieved to discover no mention of her brother Herodotus. Indeed, it occurred to her that there might yet be one man alive who could not only have brought Massingale to justice, but the elusive Samuel Butler as well—if only that remaining witness were not in India, far away from England!

''He declares Samuel Butler was his coconspirator,'' Pandora said, coming to the end of the narrative. ''He identifies Butler as the king's agent in the territory west of the Ohio River, but he does not give any other name. Indeed, it would appear the confession was never completed. See here where he writes, 'The man who was both instigator and culprit in the events detailed above was and is P—' That is all there is. It is as if he were interrupted before he could finish. The devil, Rivenoak. We are no closer to the truth than we were before.''

''On the contrary, we have a signed confession implicating one known as Samuel Butler, the king's agent, in the murder of Lord Thomas Fairley Ridgeway. I should say we are a deal closer to having the necessary proofs to convict him upon the event that we do uncover his true identity. It is, in fact, more than I had hoped to find in the colonel's Town House. Curious, do you not think, that Lady Inglethorpe should have had it in her possession?''

Pandora, sensing an undercurrent of meaning in that provocative question, glanced up into Rivenoak's stern visage. ''Curious in what way, your grace?'' she queried, the habitual tiny frown etching itself between her eyebrows. ''No doubt the colonel, her former lover, gave it to her for safekeeping.''

''Did he?'' murmured Rivenoak. ''Would you, if you were the colonel?''

"No, I daresay I shouldn't," Pandora said, with the faintest of smiles. "Not if it were meant as an assurance my coconspirator would not cut my stick for me, which was obviously Massingale's purpose in recording the details of their heinous crimes in the New World. I should have made sure my less than trustworthy partner was aware the book would come to light should anything happen to me."

"You are as acute as ever, my dearest confidential inquiry agent," observed Rivenoak, rewarding her with a buss on that lovely forehead. "Were it I, I should have left it with my solicitor to be made public upon the occasion of my sudden demise by foul means. At the very least I should have included it among my personal effects in a strong box with similar instructions for its reading by my surviving relatives. And so I ask you again, how did it come to be in the bust of Lady Inglethorpe's late husband?"

"It came there because the murderer interrupted the colonel when he was writing it and then, seeing what it was, removed the book from the premises when he or she left. Either Lady Inglethorpe was the one who killed him, which would seem singularly unlikely considering the strength required to sink a knife of that size to the hilt in a man's chest, or she obtained it from the murderer in some fashion. The devil, Rivenoak," Pandora said suddenly, "you cannot think 'P' stands for Percival, as in Percival Ridgeway, can you? I should dislike it above all things should your cousin prove to be Samuel Butler. I fear I cannot help but like him, even if he is a reprobate. And I had firmly convinced myself that, if he had killed Massingale, he did it to protect you or even Lady Inglethorpe and not for any purely selfish reasons, never mind that the evidence would seem to be all against him. Please do tell me he was never in America."

"I should be happy to do," replied Rivenoak with a singularly grim aspect. "Unfortunately, I should not be able to guarantee it was the truth. As it happens, Percival was persuaded to spend some time abroad. An incident concerning a lady's virtue, which led to some rather unpleasant complications. Aunt Caroline never mentioned where he had gone, only that he was out of the country and had been for no little time when the news arrived of my father's demise.''

"Dear, that is hardly what I wished to hear," declared Pandora, trying to picture the charming ne'er-do-well as the sort of man who, out of greed, could willfully murder innocent men, women, and children, not to mention his own kinsmen. "I'm afraid I have some more incriminating evidence to tell you concerning your Cousin Percival. Were you perhaps aware that he had accrued a considerable gambling debt?''

"It is nothing to signify," Rivenoak said with a shrug. "It is always low tide with Percival. When it becomes a pressing matter, he comes to me to settle the account. Why do you ask?''

"Because I'm afraid this time your considerable fortune will not be enough to bail him out of his present difficulties. I overheard Estridge tell Lady Inglethorpe he had got possession of Percival's promissory notes. Unfortunately, the only payment he will accept is the return of Claverly.''

"Claverly!" Rivenoak's eyes flashed steely sparks. "Why, I wonder, am I not surprised. I suppose I need not point out that Claverly is not Percival's to give.''

"It is not at the present," agreed Pandora with a significance that could hardly be lost on Rivenoak.

"The viscount, it would seem, has gone to a deal of trouble and expense to place Percy in what would appear an intolerable situation. The irony is that I should be glad to be rid of the miserable pile if it were not for its tenants.''

"Its tenants?" echoed Pandora, mystified. "What have they to do with it? Claverly is one of the most imposing houses in England. I daresay it is little wonder Estridge would go to great lengths to have it back again.''

"You may be sure of it," Rivenoak said coldly. "Claverly

is a palatial monument to the arrogant self-indulgence of its previous lords, who created it out of their own overblown vanity. The former viscount, like his father before him, sank every penny into it without a thought to the land that supported it, until there was nothing left upon which they could draw to maintain its grandeur. The tenants, whose livelihood depends upon the wise stewardship of their landlords, have everything to do with it. As it happens, those at Claverly are only just beginning to profit from the improvements to the land, which I have caused to be made at considerable expense to myself. You may be sure Estridge is well aware I should sooner turn it over to them than let him get his hands on it, only to bleed it and them dry again.''

"If there is one cooking pot that is empty, then all are empty," murmured Pandora softly, only just beginning to understand the complex nature of the nobleman who had captured her heart. "It is the way of the People. Everything you have done, your generous endowments to feed the poor, the legislation you have tried to see enacted for the benefit of the needy, your work at Claverly—all of it. You did it because of that one tenet."

"You are mistaken, Miss Featherstone," Rivenoak answered, ruefully aware of the look in her eyes as she gazed wonderingly up at him. "To say it is the way of the People is a far cry from the English concept of tenets. The People live according to the dictates of the land. They do not own it. They are one with it. What I have done is to acknowledge the responsibility that is mine as a titled man with power over the lives of a great many others. It is the duty of the Duke of Rivenoak to use the wealth and influence at his command for the betterment of those who have neither. Otherwise, he should be little better than a parasite on the land."

"That, I daresay, you will never be, my dearest Rivenoak," said Pandora, tenderly lifting her hand to cradle the side of his face. "Faith, it is little wonder that I love you. What, may I ask, will you do about Percival? You must know Estridge depends on your cousin to cut your stick for you.''

Rivenoak, who could not have cared less at that moment what Percival might do, closed strong fingers about Pandora's wrist. "That is the second time today you have said that you loved me," he pointed out, drawing her hand down between them. "I should take care, Pandora, if I were you. I am not the sort of man who takes teasing lightly."

"And I am hardly the sort of female who takes pleasure in teasing," she said, thrilling, in spite of herself, to the fierce glitter of his eyes in the dim light. "Indeed, if you must know, my brother Castor is fond of saying I am utterly devoid of the feminine art of dissimulation. Furthermore, I shall very likely be moved in future to tell you I love you on any number of occasions. It is, after all, nothing less than the truth."

"The devil, Pandora," growled the duke, pulling her without warning across his lap. "You cannot play games with me and expect to escape with impunity."

Pandora, lifting her arms about his neck, met the smoldering heat of his gaze unflinchingly. "It is no game, my dearest lord duke, I assure you," she said soberly, smoothing the hair over his temple. "It is, in fact, the most terrible, wonderful, perplexing experience of my life—quite outside the bounds of logic. I can no more explain it than I can make it go away. I am quite at its mercy."

"You will soon be at mine, little tormentress," warned the duke, clearly near the end of his patience. "Tell me why I should believe you."

"You do not have to believe me, Rivenoak," Pandora answered, her smile awry. "Indeed, it were better if you did not. Then perhaps I should find the strength to do what I must."

"Ah, a conundrum to confound the devil himself," reflected Rivenoak, who had a very good notion what it was she felt she must do. "Why, I wonder, do I mislike the sound of that? The truth is, my impossible confidential inquiry agent, there is nothing so difficult before you that could not be speedily resolved if only you will trust me with it."

"The sturdy oak upon whom I must rely when trouble threatens?" queried Pandora whimsically. "I may be small in stature, Rivenoak, but I am neither a linnet nor a child. This is one conundrum with which you cannot help me. I must resolve it all by myself."

Grimly Rivenoak quelled the urge to resort to more forceful means of persuasion on the order of assaulting her lovely lips with his until, breathless and weak, she begged to be allowed to tell him the secret that troubled and kept her from him. Indeed, only the bitter certainty that to do so would inevitably drive a wedge between them kept him from it. "Then, resolve it, you will," said Rivenoak, lightly placing a kiss on her brow. "Much as I should like to convince you otherwise, there would seem to be little point in arguing. Only, I should warn you. There is a limit to my patience. Do not put me off for too long, Pandora. I should be tempted to take matters into my own hands."

Pandora, who did not doubt that he meant what he said, far from being either daunted or intimidated, experienced, to her chagrin, an unwitting thrill at the thought. The truth was, there was a part of her that could not but wish he might simply carry her off and put an end to all her misgivings. No doubt it was the part of her that was even now awakening to a delicious sense of her own unruly primitive passions as he pulled her close with the obvious intention of kissing her full on the mouth.

It was the voice of reason, however, that prompted her to stop him with a finger placed to his lips. "As much as I should hate to disappoint you, Rivenoak," she said, a warning light in her eyes, "I will not be threatened or bullied. I am, after all, a woman who prides herself on her independence. Now, pray stop trying to weaken my resolve by appealing to my ungovernable feminine instincts. I really am in no case to fend you off. You forget, besides negotiating third-story ledges in what has proven a memorable if noticeably brief career in burglary, I have put in a full five hours as Lady Inglethorpe's ladies' maid. I want at this moment nothing more than to crawl into my bed."

"And I should prefer nothing more than to have you climb into *my* bed," retorted Rivenoak, immediately relenting. "Since, however, you have appealed to my masculine sense of compassion, I shall let you off for now—if you tender your word you will never again undertake any investigative work, covert or otherwise, without including me in it. As your employer, if not your intended, I am entitled to that much at least."

"As your confidential inquiry agent, I am obligated to give you a full report of my activities on your behalf, and that is all, your grace," Pandora countered wearily. "Indeed, I could not possibly promise something I should very likely not be able to keep."

"Then, my dear, I fear I have no other choice but to dispense with your services."

"Dispense with my services!" exclaimed Pandora, clearly unprepared for that particular conclusion to his line of deductive reasoning. She bolted upright, moving to the seat. "But you cannot. Not now, Rivenoak, when we are so close to resolving the conundrum."

"I not only can, but I will, Pandora," declared Rivenoak, at his most maddeningly inscrutable, "precisely because we *are* so near to the end of our search. You may be sure that Lady Inglethorpe will have begun by now to put two and two together. Indeed, I should be greatly surprised if she has not already arrived at the conclusion that the stolen confession has fallen into my hands. How long do you think it will be before she realizes the abigail who took it was none other than Pandora Featherstone?"

"I do not consider that an inevitability, Rivenoak. In fact, it is entirely possible she will never make the connection. After all, it is far more reasonable to suppose you would employ an agent for that purpose rather than enlist the aid of the woman everyone believes to be your intended.''

''I, on the other hand, should say she had almost guessed the truth as soon as she saw what was missing,'' replied Rivenoak. ''Who should I send on such a mission, after all, if not a self-avowed confidential inquiry agent?'' Rivenoak arched a single arrogant eyebrow at the sound of Pandora's sharply drawn breath. ''You surprise me. Surely it had not escaped you that Massingale must have told her everything he knew about you?''

''It had occurred to me to wonder,'' Pandora admitted grudgingly. Then, at Rivenoak's unmistakably sardonic curl of the lip, ''Oh, very well. I considered it a distinct possibility, which was why I most particularly wished to put my fate to the touch.''

''Put your fate to the touch? Good God, is that what you were doing?'' Pandora gritted her teeth at the duke's harsh bark of laughter. ''No doubt you will pardon me if I question your rationale, Miss Featherstone. You have, by your actions, made yourself the target of an exceedingly dangerous and vindictive woman, who would stop at nothing to keep her evil secrets from being brought to light.''

''Worse than that, Rivenoak, I have engaged the attention of Viscount Estridge, who, if I am any judge of character, is far more dangerous than Lady Inglethorpe could ever dream of being. He wants you dead and Percival consigned to Jack Ketchum. I daresay he will settle for nothing less than the extermination of your entire line, which he might very well achieve if we do not conceive of a plan to stop him.''

''And what would you suggest, Miss Featherstone? Shall I sign Claverly over to him? Or better yet, I could set you up as bait to draw him out. I daresay all it would take would be the announcement of our marriage by elopement.''

''But that is a capital idea, Rivenoak,'' applauded Pandora, her face lighting up apparently at the mere prospect of serving as the sacrificial goat to lure the man-eating lion into the trap.

"I daresay it would serve a multiplicity of purposes. First, it would foil Estridge's evil designs, since Percival could not possibly inherit for the prescribed length of a year to insure I am not carrying the heir to the dukedom. There would hardly be any point in putting a period to the duke unless his bride were gotten out of the way first."

"A charming notion," commented Rivenoak in exceedingly dry tones. "With any luck, I might be persuaded to throttle you for them."

"I do wish you would be serious, Rivenoak," said Pandora with a comical moue of displeasure. "At the very least it might buy us some more time. And, secondly, it would be sure to throw Lady Inglethorpe into a fit of the megrims. I daresay it will make her careless. I should even go so far as to speculate that, were I to drop a few hints in her direction concerning the colonel's confession and certain things I happened to overhear in Lady Desborough's garden, she would be brought to betray herself to the man we have been seeking."

"No doubt an end to be devoutly desired," Rivenoak observed, wondering what other felicitous consequences she envisioned before them.

"But of course it is," Pandora did not hesitate to assure him. "If the mysterious 'P' of Massingale's confession is Percival, he will be forced to reveal himself in an attempt to silence me. And if it is not Percival, the same remains true of the real culprit. Lady Inglethorpe must know who he is. It would be illogical to suppose she was not in Massingale's complete confidence. After all, this evening she confirmed our suspicion she was at the very least aware of the plan to frame you for my murder that night at the Town House. I should not be surprised if she was the one who wrote the anonymous note to summon you there."

"No, I daresay you would be pleased," declared Rivenoak with a singular lack of amusement. "You realize, of course, that if all your suppositions are true, Lady Inglethorpe has known all along of your connection with Massingale, which might explain her attempt to have you abducted. She was afraid you knew a deal more about events that night than was good for her. And now she will be sure of it.''

''But that is the whole point, is it not?'' Pandora persisted, acutely aware that the carriage had pulled up before the house on South Audley Street and that she had precious little time to bring him round to her way of thinking. ''Events are already in motion to bring everything to a head. All it needs is a small push. It is what you want, Rivenoak? To bring the whole dreadful business to light. Your parents' deaths? The murder of your uncle? The man who was behind it all? This is your chance; pray do not throw it all away now.''

Rivenoak's lips thinned to a grim line at the sight of Pandora's lovely face turned up to his, her eyes lustrous with entreaty in the pale glow of the street lamp. Damn her and her dauntless courage! he thought, knowing it was too late to stop the dangerous course of events. It was the height of irony that now, having found the one woman who was indispensable to his future happiness, he was faced with the prospect of using her to lure his enemies out into the open!

''I have no intention of throwing anything away, least of all the life of the woman who is to be my wife. If we are to go through with this against my better judgment, I will accept nothing less than that. You will marry me, Pandora, now, this very night.''

It was no doubt indicative of the sort of power wielded by the Duke of Rivenoak that Pandora, hardly more than three hours after her escape from beneath Lady Inglethorpe's bed, found herself in her own room staring into her Aunt Philomena's ormolu looking glass at the reflection of herself dressed in her mama's wedding gown, which Simmons had miraculously managed to freshen up and alter in what Pandora did not doubt was record time. Furthermore, Aunt Cora, wreathed in a wholly uncharacteristic aura of serene unshakability, had only just delivered Pandora the news that, not only were the children dressed in their finest and behaving, if not precisely like little angels, then not like little scamps either, but no less a personage than the Bishop of London was belowstairs ready to perform the nuptials.

It seemed that in less than a skip of a heartbeat she had been transformed from plain Prunella Potts, abigail, into a lovely princess gowned in a Watteau gown of white silk embroidered in a sprig pattern. From the white cap with lace lappets down the back perched on top of her curls, done up in the classical style with ringlets about the face, to her white satin French heels, she was a lovely, unrecognizable stranger. Indeed, she had been closer to herself playing the part of Prunella Potts than she was now, in the guise of the Duke of Rivenoak's bride.

The truth was she did not know who she was or what the devil she was about. From the moment she had spoken the fateful words that had set into motion the bizarre sequence of events that were about to culminate in her becoming the Duchess of Rivenoak, a strange pall of unreality had seemed to envelop her. Even now, with the moment of truth upon her, she could not make herself believe she was not caught up in some fantastic dream from which she must soon awaken to find herself safely tucked away in her bed.

It was not, however, to be *her* bed in which she would be awakening, she reminded herself, sustaining a sudden sharp stab of reality which had the perverse effect of sending a hot rush of blood to her cheeks. This time tomorrow she would be Rivenoak's wife in every sense of the word.

Would she choose then to tell him the terrible secret that had been gnawing at her for a seeming eternity? she wondered with a dreadful hollow sensation in the pit of her stomach, which she attributed to its pitifully empty state. Or should she confess before he took her to bed and in so doing shatter the dream before he made the mistake of consummating a marriage he would naturally wish annulled as soon as the need for the subterfuge was past?

From a purely logical standpoint, the latter should have been the one clear choice. Pandora, however, for the first time in her life, felt herself divorced from all sense of calm rationality. Indeed, she could no longer even be sure of the purity of her motives. She did not know if she had been persuaded to her present course solely out of the unselfish desire to protect Rivenoak from his enemies or if, deep down in her heart, she was doing it only for herself. She very much feared the confused threads of logic had been somehow inextricably tangled up with the promptings of her purely feminine instincts.

The devil, she thought, angry with herself. If she were to have any hope of getting through the ordeal before her without utterly disgracing herself, it clearly behooved her to get her wits about her. Had not her papa always taught her that a rational being, when faced with a crisis, cleared his mind of everything but the known essential facts before committing himself to action? The only clear facts were that, whatever had prompted her to abandon her principles, she was about to marry the Duke of Rivenoak, that she loved him more than she had ever thought it was possible to love anyone, and that he was in danger, a danger from which she could not have protected him if Rivenoak had carried out his threat to dispense with her services.

The obvious conclusion was that truly, he had left her no choice but to marry him, and marry him she would if only for the time it took to force Samuel Butler out into the open. Somehow she hoped it would not prove to be Percival Ridgeway, the duke's kinsman, who revealed himself as the enemy.

She had always prided herself on being an acute judge of character; and, while there was a deal more to Percival

Ridgeway than could at first be seen on the surface, she had difficulty believing she could like the man as much as she did if he were so thoroughly evil as to be guilty of the crimes that Samuel Butler had committed. She did not doubt he could be an exceedingly dangerous man, but was he a cold-blooded killer?

Her instinctive answer was that, while he was indeed capable of killing in some given circumstances, he was not naturally of a murderous disposition. Her reason, however, could not dismiss Viscount Estridge's utter certainty that, with a dukedom and a fortune at stake, not to mention a considerable gambling debt, Percival Ridgeway would do whatever was necessary to extricate himself from his difficulties, would even go so far as to remove the last remaining obstacle to the fortune and title that he desired—that he would willfully murder his cousin, the Duke of Rivenoak.

If it were Percival, she told herself, she would never again trust her judgment of human nature.

A light scratching on the door, followed by Aunt Cora's reminder that everyone was waiting, brought Pandora abruptly back to the present. Good God, it was time. From this moment on, there would be no turning back again.

"Yes, Aunt Cora," she called back and, drawing a deep breath, deliberately squared her shoulders, "I am coming."

Chapter 14

Pandora snuggled deeper into the warmth of the eiderdown comforter, reluctant, somehow, to fling aside the cozy mantle of sleep that held her. She had the nagging suspicion that the morning was unconscionably well advanced, and, still, she clung to sleep like the veriest slugabed. She seemed to sense that something of importance had happened, something that she had no wish yet to face. What was it? she wondered, feeling a frown etch itself in her brow in spite of her efforts to ward off the waking reality that beckoned.

A rather fuzzy memory obtruded itself into her rousing consciousness. Curious, but she was quite certain Galatea had been weeping and that Odysseus, solemn as an owl, had run out of the house and hidden himself beneath the floor of the garden shed. There had been a veritable hubbub in the wake of his departure with everyone combing the house and grounds for the missing Odysseus and Aunt Cora giving vent to a fit of the vapors while Pandora had done her best to console the weeping Galatea. But then, it was hardly uncommon for the household to be in a tumult of one sort or another. Pandemonium was more often the rule rather than the exception at Number 3 South Audley Street. It was something else hovering just on the edge of awareness that she was reluctant to acknowledge.

It had taken Uncle Laughs-In-The-Rain to track Odysseus to his hiding place and Rivenoak to coax him out of it. She rather remembered the duke hauling the little rogue into the house dangling from a powerful fist clamped at the back of the boy's waistband. What then? she wondered.

How odd that she should have an image of everyone gathered in the parlor with Rivenoak, tall and commanding, at the center of attention. He was not taking Auntie Pan anywhere, he was saying, not for a while, at any rate. And when she did go away with him, they would all come with her, yes, even Miss Wortham and Aunt Cora.

It came to her, then, to wonder why the duke's assurances should have served immediately to quiet Galatea's tears, indeed, to banish the unwontedly grave expressions from the faces of Iphigenia and Ganymede. Odysseus, she seemed to recall, had gone so far as to give a whoop, which had earned him a gentle reprimand from Miss Wortham. She, Pandora, however, was not going anywhere.

Really, it was all very vague and would seem to make little sense, decided Pandora, trying ineffectually to ignore a persistent tickle at the nape of her neck. Certainly, the children had no need to worry. She was perfectly content to remain where she was, safe and snug in her own bed.

It was that thought, the thought of her own bed, that served, where all the other impinging threads of memory had failed, to bring her wide awake, her eyes flying open with instantaneous and total recall.

Good heavens, she *was* in her own bed! And how not, when she remembered quite clearly Rivenoak carrying her up the stairs and across the threshold of her own bedchamber. A slow heat pervaded her veins at the memory, and, no longer in the least prone to sleep, she went suddenly rigid with awareness of the solid weight of a hard, masculine body unmistakably at her back.

Faith, she had done the unthinkable. She had married Rivenoak! And she had not told him her terrible secret!

It had been on her tongue, as he carried her up the stairs, to tell him all about Herodotus, but he had held her with a possessive tenderness that was unlike anything she had ever known before. It had quite robbed her of the courage to speak. And then, when he had set her on her feet and, framing her face between the palms of his hands, had gazed down into her eyes, the words had seemed simply to evaporate, rather like the moisture in her mouth. Nor had the words come back to her when he kissed her, slowly, deeply, endlessly, almost as if he might draw upon her soul. She had felt ridiculously that her bones must melt. If she had been tempted to voice the words afterwards, when he released her and, holding her with the strange, smoldering intensity of his eyes, began to undress her, she could no longer recall it. Very likely he would only have told her, "Hush, my darling," the way he had done when she had tried awkwardly to thank him for quieting the children's fears.

Wordlessly, he had laid her in her bed and covered her nakedness with the eiderdown comforter, and then he had undressed himself, swiftly, with a sureness of purpose that had struck her even then as singular. Still, no doubt she should have told him the moment he turned and, slipping into the bed beside her, had leaned over her; but how could she, when his gaze moved over her face, slowly, searchingly, a sensuous caress that caused her breath to quicken even as it robbed her of the power of speech? The answer was that she could not, any more than she could have stemmed the swell of emotions that rose up in her as she met the look in his eyes.

Unguarded passion, tenderness, a fierce pride of possession—it was all there for her to see. She was his wife, and he meant to make certain nothing could ever alter that. That realization, rather than freeing her tongue, served instead to paralyze her with sudden swift comprehension.

Rivenoak had not married her out of any sense of honor, much less to use her as bait to draw Samuel Butler out. He had married her because he truly wanted her, perhaps even needed her. Why had he never told her? flashed through her mind, even as it came to her to wish that it might have been love.

The moment for confessing the truth had been wholly and irrevocably lost before Rivenoak had ever lowered his head to cover her mouth with his.

How very strange that she should never have imagined that making love in something so mundane as a bed in the conventional circumstances of a husband and wife on their wedding night could possibly be more magnificent, not to mention enlightening, than any purely investigative excursions into the conundrum of instantaneous arousal of the primitive passions between a man and a woman of mutual magnetic attraction could ever be. She doubted that nothing could compare to the exquisite passion that she had experienced only hours ago when Rivenoak had claimed her as his wife.

It had never once occurred to her that a simple ceremony and a piece of paper could produce a change between two people that was both dramatic and yet almost impossible to define. Perhaps it was in the way he had touched her, as if he were only just discovering her. Or perhaps it was in the way he had made her feel as if she were someone rare and beautiful. Or perhaps it was in the gentle caress of his voice whispering things she instinctively knew he had never before told any woman. In the land of the Three-Rivers People, they would have strolled, naked, in the moonlight, their hands clasped, in the hopes the gods would smile on their joining. They would have lain on a bed of soft pelts spread among the cornstalks to insure the fertility of the land and their union together as husband and wife. All this would have come after the wedding ceremony performed by the Christian missionary, but it would have been the way of the People to honor the old gods as well, the Sky-People, to whom they owed thanks for the gifts of fire and agriculture.

When at last he had taken her, she had felt for the first time in her life what it was to be truly one with a man. Indeed, her heart had ached with the vision of happiness that might have been theirs, if only she had not kept the secret from him.

And now what was she to do? she wondered, tingling to the feather-light touch of Rivenoak's lips against the exquisitely tender spot at the nape of her neck. She could hardly feign sleep indefinitely, especially as his gentle caresses were proving distractingly stimulating.

A helpless smile trembled at the corners of her lips as it came to her that she would like nothing better than to be awakened in such a manner every morning for a very long time to come. At last, breathing a deep sigh, she turned over in the bed to face him.

"Good morning, your grace," she murmured, slipping her arms about his neck. "Would you think me terribly depraved were I to confess I find something deliciously wicked about awakening to a man in my bed, even if he is my husband? I half expect Castor to come crashing through the door at any moment in a high dudgeon demanding to know your intentions."

"No, crashing?" queried Rivenoak, lifting a single, disbelieving eyebrow.

"Indeed, crashing. He has a dreadful habit of going off half-cocked at the least little thing. It is one of the reasons I am grateful not to have to live beneath his roof."

"I shall remember that when you come to live beneath *my* roof," promised Rivenoak, dropping a kiss on the end of her nose. "You will find that I am never prone to go off half-cocked."

"No, you are far too logical-minded for that," agreed Pandora, marveling how young he looked when he forgot to don the Duke of Rivenoak's iron mask. "I daresay you are far more likely to withdraw behind a wall of impenetrability. I warn you I shall very possibly do all in my power to break through the barriers you erect around yourself. I could never stand to live with an enigma without trying to resolve it."

His smile strangely awry, Rivenoak brushed a stray curl from her forehead. "But then, you have never had the least difficulty penetrating my defences. I fear I shall not prove much of a challenge for you."

"Now you are roasting me, Rivenoak," scolded Pandora, who had never seen any evidence of that particular talent. "Speaking of enigmas, there is one conundrum I have yet to understand. I have been terribly curious to know the reason for Lady Inglethorpe's extreme disaffection. I thought at first that she must have loved you very much, but, after five hours as her abigail, I have come to doubt that she is capable of loving anyone but herself."

"A pity Percival cannot be made to see it," said Rivenoak, surprised to find that he himself felt nothing but an odd sort of detachment, as if last night with Pandora had served to distance him forever from the old, haunting memories. "You are right about Diana. She is incapable of that finer emotion, as was made painfully clear to me upon the event of my first Season in London. I confess I was wholly enamored of her beauty and the delicacy of her manners. I was even young and foolish enough to entertain the notion of making her my wife in spite of, or perhaps because of, my grandfather's insistence that she was a scheming little fortune hunter. I believe if he had left matters alone, I should have come sooner to the realization she was hardly the paragon of virtue I imagined her. Certainly, I should have been less determined to fly in the face of his dictum never to see her again."

"It has been my experience that there is nothing that renders something so appealing as the disapproval of a parent figure or an older sibling,'' agreed Pandora, who, well able to read between the lines, was beginning to see the former duke in the light of a rather harsh and patently unwise guardian. ''I myself could never resist developing a *tendre* for anything my brother Castor judged ill-advised. It is so very tiresome, after all, to have someone always delivering curtain lectures on what is good for one. I daresay it is a quirk of human nature to react with perversity.''

''Oh, indubitably so,'' said Rivenoak, throwing back his dark head in laughter, which had the curious effect of sending a soft thrill through Pandora. Indeed, she could not recall ever having heard Rivenoak laugh before with such unaffected ease. ''Still, I should no doubt be grateful that my grandfather had the foresight to intercept a billet-doux Diana sent me entreating my attendance at her cousin's house party in the country. I should even go so far as to thank him for arranging to be present when she staged what was meant to be a fool's trap. I believe I shall never forget the look of loathing on her face when her father broke in on us in what were intended to be compromising circumstances, only to discover the Duke of Rivenoak playing gooseberry to his heir.''

''I imagine she was no little put out,'' commented Pandora, thinking it was a shame the old duke had not had the advantage of knowing her papa's precept that a lesson kindly taught is a lesson gladly learned. It had ever been her papa's belief that, while humiliation might be an indelible teacher, the lesson learned was far too bitter a pill to swallow.

''Perhaps with good reason, as it turned out,'' submitted the duke, pulling Pandora close. ''My grandfather, not satisfied to have foiled the baron's scheme to marry his daughter off to the future duke, did not hesitate to use his influence to ruin Diana's chances in Society. In the end, she was forced to accept the hand of a man who was noted for his jealous nature. He shut her away in his castle in Northamptonshire. I could almost feel sorry for her. A woman, even one of the privileged classes,

unless she is independently wealthy, must depend upon a man
to support and care for her. For Diana, marriage to the earl
must have been like a prison.''

''Only in this case,'' Pandora pointed out, not in the least
moved to pity for the woman who was responsible for the death
of at least one man, her husband, and who would not hesitate
to add Rivenoak to her list of victims if she were able, ''it
would appear that Lady Inglethorpe succeeded not only in
freeing herself of her prison, but of setting herself up in the
not unenviable position of a wealthy widow.''

''A black widow,'' warned Rivenoak, rolling over on top of
Pandora. ''She is dangerous,'' he said, sampling the delectable
contour of her neck with a kiss that sent tiny shivers of pleasure
all the way down to her toes. He lifted his head to look at her.
''Never forget that, my little English linnet. I have assigned a
man to you for your protection. You will promise me that you
will never go anywhere without him or myself.''

''That may prove somewhat inconvenient, Rivenoak,'' Pandora objected, a frown starting in her eyes. ''As a confidential
inquiry agent, I cannot be expected to have a bodyguard forever
tagging after me. Very likely, no one would be willing to talk
to me.''

''Perhaps,'' agreed Rivenoak, who had come to know Pandora too well to point out that, as his wife, she need no longer
pursue an independent career to support herself and her family.
Not only would it have done little good, but it was, in fact, quite
possibly the surest way of forever alienating her affections, and
that was the last thing he could wish to do. ''As my duchess,
however,'' he said, taking unfair advantage of her vulnerable
state to press his lips to the rounded firmness of one of her
breasts, ''you will find any number of doors opened to you.
That would seem a fair exchange, would it not?''

Pandora, who had been anticipating a far different answer,
indeed, who had steeled herself to hear her new lord and master

proclaim the end of her career as a confidential inquiry agent, experienced a melting wave of tenderness for Rivenoak.

"I should have known you would prove as generous as a husband as you have been as an employer," she cried, forgetting, as she flung her arms about him, that she had yet to tell him about Herodotus. "I promise I shall try to make you a conformable wife, Rivenoak."

"Heaven forbid that you should do any such thing," replied the duke with a comical grimace. "I should never ask you to promise what you cannot possibly keep. Besides, I like you very well just as you are."

"Do you, Rivenoak?" Pandora queried, her voice just the tiniest bit wistful. "I was not aware that you liked me at all. After all, I have caused you a deal of trouble, and it seems I have a happy knack for arousing your temper."

"Yes, my darling," agreed Rivenoak, beginning a trail of kisses down her torso and over the firm mound of her belly. "That is what I particularly like about you." His journey having brought him to the soft triangle that pointed the way to his final destination, he pushed the comforter off the end of the bed. "With you as my wife, Pandora, I shall never be bored." Or alone, he thought, spreading wide Pandora's thighs to reveal the tiny nub set within the fleshy petals of her body. Already she was flowing with the sweet nectar of arousal.

He experienced a fierce stab of triumph at the realization that his beautiful Pandora was finally and irrevocably his. He would not allow anything, or anyone, to come between them, not ever, for as long as he breathed. And should Estridge and Lady Inglethorpe, or anyone else, for that matter, dare to threaten to harm so much as a hair on her head, he would not hesitate to bring down the full force of his wrath upon them.

He was Rivenoak and True-Son-Iron-Heart. It was time his enemies learned exactly what that meant.

Deliberately he lowered his head to Pandora in whom resided the power of the Earth Mother. Pandora, who was blessed with the magic to heal his spirit. Gentle, loving, fiercely independent, and fearless Pandora—his wife.

Bringing her swiftly to a pitch of arousal, he plunged himself in her.

Pandora felt carried on the storm of Rivenoak's passion. Indeed, she had never experienced anything so glorious as the fierce tenderness of his need to possess her. He was Rivenoak, and he was her husband. She had never known love in its physical expression could so completely shatter the barriers between two people—all the barriers save for one, the secret she could not bring herself to tell him.

Then she was arching to him, the flood tide bursting within her. Rivenoak drew up and back and, thrusting himself into her with a low cry of triumph, spilled his seed into her.

The announcement in the *Gazette* of the Duke of Rivenoak's marriage to Lady Pandora Featherstone was the talk of the Town, just as they had known it would be. After all, it was not every day that a premier nobleman of the realm, and especially one who had long held himself aloof from the marriage mart, wed in what could only be construed as haste. It was variously theorized that the duke's nursery was about to be set up rather earlier than propriety might dictate, that, properly smitten, his grace would not wait longer to claim his bride, or that, never one to indulge in pageantry, his grace had chosen the quickest, most expedient means of getting himself a wife. Those who favored the first explanation could only applaud Lady Rivenoak's resourcefulness, which had netted her a prize that had long been the despair of a host of marriageable females and their match-making mamas. As to the others, it was agreed among the gentlemen in general that the new duchess was indeed a tempting morsel who could make any man impatient for the bridal bed, and, if the pomp and pother of a church wedding could be avoided, then all the better.

As for the new duchess herself, hardly had the news of her marriage time to travel the rounds, than she made sure to attend the opera with Lord and Lady Congreve, whose box had the advantage of occupying a position next to that of Lady Inglethorpe's.

Amid the gaiety that attended the steady flow of visitors to Congreve's box during the first intermission, Pandora could not but be aware of a certain prickly sensation between her shoulderblades, which she attributed to the invisible darts she was sure Lady Inglethorpe must be directing at her from the box next door.

It was not until the second intermission, during which Pandora and her companions made to depart in order to attend Lady Melcourt's ball, that Pandora had occasion to exchange words with Lady Inglethorpe and her two escorts, Lord Estridge and Percival Ridgeway. Indeed, it could not quite be attributed to pure chance that, upon stepping out of the box, she came suddenly face-to-face with the countess. Pandora had been careful to time it that way.

"Lady Inglethorpe," she lilted, with every evidence of surprised pleasure. "How nice to see you again. And Lord Estridge and Cousin Percival, too. What a pity Rivenoak could not be here tonight. I feel certain he will be sorry to have missed you."

"How very kind of you to say so, Lady Rivenoak," replied the countess, nodding to Congreve and his lady wife. "No doubt I should take this opportunity to wish you happy."

"Thank you. I daresay I could not be happier, unless it were to have my brother Herodotus come home at last to share in my happiness. The children and I miss him so. But then that is the life of a soldier, is it not? Always to be off in foreign parts—first the Americas and now the Orient. His letters are all so very informative. I was just writing him the other day to inform him of the untimely demise of his former superior officer, Colonel Massingale. No doubt you heard of the dreadful circumstances of his passing."

"Indeed, who has not," observed Estridge, his hooded gaze expressive of little more than a polite interest. "Were you acquainted with the colonel, your grace?"

"I was, indeed, my lord," Pandora replied. "It was that which has inspired me recently to do some research in the area of the colonel's experiences in the Americas. Rivenoak and I have found it to be fascinating reading."

Lady Inglethorpe appeared suddenly to blanch.

"Where is the duke, by the way?" interjected Percival, stepping in front of Estridge to offer Pandora his arm. "I looked for him this morning at Tattersall's, but he never showed. He might have tripled a pony on a dark horse out of Derby."

"Rivenoak was called to Claverly for a day or two," Pandora said, as they all turned to walk along the gallery toward the stairs. "Something to do with his project to introduce his tenant farmers to bee keeping in conjunction with planting clover to enrich the soil. I do hope you were the beneficiary of the long shot in his absence, Percy," she added too softly for the others to hear.

"Afraid I was pockets to let, Cousin," Percy smiled wryly. "Couldn't raise the wind for so much as a cartwheel at the moment."

"I should be glad to give you whatever sum you might need, and if you will not accept it from a woman, I strongly urge you to bring the matter up with Rivenoak as soon as he returns. At least promise to call on me. As it happens I should like your advice on a wedding present I wish to buy for Rivenoak."

"I should be happy to oblige you, Cousin. I am, if nothing else, very good at giving advice."

It had come as no surprise to Pandora that, upon formally being launched into the whirl of social events that constituted a Season in London, she had enjoyed a certain immediate success. She had naturally deemed it inevitable that, as the duke's intended, she would attract a deal of attention. Nothing could have prepared her, however, for the reception she received as Rivenoak's duchess.

It seemed that every hostess in London was anxious to count the young duchess among her guests at every soiree, musicale, or gala. At the theatre or the opera, Pandora found herself the cynosure of attention, nor could she leave home without being instantly recognized and hailed by some passerby in a carriage. The silver salver in the foyer was kept overflowing with calling cards, and it was immediately obvious her parlor was entirely inadequate to accommodate the steady stream of callers.

It was, consequently, with no little trepidation that she made ready to take up residence in the duke's four-story mansion on Grosvenor Square. She did so, however, only with the stipulation that her own beloved little house would be maintained with a partial staff in the event that she might require an occasional, quiet retreat in which to think. Rivenoak would have been pleased to oblige her even if he himself had not developed a fondness for the cozy, ramshackle house or had he not foreseen a time when he might like very well to withdraw with Pandora from their more elegant surrounds.

A man of no little insight, especially concerning his duchess, the duke was well aware of all that the house represented to Pandora and what giving it up would have meant to her. It was, after all, her home, which she had fashioned for herself and maintained out of her own ingenuity and profound pride of independence. That she was leaving it for him was the measure of her love for him. To have asked her to sever all ties to it would have been tantamount in his eyes to violating her trust in him.

Thus it was that three days after the impromptu wedding the elegant Town House on Grosvenor was made ready to welcome its new duchess along with four young Featherstones, a greatly frazzled Aunt Cora, who, had she been allowed to have done, would have remained behind in familiar surrounds, Miss Wortham, and Clytemnestra and her four frolicsome offspring. No doubt the staff could be excused in measure for experiencing no little relief upon being informed that the influx was of only a temporary nature, as the children, their governess, Aunt Cora, and the felines were to depart almost immediately for the duke's summer house at the seaside where Wilkins and the handful of servants had already been installed to receive them.

Fortunately, perhaps, the children were put immediately in awe of the stately mansion made splendid with its tasteful array of priceless *objets d'art* by the grand bearing of Tremley, the duke's London butler, whose starched air and grandiloquent bearing established him clearly as a being of great superiority. To their credit, or perhaps to Miss Wortham's, the children appeared to be on their best behavior, although Rivenoak was confident that, given time to adjust to his new surrounds, Odysseus must inevitably find the curving bannister of the grand staircase too great a temptation to resist. Nor did he doubt that Ganymede would eventually be given to familiarize himself with every inch of the house from the attic to the cellar. For his part, Rivenoak hoped that they would and that the girls would soon feel comfortable enough to gather bouquets from the prize rose garden. The cold grandeur of the house steeped in unbroken tradition would undoubtedly benefit from the disturbance of a youthful influence. The cursed place had ever had the air of a mausoleum.

He was not to know how soon that disturbing youthful influence was to make itself known when he retired to his rooms to prepare for bed.

Flinging off his neckcloth, he stemmed his impatience to go to Pandora in the adjoining room as he waited for Flemming, his gentleman's gentleman, to perform the staid routine of preparing his master for bed. He would gladly have dispensed with Flemming's ministrations that evening had he not known it would have hurt the loyal retainer's feelings. Having served Rivenoak's father before him, there was a time when Flemming had stood Chance True-Son's only friend. Still, Rivenoak had been waiting almost from the first moment he saw Pandora, decked out in a Tartan sari, for this night, their first together as husband and wife under his roof. He could almost have wished his old friend and servant to the devil.

"Will that be all, your grace?" queried Flemming at last, pausing to gaze with approval at the duke, whose broad-shouldered, narrow-waisted figure shone to magnificent advantage in the brocade deshabille he was wearing.

"Indeed, thank you, Flemming," Rivenoak answered, careful to keep the impatience from his voice. "I shall not need you any further tonight."

"Very well, your grace," the gentleman's gentleman bowed and, gathering up the duke's soiled linen, quietly made his departure.

Hardly had the door shut behind the valet, than Rivenoak crossed with long, purposeful strides to the door that connected the duke's suite with that of the duchess. Aware of an absurd sort of pounding in his chest at the prospect of being alone at last with Pandora, he raised the back of his fist to knock—and froze before ever his knuckles could make contact, as a sudden, faint, but unmistakable tapping sounded on the hall door.

Now, what the devil! he thought, wondering which of the servants could be so weary of his position as to dare to disobey the duke's orders that he was to remain undisturbed the rest of the evening.

The small, but distinct tattoo on the hall door came again, more persistent this time, and yet timid somehow. As well it should be, reflected the duke, vowing a dire punishment for this unexpected interruption.

Muttering a curse, Rivenoak crossed the room and, reaching for the handle, fairly yanked the door open.

"Well? What the deuce is it?" he demanded—of the empty

air, it would seem. He found himself staring straight before him at an empty corridor.

No doubt instinct and the keenly honed senses of one reared in the forest prompted him, after the space of a heartbeat, to slowly lower his gaze.

"It's only me, your grace," pronounced Odysseus, garbed in a rumpled nightshirt above bare ankles and feet, his head tilted back to manfully meet the duke's flinty glance. "Did I wake you?"

"It is only 'I,'" Rivenoak corrected, noting the telltale tracks of recent tears on the boy's cheeks. Now, what the devil? he wondered. "And, no, you did not wake me, though I must presume something woke *you,* else you would be in your bed where you belong."

Odysseus gave a loud sniff and swiped a sleeved arm across his nose. "I couldn't sleep. Not because of any bad dream, mind you. I'm too old to be scared by a stupid nightmare. I daresay the bed was too soft."

"Yes, I daresay that it was," the duke agreed with a gravity to match the child's own. "Pray come in to the fire at once, before we both catch our death," he commanded, ushering Odysseus into the room.

"It is a mite chilly, now that you mention it," observed Odysseus, glancing curiously around him at the masculine decor of polished mahogany furniture, claret-colored drapes, and Oriental rug. "I say, your grace, this is a bit of all right."

"No doubt I am glad you approve," commented the duke dryly. Snatching the counterpane off the bed, he ordered the boy to sit in the wing chair before the fire and then bundled his unexpected guest up against the chill in the air. "You are wrong, you know," he added, fetching down his pipe from the mantel and stuffing it with tobacco. "One is never too old to be frightened by nightmares. I have known grown men to cry out in their sleep. It is nothing of which to be ashamed, Odysseus."

Odysseus frowned over the mound of covers, clearly uncon-
vinced. "I should wager you've never been scared of anything.
Uncle Laughs-In-The-Rain said you tracked a wolf to its lair
when you were younger than Ganymede. He said you took a
canoe without your papa's permission and rode down the river
and nearly went over some falls. He said you were gone for
three days all by yourself and that you had to make your way
home past an enemy's camp."

"Uncle Laughs-In-The-Rain talks too much," said Rivenoak, ruefully noting the child's worshipful eyes beneath the
mop of dishevelled hair. "You may be sure I was afraid when
I saw my canoe was on the point of plunging over those cursed
falls. I was heartily wishing myself back at the village. And,
later, when I came across the Mohawk camp, I was scared out
of half a year's growth. Any man who says he has never been
afraid is either a fool or a liar."

Lighting his pipe with a burning taper, Rivenoak watched
the boy absorb that startling piece of information. How very like
Pandora he was, thought the duke, never mind the difference in
coloring. He could see Odysseus was thinking it through from
every possible angle, just as his supremely logical-minded aunt
would have done. Drawing on the pipe and exhaling a cloud
of smoke, Rivenoak waited to hear the result of the boy's
deductive reasoning.

"I dreamt that Papa came home and couldn't find us," Odysseus announced, lifting troubled blue eyes to Rivenoak's face.

"I see." It was not the answer Rivenoak had expected,
though on retrospect, he supposed he should have done. "Your
papa could not find you because you were not at your Auntie
Pan's. But that is the difference between a dream and waking
reality. Now that you are awake, does it seem reasonable to
suppose your papa would not learn where you are the instant
he called at the house on South Audley Street? You may be
sure the staff would tell him where you had gone."

"Or our uncle would, if Papa went to Havenhill first. In fact,

I daresay there are any number of people who could tell him,''
declared Odysseus, considerably brightening. ''It was only a
stupid dream, after all. I see that now.''

''It was a dream, but it was hardly stupid. It was something
you had been worried about, whether you knew it or not. The
dream only helped you to discover something about yourself.
The People believe dreams are sent from the gods. In the old
days, young men were used to endure extreme hardship and
days of fasting in the hopes a dream would come to them from
the gods. A man who receives such a dream has been granted
a vision with special meaning. He carries it with him all his
days.''

''Like Boy-Who-Walks when he died and was reborn in the
spirit of Grandfather Bear,'' said Odysseus, his eyes shining
with comprehension. ''He made the medicine pouch of things
that would remind him of it always.''

''Exactly so,'' said the duke, bending down to knock the
embers from his pipe into the fire. ''You may be sure he kept
it with him always, until an evil manitou dressed in the skins
of a man who claimed to be his grandfather took it away.'' He
straightened and went suddenly still as his gaze came to rest
on Pandora, standing in the doorway between the master suite
and hers. Smiling somewhat mistily, she pressed the side of
her finger to her lips.

''But he got it back again?'' demanded Odysseus, his attention all on the duke. ''He went after the manitou and wrestled
it away?''

''The manitou,'' replied Rivenoak, turning his glance back
to the boy, ''was a very powerful spirit. He led Boy-Who-
Walks on a long and perilous journey into a deep, dark and
lonely place where not even Grandfather Bear could help him.
For many years he wandered, blind, in the dark, but he never
gave up trying to find his way out again. Then one day, when
he had thought he would never see Father Sun again, the Earth
Mother took pity on him. She opened a fissure in the walls of

his prison. A single ray of sun burst in upon him, and he was able to see his way past the walls of darkness to freedom."

"And the medicine pouch?" asked Odysseus, struggling to keep his eyes open. "What happened to it?"

"Ah, yes, the pouch," Rivenoak said, his glance lifting to Pandora. "The evil manitou had long since flung it into the heart of the fire that burns eternally at the frozen core of darkness. The pouch was destroyed, but Boy-Who-Walks had been given a medicine far more powerful than anything he could ever have imagined—a constant beam of sunlight to keep with him always that the darkness might be forever banished."

A silence fell over the room, disturbed only by the soft susurrus of Odysseus's breathing and the crackle of the fire, as Rivenoak and Pandora stood locked in a long embrace of glances. Then at last, Rivenoak wordlessly gathered Odysseus up in his arms and laid him in the ducal bed.

The boy was asleep, and Pandora, limned against the light of the adjoining bedroom, was waiting.

"He put the child to sleep with a bedtime story? And in his own bed at that? Rivenoak?" demanded Lady Congreve, regarding Pandora in no little astonishment at the breakfast table the following morning.

"Is it so difficult for you to imagine?" asked Pandora, who saw nothing strange in the duke's rapport with the children.

"Good heavens, yes," Lady Congreve affirmed. "On the other hand, I have sometimes suspected he might make a wonderful father one day, if only he could be brought to set aside the bitterness and distrust fostered by his grandfather all those years ago. It would appear that you have worked a miraculous transformation in him, my dear. Indeed, it is just what I have always hoped for him, and I have you to thank for it."

"What do you mean—bitterness and distrust?" Pandora

said, a wrinkle in her brow. "I'm afraid he has told me very little about his grandfather."

"No, I daresay he has not spoken of it," agreed Lady Congreve, taking a long time to stir the cream in her coffee. "It is not something he cares to remember. My father, I'm afraid, was not the most patient or understanding of men, especially after he lost both of his sons to violence, one after the other. But then, he was right about one thing. Chance was hardly equipped when he first arrived in England to take on the responsibilities of a great dukedom. Perhaps I should not have chosen the methods my father employed to prepare the heir to take his place in English society, but I cannot deny that the results went far beyond anything even my father could have expected. Rivenoak, you will admit, is a power with whom to be reckoned."

"More than that, Lady Congreve," replied Pandora, who had a fairly good notion of what Rivenoak had been made to endure from his grandfather without her having been given the specifics, "Rivenoak is a man of strength and integrity. I daresay he would have made a duke of whom his grandfather could be proud without the indignity of being forcibly persuaded to forsake the heritage of his mother's people. That is what his grandfather wanted from him, was it not? An heir who was in all ways English?"

"I'm afraid so, my dear," admitted Lady Congreve, noting with a deal of satisfaction the sparks of outrage in Pandora's marvelous eyes. She had been right. The child *was* head over ears in love with Rivenoak, a sentiment that, unless she missed her guess, was more than reciprocated by the duke. "And you are quite right. I believe my father never did understand the strengths that came to Chance from that other heritage."

"No, I daresay he did not. What a pity that was, for I am convinced that despite his harshness the former duke must have cared a great deal for his grandson. Certainly, he did all in his power to grant what protection he could to Joyfully-Sings and

her other children. That it came too late to save them must
have been a bitter pill for the former duke to swallow.''

"I believe it occasioned him no little grief. I know he
instructed Selkirk to spare neither effort nor expense in investigating the incident. My brother told me himself the duke would
settle for nothing less than having those responsible brought
to justice. Unfortunately, Selkirk was killed before he could
carry out that final mission. A pity, for I suspect from certain
things at which he hinted to me that he had received information
that led him to believe there was a deal more to the incident
than had at first been suspected.''

"What information?'' demanded Pandora, leaning suddenly
forward in her chair. "You must remember. What exactly did
he say?''

Lady Congreve gave a fluttering wave of a hand. "Dear, it
was a very long time ago. I cannot possibly remember exactly.
It was something about a parcel delivered to him by one of the
soldiers who had been witness to all that happened. Selkirk
was hardly the demonstrative sort, but I could tell he felt he
was very near to bringing the entire matter to a close. Only,
that very night he was killed. I never heard anything more
about the soldier or the parcel, and then, with Selkirk gone,
there was no one to carry on where he had left off. Save, of
course, for Mr. Pinkney. He was the Bow Street Runner my
father employed to investigate Selkirk's unfortunate demise,
an odd sort of fellow who refused to believe my brother was
the victim of a burglar, as was, for want of a better explanation,
the commonly accepted theory. He insisted it had to be someone
of the household or the family, if you can imagine that.''

"Given the peculiar circumstances of the crime,'' observed
a masculine voice from the doorway, "I should think Mr.
Pinkney was not being in the least preposterous or presumptu-
ous. I should even go so far as to say he was exceptionally
good at his job.''

"Rivenoak!'' exclaimed Lady Congreve, clapping a hand to

her bosom. "Good heavens, must you sneak up on people that way?"

"I beg your pardon, Aunt Caroline. I'm afraid you and Pandora were so engrossed in your conversation you simply failed to note my arrival. You are looking particularly fetching this morning, my dove," he murmured, bending over to place a kiss on Pandora's cheek. "Is that a new gown you are wearing?"

"You know very well it is," Pandora chided, wrinkling her nose at him. "How long have you been standing there?"

"Long enough to hear about the soldier and the mysterious parcel. Indeed, I cannot but wonder that you never mentioned them before, Aunt Caroline."

"At the time, my dear, you were hardly of an age to do anything about them, and, later, I'm afraid they simply slipped my mind. I cannot see that it matters now, Rivenoak. The parcel, whatever it was, must have been lost long ago. And, as for the soldier, you cannot possibly think to find him after all these years. Why, we do not even know his name."

"Are you sure it was a 'parcel' Selkirk mentioned?" queried Pandora, her gaze on Rivenoak's. "Might it not have been a box or a trunk?"

Lady Congreve, aware of a sudden undercurrent in the room, glanced from one to the other of her companions. "Now that you mention it," she said slowly, "I believe it was a box. Yes, a-a puzzle box. That was what he called it. I thought it very curious at the time, but Selkirk would only say he was sure it was the key to the whole sorry mess, if only he could figure out the secret to 'Tom's bloody demmed puzzle box.' Good heavens, that was it. Indeed, I cannot think how I should have forgotten. Tom was used to have a puzzle box when they were boys. It was a standing joke between them that Selkirk never could figure out how it worked."

"But that is it, then," exclaimed Pandora, pushing back her

chair and shooting to her feet. "The box must contain the answers to the puzzle, Rivenoak. We only have to find them."

"It would appear a strong possibility," the duke agreed, "unless, of course, Selkirk was only speaking figuratively."

"What box?" demanded Lady Congreve, considerably baffled by the exchange between her two companions. "Do not say that you have Selkirk's puzzle box."

"We have," affirmed Pandora, her womanly instincts, not to mention her strong disbelief in coincidences, having thoroughly precluded any other possibility. "And you may be certain the marquis was not speaking in abstract terms. The resolution is in the box, Rivenoak. I can be ready to leave for Briarcroft in twenty minutes."

"Briarcroft!" exclaimed Lady Congreve, greatly taken aback. "But you cannot. Indeed, it is out of the question. My gala is tonight. Surely you cannot have forgotten. Prinnie himself has promised to drop in to pay his respects to the new Duchess of Rivenoak. I should be ruined if you failed to put in an appearance."

"Aunt Caroline is right, of course," Rivenoak said reflectively, to Lady Congreve's heartfelt relief and Pandora's consternation. "While the box can wait until tomorrow, the prince, I fear, cannot." Nor could he, Rivenoak thought grimly to himself. Not if the box held the key to the bloody damned conundrum and possibly incontrovertible proof of Herodotus Featherstone's culpability. He would save Pandora that greatest of all disillusions if he could—Pandora and Herodotus Featherstone's four innocent children. It would be a simple matter to drive to Briarcroft, search the box, and be back in London in plenty of time for Aunt Caroline's gala and, if he discovered the secret of the box, perhaps to confront his enemies with the truth once and for all.

"You may be certain I shall not find it easy to wait either," Pandora pointed out with a comical moue at the duke which changed to a darkling look. "The first thing tomorrow, Rivenoak, promise me."

"You have my word, naturally, *enfant*," Rivenoak assured her. "We shall leave first thing in the morning. And, now, if you will both excuse me, I'm afraid I must be off. I shall see you tonight at the gala. If you should go out today," he added, dropping a kiss on Pandora's forehead, "you will, of course, remember to take Higgens with you."

"If you insist," agreed Pandora sweetly, an idea having taken root in her fertile mind. If she could not make haste to Briarcroft, she could at least put her time to good use. Only a few days ago Percival had offered, after all, to advise her on the finer points of choosing a wedding gift for Rivenoak. She might as well take him up on his offer. "I am sure Higgens will be indispensable carrying parcels. As it happens, Aunt Caroline and I are going shopping in Bond Street."

Rivenoak, who should have been pleased at her ready compliance with his request, felt, on the contrary, an inexplicable frisson of warning, an uncomfortable feeling that was not made any easier by his glimpsing a flicker of surprise cross his aunt's face, quickly to be hidden behind a vacant smile. Pandora was up to something; he would wager half his bloody fortune on it. "Then, no doubt Higgens will be put to good use," he said, vowing to have a word with his wife's bodyguard before departing for Briarcroft. "Until this evening, my dear," said the duke, turning to take his leave. "Aunt Caroline."

"You know very well I cannot possibly go shopping today, Pandora," declared Lady Congreve as soon as she and Pandora were alone again. "I still have far too much to do before the gala tonight. I only dropped by this morning for breakfast to see how you went on."

"I know, dearest Caroline," Pandora said. "Pray think nothing of it. All that was purely for Rivenoak's benefit. As it happens, I have yet to buy my husband a wedding present, and Percival has been kind enough to advise me in the matter. I daresay he shall be here at any moment to take me shopping.''

"A surprise present, how splendid," Lady Congreve beamed. ''I daresay you will be safe enough in Percival's company. And now, my dear, I shall bid you good morning. I really must be getting home.''

Pandora, after seeing Lady Congreve to the door, hastened to send a note to Percival reminding him of his promise in the matter of a wedding present for Rivenoak. Instructing the messenger to await a reply, she hurried upstairs to prepare for his arrival.

Percival, as good as his word, not only sent a reply in the affirmative, but chose to deliver it in person.

"It seemed the perfect opportunity to pay my respects to the new Lady Rivenoak," he said, bowing gallantly over Pandora's hand. ''And to apologize for what must seem my dereliction. I should, of course, have called before this.''

"Naturally, I forgive you," smiled Pandora, who could not but note the duke's cousin presented something less than his usual impeccable appearance. Not that his plum cutaway coat and dove grey pantaloons were not cut and pressed to fit to perfection, for they were. Nor was his neckcloth, tied in the Waterfall, lacking in its usual elegance. In his dress, Ridgeway was, as ever, the model of the fashionable gentleman. Rather it was a somewhat worn look about the eyes, which evidenced lines at the corners she had never noticed before. There was a tightness about the lips as well that was new to the normally insouciant Man About Town. Moreover, she was certain he bore the distinct air of a man who was in some manner distracted.

Poor Percival, thought Pandora, all too aware of the probable source of his anxiety. It would seem his luck at the tables had yet to demonstrate a turnabout. Indeed, she could not but wonder what sort of pressures were being brought to bear on him by his major creditor to meet his obligations.

"May I say you are looking lovelier than ever, your grace," Percival was saying as he helped Pandora into her pelisse in preparation for departing. "It would seem that marriage agrees with you."

"Yes, I must suppose it does," replied Pandora, drawing on her gloves. "But then how could it not, when I am married to a man like Rivenoak. He has quite swept me off my feet."

"So one would imagine," observed Ridgeway, escorting her out the door to the waiting carriage. "As I recall at our first meeting, you were set on holding off for a June wedding." Opening the carriage door, he took her arm to help her mount the step. "A pity you did not adhere to that resolve, my dearest cousin. You cannot imagine the trouble you have caused for us both."

Pandora realized too late that the conveyance was not one of those that belonged to Rivenoak and that, further, the comfortingly stolid figure of Higgens, the man who had been assigned to insure her safety, was not perched on the seat beside the driver. Worse, she glimpsed another figure, sinister somehow, in the darkened interior of the closed carriage.

Instinctively, Pandora drew back. Before she could utter the scream that rose to her throat, a powerful hand closed over her mouth. The next instant she was forcibly lifted and thrust into the carriage. Never one to lose her head in a crisis, Pandora sank her teeth into the hand over her mouth.

There was a blistering oath, and she was precipitously released. Only, just then, Percival had leaped in behind her, cutting off her single avenue of escape. As the carriage lurched into motion, a heavy fist exploded against Pandora's jaw, igniting a burst of lights, and Pandora was plunged into darkness.

Consequently, she did not see the little man in the canary-colored waistcoat bound into the street and leap onto the back of the carriage.

Chapter 15

It was made immediately apparent to Rivenoak, upon descending from his carriage in front of the Earl of Congreve's Town House, that his aunt's gala was a shocking squeeze. But then, with rumors rife that Prinnie himself intended to make an appearance, it would have been odd had not everyone who was considered to be Someone been sure to be in attendance, he told himself ironically.

Having unlocked the secrets of the puzzle box only a few hours before, however, Rivenoak was interested in seeing only one of the guests, and *she,* hell and the devil confound it, would seem to be peculiarly difficult to find, he reflected, gazing down on the milling ballroom below him with a mounting disquiet.

His hurried flight to Briarcroft had taken him longer than he might have expected. He had arrived at his aunt's gala during the second intermission. If Prinnie were coming, it would no doubt be before the hour was out. Where, then, was Pandora? he wondered, feeling the pressure start to build in his chest as he swept the room with a piercing glance. She should have been at the center of a bevy of admirers.

Rivenoak turned sharply at the sudden rustle of skirts behind him.

"Rivenoak! Thank heavens!" exclaimed Lady Congreve, hurrying up to the duke. "You are here at last. Prinnie is due to arrive at any moment."

"Pandora, Aunt Caroline," said Rivenoak, who did not at the moment give a tinker's damn if the entire royal family had decided to honor them with their presence. "I must see her at once. Where the devil is she?"

"But I thought she must be with you," Lady Congreve answered, considerably taken aback. "I have not seen her since this morning at breakfast."

"You mean since you went shopping with her in Bond Street, do you not?" demanded the duke, feeling a hard clamp on his vitals.

He was not made any easier to see Lady Congreve go suddenly pale with apprehension. "There never were any plans for you to go shopping with her," he said with steely conviction. "The devil, I knew it was a Banbury Tale, and still I left her."

"She said it was to be a surprise, my dearest, or I should never have allowed her to go without me. A wedding present for you. Percival was to help her pick it out. I never dreamed she might—"

"Percival! Hellsfire, I've been a bloody fool." Grimly, Rivenoak drew Lady Caroline into an empty room. "Quick, tell me, is my uncle here?"

"He was earlier. As always, he was the center of attention. I believe, when the dancing started, he retired to the billiards room. Rivenoak, pray tell me what is going on? What has happened to Pandora?"

Rivenoak's strong hands closed urgently on Lady Congreve's arms. "I haven't time to explain. Find my uncle and tell him the man he knew as Butler has made his move much sooner than we anticipated. Tell him I have gone home to try and discover what I can. He will find me there if he hurries.''

As this last was flung over his shoulder, Lady Congreve made as if to follow after him.

''Rivenoak, wait,'' she called in no little perturbation. ''Tell me what has happened!''

The duke, however, was already out the door and making his way swiftly along the gallery toward the exit.

It was patently obvious Pandora had fallen into the clutches of his enemies, he was grimly reflecting some moments later as he stepped into his carriage. The question was where had they taken her? And, more tormenting, how long would they keep her alive?

He would have given a great deal to know what had happened to Higgens. The former pugilist would not have been an easy man to take down in any sort of a fight. Why the devil had he, Rivenoak, not thought to inquire about Pandora when he slipped in to change, not more than forty-five minutes ago? There had not been an inkling of anything out of the ordinary about the household. Surely someone must have realized the duchess had not returned to the house all that day.

Bitterly, he cursed himself for a bloody fool for not having followed his instincts to put Briarcroft off for a little while longer, never mind that he now had the answers to the whole plaguy business. If he lost Pandora, the rest would hardly matter.

Instructing Fisk to walk the horses, Rivenoak stepped down from the carriage and strode briskly into the house. Immediately, he summoned Tremley and gave the order to assemble the entire household. Hardly had they gathered than it was made immediately apparent that two of their numbers were missing—Simmons, the abigail, and Higgens.

''Search the house and the grounds,'' ordered Rivenoak, exceedingly grim-faced. ''Find them.''

''I beg your pardon, your grace,'' spoke up Tremley, as everyone from the scullery maids to the footmen in livery exited

the library to initiate a search of the premises. "But there would
seem to be a—er—lady to see you. I tried to tell her you were
not in to callers, but she was quite insistent. She claims to have
information on a matter of utmost importance to you."

"The devil, she does," snapped Rivenoak. "Show her in,
then. I should be pleased if someone has something of import
to tell me."

"As a matter of fact, your grace, what I have to report is of
too great an urgency to wait," interjected a woman's voice
from immediately behind Tremley. "It concerns the safety of
your duchess."

Rivenoak, turning, went suddenly rigid with startled recognition. "That will be all, Tremley," he said, never taking his
eyes off his female caller. "Lady Inglethorpe and I will not
require your services."

It occurred to Pandora, struggling to a sitting position on the
bed onto which she had been deposited with a shocking lack of
ceremony, that there was little to recommend in being forcibly
abducted by an obviously desperate man who was utterly lacking in scruples. Not only had she been forced to endure the
indignity of having a woolen sack thrust over her head, but she
had been left, trussed up like a lamb for the slaughter; and that
did not even take into account the matter of being brutally
rendered unconscious and then dosed afterwards with what
could only have been laudanum.

Pandora felt a slow-mounting rage at those final two ignomin-
ies. Not only did her jaw ache abominably, a constant reminder
of the cruel blow to which she had been subjected, but her
mouth felt stuffed with cotton, her head ached, and her limbs
were trembling from the aftereffects of the drug. No doubt she
should be grateful her teeth were apparently intact and that
nothing was broken, no thanks to Percival, who presumably
had delivered the blow that had consigned her to oblivion for

no little time. Indeed, she had not been allowed to regain her senses until she had felt herself borne in a man's arms up what she calculated to be three flights of stairs to her present unenviable circumstances, only then to have been dosed into unconsciousness again—with the result that she had not the slightest notion how long she had been in the carriage or how far they had traveled to reach their destination.

Still, she was not utterly without the means to determine a great deal about her surrounds. She was in the country, of that much she could be certain from the utter lack of the telltale noises that must inevitably be associated with the City. Besides, she could hear the persistent hoot of an owl, which, besides being associated with rustic environs, informed her that the sun had set sometime since. Percival had arrived at the Town House at ten that morning. Good God, if they had traveled steadily from the time she was so rudely thrust into the carriage, then they might be anywhere within the radius of fifty to sixty miles of London!

Pandora fought down a moment of panic. It would be nothing short of a miracle, she realized, if Rivenoak found her, in which case, it was patently up to her to get herself out of the coil in which she had landed herself.

That particular realization was enough to spur her to a determined effort to better her circumstances. Fortunately, whoever had bound her had been considerate enough not to tie her hands together at the wrists, she realized, testing the restraints that held her hands at her back. Fashioned in the manner of manacles, the leather bonds allowed her perhaps seven or eight inches of slack, with the result that some few minutes later she had managed to work her bound hands down over her derriere and, from that exceedingly awkward position, to draw her legs through so that at least her hands were tied at her front. After that, it was a simple matter to pull the woolen sack off her head, which she did, flinging the wretched thing from her in disgust and drawing in deep draughts of air.

The chamber that leaped into view was hardly prepossessing. Obviously an attic room of the sort occupied by servants of the lower orders, it and its sparse furnishings, which comprised little more than a cot and a vanity, would have profited greatly from one of Aunt Cora's cleaning flurries. Covered with dust and showing distinct signs of cobwebs against the moonlight filtering in through a single, small, dirty window, the chamber had the musty scent of long disuse. Worse, it was tucked under the eaves, which meant the only avenue of escape was through the door.

As a female trained almost from the time she was in leading strings in the finer points of criminal investigation, it was hardly in Pandora's nature to wait for her abductors to return. Logic alone dictated that the villains (she distinctly recalled another figure shrouded in darkness in the carriage) could not possibly leave her alive to identify them for Rivenoak's certain vengeance. Untying her feet was quickly accomplished. Her hands were rather more difficult, since the task necessitated the use of her teeth, a process that occasioned her no little discomfort. Still, the thing was eventually done.

Pandora, freed from her fetters, scrambled off the bed, only to stand, reeling, on her feet while she waited for the room to stop its disconcerting tendency to spin. It came to her, feeling that at any moment she must be sick to her stomach, that she would gladly have consigned Percival Ridgeway to the devil and never have suffered the smallest twinge of remorse.

Unfortunately, that thought served only to sharpen the pain and disappointment of Ridgeway's villainous betrayal. How thoroughly she had misjudged him! Even now she had the greatest difficulty believing he had actually abducted her in the most ruthless manner possible. She did not doubt her entire faith in the innate goodness of her fellow man was forever shaken. For that alone she would not soon have found it in her heart to forgive him, but to think that he was the heinous Samuel Butler, who had sunk so low as to murder innocent men, women, and children, placed him beneath contempt. And, if that were not all or enough, he had the blood of his own kinsmen on his hands! She could not find the words to describe him. Indeed, *loathsome* and *vile* did not begin to do him justice.

If only she knew for certain that Herodotus had not been a party to his villainy, she thought, lifting her skirts to retrieve the pocket gun she had taken the precaution of concealing in her garter. And if only she did not have to face Percival one last time to demand the truth from him!

Turning the door handle, she sent a small prayer heavenward in thanks that Ridgeway had not thought it necessary to lock the door behind him. The next moment, she slipped quietly out into the darkened corridor.

Rivenoak, schooled at an early age to stalk game in the forest, tethered his horse out of sight and slipped, silent as the wolf-dog trotting at his heels, along the wooded path that followed the stream. Clad in the buckskins of his mother's people, his every sense attuned to his surroundings, he stole through the trees, a sinister figure with a singleness of purpose in his every movement.

The house loomed out of the darkness, the house that was as familiar to Rivenoak as the grounds around it. Briarcroft, the duke's hunting lodge! Percival had brought Pandora here, he thought. Why? Unless Samuel Butler, Rivenoak's deadliest enemy, wanted the box and its damning contents along with the one person who stood in the way of his ambitions. Pandora!

Rivenoak's stomach clenched with terrible apprehension. Had Percival kept her alive? Or was it already too late to save her!

Grimly, he banished the unthinkable as he crouched in the shadows at the edge of the glade and probed the gloom for the furtive movement of guards posted to sound the alarm. He was looking down from a low promontory onto the south side of the house, bathed in the silvery sheen of moonlight. A yellow glow of lamplight framed in a second-story window issued from the study. The villains were not lacking in gall, he thought, his hand clenching on the haft of the knife at his belt. But then, Percival, naturally, had known Wilkins and the other servants had departed some days ago for the house in Brighton. Briarcroft had been deserted, save for the old caretaker, who lived in the cottage away from the main house.

It had been deserted until now, that was, he amended with a hard gleam of a smile. The duke was come to reclaim all that was his.

Drawing the knife from his belt, Rivenoak half rose from his crouch. Suddenly, he froze, his gaze riveted on a small, shadowy form that had seemed to appear without warning out of nowhere to dangle precariously from the wall of the house itself. It was only as he watched, his breath strangely suspended, the figure begin to descend that he realized the insane fool was shinnying down the drainpipe. Now, who the devil—?

He knew the answer to that question before it had finished formulating in his head.

Good God! Pandora! And there, at the corner of the house, the stealthy form of a guard!

Instantly, he was up and running.

Pandora, who had entertained a healthy dislike of heights ever since her one and only exposure to the uncertainties of life inherent in a career of burglary, kept her eyes glued to the wall in front of her. For the first time it occurred to her, as she clung with grim determination to the leaded drainpipe, that henceforth she really had ought to make more time for vigorous forms of exercise instead of forever burying her nose in books. The existence of a confidential inquiry agent would seem to be proving rather more physically demanding, not to mention taxing to the nerves, than she had previously imagined. Indeed, she was becoming acutely aware that her ability to grip with her hands might not be quite equal to the task to which she had committed herself.

Hardly had she allowed the admission of that particular uncertainty to creep, unbidden, into her mind, than she felt, to her horror, her feet slip off the treacherous pipe, leaving her solely dependent on her hands to keep from falling.

It was not enough. A scream of horror rose to her throat, as she slid out of control down the pipe—and landed, little more than a second later, considerably shaken, but quite safe, on her feet.

Breathless and trembling with reaction, she leaned her forehead against the pipe and struggled not to give in to hysterical giggles. Thank heavens there had remained only half a dozen feet to drop when her precarious grip had failed her, else she would very likely now be suffering at the very least from a broken bone or two. It really was too absurd.

Still, she sternly reminded herself, she was not out of the briars quite yet. Drat the luck! There *would* have to be a guard posted at the head of the stairs. While she had been perfectly prepared to face Percival with a single-shot pistol as her only protection, the addition of a henchman, one, moreover, whom she had recognized from her near escape from abduction in the museum, had clearly presented untenable odds. If *one* of the rogues from the museum was there, then it was entirely possible the others were as well. The only logical deduction had been to retreat to fight again another day. The startling discovery that she was not beyond Rivenoak's reach, that she was, indeed, being held captive in, of all places, Briarcroft, had made escape seem all the more possible. After all, she had the advantage of being familiar with the countryside. She also had a two-mile walk in the dead of night before her, she ruefully reminded herself, and willed her limbs to cease their trembling.

Made suddenly conscious of a peculiar tingling at the nape of her neck, she stiffened, her hand stealing to the placket

pocket of her dress. Her fingers closed around the handle of
the gun. She turned—and was instantly bowled backward
against the wall by a large, pouncing shape with great paws
that landed on either of her shoulders.

"Stalker!" she cried in a gleeful whisper, as she was made
the recipient of an effusive tongue against the side of her face.
"Where is Rivenoak, you big, wonderful dog? Where is your
master?"

Stalker, dropping to all fours, cocked his head to one side
and gave voice to an inquisitive whine.

"I know he must be here somewhere," Pandora offered
encouragingly. "Else you would not be. Rivenoak, Stalker.
Take me to him."

When it seemed the wolf-dog was stubbornly determined to
keep that information to himself, Pandora moved away from the
wall, her eyes searching the shadows for that tall, comfortingly
familiar figure. The duke was somewhere nearby; she did not
need logic to tell her that. She could feel it.

Hardly had she taken a step, however, to look for the elusive
duke, than Stalker came to his feet with a low, menacing growl
wholly at variance with his earlier ecstatically affectionate
greeting. Pandora precipitately came to a halt.

"What is it, Stalker?" she whispered, kneeling to pull the
dog to her. "Did Rivenoak command you to keep me here?"
Then, at the dog's low whine, "There is someone out there, is
there not? Rivenoak has gone after him."

The dog bristled, baring its fangs in a menacing snarl. A
hulking shape armed with a heavy club stepped around the
corner of the house. Pandora hastily straightened. The hulking
brute came to a halt, a look of astonishment crossing his grimy,
bewhiskered face to be replaced by a leering, gape-toothed
grin.

"Blimey, if it ain't—"

The haft of the knife, descending on the brute's skull, landed
with a sickening thud. The brute straightened, his heavy jowls

going slack in a curiously vacant expression. Then all at once he collapsed, his knees buckling beneath him.

Pandora breathed a sigh of relief, as Rivenoak stepped into view, his hand sheathing the long knife at his belt. The dog bounded forward, followed by Pandora.

"Rivenoak," she cried softly. "Thank heavens you have come." The next instant she was in his arms.

"I still cannot believe it," said Pandora some moments later, her hands yet clinging to Rivenoak. "Even after everything he has done this day. All along it was Percival."

Rivenoak, his face grimmer than she had ever seen it before, seemed not to have heard. Lightly he touched his fingertips to the bruise along her jawline.

"Oh, that." Pandora, embarrassed by the bleak look in his eyes, blushed. "It is nothing. As soon as I realized what was happening, I made something of a nuisance of myself. I daresay they did it to quiet me."

"They?"

"Percival. Or at least I assumed it was Percival. It might have been the other man in the carriage. I did not perfectly see what happened. At any rate, I am all right, Rivenoak, really I am. I wish you would not look at me that way."

"My uncle will be here soon with the carriage," replied the duke, his voice sending an involuntary chill down Pandora's back. "You will wait here for him with Stalker to protect you. No doubt he will do as well as Higgens. At least you may be sure no one will steal up on Stalker from behind."

Pandora, wanting to shake him for even thinking of leaving her behind, pulled away. "Dear, is Higgens all right, then? They did not kill him?"

"He is suffering nothing worse than a headache and bruised sensibilities. The villains knocked him unconscious and managed somehow to dose Simmons with a sleeping draught to keep her from sounding the alarm that you were missing.''

''Poor Simmons. It is no pleasant thing to be dosed with a drug. Any more than it is to be told one must wait behind when one has demonstrated one is perfectly able to take care of oneself.'' Lifting her head in unconscious defiance, she turned to face Rivenoak. ''I am going with you, your grace. There is little sense in ordering me behind, when I shall only follow you anyway. Besides, my dearest Rivenoak, I have earned the right to be there when you meet Samuel Butler. Or had you forgot I am your confidential inquiry agent?''

It was true, she had earned the right, Rivenoak acknowledged grimly to himself. Furthermore, she *would* find a way to follow him, even if he ordered Stalker to ''guard.'' Deciding that at least he would know what she was up to if she were with him, Rivenoak surrendered to the inevitable.

''Very well, you win,'' he said, hoping he would not be made to regret those words. ''We agreed to work together to solve the conundrum of Colonel Massingale and Samuel Butler. We shall finish it together.''

''I am glad, Rivenoak,'' exclaimed Pandora, flinging her arms about his neck. ''For you must know I should not have liked to be an inconformable wife.''

''I should never ask you, my dear, to be anything other than what you are. Only, promise me you will not take any unnecessary chances and that you will do precisely as I tell you.''

''I give you my word, Rivenoak,'' Pandora solemnly promised. ''And you must promise you will not allow yourself to be distracted by any anxiety over my safety. I'm afraid I did not completely trust Percival. You see, I brought my pistol.''

Rivenoak smiled grimly, seeing the flash of the gun in her hand. He might have known she would have come prepared, his brash, indomitable love.

Having bound the downed henchman and left him concealed

in the shrubbery, Rivenoak led Pandora into the brooding stillness of the house. With Stalker a silent shadow at their heels, they made their way up the narrow staircase.

It occurred to Pandora, gritting her teeth at the unavoidable creak of the stairs beneath each careful step, that resolving conundrums, even those of a criminal nature, was a far cry from actually apprehending the criminals. Though she could not deny that she felt uncommonly stimulated by the sense of danger all around her, she was not in the least certain that the sensation of having one's stomach clenched in knots or one's hands clammy with misapprehension was altogether to be desired. Indeed, she had decided she vastly preferred the intellectual excitement of pursuing the threads of logic presented by a stimulating criminal conundrum to the physical stimulation of emotions more closely akin to fear, when the silence was shattered by the thunderous crash of a gunshot.

She heard, in the aftermath, Rivenoak utter a blistering curse beneath his breath and seemingly her own heart pounding within her breast.

"Stay, Stalker. Watch," commanded Rivenoak harshly. With a low whine, the wolf-dog sank down on its haunches.

Rivenoak reached for the door handle and thrust the door open. Without waiting for an invitation, he stepped through the doorway.

Pandora, following quickly in his wake, was not altogether certain what she had expected. Certainly, it was not to behold Percival Ridgeway, seated at the desk, his face alarmingly pale and a crimson stain spreading slowly over the powder blue of his superbly cut coat.

"Ah, Cousin," Percival Ridgeway smiled wryly in acknowledgment of what would seem some grisly joke. "And Lady Rivenoak. A pity. I had hoped to spare you both this unpleasantness. I'm afraid, however, I have made a botch of it."

"Percy, you are wounded," exclaimed Pandora, yielding to

the impulse to go to him. Instantly she set about ridding him of his coat in order to bind the wound with strips of his shirt.

"Perceptive, as always, Duchess," agreed Percival with an involuntary grimace of pain. "I do most humbly beg your pardon for this deplorable state of affairs. I daresay I must present a frightful sight. But more than that, I apologize for the company."

"Really, Ridgeway," interjected a new voice, which had the peculiar effect of causing Pandora to clench her hands into fists at her sides. "I see no need to be insulting."

"Good God," exclaimed Pandora, not bothering to hide the loathing in her tone. "It is you! *You* are Samuel Butler. Faith, I might have known."

"Patrick Algernon Wroth, Viscount Estridge, at your service, ma'am." The slender figure bent in a bow that was meant to be mocking. "Butler, you may be interested to learn, was my mother's name. Samuel I picked out of the air; it sounded so American. Pray do come in and have a seat, Lady Rivenoak. You, too, my lord duke. I shouldn't try anything foolish, if I were you. I fear Mr. Phineas Wake, here, or his elder brother Jonas, over there, would not hesitate to shoot you if you so much as make an unwarranted move."

The two Messers Wake, unprepossessing specimens from the lower dregs of humanity, grinned in apparent anticipation.

"No doubt I should apologize, Cousin," said Percy with undisguised contempt for Estridge and his underlings, "for this glaring breach of conduct. I most exceedingly regret that I allowed myself to be a party to it. Foolishly, I underestimated the viscount's capacity for treachery. I hope you believe, in spite of everything, I should have done all in my power to secure Pandora's safe return to you."

"But I do believe you, Percy," said Rivenoak meaningfully. "I never doubted your loyalty. How could I? You are a Ridgeway, as was my father. You have done just as I should have expected, what I should had I been in your place."

"Just as you expected!" exclaimed Pandora, staring from Rivenoak to Percy. "But the gambling debts. Claverly. Surely you cannot just dismiss them, Rivenoak. Faith, Percy forcibly abducted me to make sure of the succession. Are you going to tell me now that he did not do it all for the title?"

"Good God, no," Percival said with a shudder. "Why should I want the bloody title? I am perfectly happy living the unencumbered life of a ne'er-do-well, supported by my cousin's largesse. I should find playing the role of duke far too fatiguing. Besides, I am genuinely fond of Rivenoak. I daresay I have never been so entertained since he introduced himself to Uncle Quincy—a young savage with the bearing of a prince. Faith, I thought it would send Uncle into an apoplexy."

"But Lady Inglethorpe," Pandora persisted. "I overheard her and Estridge. She hates you, Rivenoak, enough to wish to see you dead. You yourself said Percy could never deny her anything."

"I believe Lady Inglethorpe has undergone a change of heart since she, too, has been made patently aware of the extent of her coconspirator's treachery. You will no doubt be relieved to learn, Percy, that your lady, far from residing in a cellar somewhere, came to me for protection. She is at home, packing her trunks, as it happens, for an extended tour of the Continent, I'm afraid at my suggestion. I daresay she will be waiting for you somewhere on the Mediterranean when you are well enough to travel."

Pandora, who had been rapidly putting two and two together, or, in this case, Percival and Lady Inglethorpe, was given to see a beautiful light come to Ridgeway's eyes. "As ever, Cousin," he said with a twisted smile, "I am in your debt."

"How very touching," obtruded Estridge. "I'm afraid Lady Inglethorpe, however, will have a very long wait. As a confidential inquiry agent of no little talent, Lady Rivenoak, I daresay you must have any number of questions you would like to have answered before all of you are made to meet with an unfortunate

Sara Blayne

accident. I myself am dreadfully curious to learn, Duchess, how you managed to escape from the room above. In anticipation of the duke's arrival, I made certain you were rendered harmless."

Pandora sustained a shock of surprise. "You knew Rivenoak would come."

"But how not? When Mr. Wake was so clumsy as to lose Lady Inglethorpe, I made sure of it. As it happens, she saved me the trouble of contriving a means of bringing the duke to you. This way she has become little more than a minor inconvenience, who served her purpose. Really, she should not have tried to blackmail me. I did attempt to warn her I was cut from a different mold than the unfortunate Colonel Massingale. By the way, Percival, I believe I have never thanked you properly for ridding me of the only man who could still identify me as Samuel Butler, the man who was instrumental in removing Thomas Ridgeway and his mixed-breed family from this earth. All, of course, but for the duke himself, and he is about to join the rest. I believe I should be congratulated for a clean sweep of the board. After tonight, there will be no one left to carry on the Ridgeway name."

"You are mistaken, surely," observed Rivenoak coolly. "There is one honest man who can still point the finger."

"Ah, yes, the courageous Captain Featherstone. Only, he was a mere leftenant then. He has caused me no end of trouble with his cursed sense of integrity. First, in almost succeeding in warning your father in time of my scheme to turn a healthy profit. Unfortunately, the king's intercession on behalf of the Three-Rivers People came only hours too late. Not that it would have mattered in the end. I should still have done what I did. A pity they came back. They had been warned, after all, what would happen to them. We disarmed them and executed them, every one of them, with their own weapons to save ammunition. The bloody damned savages."

"Savages?" Rivenoak murmured in a voice of death. "They

were Christians, with their own church and a school. They prayed and sang hymns while your men cut them down."

"They would have murdered us, given half a chance. Cut our throats in our sleep. They were Redskins, the whole bloody lot of them."

"One of them was Rivenoak's mother, a literate woman of great nobility," protested Pandora. "You are not fit to speak her name."

"Another was a missionary," added Rivenoak, "an old man who spent his entire life helping others. You killed him, along with the others, because he tried to stop you. And my father. You could hardly leave the son of an English duke alive to bring you to justice for what you had done."

"Killing Thomas Ridgeway was in the way of an unlooked-for boon. I had never thought to find one of his cursed breed in that forsaken land. As it happens, it was rather like killing two birds with one stone."

"You hunted him down and murdered him. We have Herodotus Featherstone to thank for the truth and for the evidence that will convict you of murder and treason. It was he who sent Selkirk my father's box with the proof concealed in the false bottom—a letter recording my father's dying words and bearing his seal. Massingale killed Selkirk for it."

"So that is why Herodotus would not speak of what happened," exclaimed Pandora. "I was afraid . . ."

"Your brother was not there when it happened," Rivenoak was quick to assure her. "He slipped away to find my father at the new camp. They arrived too late. Captain Featherstone helped my father bury my mother, and he was with him when Massingale shot from ambush. He did what he could to save my father, and then he must have made his way to the coast and from there to England. Selkirk would naturally have cleared him of all culpability had he lived. With his only ally dead, Herodotus had little choice but to keep his silence. What chance
̲inst men of power and influence?"

"None, I should think," Pandora said slowly, feeling the terrible burden lifted from her. "Massingale must have thought he was safe until the letters started arriving," she theorized. "He must have thought they came from me, Herodotus's sister who just happened to be a confidential inquiry agent. He meant to put me out of the way and place the blame on you. You, after all, had begun to look into the massacre. He must have been sure you would not stop until you found out everything. But who sent him the letters and why?"

"I'm afraid I am responsible for that, Lady Rivenoak," confessed Percival somewhat sheepishly. "It was, after all, an opportunity I could hardly resist. I must say I rather enjoyed seeing the colonel sweat while I milked him dry. Unfortunately, he came to the mistaken belief that you and Rivenoak were in it together to ruin him before you made public his part in the massacre. I really could not allow him to kill the duke, now could I? That night I went to the Town House to warn him off. You see, I saw the lad who delivered Rivenoak the letter. It took only a copper to persuade the little bugger to describe the man who had paid him to deliver it. It was Massingale, of course. The colonel took exception to my interference—tried to throttle me, the brute. I really had no choice but to defend myself."

"You did that for Rivenoak?" Pandora beamed. "And then you went through the charade of abducting me in order to be here to insure my safety until you could find some way to discover where Estridge had taken Lady Inglethorpe. Really, Percival, you make me ashamed that I ever thought you might have been the archplotter."

"I gladly forgive you, if you can forgive me for my part in these proceedings tonight. I deeply regret I could no̶t̶ ̶̶̶ ̶̶nt Estridge from rendering you unconscious or fro̶̶ ̶̶̶ ̶̶ with laudanum. In light of the fact that the ̶̶ ̶̶̶ quicker with a gun than I, I fear I have f̶̶ ̶̶̶

"No doubt I find all this excee̶d̶'̶

interjected. "Unfortunately, it is scarcely an hour to dawn—time, I fear, you were joining your ancestors."

"I never heard such nonsense," declared Pandora, unobtrusively slipping her hand in the placket pocket of her dress. "You cannot really intend to kill all of us. I'm afraid you have not logically thought this through, my lord. The death of a duke under suspicious circumstances is bad enough, but all of us? You haven't a prayer of getting away with it."

"I do not have to, Lady Rivenoak. You will all be the unfortunate victims of a carriage accident. Now be so good as to get to your feet—all of you. Mr. Wake, I suggest you call the others in."

Pandora, allowing her gaze to follow Phineas Wake as he crossed to the door, was keenly aware of Rivenoak, undoubtedly tensed and waiting, as was she. "I wonder, my lord," she said calmly, "what will be made of the bullet wound in Ridgeway's shoulder when we are found."

"Why, undoubtedly that he was wounded by highwaymen, Lady Rivenoak, just before the horses, panicked by the shot, bolted. You see, I have thought of everything."

"Not quite everything," Pandora murmured, closing her fingers around the handle of the gun. And then Phineas opened the door.

Rivenoak's shout rang in the silence. "Stalker, attack!"

Pandora drew the gun and fired. Estridge, flinging a hand to the side of his head, dropped. Stalker, a gliding grey shape, hurtled through the door at Phineas. Rivenoak lunged for Jonas.

Phineas, screaming in terror, was bowled backwards to the floor beneath the snarling attack of the wolf-dog. Rivenoak, in no mood to prolong the engagement, drove his fist into Jonas's jaw. There was a bone-crunching crack, and Jonas's head snapped back, followed in quick form by the rest of him.

In the wake of the jarring impact of Jonas's body striking the floor, Rivenoak called off the dog. Then, as Percival's voice cut through the sudden silence, Rivenoak's blood ran suddenly cold.

"Estridge," gasped Percival. "Quick. He has Pandora!"

"Stalker, watch," commanded Rivenoak, flinging through the door in pursuit of his duchess.

The guard, who had the misfortune to be hastening down the stairs in response to the din of battle, hardly knew what hit him as Rivenoak, in something of a hurry himself, flattened the one remaining obstacle to the fleeing Estridge.

"Rivenoak! Hurry!"

Pandora's scream from somewhere below sent the duke flying with reckless abandon down the stairs to the foyer.

He had not far to go. The viscount, hampered by the struggling captive, was limned against the open doorway, his arm in a strangle hold about Pandora's neck.

Rivenoak's knife flashed, silvery, in the moonlight as, a hand on the bannister, he vaulted over and dropped, light as a cat, to the floor.

"Estridge! Let her go."

Pandora felt a cold chill knife through her midsection as Rivenoak's tall, lithe figure deliberately straightened. There was something unspeakably menacing in the way he stood, loose-jointed, his weight slightly forward on the balls of his feet. There was little to see of the Duke of Rivenoak in the man who had come to her rescue. Clad in a buckskin shirt and leggings, the long raven hair unloosed from its bonds—he was in truth the shaman of the Three-Rivers People, come to wreak a terrible vengeance. Even without the knife, he would have loomed as something elemental and infinitely dangerous. Almost she felt sorry for the man who had incurred his wrath. Estridge, Samuel Butler, was about to make reparation for the evil he had wrought.

Estridge must have felt it, too. She could smell his fear and sweat. She winced as the viscount's arm tightened about her throat.

"That's far enough, Duke, or whatever the devil you are. You've the look of your savage race."

"And you've the look of a man who is about to meet his Maker. Let her go, Estridge, and perhaps I shall let you live a little while longer."

"Rivenoak, no," Pandora gasped. "Let the law have him. It was what you always intended."

"No more, Pandora." Rivenoak moved forward. "He has lived too long."

Pandora, faced with the inevitable, brought the heel of her foot down with all of her strength on Estridge's instep. The viscount uttered a blistering oath and flung her from him. Rivenoak sprang.

It was all over in a matter of seconds.

Estridge, no match for the silent fury of Rivenoak's attack, lay sprawled on the floor, the duke's knife at his throat.

"The devil, Rivenoak," Estridge gasped. "End it."

"It is ended, my lord," said a voice from the doorway. "Beggin' your pardon, your grace, but I'll just be taking it from here."

Pandora tore her eyes from Rivenoak, to be met with the sight of Canary Waistcoat and, with him, Laughs-In-The-Rain.

The tall, silver-haired warrior laid a hand on Rivenoak's shoulder. "The White Eyes is right, True-Son. The blood quest is ended. Let it be over."

"Rivenoak? Chance. Pray let him go."

It seemed at last that Pandora's voice penetrated the red mists of hatred and anger. Rivenoak's shoulders dropped. He pulled the knife away and in a single, lithe movement stood. His arm going about Pandora's waist, he pulled her to him.

"That's right, your grace," said Canary Waistcoat, drawing forth a pair of manacles with a deal of satisfaction. "Let the law have 'im. No sense in startin' your nursery with blood on yer 'ands.''

Pandora, feeling herself blush at the mention of something even she and Rivenoak had yet to discuss, turned mystified eyes on the strange little man. "Who are you?" she asked. "And why have you been following me all these weeks? You must know I thought you were one of Estridge's men."

"Obviously you are more shaken than you are willing to admit, my love," said Rivenoak, the stern features losing some of their hardness, as he drank in Pandora's loveliness. "I should have thought your impeccable sense of logic would have led you to the answer to that particular conundrum."

Instantly, he was rewarded with the soft radiance of her smile. "It is Mr. Pinkney, is it not, the Bow Street Runner. Mr. Townsend sent you to watch after me."

" 'E did at that, your grace," Pinkney admitted with a grin. "Right taken with yer, 'e was. Says 'e never seen a finer piece of investigatin' work, yer grace. It ain't often Mr. Townsend says that about anyone."

"Be pleased to tell Mr. Townsend thank you for me, Mr. Pinkney. And I do beg your pardon for pulling your thumb. By the way, there are four other felons for you to collect. We should be exceedingly grateful if you would see to them before they wake up."

"With Mr. Laughs-In-The-Rain's help, I shall get right on it, yer grace. I expect there will be a promotion in this for me."

"Dear," exclaimed Pandora, reminded suddenly of Percival, "someone must go and fetch the doctor immediately. Poor Percy, I forgot all about him."

It was consequently no little time later that Pandora found herself being borne up the stairs by her determined husband, who, having taken time to change out of his clothes, was once again her dearest Rivenoak—and Chance True-Son, too—both of whom she loved with all of her being.

Rivenoak, at peace with himself for the first time since he

had taken the long voyage from the land of the Three-Rivers People to England, the cold land of his father's father, laid her in the bed and, with a tender passion unlike anything Pandora had ever felt in him before, made love to her.

"Grandfather Sun is smiling down on us," sighed Pandora, as she lay, languorous from their lovemaking, in Rivenoak's arms. "A pity we cannot walk naked, hand-in-hand, or make love on soft pelts in the cornfields. I think I should like to be blessed with strong, happy children. Which reminds me, Rivenoak, we have yet to resolve the final conundrum. I should be greatly surprised if Estridge had the things of power. He did not strike me as the sort to place the least credence in anything of a supernatural significance."

"Fortunately, my father did, however," replied Rivenoak, drawing Pandora close to his side. "He preserved them, along with his papers, in the false bottom of the wooden box. The question is what should be done with them? They do not belong here in the land that is foreign to all that they represent. As the last of my mother's people, I should be the one to return them to their final resting place."

"Then, naturally that is precisely what you must do. As it happens, I have always wanted to see something of the world. If only Herodotus would come home! Until then, I could not possibly leave the children."

"No doubt it is fortunate, then, that I have already sent for your brother."

"No, have you?" Pandora lifted herself on one elbow, her eyes alight with excitement. "When? How long before—?"

"If it is a fast ship, by Christmas with any luck."

"Christmas." Pandora stared at him as she obviously went through the computations. "But that is little more than six months away."

"Six and a half, to be precise. I said, if it was a fast ship. I should not get my hopes too high. It could very well be longer."

"But that means you sent for him at least two months ago, before you knew—"

"Before I knew he was not a man to betray people who had taken him in and befriended him. I sent for him in March, the day after you brought me my father's box."

"But why, Rivenoak?" Pandora demanded, gazing at him with suddenly probing eyes. It would, after all, seem a wholly illogical thing to do, unless he had been motivated by something that had little to do with logic.

"Because, my little English linnet," replied Rivenoak, who could see very well where her deductive reasoning was leading her, "I had begun to suspect there must be a deal more to Herodotus Featherstone than I had been led to believe if he commanded the love and loyalty of one empowered by the Earth Mother to make me forget who and what I was. You were like a dazzling ray of sunlight blinding me to what I had sworn to do. I had to know, Pandora. You see, I had determined I must have you as my wife."

"But you did make me your wife, Rivenoak," prodded Pandora, not yet satisfied that he had told her all. "Against my better judgment, I might add. For if you must know, I was not at all certain you would not soon grow to despise me and the children once you knew of Herodotus's involvement with Massingale. But you knew that all along, did you not. And still you forced me to marry you. Why, my darling?"

"Why do you think, Pandora?" Rivenoak countered, his marvelous eyes alight with a warmth that took her breath away. "I was prepared to lay down the blood quest against the man I believed was the traitor to my people. All you had to do was tell me the truth, Pandora."

"The truth is, my dearest Rivenoak, that I married you knowing you had every reason to despise me. What I do not know is why you married me."

"Because, my implacable confidential inquiry agent, I fell in love with you almost from the first moment I saw you in that ridiculous tartan sari. I shall always love you, my dearest, most maddening Pandora. It is a conundrum that will take a lifetime to resolve.''

"Are you quite sure, Rivenoak?" Pandora persisted, a gleam of mischief in the look she bent upon him. "You know I could never resist a conundrum. On the other hand, I cannot but wonder if you have considered all the ramifications of having a confidential inquiry agent as your wife. I am most certain to cause you no end of trouble.''

"Little devil. I have never been more certain about anything in my life. And you may be equally certain that I have considered it—from every possible angle—with the result that I am reasonably convinced that being wed to a confidential inquiry agent is far preferable to living my life without the only woman I shall ever love.''

"Well, in that case, I daresay I cannot refute your logic," declared Pandora, who, indeed, had no wish to have done. Her dearest Rivenoak loved her, had loved her enough to lay down his vengeance against her brother, enough to marry her in spite of all the rational arguments against it. It was truly a most magnificent conundrum, the conundrum to last a lifetime.

ABOUT THE AUTHOR

Sara Blayne lives with her family in Portales, New Mexico, and is the author of nine Zebra Regency romances. She is currently working on her next traditional regency romance, *A Noble Heart*, which will be published in March, 2000 and her next historical romance set in the Regency period (to be published in 2000). Sara loves to hear from readers and you may write to her c/o Zebra Books. Please include a self-addressed stamped envelope if you wish a response.